D1520890

A LAWLESS MOUNTAIN TOWN BORN OF GOLD AND BUILT BY
GREED IS BESET BY ANCIENT HORROR

CLAW
EMERGENCE BOOK 3
RETURN TO DARKNESS

KATIE BERRY

Copyright © 2023 Katie Berry

All rights reserved.

ASIN: B0CQWRM7N1

Print ISBN-13: 9798873153558

No portions of this book may be reproduced without
permission from the publisher, except as permitted by
Canadian copyright law.

Published by Fuzzy Bean Books

Cover Art Copyright © 2023 Katie Berry

This is a work of fiction. Names, characters, businesses,
places, events, locales, and incidents are either the products of
the author's imagination or used in a fictitious manner. Any
resemblance to actual persons, living or dead, or actual events
is purely coincidental.

ENTER TO WIN!

Become a Katie Berry Books Insider; you'll be glad you did. By simply sharing your email address*, you will be entered into the monthly draws! That's right, draws, plural.

Each month there will be two draws: one for a free digital download of one of my audiobooks and the other for a free autographed copy of one of my novels delivered right to your mailbox.

There will be other contests, chapter previews, short stories, and more coming soon, so don't miss out!

Join today at:

https://katieberry.ca/become-a-katie-berry-books-insider-and-win/

*Your email address will not be sold, traded, or given away. It will be kept strictly confidential and will only be used by Katie Berry Books to notify you of new content (or perhaps that you're another lucky winner of the monthly draws).

PREFACE

And here we are, the last book in this prequel series to CLAW: A Canadian Thriller. Caleb Cantrill, Kitty Welch, Cornelius Brown, and the rest of the cast have been so much fun to write over the last year and a half. Now that the story is done, I will miss 'seeing' them each day since they have become such a huge part of my life.

But I am sure you are not here to read about my being misty-eyed for my characters and are eager to see how everything turns out. So, I won't keep you except to say thank you for coming along with me on this journey back in time.

Your entertainment is my highest priority, and I hope I have succeeded in providing some to you once again. I will see you at the end of the book. Enjoy!

-Katie Berry

December 24th, 2023

For Emily

Your laughter, courage, music, and grace will always be in my heart and forever missed. Be at peace, my friend.

CHAPTER ONE

A gusting wind pushed impatiently at Caleb's back as he jogged down the main street toward the Golden Nugget Saloon and Kitty Welch. Small dust devils skittered down the road in step with him as he hustled along. The forest fire was burning sideways again and moving toward the ice house further downriver, but at least it gave the town a brief reprieve from annihilation.

Fortunately, with the wind change had come some fresher air as well, and Caleb's smoke-addled lungs greedily sucked it in. Had the wind not changed direction a short while ago, the town would now be a blazing inferno. In fact, many residents seemed to have realised such a calamity might yet come to pass, and a large number had fled into the hills toward the only way in and out of the valley, the Golden Mile Pass.

Caleb and the other volunteer firefighters had arrived back at the smithy just a few minutes before. With Sandy at his side, Doctor Brown had departed for his practice to prepare more peanut balls. Lucias, along with a few of the other volunteers, stayed with Fire Chief Cochrane to assist in refilling the pumper wagon. And Police Chief Dugrodt had gone to the police station to notify Constable VanDusen of the situation. They would need to gather more volunteers to aid with the advancing fire and the monstrous red ants.

The encroaching threats were something Caleb would defend Kitty against right to his dying breath. And now that he was back in town, he wanted to keep her as close to him as possible until the most immediate problems were resolved. After all, the last thing he wanted to worry about while battling the fire and the ants was her safety. Despite everything, he felt some relief with the Hole-in-the-Wall gang paid off by Sinclair. At least now, he didn't have to fear being kidnapped and tortured by the gold-toothed Jesús and his scar-faced sidekick, Antonio. All in all, he felt renewed hope and was eager to see Kitty again.

The saloon was empty when Caleb pushed through the batwing doors, save for one ancient sourdough playing solitaire and cracking open peanut after peanut from the bowl next to his gnarled hands. Muddy was busy behind the bar polishing some glasses, seeming unbothered about the calamities unfolding outside.

It was with no small amount of surprise that Caleb took in what the bartender was doing, or rather, not doing. "Aren't you packin' anythin' up? I thought your boss would have you savin' his expensive booze at the very least, and here you aren't even packin' the fine china yet!"

Muddy shook his head, saying, "Nope. The boss man says no need."

"No need? You have a blazing inferno not a mile from town, and you're saying Sinclair isn't worried about it?"

"He doesn't seem too concerned about anything going on out there."

"Well, if that wind blows the wrong way again, we're all goin' to be needin' water instead of whiskey." The value of the alcohol behind the bartender was worth a good half-dozen nuggets like the ones he'd found in his accursed cavern. But it was strange; why wasn't Sinclair feeling the need to move his valuables out of the way of the approaching fire? Caleb shook his head, figuring the man that owned this building, and currently him, must know what he was doing. Glancing toward the second-floor staircase, he asked, "Have you seen Miss Kitty?"

Muddy nodded. "Yup. Last time I saw her, she was helpin' out Maggie in the kitchen.

Caleb thanked the bartender and was soon pushing through the swinging doors into the kitchen. Though there were usually all sorts of pleasant scents coming from back here, at the moment, peanuts were the only thing he could smell, and he quickly saw the reason why: a half-empty burlap sack of unshelled peanuts sat on the floor next to the island.

Maggie was just finishing up at the sink with a large stainless steel mixing bowl. She began to dry the bowl and turned, her greying eyebrows raised in surprise. "I wasn't expecting you back so soon!" She smiled slightly and added, "I presume you're looking for Kitty and not just back here to say hello?"

With a pinched smile, Caleb replied, "You hit the nail on the head, Maggie. Could you tell me where she's gotten to?" His quest to find Kitty seemed almost at an end, and he felt his heart beginning to beat a bit faster in anticipation of seeing her again.

"She was running an errand for me. Took a couple of cans of peanut spread I'd ground up for Doctor Brown down to his office. But now that you mention it, I haven't seen her for at least ten minutes or so. Wouldn't have thought it would take her that long."

With a nod and a wave, Caleb pushed through the screen door to the alley, saying, "Thanks, Maggie. Get yourself to safety."

"Wherever that is," the cook said as the door closed with a clack at Caleb's back.

The alley behind the Nugget was on the shaded side of the building, and it was usually cooler here. Though dark storm clouds now rolled across the valley from peak to jagged peak, it was still stiflingly hot, and it didn't seem to matter which side of the building a person was on.

A sudden flash of lightning tore through the approaching storm front, shortly followed by a crash of thunder, which rumbled toward the town like cannon fire. It reminded Caleb of his time in Africa. He and his company had been on a typical patrol, but it had ended in tragedy. The Boers had gotten their hands on some British munitions during one of their frequent guerilla raids and had decided to try them out.

The company had been making their way cautiously through the Bushveld. For the last few hours, they'd been playing a game of cat and mouse with some Boer rebels hiding in the long grass that covered most of the terrain. Their first revelation that they were getting close to one of the Boer outposts had come in the form of a thundering cannon blast. The concussive explosion of the powder-filled projectile had resulted in one of the lads at the front of the line losing his head, quite literally, while several others lost arms and legs. A hail of gunfire from long-range Boer snipers had torn apart several more of his mates, the ones the cannon fire had missed. But Caleb had been fortunate to have been marching at the column's rear and thus had been spared much of the explosive's impact and most of the bullets.

As another crash of thunder struck, Caleb cringed ever so slightly, finding himself still reactive to loud noises after all these years. It was ironic, considering his role with explosives in the army and afterwards. But that was different; he was prepared for the sound of the explosions—it was the unexpected ones that made him jump in fear for his own safety. And thinking of safety right now, finding Kitty was still his priority. Once he'd ensured she was well and safe, he would breathe a little easier.

Still looking to the approaching storm clouds, Caleb continued toward the back door of Doc Brown's office. It was on the corner at the upper end of the block, just across from the smithy. If Kitty wasn't there, he wondered if she might have gone to the blacksmiths after dropping off her peanut spread to check if he was back.

As Caleb grew closer to Brown's, he turned his attention from the skies and looked groundward once again, and as he did, his eyes widened in concern.

Only a few yards short of the rear entrance to Brown's office lay an object that looked quite familiar—Kitty's new basket, which he'd purchased for her at Vicker's Five and Ten. But why was it lying in the dirt? There were two tins labelled Johnson's Finest Lard, one still in the basket, the other on its side just outside. Caleb crouched and returned the tin to the basket, wondering why Kitty would just drop everything and walk away. He knew there had to be a reason, and his eyes widened even further as he began to imagine the possibilities.

Caleb stood with the basket, feeling his recent hope blow away in the growing breeze as he did. Having changed direction again, the wind was smoke-filled once more. As the gusts tried to tear his hat from his head, Caleb looked at Kitty's basket, his heart already feeling like it had been torn from his chest.

CHAPTER TWO

The back of the horse to which Kitty was currently tied was smelly and uncomfortable, and that was putting it mildly. There were not many times in her life when she'd felt so powerless. Her job on the second floor of the Nugget was bad enough, but at least she still got some modicum of respect there. Here, there was none, and she had been largely ignored, currently seeming to be nothing more than baggage.

As the men guided their horses into the forest, she'd listened to the conversation since she hadn't had much choice in the matter. They had been discussing their dealings with the ants, presumably like the one Doctor Brown had recently added to his menagerie and the same as she'd seen down at the river eating the carcasses of the eyeless fish.

By and large, Kitty had been left to her thoughts. But her thoughts were not a place she wanted to be, either. She thought of the last time she'd felt so vulnerable. It had been the day after the Tullibody robbery. She had been out with William McLeod, and the boy had been lavishing food and alcohol upon her in an upscale public house.

Just as she'd excused herself to use the powder room, the local constabulary had come swooping in. After some resistance on William's part which resulted in an overturned table and much shouting, they had taken him away for questioning. The only reason Kitty had been spared the trauma of being arrested along with him had been thanks to her weak bladder.

Upon discovering the reason for the disturbance she'd overheard while in the powder room, Kitty had snuck out the pub's back door and high-tailed it home. She'd told her mother she had been invited to a friend's wedding in Ireland, packed a few things and hadn't been home since.

Perhaps as a way to assuage the guilt on her soul, over the last few years, Kitty had been sending money home and telling her mother all was well. She kept up the pretence that she was in Canada on a lark and touring the country, having taken a steamship to North America with her newlywed friends. Someday, she would come clean with her mother, but she didn't know when that would be. After all, she doubted she would be seeking to return to Scotland any time soon, especially with a warrant for her arrest no doubt still active.

The horse to which Kitty was bound came to a clip-clopping halt, also bringing to a halt her own interior monologue. With a grunt and a grumble, the riders of both horses climbed down from their saddles.

A voice beside Kitty's ear suddenly said, "All right, little missy." It was Scarface. He began to remove her ropes, adding, "I'm gonna untie you from this horse. Your hands are still gonna be bound, and that gag will stay in your mouth, lessen you promise not to scream, then I'll take it out."

With the rope that bound her wrists to her ankles around the horse finally untied, Scarface lowered Kitty down and looked her in the eye. "Well, are you gonna scream, or ain't ya?"

Kitty looked at the scar-faced man with frightened eyes. She shook her head negatively to indicate her lack of desire to exercise her lungs with a good scream. Just the thought of getting the foul-tasting rag out of her mouth was enough to make her promise almost anything.

Scarface nodded and said, "Good," then untied the gag, keeping her hands bound as promised.

With the filthy cloth out of her mouth, Kitty almost reneged on her promise not to scream but then just as quickly decided she didn't want to create any waves at the moment, the relief of her recently assaulted taste buds still at the forefront of her mind. Though her feet were now rope-free, it wasn't like she could run anywhere, even if she wanted. Thanks to her long dress, it would likely tangle around her legs as soon as she got to the nearest brush and bring her crashing face-first to the earth—and with her hands still bound, it was apt to be a painful fall.

Currently stopped on a low ridge above the town, Kitty was horrified to see the forest near the river almost entirely engulfed by fire. Towering flames shot high into the dark, turbulent sky now covering most of the valley. The wind preceding the incoming storm battled against the wind caused by the fire, and the flames danced and twisted in yellow-orange fury. Depending on how the wind blew, the town below came in and out of jeopardy every minute or two but seemed safe for the moment since the fire was currently moving parallel to the river and lake beyond.

Gold-tooth came sauntering up to Kitty, grinning from ear to ear. "Buenos dias, seniorita. I hope you will pardon the roughness of your treatment until now. But a rapid retreat and a compliant captive were the first priority for our little gang of two, isn't that right, Antonio."

Antonio nodded and said, "Just like always, Jesús."

Well, now Kitty knew the names of the criminals that had captured her at least. She now knew why she had feared for

8

Caleb. Judging by the gleam in their eyes, these men were capable of almost anything at any time. Usually, that would be violence against other men, men who owed them money, like Caleb. But now, she was fearful of what their other intentions might be. Unsure what to do, she said, "I'm thinkin' you boys had best return me to town."

Jesús's dark, bushy eyebrows shot up, and he gave a golden grin, saying, "Do you think that would be best?" He looked to Antonio and asked, "What do you think, amigo?"

A flash of lightning and crash of thunder in the distance made Antonio say, "I think we should get under cover."

With a nod, Jesús said, "A good idea, to be sure."

"We just gotta figure out where."

"Stay where you are, senorita," Jesús said, no golden smile on his face this time.

Kitty nodded and stayed where she was, next to the horse Jesús had stolen.

The two men moved to the far side of the horses and talked in low voices, not wanting Kitty to overhear their undoubtedly crooked business.

Stroking the horse's mane, Kitty recognised the palomino from seeing the chief of police riding it about on business to other parts of the valley. It was a beautiful animal, strong and healthy and in its prime. She was sad to see such a noble and majestic creature suffer the indignity of having such a small, smelly criminal astride its back.

Caleb would come looking for her; Kitty was sure of it. And it was something the pair of bandits were no doubt counting on. If he actually remembered the location of the gold mine, thanks to the stress of her kidnapping, these men would most likely kill him once they'd verified the location was legitimate. And judging from what she'd seen so far of the two beastly men, her always helpful imagination suggested that afterwards, she would most likely be savaged and murdered as well.

Watching the fire burn, Kitty looked to the clouds overhead. No rain had yet fallen, though more lightning flashed, followed by another distant crash of thunder. Hopefully, there would be rain soon to help douse the fires. But if it were only lightning and thunder, it would start even more fires like the one burning near the river—a fire she was pretty sure was started by—

"Jesus, Mary and Joseph!" Kitty cried as a hand fell on her shoulder.

"It is Jesús, actually," Oritz said, emphasising the Spanish pronunciation of his name.

Kitty turned, her bound hands held close to her hammering heart. "What is it you want of me?" The wind gusted around her, whipping loose strands of her chestnut hair into her face and mouth as she spoke.

The small bandit gave her another flash of yellow metal as he smiled and said, "What I want right now is some information."

Kitty looked at him through narrowed eyes and said nothing.

"Do not worry, senorita. I do not expect you to betray your Irish amante."

"Then what is it you want?"

"Just some information," he said, almost pleasantly.

Though the Spaniard's small stature made him seem too innocuous to do any harm, there was a hard edge to the smile on his face, and the twinkle in his eyes was as cold as starlight. What he tried to pass for joviality was anything but. Behind his golden grin was nothing approaching happiness; Kitty could see that now. No, there was only anger, violence and certain death.

"Information about what?"

"Your friend who died from the spider bite."

Kitty was taken by surprise and said, "What? Farley Jones?"

Jesús gave a nod and said, "Yes, that is him."

"How do you know about Farley?"

"I learned of his demise from one of my now late gang members, who I hired right here in this valley."

When Kitty had first started at the Golden Nugget, before she'd been told she could refuse service to anyone she found too undesirable, she'd had the unfortunate experience of doing the 'business' with the taller of Jesús's local hires, the one with the bad haircut. Vern had been the man's name if her memory served correctly. But no matter which way she remembered the man, 'undesirable' was too mild a word for a person of his hygiene-challenged ways, and that included his friend with the potato-shaped head.

Antonio was now at Jesús's side and added, a slight leer on his face, "Yeah, one of them said Jones was a friend of yours."

"If he was or wasn't, what is it to you?" Kitty asked tersely.

Jesús nodded to the flames shooting up near the river. "We need a place to lay low. We were going to camp out at the far end of the valley near the glacier, but unfortunately, there is a fire in the way at the moment." He flashed her a grin and added, "And so we are in need of something a little more central for the time being."

With a scowl, Antonio stepped uncomfortably close to Kitty, adding, "And we heard from those local boys that Jones's house was empty since he was dead and lived there alone."

Vern's potato-shaped friend had been Claude Habner, and he had known Farley, Kitty now recalled. Claude had worked part-time at the ice house and had been hired by Jones. It was something she and Farley had discussed during one of her many conversations with her father-like friend. Habner had been caught stealing fruit and produce from the ice house, and Farley had been forced to let him go. Since that time, Farley had had continuing trouble with the man. Habner had tried to tell anyone who would listen around town that he'd been owed some unpaid wages by Farley, which wasn't true, Jones had assured her. And so, Kitty didn't respond to the bandit's information request and only tightened her lips, refusing to say anything further.

Staring into Kitty's eyes, Antonio brought his arm up between them, a wickedly sharp blade suddenly in his hand, seeming to spring from out of nowhere. "If you don't play ball, I'm goin' to start doin' some whittlin'." He brandished the blade before Kitty's eyes and continued, "I'll start with your little toes. Then I'll move to your little fingers. And then I'll take turns and go back and forth and work my way toward your thumbs and big toes. Do you understand what I'm sayin' to ya, little missy?"

Kitty didn't back up, refusing to let the man see he intimidated her, which he did—they both did. The jagged white scar that ran from beneath Antonio's eye down to his jawline was more than enough to convince Kitty he was very familiar with the use of a blade. Out of the blue, part of her mind wondered if the person who had given him that scar was still alive, and she realised it didn't matter because if she didn't comply, she was sure she'd be dead or disfigured for life regardless.

With wide eyes, Kitty nodded to Antonio but remained silent. It wasn't that she wouldn't speak. No, it was because she couldn't speak at the moment, her voice seeming to have deserted her as she envisioned Antonio carrying out his threats on her hands and feet every time she didn't respond to a question truthfully.

"And do you believe what I'm sayin' to ya?" Antonio wondered, the blade still gleaming between their faces.

"Yes," Kitty managed to squeak out.

"Good, then you're gonna show us where Farley's house is." Antonio held the knife sideways before Kitty's eyes and pressed the blade back into the knife's hilt with the palm of his hand, the pointed tip drawing a bead of blood as he did.

"I am glad it is settled then!" Jesús proclaimed gleefully, rubbing his hands together and moving to mount his horse.

Moments later, Kitty was sitting upright in front of Antonio on his horse, who was jammed in behind her in the saddle. They rode in front of Jesús so Kitty could guide the way to Farley's.

Antonio leaned toward Kitty, his fetid breath in her ear as he whispered, "And if you try anything funny, I'm gonna start whittlin' away on you right here in this saddle while we're ridin'."

As they wound the horses down the path toward town, Kitty realised she had never felt less funny in her entire life.

CHAPTER THREE

"Make them a little smaller, my boy."

"I'll do my best, Doc," Sandy replied.

Cornelius had been busy with Sandy making peanut balls since they'd returned from trying to extinguish the forest fire. His ant bait idea seemed to have worked rather well, but its only drawback was that it took time, something which they didn't have. The creatures would be upon the town very soon, and depending on how the wind was blowing, if the ants didn't kill everyone first, the fire would surely finish off whoever remained.

Taking another handful of the ground peanuts mixture, Sandy said, "It's hard to make the balls small when I got such a big hand. Plus, I only got one workin' at the moment." Sandy squeezed his good hand closed and then opened it again, dropping the solid, egg-sized ball into the growing pile in the bowl at the centre of the examination table. When the boy closed his fist, it was like Mother Nature forging a diamond in the bowels of the earth through intense pressure. With some slight amusement, Brown realised whichever ant got the balls made by Sandy would be in for a challenging chew.

"Don't worry, my boy, you'll be as right as rain soon." Looking at the pile of peanut balls on the table, Brown said, "I think I should be okay finishing up here by myself. Caleb will be along shortly with Kitty, and they can both help finish off these balls. Angus should have everything ready for you by now."

The doctor retreated to his small office at the back and returned with a ten-gallon galvanised steel milk can, struggling to carry it into the room. "I'm going to give you what I have, and once you've delivered this, you need to get to the kitchen at the Nugget and see how much they have. Any kind will do. But be very careful with what's in this can. Though it may smell like it, it's not regular vinegar—this is acetic acid. In fact, I shouldn't even have it in this can, but it's all I have at the moment. It's extremely caustic."

"It causes ticks?" Sandy looked at the container in disbelief.

Brown shook his head and explained, "No, it's caustic, as in 'causes burns'. At the concentration I have achieved, it will melt through your skin in a matter of seconds, so be careful!"

Sandy nodded solemnly, "Yessir, I will."

Brown nodded toward the boy's right arm, still dangling limply at his side, and admonished, "And for heaven's sake, don't try to do it yourself; have Angus help you!"

Sandy effortlessly picked up the galvanised milk can with his good hand, saying, "Sure enough!" He pushed through the door to the street with a jingle, ducking his head but still grazing the door's bell slightly.

No sooner had Sandy departed when there came a pounding at the office's back entrance, and Brown hurried to answer it. Opening the door, he was surprised to see Caleb. He looked shocked and carried a wicker basket with a lid in one hand.

"Caleb, my boy, what's the matter?" He stood back from the door to allow the other man to enter.

"Have you seen Kitty?"

"Kitty? No, I'm sorry. At least, not in the short while I've been back here."

"Well, I don't know where she is then. This was lying in the dirt outside your door." He held the basket out, and Brown took it, opening the lid as he did.

"Ah, the peanut spread!" Basket in hand, the doctor moved toward the front of the office.

"Maggie said Kitty was just running that down to you," Caleb said, trailing behind.

Brown nodded his head and said, "That's correct. When I saw the commercial product I'd commandeered running low, I asked Maggie to grind up some peanuts for more ant bait. But as for Kitty, I don't know what to say at this point, except with all the other events currently unfolding around us, her disappearance is not something we have time to deal with at the moment."

"I know, I know! But part of me wants to run outside and start lookin' everywhere for her regardless, but I wouldn't even know where to start. I'm worried the ants or spiders might have gotten to her!"

"I understand that, my boy. But there's nothing else we can do right now. Your assistance with the incoming ants and that raging fire is very badly needed here."

Shaking his head in frustration, Caleb said, "You're right, Doc, of course. But still..."

Katie Berry

Brown patted Caleb on the shoulder and said, "Once we can get some of our other situations dealt with, we will make finding Kitty our top priority, I promise."

Caleb nodded slightly, sighed, and said, "Okay, what do we need to do?"

"We need to get to work."

"Work? Doin' what?"

"Why, making more treats for our red menace in the forest, of course." Brown removed the cans of Johnson's Lard from the basket and placed them on the examination table.

"Like the ones you used at the fire?"

"Yes, exactly the same." The doctor popped the lids off, saying, "This is something I discovered our little red friends enjoy." He stuck his finger into one of the cans, withdrew it, and then licked it clean. "It's surprisingly tasty, though personally, I think it needs a little salt. Anyway, with that said, I've been spicing it up for them with a little something extra."

"What's that?"

Brown held up his now peanut-free finger and pointed to a small sack filled with white powder next to a metal bowlful of beige balls, saying, "Boric acid."

"Boric acid? Is that the same as borax used for doin' your laundry or cleanin' your house?"

"Amongst other things." The doctor picked up a wooden spoon and then scooped the peanut paste from the cans into another large bowl, this one empty. When he was done, he poured some white powder over the peanuts. "Until now, I've been using it as a flux to separate the impurities from the gold

17

extracted in my ore experiments." Satisfied he'd added enough boric acid, he began mixing everything together.

"And you just figured you'd feed some to those buggerin' ants?"

The doctor shook his head and said, "Well, no. I'd heard previously that it could be used with some success as an edible insecticide. And when I saw that the ants were crazy for that ground peanut spread Maggie had bought for the restaurant, I put two and two together, so to speak."

"And made a poison for them."

"Exactly! However, it's not fast acting."

"That's right, you said it could take a while, didn't you?"

"Yes, it can take several days, at least on smaller ants. However, with the ones in the forest being over forty times larger than average, it might be even longer. Ultimately, it should still have the same effect."

"So if you can get enough of that inside them, we should be rid of them in short order, if we can survive that long."

"Precisely. If they share these with the queen and add them to their food stores, then we should be free of their presence within a week, I would hope."

"How does it work, Doc?"

"It's a desiccant."

"A what?"

"It dries out their exoskeletons and affects their ability to absorb nutrients."

Brown finished mixing the ant bait together and rubbed his shoulder briefly, feeling the repetitive effort in his ageing joints. "We need to make as many balls as possible since there must be hundreds of ants, perhaps thousands."

"Will this also work on the spiders, Doc?" Caleb wondered.

"Sadly, no. As far as I know, ground legumes are not something an arachnid can appreciate or digest." He looked over to the side of the room and asked, "Isn't that right, Mama?"

Near the pail containing the little black beast, the spider hung upside down from the top of its cage, its plenitude of eyes regarding the men unblinkingly.

Brown continued, "If we can get those ants under control when they arrive, then we can search for Kitty as we deal with her offspring. So, let's hope things go smoothly."

The pair worked silently for several minutes, gradually adding more and more little beige balls to the growing pile in the bowl.

From outside came several gunshots, and Caleb said, "Sounds like we're goin' to find out how smooth things are goin' to go right about now!"

Seconds later, the door to the office flew open, the bells slapping frantically against the wood as Lucias stepped quickly into the room. He squinted at the men, his face an emotionless mask as usual, and said gravely, "The first of the ants have arrived."

CHAPTER FOUR

After dropping the acetic acid off at the smithy, Sandy was on his way to raid the Golden Nugget's kitchen pantry of any vinegar it contained, whether Maggie liked it or not. He'd retrieved Rufus while at the smithy, and the large dog now snuffled and snorted alongside him as they moved down the back alley toward the saloon.

The screened entrance to the kitchen was close at hand, and Rufus had stopped briefly to sniff around the garbage and compost bins. Sandy sneezed; the smoke seemed thicker, which was not a good sign. That meant the fire was getting closer, and the ants would be arriving all too soon.

Beyond the smoke, the thick, dark clouds seemed to be building into a storm of note. He found that unsurprising, especially with all the things happening. With spiders, ants and black water beasts, it certainly seemed that anything was possible around this valley now. In fact, he wouldn't have been surprised to have seen a tornado spout out of the towering clouds.

The screen door creaked like a coffin lid as Sandy and Rufus entered the kitchen. There was no sign of Maggie, and he presumed she'd gone to make ready for bugging out of the area if the fire hit town. "Maggie?" he called out, just in case, but there was no answer.

Sandy had allowed Rufus to follow him into the kitchen and saloon since he figured there wouldn't be anybody around to get the dog excited. Most everybody was probably taking care of their own business at the moment, thanks to the approaching calamities. He'd glanced into the bar as he exited the kitchen and saw with some satisfaction that he had been right; it was empty, and even Muddy was no longer behind the bar. Fortunately, he had a pretty good idea where Maggie kept the surplus vinegar, and he and the dog moved down the hall to the storage room near Mr. Sinclair's office.

Though it still hung loosely at his side, Sandy's arm was starting to have a tiny bit of sensation come back to it. He massaged it slightly as he entered the storage room and scanned along the shelves for the vinegar.

Suddenly, Sandy discovered that, for whatever reason, the dog was no longer with him. He heard it just outside the storage room door, growling for some reason. Sandy called out, "What is it, boy?"

Abandoning his search for the moment, Sandy poked his head into the hallway.

Rufus was pawing at the bottom of the door to Mr. Sinclair's office, trying to get into the room for some reason.

Fearing his boss might not take too kindly to his door suffering that kind of treatment, he pulled the dog back by its scruff, saying, "What's got your fur in a ruff, boy?"

The dog whined and looked toward the door to the office. Like many things around the Golden Nugget Saloon, it was branded with a golden letter S that shone brighter than a September sunrise. And so, he sometimes thought of his boss in the abbreviated form as it was on the door, 'Mr. S'. Of course, he would never call him that to his face.

Shaking his head, Sandy said, "I'd best let Mr. Sinclair know what was worryin' away at his door." Pointing a finger at the dog, he said, "You stay put and no more scratchin'." He turned around and rapped on the door. There was no response, and he knocked again, this time gently turning the handle and peering around the door's edge.

The large office lay empty. Cigar smoke hung heavy in the air as if his employer had recently departed. A single lantern was the only light source in the room, but its wick hadn't been trimmed back, so he thought the boss might return shortly. But wherever Mr. S was, he most certainly wouldn't appreciate a dog scratching up his shiny office door.

Seeming not to understand English as well as Sandy thought, Rufus brushed through the gap between his muscular leg and the door. Sniffing along the floor, the dog snuffled to a darkened corner of the room where Mr. S kept some of his most prized possessions in his display cases.

Whether it was the room's smokey haze or his fanciful imagination from the books he'd been reading, whatever the cause, the office seemed to carry an air of mystery to it for some reason. What conversations had taken place in here, he wondered. Probably things that he was better off not knowing about if he was any judge of Mr. S's business dealings with people around this town.

Though Sandy usually feared no man, he feared the small Scotsman. Sinclair seemed a force to be reckoned with, and as such, Sandy didn't want the man to be angry at him and did his level best to please him. Of course, sneaking into Mr. S's office when he wasn't there was not the brightest idea he'd ever had. But despite those concerns, something was drawing him deeper into the office. Perhaps the same thing that had drawn the dog in.

Rufus pawed at the bottom of a tall, dark walnut cabinet

with dual glass doors secured with fancy brass fittings.

"What is it, boy?"

The dog didn't reply, of course, and kept pawing at the base of the case.

"That's enough, Rufus," he said in a commanding tone, or as close as he could come to one. His voice wasn't the deepest; Sandy knew that, but he could make people pay attention when he wanted to. And this time, the dog did, and it sat back on its haunches with a grunt.

Sandy peered inside the case's dim interior. It was rather narrow and only contained a few things on each of its shelves, and they all looked awfully strange.

On the top shelf were three dark stones in the centre of a black velvet nest, like irregular eggs no bird would ever lay. But these egg-sized stones were much more than that. In fact, he could feel something coming from them, and he found them almost hypnotising. The flickering lamp light from across the room wavered back and forth, reflected on the surface of the dark stones, but just barely, the gems seeming to swallow the rest. It was very peaceful to look at them, lulling him into a state of calm acceptance.

The strangest thing, however, had to be the item on the next shelf down. It was a small black box, about a foot square. It looked like it was carved from ebony or something like that, and white pearl trim ran around its sides, which seemed to glow in the limited light.

Sandy's gaze shifted back to the stones. He took in every angle, every facet of their surface, feeling drawn down and down into their dark centre. Seeming of its own volition, his left hand slowly reached for the brass handle of the display case.

Sounding explosive in the calm silence of the office, a gruff voice at Sandy's back said, "I wouldn't recommend doin' that, lad. It's very dangerous."

"Huh?" Sandy started, unsure how long he'd been standing there looking at the obsidian stones. He jerked his hand back and spun around to see Mr. S staring intently at him.

"Can you feel it?" Sinclair asked from the doorway, his head cocked slightly.

"I'm real sorry, Mr. Sinclair. I don't know what I was thinkin'."

Sinclair waved it away and said, "I know you don't. But did you feel it just now?" The Scotsman still studied Sandy closely, making him feel uncomfortable.

With a nod, he said slowly, "I felt drawn to this cabinet, like a magnet almost."

"Yes!" Sinclair hissed.

Angeline moved out of the darkness behind the Scotsman to stand next to him. She, too, stared at Sandy in fascination for a moment, then said, "Most people, if they get close enough, are repelled by those stones. And yet you were drawn to them. Why?" She moved closer to Sandy and cupped his chin in her hands, angling his head down so she could better look into his eyes.

Though a tall woman, Angeline was not as tall as Sandy's six foot five. She was perhaps six feet tall, but with high-heeled boots like she now wore, she could almost look him in the eye, so she didn't have to angle his head down by much. Her hazel eyes seemed to burn into Sandy's, and he had a hard time meeting her gaze. In a soft, almost seductive voice, she asked, "Do you know what those stones are, boy?"

Sandy shook his head, his chin still clasped in Angeline's thin, bony fingers.

"They are power," Angeline said in a low voice.

"Aye, that they are," Thomas added. "I can feel it somewhat, but not like Angeline can."

"The stones pull me in and tug at the very core of my being." Angeline placed her free hand on Sandy's muscular chest, saying, "Do you feel it here? Deep down in your soul?"

Sandy nodded again. Though Angeline still held his chin, he managed to utter, "Yeah. Like it's callin' to me."

Angeline let go of Sandy's chin and turned to Sinclair, saying, "You did well choosing this one. There's much more to him than there seems on the surface."

The pair moved off toward Thomas's desk, talking in low voices that Sandy couldn't hear, except for some odd words like 'exceptional' and 'encourage'. But he wasn't paying much attention and turned back to face the stones again. They were truly amazing! Why had he never noticed them before, he wondered. Were they somehow a magnet like he'd said to Sinclair? But what part of him was being pulled toward them? He wanted to touch them and feel their power. But it was more than that, and he began to feel as if he might lose himself completely as he stared into their dark depths and never resurface.

Rufus was suddenly nuzzling at his hand, attempting to wash his fingerprints clean off, or so it seemed. But it was enough, and it broke Sandy out of his trance.

"Yes, boy, I see ya. You're right; we've got to get that vinegar." Sandy turned to Sinclair and Angeline, still deep in conversation, and said, "Sorry to interrupt, but Doc sent me over here for vinegar from the kitchen to help with those ants."

Thomas tore himself away from Angeline and said brusquely, "Do what ya need to do, lad. Help yourself to whatever you need from the store room."

Sandy nodded and said, "Yessir." He began moving toward the door and was almost to the handle when Sinclair spoke again.

"And make sure you do whatever the doctor asks of you to help with those buggerin' ants and spiders."

From beside Thomas, Angeline said, "And trust in the feeling you had just now. Let it guide you."

Sandy nodded and stepped from the office, the dog following him out. He began to close the door when Sinclair called out a final time, "And when you're done, come back and see me. We need to speak further."

As the boy closed the door and moved to the storage room, his mind was awhirl with thoughts of what had just happened. But after a moment, his mind settled, and he could think more clearly. He located two ten-gallon jugs of Heinz White Vinegar. He nestled one in the crook of his arm, and the other hung from his finger through the loop handle in the glass vessel's top.

Once in the alley and moving back toward the smithy, Sandy found himself suddenly alone. Rufus bolted away and headed in the direction of the downtown. Perhaps the dog smelled the ants approaching? Well, whatever it was, there was nothing he could do about it right now.

With a shake of his head, Sandy carried on toward the smithy, wondering what had just happened in Sinclair's office. Apart from the dog leading him there, why had he been drawn to those black stones and that mysterious box beneath? He still felt kind of strange at the moment, kind of 'off' and a little queasy. After drawing a long breath, he passed it off as being anxious about the valley's current collection of calamities, but still, he knew it was more than that. Because part of him now wanted to return to Mr. S's office and see more of those wonderous stones. Whatever they were, as Mr. Holmes would say, they were something that needed further investigation.

CHAPTER FIVE

"What's that you say?" Cookie asked, squinting in confusion.

"I said I don't have a place to put you," Chief Hildey replied somewhat loudly as he attempted to communicate with the deafened bandit.

The old man put one hand to his bushy white-haired head and cupped one ear, saying, "Eh?"

Hildey shook his head in frustration and pointed to a chair in the office lobby. It was the only part of the building undamaged by the blast from the jailbreak. When Sandy had brought the horse thieves around last night, Hildey had been worried about what he'd do if he arrested any more miscreants, thinking he'd have to start putting them in the broom closet. He now shook his head at the irony. Thanks to the jailbreak, not only did he no longer have a broom closet, but he no longer had a jail either and was reduced to locking his prisoners to the waiting room furniture.

Cookie moved to the chair and sat down, then Hildey cuffed him to one of the wooden side arms. Until recently, they had left the man handcuffed to the jail cell bars in the back of the station. But Hildey had decided he wanted to keep an eye on the bandit and have him nearby, just in case, especially if the fire or the ants made their way here.

Shouting at the old bandit once more, Hildey repeated, "I said I don't have anywhere to put you! So, you'll have to come with me when VanDusen gets back!"

The man cupped his ear again and scrunched his face as he tried to understand what was being said.

Whether the man really was as deaf as he pretended to be, there was no way to tell, and Hildey walked away, too frustrated to continue.

Several moments later, a clatter of footsteps sounded on the wooden walk out front, and Constable VanDusen hustled through the entrance. Crowding around the door at his back were perhaps a dozen men. VanDusen nodded over his shoulder and said, "Got as many as I could, Chief!"

Once he'd returned from the fire in the forest, Dugrodt had sent VanDusen out to round up volunteers to help with the conflagration and the approaching ants. Like Hildey, Albert had already had a long day. Unfortunately, he'd also had a long night before even starting his shift. He felt sorry for the man. The constable's brother, Horace, and his wife and newborn child had finally made the move from Holland to 'The New World'. Unfortunately, the constable had been kept awake most of the time he'd been home to sleep due to Horace's infant son having a touch of colic. Already exhausted, Albert had then had to come to work and look after the old man, only to have the chief relieve him and send him out to round up volunteers, which he would also need to babysit.

Dugrodt moved to the door and silently surveyed the motley group for a moment, then addressed them, saying, "As Chief of Police and Deputy Fire Chief, I hereby deputise you all as members of the local volunteer fire department."

A couple of the men groaned slightly, and one coughed, but that seemed about the extent of their enthusiasm. Hildey wasn't expecting much more than that. The men had basically been shanghaied by VanDusen into helping, but Hildey realised beggars couldn't be choosers, as his dearly departed mother used to say.

"You men need to hustle down to the smithy with Constable VanDusen and help Fire Chief Cochrane do whatever he tells you to do."

"What are you going to be doing, Chief?" VanDusen asked.

"I'm going to go door to door with my prisoner here and notify everyone about the emergency. Might be some who haven't heard the fire bell for whatever reason." Dugrodt looked to the group of men and asked, "Are any of you men armed?"

A half dozen hands went up.

"Good, keep your weapons ready. Because not only do we have a fire to contend with, we also have some oversized ants to deal with! And a word of warning right now: unless they attack you directly, give them a wide berth."

There was a rumble of voices as the men expressed their surprise at this development. From the back, a man asked, "What if we don't have a gun?"

With a glum expression, the chief replied, "I would lend you one from our armoury, but the half-dozen rifles we had were caught in the blast, and now they're bent all to hell. So, I'd suggest you find yourself a weapon when you're down at the smithy. I'm sure Angus has something pointy and made of metal that you can use."

As VanDusen and his volunteers filed out the door, a crash of nearby thunder caused the shoulders of a couple of the men to flinch.

No sooner had the men departed when there came a scratching at the closed door leading to the jail cells. But what would do such a thing, Hildey wondered. Not the ants or the spiders, surely. His hand on the butt of his revolver, Hildey popped the door open and staggered back as he was leapt upon by the beast on the other side.

Rufus stood on his hind legs, paws on the chief's shoulders, and gave Hildey a thorough face washing.

"All right! That's enough, Rufus!" He took the dog's paws and placed them on the floor, asking, "Where did you come from all of a sudden?"

Rufus gave a hearty 'woof' in reply.

"That's not much of an answer."

The dog looked expectantly at Dugrodt, then plopped its bum down and proceeded to pant heavily. It looked from the chief to the bandit and then back again as if wondering which would pet him first.

"Well, I guess an extra hand, or paw in this case, is always good." The chief scruffed the dog's head, and it grunted, then went back to panting.

Dugrodt looked over to his prisoner, tempted to leave the bandit handcuffed to the chair. But he knew he couldn't do that. If the fire broke through and he wasn't here to release the man, he'd be roasted alive. And if the fire didn't get him, the ants might, so he couldn't leave him here defenceless either. With a sigh, he unlocked the handcuff from the arm of the chair and slapped it on the man's other wrist. The chain between the iron cuffs was not long, less than a foot, so his prisoner wouldn't have too much freedom of movement.

"Hey! What're ya doin'?" Cookie asked with a startled expression.

"We're going for a walk!" Dugrodt hollered.

At the mention of the word walk, the dog jumped back up, put its paws on Dugrodt's shoulders and attempted to give his face another cleaning.

"A talk? About what?" Cookie asked, perplexed. "I can't hear ya worth a damn but go ahead."

"No, no! A walk!" Hildey removed the dog's paws and gave it another scruff on the head. He turned to face his prisoner, held up one hand, and then walked the index and middle finger across the palm of the other to pantomime the action of walking for the deaf man.

"Oh, a walk! Why didn't you say so!"

Dugrodt gave a frustrated sigh and helped the manacled man to his feet. They moved through the front door, Rufus in the lead, the prisoner in the middle and Hildey following behind.

"Ain't ya gonna close the door?" Cookie asked as he looked over his shoulder from the top of the steps.

Hildey looked to his prisoner, his eyebrows raised, wondering how the man could ask such a question after being involved in the explosion that had demolished the back half of the jail. He pointed through to the door to the jail cells, which he'd left open after receiving the dog's affection. Evergreen forest lay visible beyond. Shaking his head sadly, the chief said, "I think that blast affected more than your hearing."

Once down at ground level, Hildey surveyed the dusty main street. With most of the populous either preparing to flee the fire or having already done so, things looked quite deserted. A small dust devil kicked up a block away, spun dizzily in the growing wind, and moments later dissipated as quickly as it appeared.

The police station was located next to the undertaker's new building. Beyond that was forest extending to a low ridge which led up to the Golden Mile Pass into the valley. When Hildey had arrived at the smithy in response to the fire bell, Sandy had told him of his spider bite and how he'd discovered Ezra Randall. Bearing that in mind, for right now, the mortician's was one door on which they would definitely not be knocking.

Across the street, the bakery was closed, only open until noon today when the horse races ended. With prisoner in tow, Hildey moved up the block, trying the neighbouring businesses as they went: an outdoor supply store, a hatmaker, a haberdasher, and an assay office, but found them all closed, either because of the holiday or due to the incoming threats. Whatever the reason, it made his job easier, which was a good thing.

When they arrived at Vicker's Five and Ten, things took a turn, but it was not for the better.

The double doors were propped open, just as Melinda Vicker usually left them when open for business. Various wares and assorted dry goods were displayed on a couple of low tables out front to either side of the doors. But with everything happening, Hildey was surprised to see them still so. He escorted his prisoner and dog through the doors, calling out as they went, "Melinda? Aren't you gonna close up and pull back until the fire settles down?"

There was no reply from within the store; the only sound was the gusting wind that whistled down the main street behind them, kicking up dust clouds as it went. The pair were stopped next to the candy counter, its sugary contents a kaleidoscopic spray of colour made all the brighter by the threatening skies outside.

Rufus paused next to the men for a brief moment, then continued into the store.

A sudden rustling made the chief turn, and he slapped the old bandit's trespassing fingers away from a bucket of saltwater taffy on top of the counter. Surprised, he noted the man had already managed to unwrap two candies and jam them into his mouth. Around the glob of sugary goo, a smug look on his face, the ornery oldster said, "What're ya gonna do, arrest me?"

Hildey shook his head, a fierce squint his only reply. He tilted his head away from the Candy Corner toward the store's interior, and the old man reluctantly acquiesced to the chief's silent suggestion.

The store was hot and silent, with several aisles for them to explore, but there was no sign of Melinda Vicker.

Rufus was the only living creature inside, currently standing rigidly at the top of the cellar stairs. His fur was ruffed up along his back and neck, and he stared fixedly into the blackness beyond. Seeming to come from some deep, feral part of the dog, a guttural growl rattled from its mouth, and both men started slightly at the sound, surprised at the animal's sudden change in demeanour.

"What is it, fella?" Hildey called.

The dog didn't respond and continued to growl and look down the steep stairs.

Concerned, Hildey gave his prisoner a gentle shove to keep him moving along and together, they moved closer to the dog.

"What's got your tail up, old boy?" the chief inquired of the canine. The cellar stairs were as dark as the India ink he used to fill out his police reports. A lamp hung from a peg on the wall, and the chief took it down and lit it.

Dugrodt turned and shouted to Cookie, "Stay here!" He then looked at the dog and scruffed its head, saying, "You stay, too."

The dog tore its gaze from the cellar, looked up to Hildey, and wagged its tail briefly. Now that he had Rufus's attention, he pointed to the old man, and the dog tracked his hand. Its intelligent eyes locked onto the cook briefly, and it growled. The chief patted the dog's head again and said, "Good boy." Taking a final glance at the old man, he also patted his shoulder and added, "And you be a good boy, too."

Cookie swallowed slightly and cast an uneasy glance at the wolfhound at his side. His hearing suddenly seemed to improve dramatically, and he nodded slightly, saying mutedly, "Yessir."

Lamp in hand, Hildey descended into the cellar, the darkness swallowing him up.

The cellar smelled damp thanks to the presence of the 'pet rock' in the corner and the constantly running trickle of water. Storage shelves covered the walls, and a tall divider with more shelves ran down the middle, separating the room in two.

No one was in immediate view, and Hildey called out, "Melinda? Mrs. Vickers? Are you here?" but there was no reply.

This was very unlike Melinda. In fact, Hildey and his wife, Nell, had been very concerned for Melinda's wellbeing after her husband had passed away from a heart attack last winter. They'd become friendly and had been to each other's homes several times for meals over the past few months.

"Melinda!" Hildey called again as he moved along the

middle row of shelving. As he approached the far corner, he spotted several empty, torn cardboard cartons on the floor. Visible on them was lettering, which read, 'Chiodo Candy Corn-Made in Bronx, USA'. Like the others nearby, it was torn and empty. There were several on the shelf still, but most looked similarly damaged as the ones on the floor.

Just a little past the mess at the edge of his light lay Melinda. At least, he thought it was Melinda. The only way he could tell was from her grey hair and the dress she usually wore when working at the store, what remained of it, at least. Most of her clothing, along with all of her flesh, had been stripped from her body. The only thing remaining was some of her hair and the lower part of one side of her dress where it hadn't been covering her legs as the ants had eaten her alive.

"Oh my Lord, Melinda. I'm so sorry." Hildey shook his head sadly, his face a mask of disgust at what had happened to this poor, gentle woman who could rattle on for seemingly hours about the numerous candy varieties she sold in her Candy Corner.

From a shelf at his side, a flicker of movement caught Dugrodt's eye, and he thrust the lantern in that direction.

It turned out he had indeed seen movement, and the thing moving had also seen him. A giant red ant scuttled toward his outstretched arm and crawled onto it with lightning speed.

The chief stifled a cry of disgust and shrugged his arm sideways to dislodge the creature, but the lantern flew from his hand as he did. It shattered on the ground, and the room was suddenly ablaze with light as the kerosene flowed along the floor and under the wooden shelves, its greedy, yellow-blue flame devouring the tinder-dry wood and cardboard.

Dugrodt found himself thankfully free of the ant, having successfully dislodged it when he'd flung out his arm. However, that was of little consequence because he could now see, illuminated by the licking flames, that he was not alone down here.

Dozens and dozens of multifaceted eyes glittered back at him in the firelight, and they all began moving away from the flames in his direction.

As he backed up the stairs from the basement, Hildey pulled his service revolver and began shooting at the closest ants, and they exploded as the lead slugs tore into them. But this only made the remaining ants more aggressive. It was just like he recalled Caleb saying, and he now regretted his decision but kept firing anyway as he arrived at the top of the stairs. His Enfield began clicking on empty chambers as a multitude of ants scuttled up from the darkened basement and into daylight toward him.

Cookie still stood at the top of the stairs, seeming paralysed with fear, his eyes wide and unblinking.

"Get out of here, now!" the chief roared.

This was something that the cook had no problem hearing, and he said, "Don't have to ask me twice!" With surprising speed, the old man fled from the store with his wolfhound escort in close pursuit.

"Well, shit on a shingle!" Dugrodt said. He began backing quickly toward the front door, at the same time trying to reload his weapon with the ammunition on his belt. He only had a dozen rounds between the two pouches, and from the looks of things, there were many more ants than he had ammo.

CHAPTER SIX

Kitty's hands throbbed from the rope that cut into the tender flesh of her wrists and ankles. The scar-faced one, Antonio, hadn't been too gentle and had left her like that, tightly tied in the loft bedroom of Farley Jones's house. After listening to the men clump down the narrow stairs, she could just hear their low, rumbling voices, most likely in the kitchen directly below where she was being held captive. She'd strained to listen to what they'd been saying but had given up and presumed they were just up to more scheming and conniving regarding Caleb's gold and her ransom.

It was hot up here. Kitty's heavy cotton dress caused her to sweat profusely, and she was getting quite thirsty. The gag was back in her mouth, but at least this one wasn't some grime-filled handkerchief from a filth-ridden pocket of one of the gang members. Instead, torn in half and wrapped around her mouth several times were layers of fabric from Farley's rather oily pillowcase. It was an improvement, but not by much.

A screened hatch allowing access to a small attic in the pinnacle of the roof lay closed overhead. It was near the wall and hard for her to see into without craning her neck because of the angle. Behind the screened hatch was a solid wooden door which would be closed in winter but was now propped open to let some of the heat from the room exit through soffits in the eaves.

Unfortunately, it did little to move or exhaust the hot air in the loft of the small house since the window was shut, Antonio having closed it after tying her up, saying, "We wouldn't want anyone to hear you scream and come runnin'." Outside the window, the leaves of a large elm rustled energetically in the growing breeze from the approaching storm. There'd been several more flashes of lightning and crashes of thunder from the far end of the valley, but no rain had yet fallen.

Thinking of rain, Kitty's thirst reared its head again, and she realised if she was going to spend any length of time in this room, water would be a necessity. However, an extended stay was not something she was planning on, thanks to an accessory she usually wore, one which was currently proving itself invaluable.

On most days, a nickel-plated comb swept Kitty's luxurious, auburn-coloured hair back on one side of her head, making her even lovelier than Lillie Langtry, according to Caleb. She was very thankful that today had been one of the days she'd chosen to wear the accessory. It had a very sharp edge, one which she'd cut herself on in the recent past. Shaped like a sea shell, the top was scalloped, which, thanks to the thinness of the metal, was almost like a serrated blade if held at a certain angle.

As her recent injury sprung to mind, Kitty realised her unfortunate accident had instead been a fortunate incident. She'd struggled to reach the comb at first since both hands had been bound together, then draped over one of the bed posts.

After much contortion, she'd managed to lift her arms over the bedpost, then freed the comb from her hair. Holding the side of the hair accessory at the correct angle, she'd been able to just reach the rope on her wrists and begin to saw slightly back and forth. She'd been at it for several minutes now and could feel it beginning to loosen as the rope's strands were gradually cut.

While she worked, Kitty thought she could hear something over the slight noise of her cutting, and she stopped, her head cocked as she listened. It was a very soft tip-tapping noise. She had been entirely focused on her bondage removal and hadn't been paying attention to the world around her. That wasn't surprising since she was normally bad for tuning things out, thanks to her wandering mind. But it was especially problematic when she was focused on a task as intense as she currently was with her bondage removal. On top of that, the wind was getting stronger outside, whistling around the eaves and adding to her inability to hear slight sounds.

Tip-tap, tip-tap, tip-tap, over and over and over again. What was it, a tree branch tapping against the window? From what she could see, there didn't seem to be any branches close to the single pane of glass that might cause such a noise. She listened a moment longer. No, it wasn't from outside the window. She listened intently once more. It wasn't outside the bedroom door or from the closet at the foot of the bed either.

Kitty shook her head, unsure if the sound was something she needed to be worried about at the moment. Another crash of thunder came from outside the bedroom window, and she jumped slightly, then continued to work on the thick rope around her wrist, sawing away with the shell-like edge. In the kitchen below, the men's voices continued their low rumble.

***

"I am going out," Jesús proclaimed.

"Out? Out where?"

"To get some supplies. Being in the situation we now find

ourselves in, I think we will need certain items in order to have an advantage."

"An advantage? Well, we got more than enough ammo now." Antonio pointed to the sacks on the kitchen table.

"Yes, but that is not the problem. I need different supplies for something else in the near future. If we get the information out of that Irishman about the location of his cavern, we will need more than just ammunition."

"Well, what do you want me to do?"

"Stay here and look after our little senorita."

Antonio's eyes narrowed, and he gave a small laugh, saying, "Oh, don't worry, I can look after her all right."

"No, not in that way, you fool!"

Antonio cringed slightly from the harshness of Jesús's voice.

Oritz continued, his voice rising slightly, "I do not need another mess like in Santa Fe, so you leave her alone, for now."

Antonio grinned, his scar becoming even more jagged as he did, and said, "Yes, that was a bit of a misunderstandin', wasn't it?"

Misunderstanding was putting it mildly, Jesús realised as he thought of the last time he'd left Antonio in a similar situation with a captive. The things that man had done to the girl they'd kidnapped for ransom, a wealthy agriculturalist's daughter, had been horrific. And though Jesús was not unaccustomed to violence, there were still some lines he would not cross. But Antonio, it seemed, held no such reservations, so Jesús felt the need to clarify before he left, adding, "I want no misunderstandings this time, or the blood shed will be yours."

Though it was only mid-afternoon, the day outside had grown exceedingly dark. Lightning flashed, and thunder rumbled, but no rain had fallen so far. The wind was so strong it almost pulled the door from Jesús's hand when he exited the kitchen's back door. He found the key in the lock and used it now, not wanting anyone wandering in unexpectedly and ruining their little party.

Thanks to the many trees and bushes surrounding the property, it was quite private here, and he couldn't have asked for a better place to hide out. Once they'd gotten inside, they'd scared their stolen horses away. They didn't want the animals tied near the house in case nosey neighbours wondered what was happening and came to investigate. And though this meant they would need to use their legs to get around the town, he figured it was safer that way.

Thankfully, they had seen no sign of spiders in the house so far. When they'd arrived, Antonio had dropped down into the crawl space under the house to check but found nothing except a few spider webs. And so, he was quite pleased. This looked to be an excellent place to hole up until they could extract the location of the cavern from the Irishman and get everything they were due.

His latest cunning plan beginning to coalesce in his mind, Jesús Oritz exited the property and took to a nearby back alley as he made his way toward the downtown. Though the wind tried to pry his bowler from his head, and the smoke from the fire choked his every breath, Jesús was quite happy. With the Scottish senorita now in their possession, he was sure he could uncloud the Irishman's mind quite quickly. And if that didn't help, maybe he would allow Antonio to do some more whittling.

CHAPTER SEVEN

As soon as he stepped out of Doctor Brown's office, Caleb could see the ants were not coming from up the main street and the direction of the forest as he'd expected, but instead from Vicker's Five and Ten down the street. "Bugger me! How'd they get in there?"

"I wonder where else they've gotten into," Lucias questioned.

"There must be more than one colony," Brown said. He had an extinguisher slung under one arm and handed the other to Caleb as they began to hurry down the street, and he added, "Looks like we'll need these again. I'm glad I filled them as soon as we got back!"

They hurried down the street, which seemed dustier than usual thanks to the wind gusting behind them. Closer to the store, they could see smoke begin to billow out the entrance, and Caleb said, "That's not a good sign."

Hildey was down at street level in front of the Five and Ten, firing on the ants flooding out of the store, but soon was out of ammo.

Lucias stepped in for Hildey and began to unload both his

Colts, picking the creatures off with relative ease as they emerged.

However, the ants were not overly interested in the people outside the building despite the aggression against them and the growing fire inside. It seemed something else had attracted their attention on the way out—the Candy Corner at the entrance to the store. It was currently swarming with the red beasts, and they burrowed into seemingly every open bin that contained something sweet. More and more smoke poured out of the store's front door but was quickly whisked away by the growing wind.

"In addition to legumes, it appears our red friends have an appetite for sweets as well," Brown said. He had his satchel with him and had grabbed some of the peanut balls before leaving his practice. However, he didn't lob any of the balls at them, saying, "They have nowhere to retreat to, so feeding any bait to them would be a waste." As it was, once the creatures filled up on sugar, they came scuttling out of the store only to get shot by Lucias and Hildey.

Had things remained like that, they might have eradicated many of the ants, killing a few at a time. But the building was now fully engulfed in flames toward the back where the cellar stairs were located, and more ants were being forced out. These animals chose to ignore the candy due to the growing conflagration. Caleb realised if something wasn't done about the building soon, the rest of the block might go up as well, and then they wouldn't need to worry about the forest fire burning the town down.

"Where's Mrs. Vicker?" Sandy asked breathlessly as he arrived on the scene with Angus Cochrane and the pumper wagon.

The police chief shook his head, shot another ant that scuttled toward him out the door of the store, then said, "She didn't make it, Sandy. They ate her alive."

Sandy's face clouded with anger at this news. He looked like he was preparing to run into the store to search for the woman, but instead, he picked up a stone from the street and threw it at one of the ants with his good arm. With unerring accuracy, the ant was knocked back, its hard shell exploding in cream-coloured goo from the rock's impact.

"Volunteers get pumping!" Angus called.

There were a half dozen men on both sides of the pumper, most of them volunteers which Albert VanDusen had rounded up. As one side pressed down, the other pulled up and began to expel the contents of the wagon's water reservoir.

Brown said in concern, "Don't waste the contents of that tank if you can help it!"

"Don't worry, Doc!" Angus said over his shoulder. "It's just water! I didn't get a chance to mix in the acid yet. Only just got the tank refilled from the creek, and I hadn't had a chance to do it when I heard the gunshots and saw the smoke."

Brown's look of concern changed to a one of relief, and he said, "That's most fortunate!"

With the volunteers pumping, Angus began to mount the low steps to the store's front doors, spraying and pushing back the ants with the jet of water from his hose as he went. He moved into the smoke-filled store, washing away the ants covering the Candy Corner's display case. Other ants scrambled to get out of the way of the stream of water and scurried out of the smoke-filled entrance, only to get shot by Lucias and the police chief. Having run out of ammunition, Hildey was now using a chopped-off Winchester, currently on loan from the man in black.

Any remaining ants that didn't get shot or sprayed by the pumper got sprayed by Doctor Brown and Caleb, both of their extinguishers containing the highly concentrated acidic solution. It sent the creatures into a frenzy, blinding them as it burned into their hard, red exoskeletons. Within seconds, they curled their legs under themselves, eaten from within by the absorbed acid now inside their shells.

"Yes! The added strength is working!" Brown cried excitedly.

A brick wall served as a firebreak between the Bank of Montreal and Vicker's Five and Ten. However, the flames had found their way to the roof of the bank building, and it, too, now blazed into the overcast afternoon.

Angus moved out of Vicker's temporarily to deal with the growing fire and concentrated his stream onto the bank's roof, dousing the building with as much water as he could spare, then he turned his attention back to Vicker's.

The Five and Ten's roof suddenly collapsed in on itself just as Angus prepared to move back up the front steps. A fresh surge of panicked ants came rushing out, a trio of them quickly climbing the fire chief, their mandibles snapping fiercely.

Chief Cochrane dropped the hose, and the spring-loaded lever shut off the water immediately. He tried to swat the ants from his person before they could do any damage, but they were fast and tenacious.

Suddenly, one after the other, each ant was knocked back into the burning building in rapid succession as three precise blasts rang out from Lucias's Colt Lightning.

"Thanks!" Angus called.

Lucias didn't say anything and merely nodded, then blasted two more ants that scrambled from the building behind Angus.

The brick wall between the bank and the Five and Ten had done its job well; the bricks were scorched, but that was all. The fire in the bank's roof was now only smouldering, and it seemed Angus had hosed it down enough. But on the other side of the wall, the store was almost completely gutted. The fire chief gave it more spray for a moment when the hose suddenly began to hiss and sputter as the pumper ran dry. "I figured we were getting low!" he called over the gusting wind.

Looking at the dead ants surrounding them, Caleb said, "These beasts washed ashore at the river just up from where I landed. How could they have tunnelled all the way up here?"

Brown shook his head. "I don't think they could have tunnelled this far. They must have found some natural access that allowed them to have made it so far so quickly with the ground as rocky as it is around here."

Not seeing any more ants coming from the remains of the Five and Ten, Lucias asked, "Is that it?"

"You mean, apart from the other horde of red devils approachin' from the forest?" Caleb asked.

"Yeah, I guess," Lucias replied, holstering his revolvers with a flourish.

Doctor Brown said, "Those creatures will be here shortly, and I'm sure they'll keep you more than occupied.

"Well, they seem pretty easy to take out with a sidearm," Chief Hildey observed.

"You ain't seen nothin' yet," Caleb replied.

"What do you mean," Lucias asked.

Caleb shook his head and said, "I mean when the ones

from the forest fire get here. It'll be much harder to hit them when a couple of dozen swarm over you all at once. So, you better be sure you're a fast reloader, my friend, or have guns hidden in places I've never seen."

"You'd be surprised," Lucias replied with a squint.

CHAPTER EIGHT

Kitty cast another fear-filled glance at the screened hatch in the bedroom ceiling and began working even harder to free herself.

While she'd sawed away at her rope, the tapping sound had come again, and she'd looked to the one place she'd neglected earlier. When she craned her neck and discovered what it was, her heart almost stopped in her chest.

Over a dozen hand-sized spiders tipped and tapped across the screened attic hatch over her head, sounding like a gentle rain falling on the tin roof above. The screen separating them from Kitty wasn't the sturdiest, and though the arachnids' weight was minimal, she could see it sagging nonetheless.

Her hands finally free, Kitty had been working on her feet when she heard the heavy tread of boots on the stairs. Ceasing her escape attempt, she leaned back, the comb clasped tightly in one hand and draped her arms over the bedpost once again. With that done, she angled her feet underneath a bit of untucked blanket to hide the part of the rope she'd been worrying at with her serrated hair comb.

Antonio clumped into the room, a glass in one hand. "Hey, little missy. I brought ya some water. Figured you must be right parched up here." He sat next to Kitty on the edge of the bed, then began to remove the gag from her mouth, but suddenly stopped and asked, "Are you gonna be peaceable?"

Kitty nodded, her eyes fixed on the glass. She was so thirsty she was willing to agree to almost anything.

Antonio held the glass toward Kitty. She tilted her head forward to be able to drink properly and started a long, grateful swallow.

With a choking cough, Kitty gagged and spit out some, but not all, of the liquid, unfortunately swallowing some before she knew what it was. "Vodka!" she gasped.

Grinning broadly, his scar a jagged white reminder of his wicked ways, Antonio nodded and said, "Thought you might like a drink to loosen up."

"What do you mean?" Kitty wheezed. The vodka burned its way down her throat, its fire seeming hotter than what burned in the forest. Rarely a drinker, the strongest thing in which she usually imbibed was wine or beer, and only then when a sourdough insisted on buying her a drink. But now, in her eagerness to quench her thirst, she had taken in several ounces of the clear alcohol before her brain registered what she was actually drinking. Already feeling the vodka's effects, her voice was hoarse from the bite of the booze, and she asked again, "Loosen me up for what?"

Adjusting his position, Antonio placed a hand on Kitty's thigh and said, "Well, we got a few minutes while Jesús is out and about, and I thought we should get to know each other a little better. Like the sayin' goes, when the cat's away, the mice will..." Antonio trailed off, seeming unsure of the adage's end.

"Play," Kitty finished. Her eyes grew wide as she imagined what play would be involved in getting to know better the scar-faced man currently holding the glass of alcohol in one hand and stroking the side of her breast with the other. In a calm voice that was no doubt enhanced by the vodka, Kitty said, "I'll give you a turn if you get me a glass of real water first." She smiled sweetly as she spoke and felt relieved that her feminine wiles had not deserted her in this time of need.

The scar-faced bandit stood and said, "All right, little missy. There's a hand pump in the kitchen of this place, so I'll go get you your desire, and when I come back, you can have some of mine." He chuckled at his joke and moved toward the door.

Antonio turned back, his face now solemn. He removed the spring-loaded knife from his pocket and held it up before his eyes so he could look closely at the gleaming blade and then past it to focus on Kitty at the same time. His eyes were as wide as Kitty's, but they contained something completely different than hers—while hers were filled with fear, his seemed to hold nothing but madness. His smile returned briefly as he focused on his knife once more and murmured, "Yeah, we're gonna have some fun real soon," as if promising his blade there would be blood upon its glistening surface in the very near future.

Kitty sprang into action as soon as her captor's feet began clumping down the narrow stairs. She unlaced her hands and sat up, then began to saw at the rope around her ankles with renewed fervour. She'd tried to untie them once she'd freed her hands, but the knot was too tight, and so she'd been forced to use the comb as she had on her rope-bound wrists. The whole time Antonio had been sitting next to her, she'd held the hair accessory tightly clasped in her hands, sharp edge outward and ready to wick it out at a moment's notice and give her kidnapper more than just another scar.

When Kitty had sat up to work on her feet, she'd felt the room spin slightly from the alcohol she'd inadvertently drunk. But apart from that, she was feeling pretty good, in fact.

Somehow, it seemed the alcohol in her system gave her a boost as she sawed through the rope. It was something she'd noticed over the years, but there seemed a fine line. A certain amount of booze could sharpen her reflexes, while just a little too much, and she actually performed much worse. Throwing or catching things, along with many other digitally intensive tasks, sometimes seemed much easier, or at least she found she could perform them more quickly with a single drink, the odd time she imbibed. This felt like one of those times, and as she sawed through the rope, she was surprised she hadn't seen any smoke from her vigorous motion.

Another flash of lightning outside the window was followed shortly by a heavy crash of thunder. Downstairs, Antonio had been whistling away to himself, and immediately after the thunder's rumble, he called out from the kitchen, "Yeehaw! That was a good one! Just like the big bang I'm gonna give you, little filly!"

This proclamation from below induced Kitty to increase her rapid sawing motion, and suddenly, the rope snapped in two. And none too soon because everything suddenly seemed to happen all at once.

While she'd worked, Kitty had resisted the urge to do so, but now that she was free, she glanced up and back at the screened hatch in the ceiling and bit back a horrified scream.

The spiders that had previously been few were now many, and the thin screen was loaded down and sagging with the scuttling creatures, crawling overtop each other in their eagerness to turn Kitty into their latest broodmare. Mixed in with the growing number of hand-sized spiders were some much more monstrous ones, and it wouldn't be long before their combined weight proved too much, and the screen pulled out of the frame.

With a loud clump from below, Kitty was torn from one terror to the next as Antonio began to climb the narrow stairs.

His footsteps faltered, followed by a crash of glass.

"Son of a bitch! I dropped the water! Guess I drunk too much of that vodka you didn't want. But don't you worry, little missy," he called up the stairs, "I'll be right up as soon as I get you another glass. And it won't take long since the pump is primed!" He clumped back down the stairs into the kitchen, adding as an afterthought, "And so is mine!" He hooted laughter at his innuendo, and Kitty could hear him begin to work the pump at the sink.

Take your time, Kitty thought with a grim smile. She looked about the room as her plan began to form. She felt strangely calm considering her situation but realised the alcohol was making her more relaxed than she would have otherwise felt. In a way, it was a good thing, because without her inadvertent drink, she was sure she'd be in more of a panic than she now was.

With the two bed pillows stuffed under the sheets, Kitty made it look like she'd somehow managed to free herself and was now hiding under the covers. At least, she hoped that was how it looked.

Just as she finished tucking the blankets, Antonio was suddenly mounting the stairs again, calling, "I'm comin', little darlin'!"

The closet had been her objective in which to hide, but the more she thought about it, the less she liked it. She'd have to cross the room to get to it, possibly making noise as she did. On the other hand, the bedroom door was open wide and also much closer. Wanting to keep her element of surprise, Kitty grabbed what she wanted from the night table, slipped behind the bedroom door, and held her breath.

CHAPTER NINE

Another crash of thunder sounded as Caleb approached the Glacier Mining Supply. It seemed like the storm had settled over the valley, the wind still gusting and kicking up clouds of dirt from the unpaved street, but the rain was holding off for a while longer. Thankfully, the wind was blowing away from town for the moment.

Doctor Brown had sent him down to the mining supply store to see if they had any other chemicals that could possibly be mixed into a lethal solution for the dreaded moment when the acetic acid and vinegar ran out.

But as Caleb drew closer, he began to wonder if the store would, in fact, even be open today. He'd completely forgotten it was a holiday with everything that had been going on. If they weren't closed for Dominion Day, they might be closed because of the approaching fire. Either way, he'd know very shortly since he was almost there. He had taken a shortcut, using the back alley running parallel to the main street.

Moving quickly, Caleb wasn't paying attention, and he almost knocked over a short gentleman in a bowler hat coming around the corner from the rear of the supply store. Their collision had caused the man to drop his sack, and several bundles of dynamite rolled out. About to excuse himself and assist the man in picking them up, Caleb looked more closely at the man and said, "You!"

Jesús Oritz's eyes widened, and he started pounding his feet back the way he'd come, moving surprisingly fast for a man of his size.

But Caleb's new, unbroken leg was working quite well, just like the rest of him, and he caught up to the small man in a matter of yards. His hand slapped down on Oritz's shoulder, and he wrenched the man violently around.

"What have you done with Kitty, ya bastard!" Unable to resist, Caleb punctuated his question with a fist to Jesús's face.

Oritz tumbled to the ground and lay there for a brief moment as he shook his head to clear the stars he was no doubt seeing. He grinned, wiping blood from his split lip. "What makes you think I have done something with your little Scottish senorita." With seasoned speed, the Spaniard reached for the gun in the holster at his hip.

Perhaps it was out of habit, but as Oritz withdrew his firearm, Caleb's first reaction was to disarm the man rather than retreat with his hands up. The Spaniard had been quick, but Caleb's new leg was faster, and he kicked it out reflexively and knocked the revolver flying from Oritz's hand. "It's not gonna be that easy, ya bugger. Remember, if you shoot me, you'll never see the gold. Now tell me what you did with Kitty!"

Oritz began to stand, wiping the blood that dripped from his lip with the back of his hand as he did. He used the motion by way of distraction as he withdrew another weapon, hidden in a place where Caleb had seen many men conceal weapons over the years just as the Spaniard had.

In one fluid motion, Oritz drew a blade from the top of his

boot, unfolded it and locked it in place with a ratcheting clack. He brandished the foot-long blade with menace, the gold of his grin reflecting murderously in the shining steel.

Glancing down at the razor-sharp knife and then back into Caleb's eyes, the bandit finally spoke, "This navaja has tasted the blood of many men, both back in Spain and here in the Americas, and yours looks to be next." He easily tossed the blade from hand to hand as if quite familiar with its heft and balance.

Oritz charged, lashing out with the knife, its blade dancing in menacing arcs as he lunged and swiped, each movement filled with deadly intent.

Caleb danced back out of the way, avoiding the lethally sharp blade by mere inches.

The Spaniard was far faster than he looked and lashed out again almost immediately. The knife sliced into the sleeve of Caleb's cotton shirt and scraped shallowly along the skin of his forearm for several inches. It was more than deep enough to draw a substantial amount of blood and stain his shirtsleeve crimson.

"That was my new shirt, ya bugger!" Caleb cried. And as he did, he noted he wasn't feeling anything approaching fear despite getting cut just now. Perhaps it was his determination to save Kitty from this man, or maybe it was his decision to stop running from his life and finally stand for something. Well, he figured, the love of a good woman stuck in a bad position was as good a reason as any. With this newfound confidence, he was determined to make the Spaniard talk, or else the man would be in for a world of hurt.

With a growl, Oritz decided to use his minimal height to his advantage and came in low, slashing out at Caleb's legs and scoring a red gash across his right thigh.

"All right, that's enough!"

The gang leader jabbed the shining blade toward Caleb's gut, and he felt it pierce his skin painfully, but didn't know how far it had gone in. As the Spaniard tried to poke him again, Caleb dodged back with athletic grace and grabbed Oritz's forearm. He continued to pull the man forward while twisting his arm at the same time, and the weapon fell from the bandit's grasp. Adding insult to injury, as the round little man tumbled by, Caleb drove his fist into the side of his bowler-clad head, and Oritz crashed to the ground.

Holding the knife, Caleb gathered up the errant pistol and then moved toward Jesús, who lay in the dirt shaking his head, still stunned by the blow.

"Where's Kitty? And don't think for a second I won't use either of these on you without hesitation."

Jesús grinned and rubbed the blood from his lip once more, then said, "How do you know I am involved in her disappearance?

"Because it just seems too convenient with everything else going on. Despite the spiders and ants here on dry land, neither is big enough to carry her away, at least not without leaving a trace of web or a scrap of flesh. And to me, that means only one thing."

"And what is that?"

"That you were involved."

"I am flattered that you hold such a high opinion of me."

"It's low, not high."

"Either way, you are quite correct, Mister Caleb Cantrill. Normally, I would play with you a bit more and string you along since that would be most enjoyable. However, I will keep things moving along out of expediency, and I will tell you honestly right now, yes, I have your little Kitty."

Oritz began to stand, but Caleb pointed the gun at him, saying, "You can do your talkin' right there on the ground."

Jesús shrugged and sat back down.

The urge to give the man on the ground a solid thrashing with just his bare fists and no other weapons was an intense urge Caleb had to resist. He was not a violent man, but he knew if he succumbed to the impulse, he might just beat this man to death. No, what he needed was to think of a way to outwit Oritz to get Kitty back. Inspiration came to him, and he said, "I've remembered where the cavern is." It was partially true, at least. The plan sitting on the back burner of his mind seemed like it might be worth a try, and he had nothing else at the moment.

"If this is true, then that is wonderful news. As soon as we can verify this, I will have my compadre release your woman."

"You know as well as I do that there's only one way to verify it, and that's to go up the mountain."

With another grin, Oritz said, "Then that is what we must do."

"How do I know that Kitty is all right?"

"You do not. But I never harm my hostages unless the person I am demanding the ransom from does something stupid." He squinted into the wind as another gust of dust blew down the alley and asked, "Are you going to do anything stupid?"

"No, I already did that the day I agreed to come on board your gang's little bank heist." That was more than accurate,

Caleb realised. If he hadn't done that, he'd probably still be in Alberta, working as a ranch hand or maybe a cowboy on cattle drives. Such an uncomplicated life seemed almost fanciful to him at the moment, all things considered.

Tilting his head slightly, Oritz said, "Good. But don't tell me you regret our meeting so soon?"

Caleb said with a sad shake of his head, "No, I only regret the day you were ever born, but that doesn't help me much right now."

Still grinning but narrowing his eyes, Jesús said, "There is no need to get personal. All of this is just business, you know.

"No, I didn't know that. I'd hate to see what it would be like if it were personal." He cocked the revolver, a gleaming Remington, and kept it trained on Jesús as he did. Caleb was not unfamiliar with firearms thanks to his time in the army and was, in fact, a good shot, though not as deadly as Lucias. Not quite able to shoot fleas off a rat's ass, he still did pretty well when it came to handguns and rifles. He concluded, saying, "You know, now that I think about it, I might just take you to Chief Hildey and see if he can find a place to lock you away for a while until you tell me where you've stashed Kitty."

Jesús shook his head sadly, "You know you cannot have me arrested."

"Why not?"

"If I do not return within a certain time, Antonio will begin to do unspeakable things to your woman."

As if to accentuate Jesús's statement, a crash of thunder echoed through the valley, sounding closer than ever now. Caleb was torn. He was loathe to let the little man go. But he didn't want any harm to befall Kitty either. "All right, what do you suggest?"

"May I stand now?"

Caleb gestured with the revolver, indicating the man could do so.

Oritz collected his dynamite and stuffed it back in the sack, saying, "I need this for later."

"So it was you who set the forest on fire, wasn't it?"

Oritz shrugged and said, "If that is what you want to think."

"Are you saying it wasn't you?"

"No, but I was doing the valley a favour. I despatched some creatures assaulting me and my men."

Shaking his head, Caleb said, "It looked more to me like you 'despatched' your men when you blew their heads off and sent them to whatever burning place in the afterlife they were due to visit!"

"That was unfortunate but necessary," Jesús said, shrugging again.

"Necessary? When is murder necessary?"

"They were beyond saving when we got to them. It was mercy. And if I inadvertently started a small fire, it is of little concern to me."

"A small fire? You've threatened the lives of everyone in this valley with your recklessness!"

Jesús shrugged and held his hand out, apparently expecting Caleb to give him back his knife and revolver.

With a shake of his head, Caleb said, "I'll keep these as a memento until I see Kitty again."

"Do not think we are done here, compadre," Oritz said, wiping at the blood still oozing from the corner of his lip.

Caleb looked down toward his own body and the cuts and gashes he'd received, saying, "You're tellin' me? You'd better not believe for a moment that the opposite isn't also true, compadre."

Oritz said, "I will be in contact with you soon." He turned and hurried down to the corner of the building.

"How will you find me?" Caleb called.

Speaking over his shoulder, Oritz said, "I will just look for the place in this town experiencing the most trouble. You seem to attract it."

CHAPTER TEN

Despite his numb arm, Sandy still had another, along with two good feet, one of which had ant guts all over it. At the moment, he was trying to wipe the goo from his boot tread onto the front steps of the smouldering Five and Ten. Just after Caleb departed, several more ants scurried out of the wreckage. He'd been surprised to see anything alive, but the creatures had been streaked with soot and not moving very fast, perhaps half dead already from the smoke and heat of the fire. Whatever the reason, they'd been easy prey for his size fourteens.

Shaking his head as he looked at the mess, Sandy still couldn't believe that Melinda Vicker was dead. He felt somehow responsible like he should've been there to defend her or perhaps done a more thorough job in the cellar of the store when he had explored it the other day. If he'd found the ants and hadn't been in such a hurry to get to work, she might still be alive.

And keeping people alive was what some of the other volunteers had offered to do. Several had gone on lookout from the rooftops of the tallest buildings in town. They served a dual purpose, both as fire spotters and ant locators. If there were any changes in either the direction of the fire or the ants, the fire bell would be rung by another volunteer on the ground.

Unfortunately, the man currently assigned that job was not the one who was supposed to have been doing it. Chief Hildey said the old bandit he'd had with him at Vicker's should have been relegated that duty, but in all the confusion, the man had managed to disappear.

With his boot now relatively clean and everything seeming under control for the moment, Sandy felt his own need to disappear. He approached the fire chief, who was currently rolling up the hose, and said, "If'n you can spare me for a few minutes. Mr. Sinclair wanted to see me when I was done. And since things were quiet for the moment..."

Nodding at Sandy's unfinished request, the fire chief said, "You go ahead, son. I should be okay for a few minutes, but remember, those other ants from the forest will arrive soon. And with Caleb running that errand for Doc Brown and Lucias also gone for the moment, I don't want to be short-handed, so don't be long!"

"Sure enough!" Sandy exclaimed, then began to dash back toward the Golden Nugget. As he hurried along, he felt a strange sensation in the pit of his stomach, part excitement and part dread.

There were things that Mr. Sinclair did that were for the benefit of the greater good in the town, providing many services and employment opportunities. And that included Sandy's own position and his indebtedness to the Scotsman for hiring him, an uneducated country bumpkin, and giving him a position in his fancy establishment. But he also knew that his employer did other things solely for his own benefit, despite what their effects might be on others.

And it was these less generous aspects of Mr. S which made Sandy wonder what he was getting himself into. After all, there had been things he'd pretended not to overhear during his employment at the saloon, and many of those things hadn't been good. Though he seemed a simple country boy, Sandy was aware of the bigger picture of the world, thanks to his reading. Though he knew that Thomas Sinclair could be generous on occasion, especially regarding the good of the town, at other times, he was downright cutthroat.

There'd been more times than Sandy could count when he'd witnessed one unfortunate sourdough or another run out of gold, either through gambling downstairs or running up a huge bar tab upstairs. More often than not, these men found themselves needing to speak to Mr. Sinclair. Most left his office a short while later with nothing left in the world, Sinclair taking their land and mining rights as payment for their debts.

Some of them, Sandy believed, gave more than their land and gold to cover their indebtedness to Sinclair—though he'd not witnessed it, he was pretty sure they sometimes gave their lives. In fact, he figured he needed two hands and both feet to count the number of men who were never again seen anywhere around this town after being escorted out the batwing doors by Mr. Lucias.

When Sandy arrived back at the saloon, the door to the office was open, but there was no sign of Mr. S or Angeline. He had been surprised, however, to see the girls from the second floor show up just after he did. They said they'd seen the smoke and had come into town to see what was happening. He told them they should grab whatever they might need from their rooms and then head to the hills until they could get things sorted out here in town.

After that, having no guidance or direction, Sandy returned to Sinclair's office and the display case with the black gemstones and ebony box. What was it about them that so drew him in, he wondered. He reached his good hand out and touched the glass of the case. It felt cold. So cold, in fact, that he was surprised there wasn't frost on the glass.

Sandy flipped the latch on the case and opened the door slightly, just enough room to get his oversized hand inside. He reached for the Ebony box, his fingers within inches of its cold, dark surface, when a jingle of spurs came from the hallway, moving quickly in his direction. He closed the cabinet door and jerked his hand back from the case, whirling around just in time to see Mr. Lucias standing in the doorway to the office.

"I-I was just lookin' for Mr. Sinclair."

Lucias nodded toward the cabinet Sandy had been closing and said with a slight smirk, "Well, you're not going to find him inside there because he's downstairs and wants to see you."

The gunman turned and moved back down the corridor toward the basement stairs. Sandy followed along behind, saying nothing. He and Lucias were never much on speaking terms. The man in black usually said very little and spent most of his time with Mr. Sinclair. Apart from his legendary shooting skills and abilities with various kinds of bladed weaponry, he knew little of the man.

Lucias moved quickly and lightly down the stairs, Sandy clumping behind, his large boots easily filling each tread. His mind was still preoccupied with everything he'd felt moments ago when he'd almost made contact with the ebony box. Like the stones, the box seemed to draw him in, and he wanted to be in its presence and feel the power it seemed to contain. He also wanted to see inside it, wondering if it held more amazing black stones.

Following Lucias through the heavy steel door into the lower gambling bar, Sandy found it strange how the room felt without the customers that would usually be here at this time of day. Most sensible folks were home packing their belongings or already heading up toward the Golden Mile pass to camp out, just in case the fire got too close for comfort. And so, it meant no customers.

They entered Mr. Sinclair's lower office, and Sandy marvelled at what it contained, his mouth agape as he looked around. This was a room he'd seldom entered, and it seemed filled with even more weird and wonderful things than the office upstairs, with some items that looked like they'd be at home in a castle dungeon. Though Sandy swept the Nugget's floors each night before the end of his shift, he never did so inside Sinclair's offices. That was done by someone else, perhaps Lucias or Angeline. Up until his recent exposure to the dark things in the cabinet upstairs, and now seeing these other wonders, he'd never spent any appreciable time in his boss's office.

At the other end of the room, Lucias walked around a massive desk that looked almost as large as the one upstairs and just as polished. However, it didn't seem like they would spend time admiring it.

His jaw dropping even further, Sandy watched as Lucias twisted the stone head of an angry-looking Chinese fella, and one of the bookcases swung out, opening like a door.

"What in tarnation?" Sandy wondered as he gaped at the wrought iron cage beyond the bookcase.

Lucias slid a metal gate aside and stepped into the cage, gesturing with his hand as he said, "It's an elevator. Hop in."

Sandy did as instructed and jumped lightly into the elevator cage, shaking it mightily. There was a metallic 'clang' from somewhere far below, and it reverberated throughout the elevator shaft.

His face flashing with anger, Lucias said, "I meant, step inside."

Bowing his head slightly in contrition, Sandy said, "Sorry, Mr. Lucias. I take things the wrong way sometimes."

Lucias didn't respond and slid the gate closed. "Okay, now relax, big boy. We're going for a little ride." The black-clad man pulled a lever, and the metal cage descended into darkness.

CHAPTER ELEVEN

With a shuffle of stumbling feet, Antonio staggered into the room, saying, "Whoops, that was close! Almost dropped it again! Definitely shouldn't have had that whole glass of vodka. But don't you worry, little missy, I'm still more than—" He broke off as he looked at the bed. "Hey, how'd you get loose, little filly? Guess it don't matter none. You're already under the covers and ready to get down to business. I like that in a woman!"

As she'd fled from the bed, Kitty had grabbed a heavy pewter candlestick holder from the bedside table, one which matched a picture frame containing Farley's dearly departed daughter, Emmaline.

Kitty now brandished this heavy candle holder as she stepped out from behind the door.

Antonio began to turn as she approached, but Kitty was faster. The man's eyes widened, and he uttered a grunt of surprise as the candle holder made contact with the side of his head. He collapsed onto the bed and rolled onto his back.

Not waiting to see if she'd knocked him out or not, Kitty moved to the open doorway and squinted her eyes slightly as she lined up her shot and let the candlestick holder fly.

Whether it was her natural ability or the slight relaxation the alcohol provided, Kitty's aim was straight and true, and the pewter holder flew up to the ceiling and crashed into the brass latch that kept the screened hatch closed. The flimsy latch broke off, and a sudden rainfall of spiders poured down, covering Antonio's semi-conscious form with a blanket of creeping, crawling death.

Keeping the momentum of her escape velocity, Kitty didn't wait to see what happened next and slammed the door shut, locking it from the outside with the key located conveniently in the lock. As she did, she heard her would-be assailant begin screaming as his new spider blanket began to bite every part of his exposed skin and inject him with paralysing venom.

"Omigod! Sweet Jesús!" was all Antonio could say before his wails became muted gagging. Presumably, one of the larger female spiders had thrust its breeding tube down his throat and had begun to lay eggs in the linings of his lungs, welcoming him to their wonderful webbed world.

As Kitty backed away from the door, another brilliant flash of lightning was followed by a huge crash of thunder that shook the house. Near the door's bottom edge, hundreds and hundreds of spider legs tipped and tapped around, some trying to reach under the door as they sought to escape the room, their legs looking like little hairy fingers beckoning her to unlock the door. With a shriek of fear, disgust and relief, Kitty flew down the narrow stairs, hoping she didn't break her neck in her haste.

Just as she reached the bottom, footsteps clumped across the front porch. Kitty high-tailed it toward the back door. Discovering it was locked, she resisted the urge to scream in frustration. There was no bolt to turn, and the lock required a key. In a panic, she looked about, unsure what to do.

And then Kitty saw it, the trap door to the crawlspace. She

grimaced briefly at the thought she was now thinking but nevertheless pulled the door up and looked into the darkness. No new spiderwebs were down there, at least since they'd found Farley, and she lowered herself into the trap as she heard a key rattling into the front door's lock.

Kitty lowered the trap lid as quietly as she could, squeaking it closed just as the front door creaked open. The sound of heavy tread moved down the short hallway from the front door toward the kitchen. Looking upward, she could see a sliver of light coming through the edges of the trapdoor where it met the floor. Jesús had stopped almost directly over her head.

"Antonio? Where are you, amigo?" Not receiving a response, he replied to himself, "Probably upstairs keeping the senorita entertained, I would imagine. Well, you better not be damaging the goods."

Kitty held her hand over her mouth to stifle the scream she felt wanting to escape her lips.

The bandit placed something on the kitchen table and then clomped off toward the stairs in search of his companion. Kitty listened as he climbed the stairs and stopped on the upper landing when he encountered the locked bedroom door.

***

"Antonio? I hope you are not harming our hostage, not yet, at least."

Jesús rubbed his swollen lip for a moment as he listened at the bedroom door. He expected to hear the mattress springs squeaking, but there was only silence on the other side. He chuckled and said, "Needing privacy, are you?" He tried the door handle and asked, "Why did you lock this?"

Strangely, the key was in the lock, just as they'd found with the front and back doors. What was it with people leaving their doors unlocked in this country? There were locks for a reason—to keep people like him out. Shaking his head, Jesús unlocked the door and pushed it open, then cried out in horror, "Madre de Dios!"

Antonio lay motionless in the centre of the bed. At least, he thought it was his compadre, but it was hard to tell. Although Antonio's grisly fate could only have befallen him less than an hour ago, the spiders must have been fast and efficient because he was now covered from head to foot in webbing, with only part of his face exposed around his nose and mouth. The bed was thick with scampering spiders, mostly the smaller hand-sized creatures, just now finishing their cocooning.

Unfortunately, one of the larger, head-sized spiders hung in the corner of the room. It noticed the fresh prey standing in the doorway, looking dumbfounded, and it scuttled rapidly in Oritz's direction.

With a squawk of fear, Jesús slammed the door, squashing some of the little monsters in the doorframe, but several more scuttled out to freedom.

The Spaniard danced about the floor, stomping and cussing and stomping and cussing until he'd ground each and every one of the disgusting things into the polished hardwood.

This had to be the doing of the Scottish skirt, he realised, wherever she now was. Oritz swore to himself then and there that if he ever found her, he would give her more than just a piece of his mind.

Over the years, he and Antonio had been through many adventures, stolen much wealth together and sent more than their fair share of souls into the great hereafter. And despite the man being a little slow on the uptake at times, he had been a valued and trustworthy right-hand man through it all.

Roaring, he said, "Where are you, you little bitch!" He moved into the other bedroom across the landing and wrenched the door open, only to find it empty, or at least it had no place for a Scottish floozy to hide. He cursed and slammed the door closed.

Mixed in with the anger Jesús currently felt at the Scotswoman was something else—he felt bad for his fallen compadre. It was strange since he usually never felt compassion for anyone. But his association with Antonio went back to the days when he had first come to Mexico from Spain to take over his family's business holdings.

Antonio had been a loyal and trusted ally since the beginning, and yes, now that he thought of it, even a friend. Jesús didn't have too many friends since most people lived in fear of him, and he was okay with that. But now, one of his few friends was growing spiders inside his body, and he hadn't even had a chance to put the man out of his misery since he'd been too busy dealing with the crawling monsters trying to escape the room. Yes, the young Scotswoman would pay for what she had done, and her pain would be excruciating and drawn out, just like Antonio's. He smiled again, glad to have something more to look forward to.

Stomping back down the stairs, Jesús quickly searched the house but found no sign of the woman. He'd locked the front door when he returned just now and had locked the rear entrance when he left for his dynamite. So that begged the question, if she hadn't escaped via either of those routes, where was she now?

There were no places to hide on the ground floor of the small house that he could see, and no windows were open. Apart from the kitchen in the back and a small parlour and living room in the front, there were only so many places a petite Scotswoman could hunker down out of sight.

And then he saw it. A trap door lay in the floor of the dining area near some sort of clothes drying rack.

Jesús flung the door open, expecting to see the woman cowering in the dark and blinking up at him with her big, pale blue eyes, but no one was there. He stuck his head down the hatch but saw nothing more except darkness and some wooden panels framing the support posts near the trap.

There were signs of someone being down there recently since the dirt floor looked freshly disturbed, as if someone had dragged fabric along the dirt and smoothed it out as they went. Someone most likely wearing a long dress.

Taking a deep breath, Jesús held it as he lowered his bulk into the small hole so his belly would fit down with the rest of him.

"Niñita? Where are you? Come to Jesús." After waiting a moment, there was no sign of the woman paying any attention to his pleas, and Jesús crawled further into the darkness. Did he hear something just now? He listened harder. It was hard to tell with the howling wind outside, but the noise didn't seem to repeat itself.

A flash of lightning blazed briefly through the cracks in the skirting that ran around the edges of the house. It was pitch dark down here even though it was only mid-afternoon, but it wasn't surprising since the storm clouds outside were the colour of a day-old bruise. As more thunder pealed outside, he struck a match to see better.

Waving the match back and forth as he moved to light his way, Jesús found what he was looking for once he arrived at the far corner of the crawlspace. A piece of skirting looked to have been recently broken away and then placed back crookedly. And stuck in the corner of the skirting was something that made him smile and angry at the same time—

a piece of a purple fabric the exact same colour as the Scottish floozy's dress. He snatched it from the sharp corner of the wood and stuffed it in his pocket, thinking it would make an excellent gag for when he found her again. And find her he would, that he swore to his fallen compadre.

Jesús yanked the skirting back and wiggled his bulk through the hole and into the gusting day beyond. He called out as he stood, "Do not worry, niñita, I will find you! And when I do, you will feel the pain you have caused Antonio!" A bone-rattling crash of thunder echoed throughout the valley, seeming to punctuate his call for vengeance, and he gave a golden grin of grateful anticipation.

CHAPTER TWELVE

With time running short, Doctor Brown needed to get as many more peanut balls ready for the next batch of ants as quickly as possible. Though some ants might eat the balls on the spot, as he saw from his observations at the fire, others were taking the bait back to the colony where it would be shared. And it was the ant's hive mind and their need for the collective good that he was counting on to kill them. Even a tiny bite of one of his tasty treats would be enough to make an ant seriously ill and eventually kill it. From what he understood, one of the effects of boric acid was to disrupt the ants' ability to digest their food and absorb its nutrients. Despite continuing to eat, they would eventually starve to death.

But that took time, and time was something in short supply at the moment. Between the fire and the other threats the valley now faced, he'd calculated the odds of the growing town's survival. And being a gambling man on occasion, he realised those odds were quite bad, dwelling in the cellar somewhere between low and abysmal, according to his reckoning.

The doctor stood before the spider's cage, the sloshing black beast in the bucket at his feet. Even if his poison ant bait were successful, what of these other two species of monsters from the past? How could they best deal with them? Set traps for the black beasts near the river? And what of the spiders? He'd thought of several methods and was trying to figure out which might be best.

Looking more closely at the coiling obsidian creature before him, he wondered if his eyes were playing tricks on him or if the thing had actually gotten bigger. With a scowl, he said, "Well, I'm pretty sure your bucket hasn't gotten smaller." The beast seemed to fill the mop bucket with much more black, oily skin than he remembered from earlier in the day. He hadn't fed it at all, and from his understanding, the last thing it had eaten was perhaps a bit of a small boy's arm.

"What am I going to do with you two?" he queried of his remaining menagerie. The spider hung upside down in its cage, its numerous eyes regarding him with cold, unnerving intelligence. The little black beast splashed about in the bucket some more, seeming to react to the sound of his voice.

Inside the galvanised washtub, still encased in its spider cocoon, the ant now looked more like a silken-wrapped cabbage roll. As Brown stared at the dead ant, he recalled the last time he'd stood and looked down on something dead at the hand of another. In fact, in that case, it had been something killed by his own hand—Samuel Nash's racehorse, which he'd overdosed in Vancouver at the Hasting's racetrack.

Of course, it hadn't been an intentional act. He'd only been trying to give Samuel what he wanted. And that was a horse that would win races. Due to some previous, unfortunate dealings with some less-than-savoury characters who had similar illicit goals, Cornelius had been introduced to Samuel Nash one fateful day. The man had drawn Brown aside and given him a 'business proposal'. Upon reflection, Cornelius realised the man's desire to have a winning horse no matter what the cost was something on which he should have taken a hard pass.

But that hadn't been the case since Cornelius had been wallowing in the depths of his addiction to alcohol at the time. In fact, he had felt quite grandiose in his description of his abilities to dope the man's horse. And so, he'd started the Thoroughbred on a regimen of drugs that would ultimately lead to its death by overdose at his hands.

Now, as he stared at the cocooned carcass of the giant ant, he wondered about the overdose he'd given the horse. What he was doing with the ants was similar in that he was also poisoning them, except this time, it was intentional. He shook his head, feeling somewhat like a member of the Borgia family, though he seemed to specialise in animals rather than people.

Turning to the oversized arachnid again, he wondered if he could do something similar through poison but without harming the town's population. Though he'd toyed with the idea of using the cyanide from his gold extraction process and mixing it with his acid spray deterrent, he wanted to avoid killing anything other than his targets. If he were to go the poison route, he needed to figure out a delivery method that wouldn't kill him and everyone around once it was initiated.

And then he had it, or so he thought. He recalled his conversation with Caleb about the arachnids hunting the ants in the cavern and wondered about it again. Was there a way he could lure the spiders into a trap? Could he use an ant or two for bait? But for that to work, he would need a good supply of ants, which he was trying to poison. He shook his head. More thought was obviously needed on this, he realised.

The doctor's musings were ultimately interrupted when Caleb came bursting through the front door, accompanied by a deep rumble of thunder. His eyes almost bugging from their sockets, he said, "Kitty's been kidnapped!"

Brown looked at Caleb with wide eyes of his own, his bushy white brows like startled caterpillars on a piece of yellow birch. But his reaction was only due in part to Caleb's startling statement. The rest was due to seeing the condition of his Irish friend's clothing; the front of his shirt and pants were stained with blood. "Are you sure, my boy?"

"I'm as sure as the nose on my face!" Caleb declared, then gestured toward the blood on his clothes, adding, "I just had a scuffle with her kidnapper." He removed a revolver stuffed in the waistband of his dungarees and placed it on the front counter. "That's where I got this. From our friend, Jesús."

Cornelius nodded toward the Remington, eyebrows still raised, "I was just going to say, you don't normally sport a pistol. But then again, you don't normally sport those either." Brown pointed to the bloody gashes on Caleb's clothing. He gestured to the examination table and said, "Sit up there and let me take a look at those while you tell me what happened." He shook his head, adding, " I certainly hope the other fellow is in worse shape than you."

"I laid him out flat," Caleb said somewhat proudly. He unbuttoned his shirt and removed it for the doctor to examine his wounds, then lay back on the table.

"Good job, my boy," Brown said with a nod. He moved to a tall jar containing cotton balls next to another filled with gauze. He gathered them up along with a glass bottle of iodine, asking, "Where is the miscreant now?"

"I let him go."

"You did what?"

"I let him go," Caleb repeated. "That other fella with the scarred face, Antonio, is still holdin' Kitty captive. Jesús told him that if he didn't come back, to start hurtin' Kitty until he was told to stop."

Brown shook his head, saying, "Well, they mustn't be

based too far away if one of them was out and about while the other minded the store, so to speak. No disrespect intended to Miss Kitty. I hope she's holding up."

"Me too, Doc. I don't know what I'd do if somethin' happened to her." Caleb said sadly.

"Yes, you have grown quite close over the last little while, at least from what I've seen."

Caleb's sad smile brightened slightly, and he said, "Aye, that we have, Doc."

Brown began to examine Caleb's torso as he spoke, "You do make an attractive couple."

"I'd have to agree with ya," Caleb said as he craned his neck to where the doctor currently probed. "How's it looking?"

Shaking his head, Brown picked up Caleb's cotton shirt and fingered the hole in the fabric, the bloodstain around it now turning brown as it dried in the heat of the day. "Are you sure this is your blood?"

"Of course, Doc! What're you talking about? I felt the knife scrape my arm, jab my belly and slice into my thigh. In fact, with my leg, I think I'm lucky he didn't hit an artery!"

Brown picked up Caleb's arm and wiped at the blood with some iodine-soaked cotton to clear where the wound looked to be and asked, "And how's it feeling right now?"

"I gotta say, not bad, actually."

The doctor moved lower to examine the skin beneath the blood on Caleb's thigh, wiping it vigorously with the iodine, then said, "Well, however bad your wounds were, I can't find any trace of them now, only what looks like some slight scarring."

"What? Stop kidding around, Doc! How are they?"

"Look for yourself." Brown pointed to the patch of skin on Caleb's abdominal muscles, now wiped free of blood.

Caleb sat up and probed with his fingers back and forth and up and down along his abdominal muscles but found nothing. His digits moved to his thigh, where there was a gaping hole in his dungarees. Like a robin looking for worms, his fingers probed and poked for a moment longer, then he said, "Look, I know he scraped me here and stabbed me there. There is no way that is his blood. He had a bloody lip and wounded pride, but that was all."

"Well, my boy, it seems that once again you've gone and done something miraculous because it appears your wounds have completely healed." It was true since the only evidence of the cuts were some fine white scars looking as if they'd occurred years ago rather than this very afternoon.

"But it only happened a short while ago at Glacier Supply!"

"I don't know what to tell you, but once again, you seem to be extremely fortunate in the healing department."

"I'm wonderin' about that, Doc."

"Oh, and how's that?'

"For some reason, I'm beginnin' to feel that somethin' like this condition of mine might just turn out to be a curse in reverse."

CHAPTER THIRTEEN

The elevator lowered silently into the cavern below. Sandy's eyes were as wide as could be as he took everything in. Lucias lit a lantern after the elevator began to move, and it shone on the rough rock of the shaft walls that flowed by as they descended into the bowels of the earth.

Sandy had been in a couple of caves in his lifetime but never anything like this. The ones he'd been in were low and cramped and didn't go very far into the ground. But this, this was completely different.

As they neared the bottom of the shaft, the rock face on one side disappeared as things opened out into a massive cavern. Visible through the wrought iron cage, long stalactites hung down from numerous places in the darkness above.

With a clunk of metal on metal, the elevator came to a stop, and Lucias opened the gate. Sandy stepped out in wonder, staring into the large volume of darkness surrounding them. Off to one side, Lucias worked silently at something. After a moment, he turned back toward Sandy, a newly lit lantern in hand, this one much brighter than the small kerosene lamp he'd been using. The gunman left the other lamp on a large rock that seemed to serve as a work table of sorts. With Lucias in the lead, they moved off into the darkness, Sandy following close behind.

"What is this place, Mr. Lucias," Sandy asked quietly.

Lucias didn't respond right away, and they continued to move in silence for a short distance, then he said tersely, "You'll know soon enough."

They paused when they came to a rickety-looking wood and rope footbridge across a dark, swift-moving river.

"I'll go first. I wouldn't want to trust this bridge with both our weights on it—or more to the point, with just your weight on it. Nothing personal."

"Yessir, Mr. Lucias," Sandy said with a nod. He watched as the gunslinger crossed first, then stepped tentatively onto the first slat.

Black water rushed only inches beneath Sandy's feet as he carefully followed behind, stepping only where the man in black had stepped, the wood creaking alarmingly under his muscular weight.

Heart thumping in his chest, Sandy made it to the other side of the dark river without incident, and he began to follow Lucias down a short tunnel. A faint hint of light was coming from around a corner up ahead. Voices echoed softly, becoming easier to hear as the rush of water lessened at his back.

"...and make sure no one knows." It was Mr. Sinclair's voice.

"Don't worry, if he makes it back down, it'll look like an accident." A familiar voice, but one that he couldn't quite place.

"See that you do. We don't want any further

complications," Angeline said with finality.

They came out of the tunnel into another large chamber, its depths extending into darkness. In addition to Angeline, Mr. Sinclair had a representative of the law visiting him down here, one Constable Albert VanDusen. Strange for the police officer to be here, Sandy thought. He was supposed to be rounding up more volunteers for the chief.

Sinclair said to the constable, "Come and see me later."

VanDusen nodded and then moved toward the tunnel where Lucias and Sandy had just appeared. The constable brushed by them both, nodding slightly at Lucias as he passed, but ignoring Sandy altogether, which was a pretty tricky proposition to begin with because of his size.

Mr. S and Angeline were off to one side of the cavern at a small, rough-cut wooden table. As they approached, Sinclair said, "Sandy! I'm glad you're here, laddie."

Looking around in astonishment, Sandy said, "Thanks, Mr. Sinclair, but what is this place?"

"Come with me." Thomas took the lantern from the table, another super bright one, and left Angeline with the man in black.

Thomas reached up and placed one hand on Sandy's muscular shoulder in a fatherly manner, and they moved off into the darkness together. In a kind voice, which was surprising for the Scotsman, Sinclair asked, "How long have you worked for me now, laddie?"

Thinking hard for a moment, Sandy replied, "Gosh, Mr. Sinclair, it's gotta be a whole year and a bit at least now."

Thomas nodded and said, "That sounds about right. And in that time, have you enjoyed workin' for me?"

With a nod, Sandy replied, "Yessir. It can be a trial sometimes working the front door at the saloon, but I like my job."

Sinclair laughed and said, "Yes, workin' with the public can be a challenge, but it can be rewardin' as well."

"You sure do seem to do some good business at the Nugget, that's for sure, Mr. Sinclair."

"Aye, that I do. But that is not where the real money is, as I'm sure you know."

"It isn't?"

"No."

"Where is it then?"

Thomas removed a golden nugget from a pocket in his tailored vest and showed it to Sandy. "D'ya know what that is?"

"Yessir, it's gold." That was a bit of a silly question, Sandy thought. He certainly knew what the yellow metal was after such a long time in his current position, much of it from talking with the sourdoughs in the saloon. Once in their cups, they sometimes liked to share their gold mining ordeals with him and show him some of their pouches of extracted dust or the sizeable nuggets they'd found.

In fact, after Sandy swept up each night, at the end of his shift, he would sift through the sawdust and peanut shells and sometimes find a substantial amount of gold dust and fragments in the bottom of the dustpan. There was a small sack hidden in his shed out back where he would put his findings, and it must have almost a pound of reclaimed gold in it at the moment, but it was a fact that he shared with no one. He wanted to give it to his mother and father back home in Rock Creek sometime next spring when he went for a visit. His dad was getting on in years, and his mother suffered crippling arthritis due to her time as a laundry worker and her exposure to constant cold water used in the process. Yes, a good pound of gold dust would help them out quite nicely.

"D'ya want to make some more gold for yourself?" Sinclair asked with a slight tilt of his head as if reading Sandy's mind.

Taking a moment to process the offer, Sandy said, "Gosh, Mr. Sinclair, that sounds great and all, but I don't know if I'd have time for diggin' for gold while keepin' an eye on the front door of the saloon." He sure was interested, though. Extra money for his parents was always a good thing, he figured. And he could also buy more books which was an added bonus.

Chuckling at Sandy's response, Thomas said, "You wouldn't need to do that anymore if you came on board in a different capacity for me."

"Different capsity?"

"Capacity. Yes, a different position, if you will."

"Oh. What position is that, sir?"

"Similar to what Mr. Lucias does. Sometimes, I need someone to help me go about my business here and elsewhere in the world, someone who can help people understand that they should agree with whatever position I take on a subject or whatever I propose to them."

Help people understand his position? What did that mean, Sandy wondered. "I don't know too much about business, Mr. Sinclair."

"You don't have to, laddie."

"But who'd work the front door?"

"Don't you worry about that," Sinclair said with another small laugh.

The walk had ended, and they were now standing before a hole in the ground about a dozen feet across. It seemed colder here, perhaps because of the dark opening before them, which seemed to have no bottom. Mr. S shone his high-intensity lantern into its depths. "D'ya know what that is."

"A big hole?"

Laughing again, Sinclair said, "Yes, but much more than that." He gestured around the cavern with his free hand and added, "When I built the Golden Nugget Saloon, I built it here for a reason."

"To be over a big hole in the ground?"

Thomas shook his head. "No, because of what was also located nearby."

"Gold?"

"No, it was for somethin' far more valuable."

"Diamonds?"

Sinclair shook his head. "You remember those stones in my cabinet upstairs?"

"Yessir. There's somethin' special about them."

Nodding, Sinclair said, "Yes. You felt it. D'ya know where I found them?"

"Here?" Sandy asked, still staring into the hole's inky blackness, which seemed even deeper than the black stones upstairs. He thought of the novel he'd recently loaned to his friend Caleb and wondered at the hole before him. Did it go all the way through to the centre of the earth? Were there monsters from out of time at the bottom?

Clapping his hands together, Thomas said, "Very good, laddie! Yes, here. Not down this hole exactly, but nearby, and also in similar situations in other places around the world. But wherever I've found them, they've always been near holes like this."

"Really? But how did you know where to find them?"

"We'll come to that in a moment." Sinclair guided Sandy away from the hole in the ground and moved them toward another darkened corner. Soon, they were standing before the entrance to another cavern, which sloped slightly downward, but its entrance was filled with water.

"Did you find some in there?"

"Nay, we've never explored further than this. But I've ordered a divin' suit from back East that I hope to use in that process in the future."

They began to walk back toward Lucias and Angeline. Thomas said, "But in answer to your question. I knew those stones were there."

"But how?"

"The same reason I knew where that ebony box was along with those stones upstairs."

"You were drawn to them?"

"Not me personally, but drawn nonetheless. Each of those stones is very powerful. And it's power that another person close to me can feel, the person who guided me to this spot and who can see more than is visible to most men."

"More than visible?"

They were now back to Lucias and Angeline. Sinclair nodded and looked to Angeline with a satisfied smile, saying, "Yes, all thanks to my Angeline. Not only can she feel the stones, but she can see things that others can't, just as she can know things about others without being told, things a person would never tell another soul."

Sandy looked with interest at the woman before him. Thomas had called her 'his Angeline,' and Sandy wondered at that. He'd always suspected there was more than met the eye to Thomas's relationship with the woman.

Angeline smiled coldly at him but said nothing at this revelation.

"But why are you tellin' me all this, Mr. Sinclair."

"Like I said, I want you to become more involved in my operations, and I can use a good strong back like yours in more situations than just minding the front door of my saloon. And don't forget, with your new duties will come much more money to send home to your family." Sinclair looked expectantly at Sandy as he spoke, while Angeline and Lucias only stared blankly at him, saying nothing. The Scotsman patted Sandy on the shoulder again and said, "So what'll it be, laddie?"

His mind awhirl, Sandy didn't know what to say. More money to send home to his family sounded like a great thing. But he also knew Mr. S was a powerful businessman and that some of his dealings were not quite above board sometimes, especially when it came to helping other people part with their hard-earned cash and gold. Another part of Sandy also wondered what else this new position might require of him. He didn't have a problem keeping the peace at the front door of the Golden Nugget, but it seemed that this new position may have other aspects that were much less straightforward. However, the thought of helping his ageing parents was a strong desire within him. And so, with a twinge of reluctance, Sandy nodded and said, "What do you need me to do, sir?"

CHAPTER FOURTEEN

Caleb was buttoning his torn shirt when the first screams sounded outside.

Hurriedly gathering his satchel, Brown filled it with as many peanut balls as he could manage, saying, "I think the ants from the forest are finally here."

"I'd say you're right. Those people probably aren't screamin' just for the fun of it."

His balls gathered, the doctor picked up one of the acid-filled fire extinguishers and handed it to Caleb, then grabbed the second for himself and said, "I've refilled these with the last of my solution."

"Then let's hope this is the last of those ants."

Dust was being whipped into great clouds by the growing storm, stinging their eyes as they stepped onto the wooden sidewalk. Yellow-orange flames shot high into the sky, the fire seeming closer than ever, the trees closest to the edge of town now fully engulfed. Barely audible over the wind, Caleb could hear the high-pitched keening of the ants as they grew closer.

Near the upper end of the main street, at the edge of the

forest, a wave surged into view toward them. However, this wave did not bring relief from the encroaching fire, but instead, a red flood of almost certain death.

The red beasts rushed eagerly forward, crawling overtop each other as they advanced. Whether they were agitated from the fire or keen to start filling their food stores with the town's remaining residents, whatever their motivation, the creatures looked unstoppable as they moved into the town.

A group of volunteers stood as a vanguard, defiant before the crimson wave. They had a substantial amount of firepower in their hands, including shotguns, rifles and handguns.

Caleb and the Doctor moved past them in the opposite direction, trying to distance themselves from the ants to allow the doctor to work. As they hastened along, Brown tossed his peanut balls here and there, and by the time they arrived at the front of the Golden Nugget, he'd used most of his supply.

Ester and Camille came galloping around the corner from the alley behind the saloon. Emily rattled along in pursuit, tethered to the back of the pumper wagon. It seemed whatever Chief Angus could find lying about the smithy, he'd strapped to Emily, using the small mule as a weapon supply transport. She sported an array of axes, pitchforks and other assorted smashing and stabbing implements.

The fire chief steered his rig to where the doctor and Caleb now stood in the middle of the street, extinguishers at the ready, another group of volunteers alongside them.

"Looks like I found the party," Cochrane called.

Up the block, the first group of armed volunteers met the ants. Their lead tore into the scourge, and a cacophony of ear-ringing blasts rang off the hardwood buildings on either side of the street. Sadly, their firepower was of little use against the approaching horde, and as one ant was knocked back, two more took its place. They eagerly scuttled over the corpses of their downed comrades, rushing toward the menace on two legs killing their brethren.

Unfortunately, the volunteers had been caught unaware because the ants had not come from just one direction but from the alley at their side as well. Some of the men tried to run, but the ants snipped and snapped and tore them down as they tried to shake them from their arms and legs. They shrieked in agony as the puppy-sized creatures swarmed over them, clicking and clacking as they ripped into their bodies. The poor unfortunates squealed and thrashed for several moments, but they soon stilled, now nothing more than lumps being torn to bite-sized pieces.

Caleb watched this in horror, his final moments in the cavern flooding back to him. The mass of ants looked even more terrifying in daylight, and he realised that many more must have washed out of the cavern than he'd initially thought. Either that, or they'd multiplied like, well, ants.

In his cursed cavern, Caleb had only seen the red devils dimly during his initial introduction in the small tunnel, when he'd thought their eyes had been diamonds. And though he'd glimpsed the army behind the scouts near the fire outside of town, the glade through which the creatures had marched made it difficult to judge their true number. But now, he could see them clearly, and it seemed they were legion.

Angus jumped down from the pumper, and several volunteers began to unfurl the hose. Calling to Brown as he handed out tools from Emily's back, the fire chief said, "Got some more weapons, and I filled 'er up again, Doc!" He nodded toward the pumper, saying, "And it's got the acid in it this time!"

"Tremendous!" Brown called. "I hope the combination of my remaining store of acid and the vinegar from Maggie's kitchen will be enough!"

The ants swarmed along the width of the main street as they moved forward. The men they had torn to pieces seemed to have only whet their appetite. They scuttled into any open doors or windows of the buildings on both sides of the street as they approached, no doubt searching for more food and prey to take back to the stores at the colony.

Pointing to the questing ants, Brown called to Angus, "Make sure to spray down the fronts of the buildings, including the doors and windows, along with the sidewalks in front. We want to keep them channelled in the street and don't want them going in every direction. That way, we can concentrate our firepower as we channel them toward us. After all, we want them eating my balls!"

"That sounds wrong on so many levels," Lucias said as he pushed through the batwing doors of the Golden Nugget. He was followed by Sandy, a pump shotgun in his good hand. Behind them stood the girls from the second floor, their eyes wide.

Sandy tromped down the Nugget's front steps and handed the weapon to Caleb, saying, "Here ya go, Mr. Caleb. I can't use this with one good arm anyway, and I can probably help better over at the pumper." With that, the boy moved to Ester and Camille while calling to Angus, "I'll guide the mules while you spray, Chief!"

Angus nodded and prepared to hose down the sidewalk and front of the Golden Nugget. However, the second-floor girls were still standing in front of the batwing doors, and he advised them to get back inside and stay away from the fluid. With the ladies hustling out of harm's way, Cochrane began to hose down the front and sides of the building, then proceeded to the Kootenay Saloon across the street. They moved as quickly as they could, with Sandy guiding the pumper wagon mules and the chief spritzing ant deterrent, alternating sides as they went.

Lucias and Chief Hildey joined Caleb and the Doc near the front line. The gunslinger looked at the shotgun in Caleb's hand and asked, "You know how to use that, don't you?" Lucias also held the same model, a Winchester 1893 pump-action, no doubt from an armoury kept somewhere inside the Golden Nugget.

"I've had occasion to use one recently," Caleb replied. "They're not my favourite, but then again, no weapon is." He sometimes used a rifle for hunting, the that was the extent of his firearms usage these days.

"Favourite or not, make your shots count." The gunslinger handed Caleb a belt loaded with shotgun shells, then nodded to a saddlebag over his shoulder, saying, "And I have extra ammo in here. Holler if you need some."

Caleb had fastened the ammo belt around his waist while Lucias spoke. With a nod, he reached into the saddlebag, grabbed a handful of extra shells, said, "Don't mind if I do," and then began sliding them into the Winchester's loading port.

"Wait till they get close enough," Lucias admonished as several other men nearby with firearms joined them. "We don't want to waste any ammo. There might be more ants than we have ammunition for."

A couple of large, plopping raindrops slapped the dusty ground in front of Caleb, but nothing more fell for the moment, the business end of the storm not quite upon them. The clouds were dark as midnight and towered high above the licking flames of the forest fire. Several miles away, toward the back of the valley where the clouds had originated, none of the mountains were now visible. A heavy grey sheet of drenching rain fell along the edge of the approaching front, but whether it would do any good, or even arrive in time, remained to be seen.

Another brilliant flash of lightning streaked overhead and struck a tree a half block off the main street. The elm burst into flames, the fire spreading quickly, and it engulfed a quaint little house sitting next to it as well.

The ants began to hit the poison peanut balls the doctor had dropped in the street, and they quickly snatched them up. Now laden with the bait, the creatures retreated with them through their oncoming comrades as they sought to store them for later enjoyment by the colony. The plan seemed to be working, and the animals weren't straying from the street since the acidic solution coating the buildings and sidewalks seemed strong enough to keep them moving in the right direction.

Brown grinned and shouted gleefully, "They must have enjoyed their last feed of my balls. And this new batch is even stronger, so this is wonderful!"

Caleb shook his head and said, "Maybe it'll be wonderful when another week goes by, and your poison works its magic, Doc, but I don't know so much about right now."

Checking his rifle, Chief Hildey said, "Yep. For now, we need to deal with the live ones."

Sweating profusely, the men clattered the pump handles up and down as they toiled away. Angus continued to spray the fronts of the buildings and sidewalks. The smell of vinegar was heavy in the air, making some of the men cough. As they continued backwards down the street, the ants moved inevitably toward them.

With an excited, "Woof!" Rufus came bounding out from a narrow side alley between two buildings. He saw Sandy leading Emily and galumphed toward the boy. There was a piece of something fluttering from the dog's mouth. Sandy scruffed the dog's head as he retrieved the wolfhound's prize. "What've you got there, boy?"

A piece of blue denim fabric the size of Sandy's oversized hand had been torn from someone's trousers. Sandy turned it over in wonder and said, "My, someone must have a bit of a draft right now."

"Did you find our missing cook?" Hildey asked Rufus as he approached. The chief gave the dog a quick scruff, then blasted a pair of ants scuttling from the side alley where the dog had come.

"I wonder if he treed the ol' bugger?" Caleb asked.

The chief scruffed the dog's head again and said, "Good dog. But we'll have to go get the old boy and the rest of his pants once we've dealt with our little bug problem."

Rufus basked in the chief's praise for a brief moment. But as the chief stopped petting him, he turned his attention to the approaching ants with a growl.

Suddenly, choking smoke descended on the group when the wind changed directions yet again. This kicked up more dust and debris, making it difficult to see the advancing swarm of ants. Several men had bandanas, which they pulled up over their noses, though it did little to help.

The line of men waited for the ants to get a bit closer before opening fire. Though the animals were large for their size, they were also quick, erratic and hard to track. Thankfully, the pumper's spray seemed to be keeping the creatures funnelling toward them, except for where Angus hadn't been spraying—the rooftops. He hadn't had the time or enough acid solution for the tops of the buildings, and this was an unfortunate oversight.

With a shriek, a man off to Caleb's right began swatting at

his body. An ant had dropped onto the volunteer from a section of covered walkway that ran in front of several businesses. In fact, numerous red beasts now scuttled over the edges of the surrounding rooftops toward them.

Across the street, another man roared with pain as he fell to the ground, two ants having dropped onto him from the tin roof over the sidewalk. One of the animals burrowed into his ear, another into his throat. As they snapped and sliced their razor mandibles, his blood sprayed across them, brightening their already brilliant red shells.

Doctor Brown sprayed the ground around the volunteers as well as any ants that strayed too close. However, he couldn't spray the men being attacked any more than Caleb could shoot the ants from them with his shotgun as Lucias had with Hildey. No one was that good a shot except the gunslinger, and he was busy just trying to keep himself alive at the moment. Beside Caleb, Sandy beat at the ants with a large, long-handled wooden mallet, each blow cracking the monsters beneath into white-yellow goo.

Chief Hildey blasted his rifle at ants surging over the edge of the nearby rooftops. At street level nearby, men beat at them with pokers and tongs, pitchforks and scythes. But there were too many things happening all at once, and each man was in the middle of their own life-and-death struggle, and their organised defence began crumbling away. It was also when the inevitable moment arrived as the volunteers who actually had a firearm began reporting their ammunition running critically low.

Two ants dropped off the edge of an awning onto another volunteer's back, distracted as he was by the struggles of the other men around him. One of the ants scurried around the man's body and tried to weasel its way into the folds of his shirt to eviscerate him. The other scuttled quickly over his shoulder toward his face. He squealed as the first ant impelled its mandibles into his gut, crimson gushing from around the beast as it scuttled inside him. The other took the opportunity to begin thrusting its blade-like pincers inside his wide-open, shrieking mouth. He began to gag instead as the beast began chewing its way down his throat. He collapsed to the ground in a shuddering heap, only to be quickly overrun by a swarm of the deadly creatures.

Sandy shouted in alarm, and Caleb turned to discover more monstrous ants approaching at their backs. A flanking contingent of the beasts had snuck in from an alley lower down the main street. And now, with six-legged eating machines coming from the high road, the low road, and all directions in between, the group of exhausted men were captured in a pincer of peril.

Doctor Brown called to Angus, "Spray your hose behind us to slow them down!"

The fire chief nodded in understanding. He'd been spraying the street in front of the group to slow the approaching ants, and now, he turned his attention to the flanking contingent, coating the dry, rutted dirt with the acidic solution.

The ants skittered back, and it looked like the spray might grant the town's defenders a slight reprieve when, all of a sudden, Angus's nozzle hissed and sputtered as the tank of the pumper ran dry.

CHAPTER FIFTEEN

Farley Jones had lived not too far from where he worked each day, the ice house. Located on the edge of town, his home was close to the forest, which now burned just beyond the line of trees closest to Kitty Welch.

The wind had changed again and now moved in the direction of civilisation once more. In fact, it looked like the fire was already burning into a part of town not far from here, where several new houses had just been built. The smoke was thick but could have been worse. The gusting wind was a dual-edged sword, allowing some moments of fresh air but also whipping the flames into even more of a frenzy.

The crawl through the dirt underneath Farley's house had been harrowing. She'd crawled, terrified, through the dark, moving from corner to corner in her panicked search for a way out, thinking eight-legged death would drop on her at any moment. Fortunately, it had been arachnid-free, and for that, she was extremely grateful.

Some skirting had been loose, and she'd been able to kick it out with her foot but tore her dress as she scurried into the backyard. After hastily replacing the skirting to cover her tracks somewhat, she'd fled into the stormy afternoon. It was only a matter of time, she realised, before Jesús began searching for her outside the house, and she wanted to be well away by the time that happened.

A short lane ran to the edge of Farley's property, where it met a dirt road. There weren't many other houses along this stretch since it was on the edge of the town. From here, a path led down to the river and the ice house where Farley worked, but the way was currently engulfed in flame. Not that Kitty wanted to head in that direction anyway. More forest was on the other side of the road, the land not yet developed. Luckily, there was a way through this bit of forest via another less-trodden path that cut through toward the downtown, and Kitty took it now.

Kitty's time being chased by the Red Flannel Man came flooding back to her. Jesús would soon be looking for her, and she didn't want to be out in plain view. Not following the road was her plan, at least until she could get closer to the safety of the Golden Nugget. With the fire burning out of control, ants and spiders swarming across the land, and ravenous black beasts in the water, she didn't think any place in this valley was safe now.

The trees were fairly thick and provided good cover. Lightning flashed overhead, illuminating the gloom of the dense patch of forest. As Kitty moved out from around another tree, her eyes widened in surprise. Just coming round a bend in the narrow path was the old man from the bandit gang who talked so much about his pots and pans.

Unfortunately, he saw her, too, and his eyes grew large in delighted surprise. "Well, well! I was just hidin' out here after excapin' that damned police dog and look who I should meet!" He began to advance on her, his eyes now carrying more than a hint of crazy.

Kitty backed away from the grizzled man, saying, "I don't have any quarrel with you!"

"I know ya don't. But I also know that Jesús had been talkin' about a plan to use you as leverage, and now it looks as if we're about to get our chance." He started toward her with his hands out as if to grab her.

Kitty's legs now moved as fast as they could, the tips of twigs and branches along the narrow path scraping at her arms and tugging at her gown as she ran. Though she held the fabric off the ground, she was still constrained by the dress's design and cursed its lack of function.

Exiting the small patch of forest, her troubles suddenly doubled because who should be coming toward her from the opposite direction but Jesús, a wild and wicked gleam in his eyes. He'd no doubt found the exit she'd made from the skirting at the house and gone searching for her as she'd feared.

Unsure which threat was worse, Kitty decided the small Spaniard in the bowler won that prize, but the old man, with his crazy look, took a close second. She darted off at a tangent away from both, moving swiftly into a clearing ahead. Though she hadn't run in a while, her childhood had been filled with it, and she had been one of the fastest of all her siblings. Though her lungs now burned for air, she kept up her pace and was doing quite well, having reached the middle of the small clearing.

And then, her long dress suddenly pulled free of her hand and wrapped around her legs, and she fell to the ground with a jarring thud. Gathering herself up as panic threatened to overwhelm her, Kitty was about to beat her feet further when an iron hand gripped one arm, and she was spun around.

"Gotcha, little lady!" It was the old man, and he seemed to have been surprisingly fleet of foot to catch up to her. He grinned at her menacingly, the kindly, almost simple look he wore at the Golden Nugget, now long gone.

The air smelled heavy with moisture as great splattering raindrops began to fall. But they were soon mixed with something else--small chunks of hail. They tipped and tapped as they slapped into the ground and bounced like popcorn in a hot kettle.

At the old man's back, looking winded, Jesús walked rapidly in their direction. Though he'd been moving quickly behind Kitty when she'd started her dash to freedom, it seemed the rotund little man was not much for distances. The cook, despite his age, with his longer legs, had been right behind her when she'd stumbled.

Kitty felt a sting as a sharp chunk of ice struck her neck. The pebble-sized hail that had tentatively begun to fall with the rain now began to drop in earnest, and it was getting bigger and bigger.

The old man tightened his grip on her arm as he grinned toward Jesús and said, "Yer in for it now, little lady!"

A chunk the size of a golf ball suddenly struck the old man on the back of the head, and he let his hands drop away from her with a howl. He briefly rubbed where the ice had struck his wispy, white hair and then covered his head with both hands as more and more large chunks of hail began to rain down on them all.

Kitty took this moment to bolt away and did so with a shriek.

Jesús was close by but also battered by the storm's wrath. Another flash of lightning was immediately followed by a huge crash of thunder, and a large spruce tree exploded off to one side of the clearing, cleaved in two by the blinding bolt. One piece crashed to the ground near the old man, and another substantial chunk slammed down near Jesús, unfortunately missing both men by only inches.

Though the downed tree separating Kitty from the bandits was not huge, it was enough to buy her some time, and she used the diversion to her advantage. With her forearms over her head, she fled the clearing for the safety of the forest once again.

Daring a glance over her shoulder, Kitty gave another small scream. The men were pounding their feet rapidly after her again despite their close encounter with the tree and the growing ice storm. Her plan had been to get to the Nugget, but with the hail still growing larger, she didn't think she'd make it that far. If she tried to venture out into the open, it would most certainly mean death from above.

Her dress hitched high, Kitty fled blindly through the forest, now well off the path, the brush tugging again at her dress. The old man jogged along at her back, and panting behind him was Jesús.

Kitty came out at the lower end of Main Street a few moments later, near the semi-demolished police station and funeral parlour. And it was here that her progress came to an abrupt halt.

It was not only because she'd run out of forest to protect her—up ahead were hundreds and hundreds of ants, and they all moved toward a group of men in the centre of the main street, halfway up. Caleb was among them, but he couldn't see her at the moment since he was too busy fighting for his life.

The hail continued to pound into the ground around Kitty, but she moved into the open, nonetheless. Her head was protected for the moment with an inch-thick piece of bark from a rotting tree she'd collected as she arrived at the forest's edge.

Ice chunks cracked like gunshots against the bark as she ran, and just as she made it to the covered porch of the police station, Kitty's protective headwear split in half. She cast it aside and looked in the direction she'd come. Thankfully, there was no sign of the two men pursuing her quite yet, and she hoped that some of the large pieces of hail had caved in one, or preferably both, of their heads.

CHAPTER SIXTEEN

Pumping his Winchester, Caleb Cantrill unleashed another round at the surging ants. The shell's scattering shot tore through two of the beasts, rending them to numerous pieces both at once. All around him, men blasted, stomped or smashed at the ants still coming over the tops of the buildings, and that was only part of their problem.

The largest mass of ants still moved down the main street toward them. But they were currently at an impasse on the other side of the soaked earth where Angus had sprayed to give them a bit of buffer. He'd also sprayed some behind them, though he'd laid down much less there since the pumper had run dry. But at least the acid solution was working for the moment, but how long it would last was anybody's guess. The ants were already probing and retreating and probing and retreating, and soon, they would swarm over the acid-topped earth just as they had everything else.

At Caleb's side, Lucias continued to blast away at the advancing army. Each spray of his buckshot took out several ants at once, but unfortunately, just as many took their place.

Only a block away, the forest fire had reached the buildings just off the main street. Searing flames shot high into the air as the straight, dry timbers of the newly constructed houses caught quickly and were rapidly consumed.

Before creating his own flash flood in the Kokanee River, Kitty had told Caleb of a late spring storm that had run roughshod over the valley and caused some small amount of flooding as the river had overrun its banks. Another plop of rain struck Caleb's shoulder, and he glanced quickly at the tumultuous sky, offering a quick prayer they would be that lucky today.

Seeming in answer to his appeal to heaven, the large plopping raindrops were suddenly mixed with small pieces of ice the size of marbles. They clattered and clanged as they hit the tin roofs of the buildings along the street, bouncing off the covered walkways and into the quickly darkening dirt.

Sadly, the spray Angus had been laying down on the ground was soon diluted, and it gave the ants the break they were looking for, and they surged toward the men from all fronts.

But now, the hail began to get larger and larger as it dropped, and soon, the ice chunks were the size of a golf ball, with some the size of a fist also beginning to fall. They crashed into the hard-packed dirt, some shattering into thousands of glass-like fragments and others driving deeply into the rapidly softening ground.

The men quickly holstered their weapons and covered their heads with their arms as they scattered onto the covered sidewalks on both sides of the street. The ice crashed onto the sheet metal over their heads in a deafening cacophony. Unfortunately, some sections of the walk were only covered with a thin layer of wood instead of tin, and the heavy ice chunks blasted through like cannonballs.

Meanwhile, back in the street, with no cover, the ants

surging toward them began to explode in bursts of yellow-white gore as the large hail balls battered them with concussive force. The animals scattered in all directions, some heading onto the covered walkways, now occupied by the men.

Blasting and cussing, the men repelled the ants' attempts at self-preservation, and creatures that didn't get pummeled by the hailstorm above were torn to pieces by the leadstorm below. Many of the creatures perished from the dual fronts, but many more still survived, and they crawled seemingly everywhere at once as they attempted to escape their fate.

With another brilliant flash and thunderous crash, the dark, turbulent day turned as bright as high noon for just a split second, and everything, man and monster included, seemed set in alabaster.

After several minutes, the pounding hail from the heavens began to diminish slightly, and large drops of rain began mixing with the ice. Soon, it became a deluge, the water pouring down in sheets and washing away the dead ants as well as the live ones, sweeping the creatures past the police station and morticians. The dirt that had covered the hard-packed street was now saturated, becoming a mire of thick mud topped by several inches of fast-flowing water.

Emily and the other mules had survived the hail storm thanks to Sandy. He'd unhooked them from the pumper wagon and managed to lead the team to the edge of a covered walkway whose tin roof wrapped partly around the side of one of the buildings. A bench had been set there, and Sandy had tossed it aside almost effortlessly, then led the mules mostly under its cover.

Though the punishing hail had no doubt bruised the poor animal's still exposed hindquarters, their heads and most of their bodies had been spared the concussive force of the pounding ice. As the hail had fallen, some ants had tried to scramble to cover in the mules' new safe spot, but Sandy had been standing by with his mallet and smashed to paste any of the creatures that tried to share their space. Rufus had also been there, snipping and snapping at any creatures that made it by Sandy. And even the mules were helping, either kicking the ants away with their powerful hindquarters or crushing them to death beneath their solidly-shoed hooves.

Caleb took note of Sandy's predicament as he looked after his own. His head whipped back and forth as he scanned for any of the red devils approaching his current spot on the walkway in front of a feed supply. Many ants had floated past his location as the rush of water flowed down the street. Shaking his head, he said to several of the creatures floating past the edge of the walkway, "I hope you buggers drown!"

Brown was beside him, and he looked up at the drenching downpour, saying, "There is a good chance this might do just that to these creatures. If the water floods the egg chamber and drowns the queen, this might be the reprieve we've been hoping for!"

"I hope you're right, Doc!" An ant had managed to snag its mandibles onto the edge of the bottom step leading up to the sidewalk, and Caleb blasted it with his shotgun, taking out a chunk of the step as he did.

The smoke seemed even thicker now, and Caleb suspected it was because of the pouring rain, which gushed like an open wound from the sky and doused the roaring flames from the forest fire. Whether it would be enough to extinguish the inferno was anybody's guess, but it was more than welcome, nonetheless. However, if the rain kept up like this, he feared they might just be swept away by a flood rather than burned out by a raging fire. This country was a study in extremes, he thought sadly; alternating from one catastrophe to the next seemed to be the way of the land out here.

A shriek of pain sounded from Lucias up the street. He'd

been resting his hand on the railing in front of the assay office. A little red beast had scuttled up one of the balusters when he wasn't looking and grabbed hold of one of his fingers, snipping it off almost as if the ant were a gardener and the finger an errant twig.

Roaring in rage, Lucias smashed the creature against a post which abutted the railing, and it ruptured into a spray of guts. Caleb figured losing a finger like that would be a career-ending injury for a gunslinger in the prime of his life. But perhaps the man in black was just as proficient with the other hand. Time would tell, he supposed.

As the drama unfolded up the block, Caleb thought he heard something familiar at his back. A voice was calling out his name. His eyes widened as if he'd just seen the Second Coming, and he whirled around.

Barely visible through the smoke, haze and rain, Kitty Welch stood on the walkway in front of the police station. She was waving her arms in the air in the hopes he would see her, which he finally had. Caleb waved back and moved down the sidewalk toward her, but as he moved, he saw her glance across the street.

Under the canopy of Munroe's Bakery were Jesús and his grizzled cook, having taken shelter there from the storm and waterborne ants. It seemed that the bandits, too, had their hands full. Cussing in Spanish, Oritz shot at several of the beasts trying to share their covered accommodations while the cook beat at them with a branch he must have brought from the forest. I hope the ants win, Caleb thought grimly.

Growing closer to Kitty, Caleb pumped his shotgun, ready to use it on the bandits across the street if they decided to shoot at anything other than ants. The water level was rising surprisingly fast, most likely due to the large amount of rain that had already fallen at the valley's far end. Much of it seemed to have made its way here, and water lapped against the second of three steps that led to the raised sidewalk Caleb moved along.

Though the initial rush of water had slowed somewhat, it was filling the lower end of town at a rather rapid rate. Caleb came to the end of the covered walkway, where a narrow alley separated one block of buildings from the next. He was tempted to jump across but instinctively knew the distance was too great. And so, he waded through rising muddy water that was now up to his knees, slapping away any waterborne ants that floated past.

The next section of businesses was shorter, with Kitty one block further down, just after another small break between the buildings. Unfortunately, that end of town was much lower, and the water was deeper there, now lapping at the bottom edge of the walkway where she stood.

Caleb jumped down from the raised walk and moved as quickly as he could through the murky water between the buildings. The hard-packed dirt was now soft mud which tried to suck the boots from his feet with each step he took.

Out of the corner of his eye, as he climbed onto the next block's walkway, Caleb thought he'd seen a cluster of ants floating down the middle of the street, huddled together on a piece of tree branch. However, when he turned his head to look fully, they were gone, and only the branch twirled lazily through the water as if the ants had never been there at all. He shook his head, thinking he must be seeing things, and continued toward Kitty.

CHAPTER SEVENTEEN

Monique picked through the numerous mementoes of generous benefactors she'd collected over the last year or so of her employment at the Golden Nugget Saloon. Some were trinkets and costume jewellery, but there were other items worth substantially more than that. She'd often been given golden presents from many of her sourdoughs, golden presents she'd never converted into cash at an assay office. Altogether, she figured she had about five pounds of gold that she didn't want to leave behind. But at the moment, she was unsure if she should pack it up or not due to its weight and her possible need to travel light if the fire grew any closer.

Earlier in the day, the girls had been relaxing at the cabin on their holiday off from work. Monique had spotted the smoke first and had alerted the other girls. The trio had rushed into town, arriving just after the volunteer fire department returned from the forest.

Sandy had shown up at the saloon just ahead of them and seemed quite distracted for some reason. Despite that, he'd told them that once they'd gathered their things, they should get to safety up in the hills. In addition to the fire, he'd said there were monstrous ants to worry about, just like the ones Kitty had told them of, but many more than the couple of dozen she'd reported. So, just after that encounter, Monique and the other girls returned to their 'business suites' to begin sorting through their belongings.

But a short while later, they were interrupted by shouts and gunfire from the street outside. As Monique and the other girls descended the stairs from the second floor, they saw Sandy coming from the basement with Lucias. They'd followed the men to the batwing doors to find Chief Angus with the pumper truck, ready to hose down the sidewalks and fronts of the buildings with a powerful-smelling fluid that he said was ant-deterrent. The chief had told them to stay away from the doors and windows, so they'd moved back upstairs and continued going through their things.

But even more surprising, just after that, Angeline had swept up the stairs, asking the girls what they were doing.

Monique responded they were getting ready to bug out as Sandy had suggested.

But Angeline had shaken her head as she'd told them there was nothing to worry about and that the building wasn't in jeopardy in any way.

Monique had wondered why Angeline suspected that to be the case. Whatever the reason, the woman hadn't elaborated, and none of the girls had asked further questions. But with everything happening outside, Monique found it incredible the woman could just go about her day as usual. However, it was in keeping with the strangeness of Angeline and her seeming ability to just 'know' things sometimes. Monique and the other girls had seen this behaviour on several different occasions in the short time they'd known the woman.

Right now, and despite Angeline's assurances, the other girls were in their suites doing the same thing as she, going through their possessions and knick-knacks. All the second-floor girls had their own permanent boudoir, not shared with any other girls. As a result, they all kept things of value in their rooms since they had the only keys, except, presumably, for Sinclair.

While Monique had been packing her personal knick-knacks and trinkets, she'd left the window to the street open. It was oppressively hot on the second floor in the summer, so the windows were often left ajar, and today was one of those days. It had grown progressively darker, and she'd lit a lamp to see what she was doing. Moments later, she'd listened with surprise as hail began to fall and rattle the roof above.

The storm had been pounding away at the roof and streets outside for several minutes now. Hopefully, this change in the weather would be good for the fire and help with the ants--at least, that's what Monique silently prayed for.

But the change in the weather had brought something else rather unexpected with it, which Monique quickly discovered. So, too, did Lucy and Carla, from the sounds of it, and both at the same time.

Seeming in unison, the girls shrieked as they discovered unexpected and unpaid visitors entering their business suites.

Several monstrous red ants scuttled through the window to Monique's room, snipping and snapping their razor-like mandibles and seeking shelter from the pelting ice cracking their red skins open outside. One crawled toward the ceiling, while another dropped to the floor and scurried under the bed. A third scuttled along the wall directly toward her.

Monique had been at the small dresser near her door, and she shrieked and grabbed for the door handle at the same time, slipping out just as the red beast arrived at her location. She backed away from the door as the ants almost immediately began to worry away at the sizeable gap between the door's bottom and the floor. To her left, Carla and Lucy both burst out of their respective rooms and slammed their doors.

"Lord, have mercy!" Lucy cried. "There's a bunch of ugly buggers in my room. And I don't mean sourdoughs!"

Carla held her arm where a red bite mark welled with blood, saying, "Me as well! I was near the window and didn't see the little monster until it was crawling up my arm, and then it bit me as I tried to pull it off!" She revealed the bite, a nasty-looking gash several inches long in her soft, pale flesh. Lucy rushed to Carla's aid and wrapped a hanky around it, which she pulled from her decolletage, saying, "Let me get that tended to temporarily, darlin'."

As Lucy quickly dressed Carla's wound, Monique grew more and more concerned as the ants continued to snip and snap at the bottom of the door to her room and, from the sounds of it, the other girl's rooms as well.

"We need to do something about that, ladies," Monique said, pointing to the sharp mandibles that worried away at the bottom of her door. There wasn't much in the line of items to block the ants' progress, but there were a couple of small ornamental tables. Lucy took one and Monique the other, and they placed them upside down with their thick wood backs against the doors. Hopefully, this would stop the ants from progressing through the door's gaps.

All the doors, that was, except Monique's. While she and Lucy had been grabbing a small settee near the top of the stairs to block the bottom of her door, Carla shrieked, "They've just burst through!"

But it seemed that was stating the obvious, and Lucy and Monique had already seen what was wriggling underneath Monique's door, and they joined Carla in beating their feet down the stairs to the ground floor.

The ants, unfortunately, didn't need to use the stairs, and they scuttled from between the balusters. By the time the girls arrived at ground level, so had the ants. There was a half dozen altogether, the creatures in Lucy and Carla's rooms seemingly still trapped behind the furnishings propped there.

The trio of girls shrieked again as one and fled toward the bar. It was currently unoccupied, with Muddy nowhere in sight. In fact, from what the girls could see, they were on their own. Outside the batwing doors, more gunfire erupted as the men tried to defend the town from the ants fleeing the pounding hail. Lighting flashed, and a massive crash of thunder came from down the street, sounding like a building or a tree may have been struck.

All three ladies stood behind the bar, Lucy holding a bottle of whisky high in the air and preparing to throw it at the ants. Monique stayed her hand, however, saying, "They don't seem interested in us, Lucy. Let's leave it like that for now."

It seemed Monique was quite correct. The ants appeared hardly interested in them at all. One of the creatures had approached them briefly, its antenna waving around and its mandibles slowly opening and closing as if sensing or tasting the air. And then, it moved away and joined its colony mates who were exploring other corners of the saloon. Returning from its journey through the kitchen doors, another ant began chittering and chattering in high-pitched sibilance.

The other ants retreated from their areas of exploration and regrouped, then followed the chittering ant eagerly into the kitchen.

"What're they after?" Lucy wondered.

Closest to the end of the bar, Monique moved out first, followed closely by Lucy and Carla. All three girls had eyes the size of silver dollars as they moved toward the kitchen doors.

In the middle of the kitchen, on the island, sat a tall cake with beige frosting. From the smell, Monique could tell it was made with peanuts. In fact, the whole kitchen reeked of them. A large waste barrel was overflowing with empty shells, the contents of which Maggie had been running through a grinder clamped to the corner of the wooden island.

The ants were buried head-first in the cake, seemingly oblivious to the girls as they entered the kitchen.

"We've got to do something to stop them from running to get their friends," Carla hissed.

Lucy from London whispered, "I think I have just the thing." She nodded toward a washtub propped in the corner of the kitchen and edged quietly toward it. Monique was the closest to Lucy, and she grabbed the handle on the other side.

Nodding to her tub-mate, Lucy mouthed, one, two, three, and together, they clanged the tub down on the ants like a serving cloche over a delicious but deadly meal.

One of the ants had attempted to scuttle away as they brought the tub down, but instead of escaping, its thorax had been amputated from its abdomen. However, this setback hardly seemed to phase the beast, and using its three-and-a-half remaining legs, it dragged itself across the island toward Carla.

In a panic but needing something to use as a weapon, Carla from Calgary found a freshly oiled cast iron pan on the counter beside her. Lifting it with both hands, she slammed it down on the ant. Though this part of the animal was smaller than its sizeable abdomen, it seemed almost as gore-filled, and as the pan pounded down, the creature exploded out from beneath, spraying its innards in all directions.

Under the tub, the cake-loving ants sounded as though they were trying to gnaw their way through the galvanised metal but were having little success.

"You go right ahead and try to get outta there, ya little bastards. I dare ya!" Lucy said to the tub.

Carla added, "And I hope you get indigestion while you try!"

As if in response, the ants clanked and clunked against the steel but were unable to move the heavy washtub despite their size.

Monique moved to the screened door and looked out to see if there were any other ants outside but saw only sheets of rain scouring across the alley, now a small river, running in back of the saloon. The water was getting close to the bottom of the three low steps that led up to the kitchen. Fortunately, the Golden Nugget's foundation was substantially higher than the water flowing down the alley. But if it kept up, how long would it be before it washed into the building and flooded the gaming room downstairs, Monique wondered.

Lucy called over to her, "You know, this cake is on a cutting board." She pointed to the washtub, its circumference just about covering the sides of the large board on which Maggie hacked, sliced and diced during the day.

Monique nodded in understanding, and together, she and Lucy lifted the board and moved slowly toward the back door.

Carla still held the handkerchief to her wound but was able to open the screen door and stand out on the stoop as the other girls moved through with the captive ants.

"All right, on three," Lucy called. Not mouthing the words this time, she hollered, "One, two, three!"

As Lucy counted, they swung the board back and forth to build momentum. When three was reached, they let go of the tub, and it arced several feet out over the water.

It hit with a splash, and almost immediately, the ants swam out from under and paddled about in the swirling stream as the tub sank beneath the surface. Chunks of sodden cake floated in the water for a moment, then they, too, disappeared into the murk.

The ants continued to swim against the current moving past the door, and for a moment, it looked like they wanted to head back toward the Nugget, but that thought didn't last for long, nor did they.

From out of the muddy water surged something large, black and scaly. It circled rapidly around the foundering ants for a moment, then dodged in like a viper. One by one, it quickly snatched and crushed the ants in its spiky-toothed mouth, gobbling them greedily down.

Carla cried in horror, "Now they're a meal themselves!"

"What in the name of heaven is that thing?" Lucy wondered, aghast. She stepped back from the edge of the stoop and into the doorway of the kitchen where the other girls stood.

Monique shook her head and said, "I don't know if that thing is from heaven, but it sure seems to have a *hell* of an appetite."

CHAPTER EIGHTEEN

The rain continued to pound into the ground, or more accurately, pound into the water now covering the ground. Thanks to the grade of the main street, Caleb figured it was well over two feet deep at this end of town, his concern rising in concert with the water level.

Kitty was waiting for him less than a block away on the police station's porch, the water almost lapping at the top edge of the steps. She wore a worried expression and glanced once again across the street.

Caleb narrowed his eyes as he peered through the scouring rain. The reason for Kitty's terror, apart from the monstrous ants on the loose, was now located next door to Munroe's Bakery in front of O'Malley's Outdoor Supply.

The white-haired bandit was sitting on a bench, looking wet and miserable. Next to him, leaning against the wall, his bowler hat tilted back at a jaunty angle, Jesús Oritz gave Caleb a golden grin. The corner of his mouth was still red and swollen from his recent run-in with Caleb's fist. *I'll give you more than that next time we get close to each other,* Caleb thought grimly.

Several more ants floated past as Caleb moved down the

sidewalk toward Kitty. But as before, they suddenly disappeared from sight, pulled under the muddy water by something unseen. Caleb had a suspicion what it was—the obsidian beasts. Doctor Brown's assumption that there was more than one seemed correct. A flash of black coiling through the water after the ant's disappearance confirmed Caleb's speculation, and he called to Kitty, "Stay back from the edge of the steps as far as you can! There's a black beast in the water!"

Her look of concern even greater now, Kitty nodded and called back, "I just saw it!"

But how many were there, Caleb wondered. Was there two, or three or four, or perhaps even more? Though he'd battled only one of the beasts before going over the waterfall in the cavern, there had undoubtedly been more than one of the black creatures in that lake.

Thanks to this end of town being so low, the pools must have overflowed quickly with the downpour of rain, allowing the monsters to escape their confines. The creature's stubby legs, which Doctor Brown had noted, were no doubt effective, allowing the beasts to drag themselves through shallower parts of water where they couldn't completely swim.

And that begged the question, how to get to Kitty? The cloudy water was difficult to see into, and the black things seemed able to hide just below the surface, ready to spring up and snatch any unwitting prey that wandered by. They reminded Caleb of the crocodiles he'd almost been eaten by during his time in South Africa. Like them, the black beasts could be just about anywhere beneath the swirling, muddy flood water surrounding the buildings.

Caleb knew he'd have to fight the urge to shoot the creatures the next time he saw them in the water and would only do so if he saw the whites of their eyes, so to speak. He only had a couple of rounds left in his shotgun and had used up the rest of the ammo from the belt Lucias had given him. And even if he had the rounds, he wouldn't waste them on the creatures in the water. From his time in Africa trying to shoot the crocodiles that had wanted to eat him, he knew the shot in the shells lost a lot of its punch once entering the water. And so, unless the creatures rested on the surface, shooting them as they coiled about beneath the waterline would be a waste of ammo. A rifle would have been a different story, however. And once his ammunition ran out, the shotgun would be useless, except perhaps as a club.

Fortunately, the bandits across the street had shown no desire to try and cross. Presumably, they, too, had seen the creatures that swam in the turbid water. But even as Caleb looked across to them with a grimace once again, he had a moment of inspiration.

Though the distance wasn't great, Caleb knew he couldn't walk through the water to get to Kitty, unless he wanted to lose a leg. Since there was no way to easily walk across the narrow gap between the buildings without getting eaten, he thought he could bridge the distance instead.

Along the fronts of many buildings on the main street were benches for people to stop and rest a spell, if they wished. It was one of these benches that caught Caleb's interest. Thick and sturdy, it was made of tongue and groove two-by-sixes that ran about eight to ten feet, from what he could judge with his eye. He dragged the bench to the platform's edge and began to tilt it up on end.

When she saw what he had planned, Kitty's concerned face became hopeful once again.

He shouted across the gap, "Stand away from the edge!" The driving rain and erratic wind seemed to try and tear his words away as he spoke. If the wind hadn't been blowing the right way earlier, he doubted he would have even heard Kitty call out his name.

Eyes like saucers, Kitty complied, and she backed into the open doorway of the police station.

Caleb balanced the tall bench, angling it to the proper trajectory, one end scraping the tin roof over the walkway. He let it go, praying he had a keen and straight eye left in his head.

The bench teetered momentarily, and Caleb thought it might tilt the wrong way and fall into the water between the buildings. But gravity took over, working in his favour for a change, and the bench slammed down onto the top of the sidewalk on the other side.

As soon as the bench made contact, there was furious movement in the water as something just beneath the surface slithered quickly away, startled by the unexpected noise made by the prey it was stalking near the platform's edge.

"There looks to be more than one of those damned things swimmin' around! Watch yourself"

Nodding again, Kitty gathered her skirts and moved to the walkway's edge. She bent down, trying to adjust the side of the bench and pull it a bit more onto the porch. With one hand clinging to a roof support column, her other tugged on the bench's arm.

Just as Kitty grabbed hold of the lumber, a water-soaked ant scrambled around the corner from the side of the building and up the edge of the steps. It skittered up the leg of the bench, chittering and chattering as it moved aggressively toward Kitty.

"Step away!" Caleb called.

Kitty had already begun doing so and pulled back as quickly and as far as she could.

With two shots left in the shotgun Lucias had lent him, Caleb let loose a single blast, the buckshot scattering across the gap. The corner of the bench was blasted away, along with the ant, and it was knocked back into the water. Almost immediately, the ant's remains were tugged under by one of the voracious black things swimming beneath the water's surface.

Caleb called across the storm-swept street, directing his comment to the two bandits watching his feat of derring-do with the bench, and he shouted, "You fellas should go for a swim!"

Jesús only grinned more broadly at the comment. The old cook cupped an ear and mouthed, "Eh?"

In two strides, Caleb crossed the plank and soon found Kitty in his arms. He hugged her tight as she did him. Not caring what the world knew and knowing only that he was happy to have her safe again, he kissed her. But it was not as long or as hard as he would have liked, since one eye was still on the lookout for beasts out to eat them.

Kitty kissed back passionately but chastely, her own sense of propriety perhaps getting the better of her. "Caleb!" she gasped, sounding on the edge of tears. "I'm so glad to see you!"

"And I, you, lass," Caleb replied, his voice threatening to break. Stepping back from Kitty, he saw she had blushed slightly at his forthright nature. He looked at her with serious eyes and said, "We need to get out of here. The way the water is coming in from up the valley along with what's now fallin', this end of town is likely to be underwater soon."

"I know! I got out of Farley's just in time."

"Farley's?"

"That's where they took me! I just escaped, and they were chasin' me down tryin' to capture me again!"

Caleb hugged her again briefly at that comment and cast his eyes angrily across the street.

Still in Caleb's arms, Kitty said, "And you were right, by the way."

Holding Kitty out from his embrace, Caleb looked into her eyes, asking, "About what?"

"There's more spiders in Farley's house."

"Is that where the one with the scarred face is right now?" As he spoke, Caleb tilted his head toward the two miscreants across the street.

Kitty nodded, "Yes, but I introduced that one to some of the eight-legged squatters in the attic."

Caleb suddenly recalled the sound of something coming down the stairs from the loft at Farley's that day just after they'd recovered the man from his cocooned predicament. So it hadn't been a woodrat or a squirrel after all. He placed both hands on Kitty's shoulders, looked her in the eye and asked, "Are you all right? Did you get bit?"

Kitty shook her head and said, "No, but I can't say the same for that scar-faced man."

"Well, I'm glad you're safe." He hugged Kitty close for another moment.

Kitty hugged him back, trembling slightly as if on the verge of tears.

Another crash of thunder interrupted their brief moment

of grace, and they parted. Caleb said, "Now, we need to get to higher ground, if that's even possible."

CHAPTER NINETEEN

"Hold still, man!" Doctor Brown admonished.

Lucias groaned slightly and took another shot of whisky the doctor had provided for pain relief, then adjusted his hand on the cotton pads the doctor had laid out. This was Lucias's second shot of whisky; Brown was on his third.

After everything that had happened, the doctor had needed a good few stiff drinks, and Lucias had needed some medicinal help with his pain. He'd asked the gunslinger if he wanted any morphine, but he'd deferred, saying a few shots of alcohol now and again were about all he ever did. Otherwise, it played havoc with his aim.

The pounding, fist-sized chunks of ice had worked surprisingly well in despatching the ants. The flood of water that rushed down the street from the subsequent rainstorm had also helped wash away their remains. And those that hadn't been crushed to a pulp by the hail had hopefully been drowned, including the queen and her egg chamber. If any still survived, he was hopeful that at least a few of his peanut butter treats had made it to the food stores and were now poisoning the rest of the colony.

The water at this end of town was not too deep, less than a

foot, but down at the other end, it was a different story. Due to a natural depression at the far end of the main street, any properties that weren't built above the floodplain were now partially underwater.

Once done with Lucias, more patients were waiting in the wings at the Golden Nugget. There wasn't room for more than a single patient at a time at his practice, so part of the saloon was being set up as a field hospital. Several tables had been pushed together to create a temporary hospital ward in one corner. But before he could tend to them, he needed to finish up here.

Holding Lucias's hand, he examined the wounded more closely. "I need to get a healing plaster over this before I bind it, and your fidgeting around isn't helping things any."

"Sorry, Doc. But I don't know what I'm going to do. My trigger finger was my life! I mean, I can shoot with my left hand and shoot real good too, but not as good as my right hand. That finger made me the man I am today!"

Brown shook his head in commiseration and said, "Perhaps you can find a different line of work, one where pointing a gun, or pointing in general, isn't as important."

The gunslinger didn't speak and only looked at his mangled finger with what seemed a mixture of anger and disgust.

"Maybe you can become twice as good on your other side to compensate," Brown offered helpfully as he finished securing the bandage he'd wrapped around Lucias's hand. "I'm afraid you're going to have to go easy on it for it to heal properly, however."

Glancing with a sneer at his bandaged hand, Lucias replied, "Shouldn't be much of a problem. It's useless now, just like the rest of me." With that, he climbed off the examination table and began moving to the door.

"Here," Brown said. He handed some gauze and cotton to the man in black, saying, "If you wouldn't mind taking this down to the saloon with you. I have some more things I need to bring for the patients and don't have enough hands." Realising what he'd just said, the doctor added, "No offence intended."

"None taken, Doc. At least I still have two of them." The gunslinger tucked the bundle under his arm and paused as he opened the door with his good hand, the bell jingling overhead. "Thanks for the patch job. I'll see you soon."

"No doubt, my boy, no doubt."

With Sinclair's right-hand man, now left-hand man, taken care of, Cornelius briefly studied the two bottles he'd brought out from the assortment of chemicals stored in his combination lab/bedroom/office at the back. Before returning to the saloon to treat more patients, he wanted a quick moment to review his plan.

One bottle, filled with round white pellets, had a skull and crossbones on the front, its label reading, 'Sodium Cyanide NaCN'. The other was dark brown and had letters etched into the glass, 'Con Acid Sulfuric H2SO4 - Handle with Care!'.

As he'd been battling the ants, part of Cornelius's mind had been pondering the other problem the valley faced: the spiders. He'd been thinking of possible ways of exterminating them without getting too close with the spray, and then he'd thought of it: fumigation.

In a recent science journal, he'd seen an article about combining the two chemicals to create hydrogen cyanide gas. Once released, it could be used to fumigate rooms and entire houses, clearing them of assorted pests. He'd concluded that it had to be worth a try on the monstrous spiders. But how to dispense it was the current conundrum.

He'd thought of the cyanide initially when he'd made up his first batch of spray and toyed with the idea of mixing some with the acetic acid. Apart from poisoning everything around him, the mixture would also have created an unfortunate side effect he hadn't considered at the time; even at the low levels he would have used, he would have stood an excellent chance of poisoning himself from the fumes. And that thought had led to his recollection of the scientific article.

So now, he had the challenge of figuring out how to deploy the two remotely without gassing himself in the process. Images of one possible method appeared in his mind: a candle burning under a string, the other end of which had some gauze containing the cyanide pellets suspended over a dish of sulfuric acid. It was one possibility, but he was sure he could think of others. And once he'd figured out a viable delivery method, the first place he'd be off to engage with his experiment would be Ezra Randall's funeral parlour.

As the forest fire had raged, a small part of the doctor had hoped the inferno might do the job for him and burn the funeral parlour to the ground, though it would have likely meant the entire town going up in the process. But if such a thing had come to pass, at least it would have cleaned every trace of the cavern's scourge that hadn't yet emerged from the shadows.

The shrillness of the doorbell jangled away Brown's thoughts of eradicating spiders and turned instead to thoughts of their victims as Sandy forced his muscular bulk through the door from the street.

"Sandy, my boy!"

"Hey, Doc."

"How are our equine friends doing now?"

"Sorry, Doc?"

"Emily and friends."

"Oh, the mules! Yeah, I got them out of the mud and brought 'em around the back way to the smithy. Ain't hardly any water there, bein' a little higher and all."

"Well, I'm glad you got that straightened out."

"Yeah, I was expectin' to see a few of them there ants still, but I think they got ground into the street by that hail, or they're now swimmin' out in the lake."

"Exactly what I was thinking, my boy. And speaking of swimming, how's your arm?" When Sandy had entered, he'd noted that the boy seemed to move it somewhat as he'd tried to close the door out of habit.

"It's not bad. I've got pins and needles in it now, but I still can't move it much."

Brown grasped the boy's hand and lifted the affected arm. He momentarily poked and prodded at the thick, corded muscle, then asked, "What did you feel just now as I examined you?"

"Like my arm was covered in moss and had slugs crawlin' on it."

The doctor shook his head and let Sandy's hand drop to his side, saying, "You do paint quite a picture, my boy. You should be a writer."

Sandy's eyes widened at this possibility, and he asked slowly, "D'ya really think I could write a book someday, Doc?"

"I'd dare say you could easily write one about some of the

strange things happening around this valley of late. If I hadn't seen some of them with my own eyes, I wouldn't have believed them."

"That's one of the things I came to see you about."

"What's that?"

"What I saw with my eyes... And felt in my soul."

"Your soul, you say?"

"That's kinda what it felt like, Doc. I'm not sure what a soul should feel like, but what I felt sure seemed like something was tugging at the very centre of me, deep down inside."

"What caused that?"

"I'd gone looking for that vinegar for to put in the pumper wagon..." Sandy trailed off as if reliving the events in his own little world before speaking them aloud.

"Go on," Brown prompted.

"Well, Rufus was with me at the time. But I got him with Hildey now. Anyway, I was gettin' that vinegar and the dog went into Mr. S's office."

"Did Mr. Sinclair get angry?"

"No, he wasn't there at first. And when I called to Rufus, he wouldn't come to me."

"Did he corner an ant?"

"No, he was determined to get into Mr. S's office. And then I accidentally let him in. He made a beeline for one of those glass cases. So I went over to see what it was that had got him so worked up."

"And what was it, my boy?"

"You know how Mr. S has all those gewgaws and whatchamacallits inside his cases, them things that he collects from all over the place?"

"I am familiar with those cases, yes."

"Well, the one Rufus was worryin' over had these black stones inside with this even blacker box beneath them."

"Do tell."

Sandy looked down for a moment, then back up to the doctor and continued, "Gosh, well, I went and opened the case."

"I wouldn't think Mr. Sinclair would like that."

"Me either. But I didn't seem to care for some reason. I had this urge to touch those stones. And just as I was about to lay my fingers on them, Mr. S showed up."

"And what did he say?"

"He asked if I was drawn to them."

"And were you?"

Sandy nodded, saying, "Sure enough. Like I told you, it felt like somethin' was tuggin' at my insides. And for some reason, I wanted nothin' more than to reach out and touch 'em, but Mr. S said that wouldn't be a good idea."

"But he wasn't mad?"

"Nope. He even went on to have Lucias take me to his

secret place down below to show me where he found 'em."

Sandy quickly detailed his introduction to Sinclair's underground mining operation, revealing how Sinclair had found the black stones beneath the Golden Nugget. This was news to Cornelius since the only thing Sinclair told him and Caleb of was the golden nuggets he'd discovered underneath the saloon. There had never been any mention of the black stones.

"Well, it got even stranger. After I told Mr. S that the stones seemed to pull at me, he told me they did the same to his special lady friend, Miss Angeline. Anyway, so now, Mr. Sinclair thinks I'm pretty special."

Cornelius was surprised at this news but also saddened by it. Thomas Sinclair was attempting to pull this innocent boy into his avaricious, grasping clutches and no doubt corrupt him. With a slight shake of his head, Cornelius said, "You need to know something about Mr. Sinclair..."

CHAPTER TWENTY

Caleb balanced carefully as he moved along the narrow back of the bench in order to show Kitty how easy it was. He couldn't carry her across or follow behind her since he wasn't sure if the boards would hold both their weights. Turning around, he held his hands out and said, "See? Easy as pie!"

The rain was still falling, not in sheets, but it was steady and heavy. The murky water now lapped near the top edge of the walkway in front of the demolished police station. It would be underwater within minutes at the rate the rain now fell. And then, the black things could pull themselves onto the submerged sidewalks and gobble down anyone they found.

There appeared to be many more obsidian beasts than they'd initially thought. Caleb almost laughed aloud as he recalled his earlier supposition that there might be only one or two creatures. There must have been many more of them in that cavernous lake than he'd suspected. And upon reflection, he realised he was lucky to have made it out alive. Had it not been for the explosion of his nitro scaring some of them away and the subsequent collapse of the cavern wall into the lake, he might have otherwise had to contend with more than one of them trying to sample his hide. And if that had happened, he was pretty sure he wouldn't be here right now.

With those thoughts swirling through his mind, he said to Kitty across the way, "Now, just take it easy. Don't rush! One foot in front of the other."

Kitty had watched Caleb move cautiously across the temporary bench bridge. Now, she smiled at him quizzically as if thinking he was touched in the head and wondering just how much. "Aye. I know how to walk, thank you very much!"

Gathering her skirts, Kitty glanced down at the narrow boards beneath her feet only once. She moved gracefully across the water-filled gap between the buildings, doing so as easily as if she were strolling down the sidewalk on a Sunday afternoon. As she stepped onto the sidewalk on the other side and looked up into Caleb's eyes, she said proudly, "You keep forgettin'. I have six brothers, and we used to go on adventures together."

"And I guess you've seen your fair share of narrow ledges and such in your previous career." Almost as soon as he'd said it, Caleb regretted the comment and added, "I didn't mean it in a bad way, just that you are very athletic, and that line of work must have been great practice for what you just did, and—"

Smiling broadly, Kitty said, "You can take your foot out of your mouth now. And don't worry, you didn't offend me." She flashed another quick smile and finished, saying, "And you're right, it was great exercise."

Together, they moved along the sidewalk toward the Golden Nugget, still another block past this one. The Kootenay Landing/Natánik Lending Library was located here, according to the hand-lettered sign in the window. It was running out of a small shop until the new library's construction near the park could be completed. With that not being scheduled until late fall, Caleb wondered if that was one of the reasons for delaying the naming of the town. Perhaps they wanted to unveil the name when they had the library's grand opening and celebrate both things at once.

Caleb thought of the National Geographic Magazine Kitty had told him of, which she'd borrowed from the temporary lending library. In it, she'd read of the river sturgeon here in the Kootenays. It seemed the creatures could grow as large as eighteen feet long with skin almost four inches thick, which Caleb thought must be almost equal to the horrors somewhere in the muddy water next to them. Thankfully, those giants of the river didn't share the same appetite for people as the black beasts. One thing he recalled for certain was that the river sturgeon was rumoured to have a long lifespan, possibly over one hundred years. Did the black beasts have similarly long lives, he wondered.

At first, Caleb had thought of dragging the bench with them down the walk to the other end of the block, but he knew the gap between the buildings up ahead was quite a bit wider. The water was at least a couple of feet deep here and getting close to the edge of the walkway. He looked over his shoulder and saw that the entrance to the police station was now partially submerged, and he was glad he had gotten to Kitty when he did. Wondering what the bandits were up to, he glanced across the street but saw they had disappeared, possibly having broken into one of the businesses in the block where they were stranded.

Chief Hildey Dugrodt was at the top of the steps of the walkway in the next block, standing in front of Verigin's Cigar Emporium, part of the Hanover Building. He called across the gap to Kitty and Caleb, "Watch yourself! It's still pretty deep here, and I think I saw something swimming around!"

"We know! We've seen them," Caleb replied.

"I wonder how many of the beasts from the river got into those pools in the park?" Kitty said, looking at the water-filled main street.

Caleb replied, "There might have only been a few at first. But I think there's a pretty good chance they were breeding in them. And I'm sure they grow as quick as the spiders and ants." Thanks to the hot spring aquifers that ran beneath the surface of the three pools, he knew they were as lovely and warm as he'd experienced in the cavern before being flushed away.

Kitty's eyes grew alarmed, and she said, "But if they were breeding in there, there could be dozens or even hundreds of them now for all we know."

As the words came out of Kitty's mouth, there was a splash at the edge of the walkway. Something long, thick and oily-looking undulated sinuously through the murk-filled water next to them.

The Golden Nugget Saloon was the tallest structure in town. With a false widow's walk at its top, it appeared to have a partial third floor. The Hanover building was the second-highest but had no widow's walk. Along with the cigar emporium, several lawyers and assayers were located inside. The building took up most of the block, making it the defacto business district.

But business was not something on the minds of the unexpected visitors just now departing the Hanover Building—unless it was the business of survival. Seeming protected from the hail and rain by their exploration of the large structure, several ants suddenly appeared through the open windows on the second floor, left so because of the heat.

Unfortunately, this window was just overtop the edge of the covered walk where Chief Dugrodt stood. And to Kitty and Caleb's horror, Hildey was directly where the ants dropped.

Caleb had begun to call out and warn the chief of his peril, but by the time he did, it was too late because it all happened so fast. It turned out there were four of the red beasts altogether. Two were flung off just as they dropped onto Hildey, thanks to the chief's fast reflexes. They splashed into the water and were snapped up almost immediately by the black abominations swimming about.

The other two ants were more pernicious, however. As one started to burrow into the flesh of Hildey's exposed throat, the other began to tear through his shirt to get at his stomach.

Kitty shrieked, and together, she and Caleb watched the policeman's final battle in impotent horror.

It was a painful skirmish, but it was also brief. As the ants attacked, the leather sole on Dugrodt's boot slipped on the edge of the walkway's wet wood. He began to pinwheel his arms as he tilted backwards, but his balance was gone, and he hit the muddy water with an enormous splash, then disappeared.

Kitty threw her hands to her face, and Caleb wrapped his arms about her. Though there was still one round left in the shotgun, there was nothing he could do from this distance because he couldn't even see the police chief or the black monsters beneath the surface of the cloudy water. Even if he splashed out into the muck, by the time he got to Hildey, he would have attracted the attention of one or more of the ravenous things already swimming the streets. He grimaced as he looked to the water, hoping the chief made it out and back to the elevated sidewalk before it was too late.

With a gasp, the chief reappeared, and amazingly, the ants that had attacked him were gone. But the water around Hildey grew red as he staggered upright, his hand to his throat where the ant had bitten him. Crimson leaked between his fingers as he began to lurch toward the stairs leading up to Verigin's Cigar Emporium.

Unfortunately, he never made it.

At the chief's back, an obsidian beast coiled up from the water. Its ropy, serpentine body wrapped around him like a monstrous boa. He struggled fiercely, but it was strong and held him fast. As it squeezed the life from Dugrodt, the animal's jaw unhinged, and its spiky-toothed maw clamped down over his head, stifling his anguished cry. Together, they dropped backwards into the turbid water with a huge splash, and this time, the chief didn't resurface.

Kitty screamed again, this time in Caleb's ear, and he winced but held her tight as she buried her face into his shoulder.

The water grew redder still as other black creatures swarmed to the site of the fresh kill, no doubt attracted by the blood. They tore and shredded Dugrodt's body, and within seconds, there seemed no longer any sign of the chief of police.

Caleb moved Kitty into the doorway of a haberdashery at their back, wondering what to do next. With the water still rising and the buildings along this block only a single story, they would need to move within minutes or perhaps seconds. There was no staircase to a second floor, so they would have to try and climb onto the hail-dented tin covering the walkway and, if it held them, onto the roof.

The rain seemed to redouble in strength, quickening the rising of the flood water. Caleb held Kitty tighter for a brief moment. Through her trembling, he could feel her heart beating like a hummingbird's, and he feared it might explode in her chest.

With an almost useless shotgun slung over his shoulder and nowhere to go, Caleb realised they were both well and truly up shite creek, and there were no paddles anywhere in sight.

CHAPTER TWENTY-ONE

Sandy's head was spinning with what he'd just learned from Doc Brown. Before getting into details about Mr. Sinclair, the doctor had needed to tell him a little bit about his own less-than-stellar past, and that in of itself was a shock to Sandy.

Just now, the doctor had admitted to Sandy that he wasn't, in fact, really a doctor, or a dentist, or even a barber, but merely a veterinarian and a disgraced one with a bounty on his head at that.

Back when the doctor had been a new veterinary school graduate, he'd gone by the name of Cornelius Braun. While at school, he'd made some poor choices and ended up getting in with 'the wrong crowd' through some friends he'd made. That had led to his developing a thirst for liquor, which the doctor said he could never quench despite repeated attempts. To earn some quick cash after graduation to support his gadabout ways, he had agreed to help a friend with a sick horse that needed to run for a race no matter what.

And so, like a snowball rolling downhill, he'd had more and more clients come to him and request similar 'doctoring services', mostly horse owners who wanted to race their animals at the newly built Hastings Racecourse.

Eventually, word of his exceptional abilities with horses got around, and the doctor ended up working for one Samuel Nash, who was not a nice man, it seemed. It was at that point that Cornelius's budding horse-doctoring career had ended; Nash's horse died of painful complications from the 'health tonic' he'd been giving it. Mr. Nash had been very unhappy about this and offered a large sum of money to some local strong-arms in Vancouver to have the doctor put out of his misery. And so, the doctor had fled to the interior. Moving from gold town to gold town, he'd offered his 'doctoring' services to anyone who'd pay and eventually landed here in this nameless little town. In his travels, he'd also assumed the name of Brown, not wanting to use his real name to avoid attracting the attention of anyone looking for him.

After that rather long confession, the doctor had explained that he'd needed to tell all that to Sandy so he could get to the point, which was Mr. Thomas Sinclair.

And that had brought Sandy to his next surprise: when he learned that, to get Cornelius to do his dirty work, Mr. S was holding the doctor's past over his head with the threat of turning him in to Nash for the bounty if he didn't toe the line.

This 'blackmail', as Brown called it, was something Mr. S was also doing to Miss Kitty. The doctor wouldn't say exactly what Sinclair had on his lovely Scottish friend, citing Miss Kitty's need for privacy.

With all that now in mind, Sandy told the doctor one more bit of information about his new position with Thomas Sinclair, and it was something he didn't quite understand. "And Mr. S said he'd let me know what my new duties were since they were a flower, but I don't remember which kind."

Brown blinked and pondered that for a moment. A flower? What kind of flower? And then it came to him, and he said, "Ah, yes. I would imagine what he said was, he'd let you know your duties were 'as they arose'?"

"That's it, Doc! It was a rose! They're awful pretty, you know."

The doctor nodded and said, "Yes, indeed. And that is a slippery slope, to be sure, my boy. Bear in mind, whatever you do for Sinclair, it will be something that will only ever benefit him and never you. Or, even worse, he might ask you to do something more egregious involving other people and their indebtedness to him."

"Agree just?"

"I mean something harmful to others."

Sandy now viewed his new position with Mr. Sinclair with wide-open, disbelieving eyes. He shook his head and said to Brown, "Gosh, I didn't think Mr. S was all that bad."

"He's a shrewd businessman, to be sure, and one who has helped this town grow. But it's only been for his own enrichment, even though he plays a benevolent benefactor. So, I suppose you could say his morals are lacking in some departments." Brown paused momentarily, then added, "Actually, I believe they're lacking in many departments. And I would caution you to think carefully of anything that man asks you to do."

Sandy nodded slowly in understanding and said, "Sure enough."

The doctor had finished their little conversation by saying he needed to quickly check a couple of things and then get up to the Golden Nugget to tend to more patients.

Sandy hoped the doctor didn't have any major surgery to do when he got there since he'd already had a few drinks from the look of him. But he figured that was understandable after what had just happened with the ants outside, and the doctor probably needed to steady his nerves.

If he had been a drinking man, Sandy figured he would have probably indulged himself. Though he'd tried alcohol in the past, thankfully, he'd never had much of a taste for it. Part of that could have to do with his time as the doorman at the Golden Nugget, where he had seen many good men ruined by alcohol. As a result, he was understandably concerned about his doctor friend and hoped to help the man cut back on his reliance on the devil's brew. That was the name he'd heard some temperance ladies call alcohol one time when they'd handed out leaflets to the sourdoughs coming and going from the saloon.

Rounding the corner from the doctor's office, Sandy paused before stepping off the covered walkway. The rain was tapering off a bit, the shallow, muddy water seeming to fizz and pop as the water drops hit, filling it with small bubbles like a glass of beer at the Nugget. Still, it wasn't as bad here as it was further down the main street.

He'd been forced to abandon the pumper wagon in the street when he first rescued the mules from the hail. Once it had ended, as the rain started, Sandy moved the mules out from under cover at the side of the building and up the back alley behind the Nugget to their home at the smithy. He'd planned to get them as far away from the quickly flooding main street as he could. It had taken him a little while to get them there since they kept getting mired in the growing mud, but he'd finally made it. Now, he wanted to ensure they were safe and dry since there was still the odd ant roaming around out there, amongst other things.

And with that thought of 'other things' in mind, Sandy paused on the bottom step and looked more closely at the murky water. Part of what he thought had been bubbles from the falling rain actually seemed caused by something else entirely. And this something lay in the bubbling water just up ahead.

Sandy stepped into the murky water and approached the bubbling thing cautiously. He had no choice but to approach it since the thing lay directly in his path to the smithy.

Was it a body, he wondered. Perhaps someone who had been killed by one of the ants? It wouldn't be surprising. There were a few volunteers still unaccounted for who had been battling the red monsters in the street. Sandy suspected the bodies of several may have ultimately washed down toward the lake when the flood hit.

Whatever the thing was, as he grew closer, it quivered slightly. Sandy paused to study the muddy mass more closely. The water was a couple of inches deep on the surface around the thing, but the rest of it had settled into the muddy slurry beneath, making it hard to see.

Uncoiling from the unassuming lump it had appeared, the black beast moved with lightning speed and shot up from the muck, snapping its mouthful of pointed teeth only inches from Sandy's face as it tried to grab him and pull him down into the muddy water.

Sandy backpedalled and moved out of the way just in time. The thing slapped back down into the mud and then began squirming toward him, pulling itself along in the muddy slurry on stubby little legs and moving with surprising rapidity as it did.

Lifting his muscular legs as fast and as frequently as possible in the muck, Sandy struggled toward the smithy as the black thing slapped through the mud behind him.

The fire chief wasn't around at the moment since he'd wanted to get out to the forest and see how the fire looked after the drenching rain. The flames weren't visible any longer, and thick smoke now blended with the mist of the falling rain, making the visibility quite low. Angus had said he was hopeful the fire had been beaten back. Though it hadn't made it all the way to the downtown, there'd been reports of several dozen houses on the outskirts being incinerated by the raging fire, and that was something else Chief Cochrane was checking on.

Sandy was relieved he'd left the animals in the stable with the doors closed and all its occupants out of biting range of the black things. Now, he just had to get there. As he struggled along, he wondered if the thing behind him was the same one that had killed Sam Shepherd and also responsible for the disappearance of Bill Burton from Boston Bar during the diving competition.

Plopping, flopping, and slopping along, the beast squelched eagerly through the mud at Sandy's back, sounding closer by the second.

The boy didn't try to look back and instead concentrated on putting one foot in front of the other and not slipping in the muddy water. Once he was at the smithy, he hoped to find something to use as a weapon to defend himself, praying that Angus hadn't brought everything he had to the ant fight. If both arms had been working, Sandy was sure he would have been better able to give the creature a good pounding. As it was, with only one good arm, he was almost defenceless.

Not bothering to stop and open the gate to the smithy's rear courtyard, Sandy instead vaulted over the fence, his one good arm giving him all the force and balance he needed to complete the task.

Unfortunately, the black thing was equally adept, but instead of vaulting the fence, it slithered its thick body through the mud between the foot-high gap in the cross-rails as if they weren't even there.

Knowing the thing would try to wrap around him as it bit into him, Sandy figured he needed to protect his legs and the only thing nearby that would do the trick was right in front of him.

With a splash, Sandy stepped into the horse trough just as the black thing arrived at his back. The beast crashed into the trough, narrowly missing Sandy's leg. Instead of latching onto the boy, it had bitten into the corner of the trough. In doing so, the monster appeared to have unhinged its jaws to get an extra big bite of his leg but instead got an extra big bite of the trough.

Now, its teeth were stuck into the soft pine, and it was having a hard time pulling them out since it couldn't open its jaws any wider to remove them from the wood. Instead, it thrashed and sloshed in the murky water, trying to back itself off from the trough so it could try again.

Sandy glanced for a weapon. Once the creature was free, he would need to deal with its sharp teeth again, not to mention its ropy and sinewy black muscles. His mind's eye showed him an image of the beast wrapping itself around him and crushing him to death while it ripped chunks from his body and ate him alive. That helpful image spurred him to look wildly about for anything that might be of assistance.

And then he turned and saw it, leaning against the side of the stable only a half dozen feet away, a pitchfork. With its long and pointy tines, it was just what he needed. He took one giant step out of the trough and moved through the thick mud as fast as he could toward the pitchfork.

From behind, there was a crack of wood as the black beast broke free.

Now, at his back, the creature squirmed and slapped its way through the muck, eager to make Sandy its next meal.

CHAPTER TWENTY-TWO

Kitty sobbed quietly as Caleb held her close, face buried against his shoulder. His heart ached for the poor woman, and he'd give anything to get her away from this awful situation. The last Kitty had braved a glance, another couple of the creatures had swum close by the edge of the walkway. Both had been distressingly thick and long and black. Unable to bear looking any longer, she had turned back to Caleb for further comfort.

The rain fell in a fine mist now, slowing the water's rise, but not by much—it was still flooding in from other parts of the valley. Caleb had turned them slightly from their view of the street and was thinking about kicking in the door to the haberdasher's to see if there was access to the roof when a familiar voice sounded at their backs.

"Can I give you a ride, amigo?"

They whirled as one, their mouths agape.

"You!" Caleb cried.

With a grin, Jesús Oritz replied, "You were expecting Captain Nemo, perhaps?" He tilted his head slightly in greeting, rainwater dripping from his hat brim and splashing onto his sodden shirt and jacket. He sat in the bow of a collapsible flat-bottomed boat made of canvas. At the oars behind him sat the grizzled cook, a despondent look on his face.

"I wasn't expectin' you at all, to be honest, all things considered." Caleb nodded toward the boat and asked, "And where in heaven did ya get that?"

Jesús grinned more broadly and replied, "It is surprising what this little town has available for... sale."

"Or stealin'," the old man behind him muttered.

Jesús waved a hand dismissively at his oarsman.

"What d'ya want?" Kitty asked, her moist eyes filled with suspicion.

"To rescue you, a course! Ya think we're out here for a pleasure cruise?" the cantankerous oarsman responded.

Oritz added, "It is true. After all, I didn't want to see my new partner get eaten before he could divulge the location of his fortune."

Caleb narrowed his eyes and looked the small Spaniard up and down, then said, "Partner? What're ya talkin' about? I thought Sinclair paid you off so you'd have no more claim on me."

Jesús held his hands up in a 'what-are-you-gonna-do' gesture and said, "This is true, but things change quickly around these parts. I am sure it is something we can discuss in a more civilised and safer location than this. Perhaps we can take you both to the Nugget saloon, and we can discuss it further there."

"How do we know we can trust you?" Kitty asked.

Jesús pursed his lips slightly, his dark eyebrows raising in unison, and he said, "You do not."

"Then why should we? What if you feed us to the black things in the mud instead of rescuing us?" Caleb wondered.

Shaking his head, Oritz said, "That would most certainly not be in my best interest, now, would it?" He looked over his shoulder to the small boat behind him and said, "Unfortunately, we can only take one of you at a time. I would not want to capsize this boat or have it bottom out, not in these waters." He looked to the black things curling and slithering through the shallow, muddy water nearby. "They are still looking for more ants or anything else that happens to fall into the water."

Caleb was torn but knew they couldn't stay where they were and argue for much longer since the water was now lapping over the top edge of the walkway. "You should go first, Kitty."

Looking as if he'd just slapped her, Kitty said, "I just escaped from these buggers! What makes you think they won't just row off with me and kidnap me all over again?"

A distant voice called, "I'll keep them in my sights, Miss Kitty."

The group turned to see Lucias standing on the sidewalk of the Golden Nugget, his bandaged hand resting on one hip, the other on the stock of the chopped-down Winchester rifle slung under his arm.

"You see?" Jesús said. "Everything will be all right."

Kitty looked to Caleb in question. He gazed into her eyes for a moment, then glanced to the water and the ripples that played here and there, dancing with the fine raindrops that fell, ripples likely caused by the black beasts swimming beneath. With a shake of his head, he said, "I don't think we have much choice."

Caleb helped to steady Kitty, and she gracefully stepped into the small boat, then moved carefully to sit on the single seat at the stern.

The old man spun the oars in the water, and the boat swung slowly around. With a grunt and a heave, the cook piloted them into the street and began rowing against the slight current toward the Golden Nugget in the next block.

Revolver in hand, the Spaniard sat in the bow of the boat, riding like Captain Ahab and watching the water ahead, his eyes scanning for anything large and black getting too close to their thin-skinned boat. The bandit must have gotten the handgun from the same place he'd stolen the boat. It made Caleb wish he still had the sidearm he'd confiscated from Oritz during their fight. Sadly, he'd left it on the counter at Doc Brown's office in his rush to get out the door when the ants had arrived from the forest.

As Caleb watched the boat move up the street, his heart felt lodged somewhere between his stomach and throat. Kitty looked so small, delicate and defenceless. If something happened to her now, he didn't know what he'd do. But however things turned out, he knew that she would be staying down here in the valley where it was now safe, relatively speaking.

Unfortunately, it appeared he'd be going back up the mountain with that Spanish scoundrel, if for no other reason than to get both him and Thomas Sinclair off his back. If he could ever find the cavern again, he now felt like he would gladly give it to them both and let them go at each other over it. Then, he could wash his hands of it and perhaps go somewhere else with Kitty. He really liked the Kootenays, despite his experiences here, and thought that perhaps they could move to a different city. In fact, he'd recently heard of some silver mining going on over in Nelson, another new and growing Kootenay town similar to this one.

The small canvas boat made it to the front steps of the Golden Nugget and bumped against the edge of the top step without incident. Unlike other buildings in the area, the Nugget had a brick foundation with no street-level windows for the water to pour through, and as far as Caleb knew, the downstairs bar and his hidden room were still dry.

Kitty had been safely unloaded by Lucias, who held out his hand to steady her as she departed the rocking boat. As the painfully thin old man rowed back the distance to pick him up, Caleb was reminded of the Greek legend of Charon, the gatekeeper to the underworld who ferried people over to Hades. As the canvas boat drew closer, Caleb hoped his upcoming ride wouldn't be to the underworld since he had nothing to pay the ferryman. And looking at the rising water now washing against his boots, he realised, boat ride to hell or not, this was one trip he had to take.

A few moments later, the boat nudged against the steps in front of Caleb, and he stepped on board, then moved to the rear seat where Kitty had sat. Linseed oil from the waterproofing on the canvas suddenly filled his nostrils, and he wrinkled his nose in distaste.

Jesús pushed them off with the toe of his boot, and they floated out into the channel that was now the main street. Oritz stayed in the bow, and as the cook rowed, the Spaniard drew his weapon once more.

Several obsidian monsters circled back and forth around the slow-moving boat, gradually constricting their circle of curiosity further and further until they would no longer be curious but ravenous instead.

Noting this, Caleb said, "It looks like your little ferry

service has attracted some unwanted attention.

Jesús nodded and said, "I was afraid that would happen."

Whatever attention they'd drawn, it didn't seem quite enough to cause the black things to attack at this point. But as the monsters slithered by, they gradually grew much too close for comfort.

"I'd avoid shooting at them while we're in the water," Caleb advised. "I'm sure they wouldn't like it, and I think it'd be especially dangerous if you only wounded one of them."

Cocking his revolver as one of the obsidian creatures wriggled past the bow, Oritz replied, "I will try to avoid doing so unless they decide otherwise."

After several tense moments, they arrived at the Golden Nugget, Lucias standing ready to steady the boat when it arrived.

Kitty was just behind him, wearing a hopeful expression.

Caleb smiled and suddenly experienced that warm, gooey feeling in his chest again. His heart began to flutter as he watched Kitty's expression of hope blossom into a smile of joy at his arrival.

Though she had streaks of mud on her face, and her purple dress looked like it'd been run through a thresher, she still looked as lovely as ever.

Jesús disembarked first. Cookie tucked the oars inside and stepped off next. Lucias continued to steady things at the bow as Caleb rose to begin his own journey to dry land.

At that moment, a beast's curiosity suddenly became too much, and it slammed into the canvas craft, puncturing its tooth-filled face through the boat's oiled side.

Caleb tried to steady himself, but the jolt caused the boat to rock to such a degree that he began to pinwheel his arms to keep his balance. But it was no good, and he tumbled backwards into the muddy floodwater, disappearing from sight with a tremendous splash.

All around, black things roiled and coiled through the water in his direction.

Her hands to her face, Kitty Welch began to scream.

CHAPTER TWENTY-THREE

The slap of the beast's thick, sinewy body through the muck at his back spurred Sandy to move faster. His weight was a disadvantage in this mire. The mud was sucking and treacherous, and he'd almost pulled off one of his boots on one vigorous heave of his leg as he struggled to keep going. If he were to stop, he was sure he would sink down far enough to get stuck, and then the thing at his back would be upon him.

Up ahead, the sturdy pitchfork that Angus had mended for a local farmer would serve his purpose nicely, the purpose of sticking its long tines into the black demon at his back, that was, if he got to it in time.

From inside the stable, her head peeking over the side of the half-door, Emily brayed as if in warning at the sight of the creature following Sandy.

"I know it's there, girl. Believe me, I know!"

Sandy took one more mighty step and arrived at the barn, snatching up the pitchfork as he did. As he turned, he lifted his leg and was glad he had done so.

The black beast surged through the murky water and

slammed heavily into the side of the stable just as Sandy's foot cleared the mud. With a hiss, it began to rear up against the stable wall, trying to use it as support to launch itself at Sandy.

Still on one leg, Sandy pivoted gracefully and slammed the pitchfork into the black creature with all his weight behind it, skewering the beast to the side of the stables.

Hissing and sputtering, the creature writhed and coiled against the wall, but it wasn't going anywhere. It was stuck through and through by all four tines of the pitchfork. It struggled fiercely for several moments, tearing its flesh around the tines as it tried to free itself. Black fluid began to see from the punctures the pitchfork had made, and its movements diminished further and further as it succumbed to its mortal wounds.

At Sandy's back, Angus said, "I'm away from the smithy for a few minutes checkin' on the forest fire, and you start redecorating the place with those ugly black slugs!"

Sandy whirled to see Angus slogging through the mud toward him. Taking a moment to catch his breath, he said, "The darned thing ambushed me in the muddy water!"

Angus looked about and said with surprise, "The water does seem a bit higher than when I left. But I didn't think those things could crawl around on land like that."

"Well, this one used its little legs to drag itself through the mud to get to me." With a grunt, Sandy pulled the pitchfork from the stable wall and the black thing, now stilled, dropped into the mud with a slithering plop, its lifeless body quickly hidden by the muddy water.

"I'm glad to say I didn't see any of those things in the forest, but it wasn't underwater there."

"I guess that's some good news. How is the fire, Chief?"

"That rain made all the difference. A few hot spots here and there are still smouldering, but it looks like it's pretty much out. Course, that doesn't help the dozen or more folks who lost their houses on the river side of town, or the ice house for that matter, since it's gone as well."

Sandy shook his head, saddened by the news of the number of people left homeless by the inferno, but was thankful the rain had done its job. Now, if Mother Nature could just do something about the black things slithering about. Though they were dangerous as all get out, it seemed they had served their purpose and gobbled down many of the ants in the water that hadn't been pounded into oblivion by the hail stones.

A scream came from around the corner on the main street, interrupting Sandy's momentary reverie. He and Angus looked at each other and then high-tailed it through the mud. As the boy approached the sidewalk at the corner where the Doc's office lay, the scream came again, and he thought he knew who it belonged to: Kitty Welch.

Sandy's long legs had helped him move through the mud much more quickly than Angus, and he mounted the three low steps to the sidewalk in one long stride, well ahead of the fire chief. He pounded down the walkway, almost bowling over Doctor Brown, who was just leaving his office to investigate the source of the screaming. Whatever was happening to Kitty or someone close to her, it sounded like bad news indeed.

People were crowding around the end of the sidewalk at the corner, in front of the Nugget's batwing doors. Sandy had sat bored behind those same doors for so many hours, never expecting any of the horrors he'd seen unfold in front of them over the past week. It all seemed like something out of one of the books of fantastic fiction he so enjoyed reading.

In addition to Doc Brown and Angus at his back, the girls from the second floor were also moving out front to see what was happening with Kitty.

The Holey Gang Man with the golden teeth was back, and he sported a new bowler hat. He was standing near a canvas boat, his white-haired cook tying it off to the railing along the front of the Nugget. Sandy still had the scrap of fabric stuffed in his pocket, which Rufus had torn from the seat of the old man's pants.

The dog in question was tied to the same railing several feet further along, and it growled at the old man, whose eyes were glued on the dog as he tied off the boat. Whatever the problem was, it didn't seem to have anything to do with either of the bandits at the moment, and Sandy moved into the group of people crowded at the steps.

Miss Kitty stood off to one side, her hand bunched against her mouth to bite back another scream as she stared down at the water-filled street.

A group of men stood indecisively at the top of the steps, apparently wondering what to do about the current situation. Sandy pushed them aside to see Mr. Caleb floundering about in the muddy water and getting attacked by the black river monsters.

But as Sandy looked closer, he saw that Mr. Caleb wasn't being attacked and the black things, of which there appeared to be dozens, were merely slithering and coiling past him in the shallow muddy water, some even bumping into him, but for some reason, none bit him.

One of the volunteers was wailing in agony and clutched at his hand. It looked like he had tried to help pull Caleb out and lost four fingers in the process when he'd gotten too close to the water. Another man had a bite taken out of the side of his leg. Doctor Brown moved in to tend to it first, tearing the man's shirtsleeve off and wrapping it in a tight tourniquet above the wound to stem the bleeding.

"Do somethin', Sandy!" Kitty cried as she stared at the water in horror.

"Mr. Caleb!" Sandy called. "What're you doin' out there? Those things are deadly!"

Caleb sat in the muck, his arms propping him up from behind, surrounded by the creatures but still untouched. "I know that, Sandy! I'm not takin' a mud bath here! I'm afraid to move in case these things go from swimming around me to eatin' me alive."

Why hadn't they attacked his friend, Sandy wondered. They'd had plenty of opportunity but had left him alone and seemingly untouched. Whatever the reason, it might not last for long, and he needed to do something to help his friend, now.

An image of the railing to which the dog and the boat had been tied popped into Sandy's head, and he pushed back through the crowd. With a huge grunt of effort, he tugged on the railing next to the boat and dog with his good arm, pulling it almost completely free with one massive yank. About a dozen feet long and as big around as a man's fist, the railing would hold his friend, he hoped. As the remaining nails were wrenched from the wood, they squealed like a stuck pig. And while Sandy pulled, he felt a twinge in his muscles along his side, yet he didn't stop.

The crowd parted as Sandy moved back to the edge of the steps. He slapped the railing out into the water next to Caleb with a tremendous splash, the black beasts nearby scattering as the wood hit the water.

"Grab onto this!" Sandy braced the wood against his hip

since his spider-bite arm was still not cooperating fully. The pins and needles were feeling worse at the moment, if anything, and he only had minimal strength in it. He leaned out over the water, and several men held onto his spider arm so he could extend his reach with the lumber.

Caleb grasped the lumber, and as Sandy began to pull, an obsidian beast poked its head out of the water near the edge of the stairs. There was nothing Sandy could do to kick it out of the way since his balance was shifted too far out over the water, and it looked like he was about to suffer a serious bite.

A shot rang out at Sandy's side, and a chunk of the black creature's head disappeared in a cloud of buckshot.

Lucias pumped his shotgun with one hand to reload it, then braced it on the forearm of his bandaged hand to steady his aim once again. "Better hurry up. These things are hard to hit unless they rear up like that."

"I'm workin' as fast as I can, Mr. Lucias." With a grunt, Sandy leaned back again, pulling with all his might, the muscles in his good arm standing out like corded steel beneath his skin. This time, he felt more pain shoot through his side, but he knew he couldn't stop, and he didn't.

Caleb was lifted up and out of the water and then swung over toward the steps all at once. He collided with the edge of the railing and would have fallen back into the deadly water had it not been for Doc Brown and Angus, who were able to grab hold of him before he could do so.

"I've got you, my boy," Brown said, grasping Caleb's arm. In reality, the doctor didn't have much of Caleb at all, Sandy saw. Angus had grabbed most of the Irishman about the waist and lifted him bodily over the exposed balusters that poked up from the base rail. Though not as large as Sandy, Angus was a big man and had little trouble lifting Caleb.

Though Mr. Caleb was covered from head to toe in muddy water, that didn't seem to matter to Miss Kitty. She ran to him, flung her arms around his shoulders, and kissed him hard. Sandy's eyes widened in surprise. The pair weren't hiding their romance now and didn't seem to care who knew about the two of them.

"I thought you were monster food!" Kitty cried as she wiped her eyes with the back of her hand.

"So did I," Caleb said as he hugged her hard. "I don't know why they didn't eat me."

"Or take a bite out of you," Brown added, adjusting the tourniquet on the leg of the wounded man he would soon be attending. The fingerless man had a belt about his forearm as a tourniquet, loaned by another volunteer. With these men and the ones inside the Nugget, the doctor looked like he would be having a busy day.

Standing at the edge of the group, Gold Tooth said to Caleb, "Maybe there is more to you than meets the eye."

Caleb shook his head and replied, "Whatever it is, I'm thankful there isn't any less of me, unlike poor Chief Hildey."

"What?!" Sandy exclaimed, hearing this news for the first time.

"Aye, lad. Chief Dugrodt is dead," Caleb said sadly, adding, "The ants got to him first, and then the black beasts finished him off."

Sandy's eyes were wide with shock. The police chief was a nice man, and one Sandy had looked up to. And now Hildey had died trying to help others, just as he'd dedicated his life to that same act. Of course, the black things were vicious creatures that didn't care who went into their mouths. No one, good or bad, seemed safe around them.

Well, almost no one, Sandy corrected himself, except for his strangely lucky friend, Mr. Caleb Cantrill. He recalled the bite mark the man had shown him on the dock the night they'd met. For whatever reason, it seemed as if the black beasts had decided that one taste of the Irishman was enough.

CHAPTER TWENTY-FOUR

Kitty looked from Caleb to Jesús, back to Caleb, then repeated the process over again. She was trying to work out what was going through the minds of the two men before her. For the last little while, they had been discussing the terms of a truce agreement between them. The discussion had been tense, especially since Caleb was still fuming about the fact that Oritz and his now ex-lackey, Antonio, had kidnapped Kitty in the first place.

Though they'd both been grateful for the unexpected rescue by the bandit-turned-boat captain, Kitty was still very wary of him and was quite sure Caleb wouldn't be letting his guard down either.

The bandit gang was now down to only two men, and she felt somewhat relieved by that thought. Antonio's demise had been confirmed by Jesús. Though she was not a person to wish anyone dead or cause intentional harm to them, she was fairly sure she wouldn't lose any sleep over the fact that the man's passing was her doing. In fact, she figured he probably deserved it, especially after overhearing Jesús tell him to leave her alone and that he didn't want 'another mess like in Santa Fe'. Hearing those words rise up from their conversation in the kitchen below had made her blood boil and more determined than ever to escape. Whatever had happened to the scar-faced man in the loft room after she closed him in with the spiders had been brought upon him by his own lascivious actions.

Jesús sat before her, grinning as usual, having told her he bore her no ill will for the death of his right-hand man. But Kitty knew better. In her experience, men like him never said what they really and truly meant. Given the opportunity, she was sure the gang leader would have no compunctions about doing himself whatever Antonio had planned for her while tied up in bed. No, she was under no illusions about how dangerous the small Spaniard was and how little he could be trusted. After all, he was only protecting his self-interests, as he'd freely admitted when he'd first picked them up.

There was a bit of good news, at least, and Caleb said he'd had several more flashes of memory leading up to his finding the cavern. He figured it was due to the stress he'd been under. What with her kidnapping, the fire in the forest, the ant attack, her subsequent rescue, and almost being eaten by the black mud monsters, it was a lot of stress, to be sure. He also admitted he was just as mystified as she that the creatures had paid him no heed as they swarmed around, almost treating him, he'd said, as if he were one of their own.

Of course, there was bad news. Jesús now expected Caleb to show him up the mountain. They planned on leaving just after breakfast, and she hoped the flood water would be down to a more manageable level by then.

The rain had stopped several hours ago, and the water outside had gone down a bit, at least up here at the Nugget, where the main street was now more of a mud bog. But with the downtown, it was another story and still half underwater. No matter which end of the messy main street you were on, it was deadly because of what hid beneath the surface. Presumably, the creatures would return to the river or lake when the water receded enough, making dry land once again a safe place to be.

Those that could, returned to their homes. But many still couldn't since it had either been burned away in the fire or was still in the dominion of the black water beasts. And so, those with nowhere else to go had remained camped out on a small, forested ridge near the valley's entrance, where they'd also weathered the seemingly unending catastrophes in the valley below.

The sun had slipped away for another day, making a brief appearance through the departing clouds as it settled over the ridge of rugged mountain peaks in the west. Outside the batwing doors, the sky was now deeper purple than Kitty's now rag-worthy dress.

After the ants in the boudoirs upstairs had been exterminated by Caleb and Lucias, Kitty had managed to change out of her ruined dress and rinse off most of the mud using her small washbasin. Now, she wore a red velvet dress with lace trim around its daringly deep decolletage.

Nearby, several tables had been pushed together where injured men were being treated. That was the other reason Kitty had needed to clean herself up, her new part-time job as a nurse. Earlier in the evening, she'd spent several hours assisting the doctor, who had been kept quite busy with sutures and amputations. Though now that was all thankfully behind them.

There was one patient who required no surgery, however, and surprisingly, it was Sandy. While not physically wounded, when the large man-boy had yanked Caleb from the water, he'd apparently pulled some of the muscles in his back and shoulders. For the boy to lift Caleb's slim yet muscular build using only one arm must have been an incredible strain on him, fit though he was.

Off in one corner, on recommendation of Doctor Brown, Sandy lay resting on top of a blanket on the floor to help with his pulled muscles. Next to him lay his new four-legged friend, Rufus. The dog was seemingly asleep, as was Sandy, both worn out from the day's adventures. One of the dog's legs kicked out randomly every few seconds, perhaps chasing dream rabbits across sun-filled meadows. To one side of the boy and his dog sat Lucias. He was nursing a beer, a morose expression on his face as he regarded his wounded hand.

Kitty left Caleb and Jesús to their negotiations, wanting to check on the wounded since Brown was currently at his practice. All seemed as good as could be expected, and as she'd been fluffing the pillow under the head of her final patient, some commotion caught her attention in the far corner where the kitchen lay. She hurried across the saloon to see what was happening.

The volunteers had begun returning as darkness fell. After a few complimentary drinks, most were looking for some food as well, which the saloon was also providing as thanks for their hard work. Fortunately, Maggie had returned after the ant attack and rain had ended. She'd hunkered down in her tiny house at the upper end of town and watched in terror through closed windows as the ants had marched by.

Kitty was thankful her friend had been safe and sound and now back doing what she enjoyed. In fact, the cook had been whipping up some stew and biscuits, the last she'd heard. With that being the case, Kitty couldn't understand what all the commotion could be about.

In the kitchen, the second-floor girls crowded around Maggie at the island in the centre. Kitty moved into the circle of girls, and they parted slightly so she could better see.

The cook said, "And then I looked up, and the horrible thing on the wall was just above my head! Well, I went to grab my broom, and when I returned to the stove, it was gone!"

"That's terrifying!" Carla said.

"Oui! I thought the rain had washed them all away, did it not?" Monique said.

"Seems a few have survived," Lucy observed with a shake of her head. Turning back to Maggie, she asked, "And what happened next, darlin'?"

"Well, I checked everywhere around the room but couldn't find it anywhere. So, I carried on, keepin' an eye out for it, until now."

Maggie stood next to a large pot in the middle of the island filled with what appeared to be the stew. But what the cook had fished out of the pot was definitely not something found in any stew Kitty had ever seen or would ever want to have, for that matter.

The cook continued, "I'm glad I found it, but I certainly didn't want it there!" On the end of her wooden spoon was the curled corpse of a giant red ant. "When I went for my broom, it must have tried to scurry away and fallen directly in my stew pot!"

"And that's why you couldn't find it. It'd gone and killed itself, doin' the job for ya!" Lucy said helpfully.

Maggie nodded in agreement as she placed the dead ant on a serving tray in the centre of the island, steam rising from its shiny red corpse. Its abdomen had split open during its unexpected bath in Maggie's stew, and now, its whitish-pink innards lay exposed.

The cook sniffed it and said, "It doesn't smell bad. In fact, it reminds me of boilin' a crawfish almost. Even its flesh here looks quite like it!" She poked at it with the tip of her spoon.

Though it hadn't been cooking for long, it seemed to have been enough for the ant. As the cook poked at it, a piece of meat had flaked off, looking more like poached trout than a drowned ant. Maggie gingerly picked it up, brought it to her nose, and sniffed it. With an inquisitive expression, she placed the small piece of ant flesh in her mouth, chewed it, and swallowed.

Almost as one, the girls chorused, "Eww!"

Kitty exclaimed, "Maggie! What're ya doin', girl?!" The other women around Kitty had mixed reactions, and many were not unlike her own. Lucy watched with wide-eyed amusement. Carla looked like she'd been goosed by a ghost, and Monique had her hand to her mouth, seeming about ready to be sick all over her high-button boots.

Maggie looked at Kitty with surprise in her eyes. She had another small sample of stewed ant and said, "I'm surprised you'd say that, Kitty!"

"What do you mean?" Kitty said.

"You most of all should be familiar with found food! What with your foragin' with your dad when you were little and your daily journeys in the forests around this valley."

Though Kitty had been initially shocked at Maggie's actions tasting the ant, the cook was correct. She was a huge proponent of found food. And though disgusting, that is what the cooked ant was.

Lucy said, "Well, I bet she never foraged for the likes of that!"

Maggie shook her head. "Nor have I. But my ancestors did. One of the many bounties of the land."

Carla said, "They had big buggerin' ants like that back in the day?"

Maggie shook her head. "The smaller cousins of this fella are quite nutritious in a pinch. And I'd heard of my ancestors roasting them on hot rocks from the fire, so I didn't think there'd be much harm in trying."

Still trying to hold back her stomach's contents, one hand to her mouth, Monique gestured weakly toward the ant and said, "Please feel free to help yourselves."

Gathering herself somewhat, Kitty said, "Well, to each their own, I'm sure. But I will take a pass on it at the moment. Thank ya very much."

"Yes, definitely a hard pass on that," Lucy added with a slight grimace.

Maggie shrugged her shoulders slightly and had another sample of the ant's abdominal flesh. "Are you sure? It kind of tastes like chicken."

The girls all shook their heads, and Maggie scraped the remains of the ant into a nearby garbage pail, saying, "Your loss."

The cook picked the pail up and moved to the screen door. With a sigh, she placed it on the floor and looked out at the darkening alley. "I'd sure like to dump this fella in the garbage where I found that live one, but I don't want to slop through all that mud in the dark."

Kitty nodded, peering into the dark beside her friend, and said, "That's a wise choice, Maggie. Especially considerin' what might still be slitherin' around out there."

CHAPTER TWENTY-FIVE

Caleb watched Kitty move off toward the kitchen, still exceedingly happy to have her back in his life. He felt quite unwilling to let her out of sight but knew he had to do so eventually. She'd be fine in the kitchen, he imagined. The rest of the girls were already there, so she would be in good company.

Just a short while ago, Albert VanDusen had returned to the saloon. He was the new temporary police chief and the sole remaining member. A short while ago, he'd joined Sinclair in his office to go over emergency plans for the town. At least, that's what Lucias had said when he came to collect him for the Scotsman.

Earlier in the evening, VanDusen and some of the volunteers had been on patrol scouting for ants in the drier parts of town. But now, with night having fallen, the dozen or so men had been returning in twos and threes. Anyone still wandering around in the dark might find themselves at the wrong end of a set of mandibles or pointed teeth.

When the most recent group of volunteers wandered in the doors, the previous arrivals pulled some tables together so they could all sit as a group and enjoy a friendly drink after a long and trying day. Apart from some stories about survivors they'd located, the men said they'd found relatively few surviving ants (which survived no longer thanks to the hot lead pumped into them), so that was at least some good news.

Sandy and his dog had been awakened by their arrival and had moved out to the front sidewalk, perhaps on the lookout for further trouble.

With thoughts of other threats and trouble in mind, Caleb's eyes tracked back to the man sitting across the table from him.

Bowler hat tilted back on his head, Jesús's gold teeth gleamed from both sides of his mouth. The man had been watching him observe Kitty leave the room and said with a sly smile, "You are a lucky man." His eyes ticked briefly toward the kitchen and then back to Caleb.

"I know. And I still can't believe I'm sittin' at the table with the man that kidnapped her!" Though he had brought up the fact of the kidnapping to temporary Chief VanDusen, the man had deferred doing anything about the situation for the moment. He'd said that until there was a secure place to lock up criminals once again, he couldn't do much more than make some notes and tell them not to leave the valley. And since the telegraph lines were still down, he couldn't even wire for backup from the North West Mounted Police.

Oritz shook his head and said, "And I never thought I would be sitting at a table with you again, either. But strange times make for even stranger bedfellows."

"Let's not get too intimate now."

"We should get to know each other if we will be travelling up the mountain together."

There was little Caleb wanted to know about the man across from him. He already knew all he needed to know from his experiences with the gang leader, in that he was greedy, conniving, murderous, double-crossing and all around no good.

However, across the room, getting to know each other was indeed something Doc Brown and the bandit cook were now doing. Having returned from his practice and given a quick check on his patients, Brown was now taking advantage of his line of credit with Sinclair. With a smile, he'd ordered a bottle of whisky from Muddy, then sat down at his usual table and removed his 'emergency shot glass' from his waistcoat pocket. As the doctor filled his glass, Caleb watched Cookie approach, eyeing the whisky bottle with thirsty eyes. Brown had gestured for him to sit, and so the two seniors had a meet and greet while Caleb and Jesús had a tête-à-tête.

Caleb tasted the beer before him, having waited for the foam to settle after pouring it into the glass. As he'd sipped, he watched a volunteer at the bar over the rim of his glass. The man was taking a sip of his beverage, a freshly poured draft beer courtesy of Muddy. After a good hard swallow, the thirsty man grabbed a rag and wiped his bushy moustache and lower chin. The rag was one of several hanging along the front of the mahogany bar. Satisfied he'd cleaned the foam from his face, the man hung the rag back on the hook where he'd found it.

That was something Caleb never did. The last thing he ever wanted to do was wipe his face with a rag that, despite the relative cleanliness of the Golden Nugget, had already been used by dozens of men and likely went for hours at a time before being changed. Over the years, he'd met men from all over the world, from all walks of life, with many carrying some sort of communicable disease or other.

It was an association Caleb had made a few years before after reading an article in a newspaper about some new things called 'germs'. He'd been out with a couple of friends the previous night, and the next day, his companions had woken up with a sore throat and a cold. They couldn't figure out how Caleb hadn't picked it up since they had eaten and drunk the same things. But in a flash of realisation, Caleb recalled that he'd been the only one of the group who'd favoured his shirt sleeve over the communal beer rag on the table where they'd been drinking.

Thoughts of sickness on his mind, Caleb placed his glass on the table before him, looked over to what was surely a communicable disease on two legs, and said, "About us going up the mountain together."

"Yes?" Jesús leaned forward slightly.

"I know I said otherwise, but I'm still unsure if I can remember exactly where the entrance to the cavern is."

Oritz shook his head and said, "This is most unfortunate news."

"But it's not all bad," Caleb responded. "Though the cavern is still hazy, I might have recalled where your gold sovereigns are now." That was a bit of a lie. He still had only flashes of memory, but at least it was something to go on. Once he was closer to the location, he hoped more might come to him then.

The bandit perked up in his chair and said, "Do tell, amigo!"

Frowning, Caleb said, "We need to get some things straight first."

"And what are they?"

"First of all, I'm not your amigo, your compadre, or your friend. In fact, I trust you about as far as I can throw you. And judgin' by your build, that wouldn't be very far."

Jesús pouted slightly, then said, "No need to get personal.

This is all purely business."

"Say what now? You were just doin' your job? For whom?" Caleb's eyes narrowed, and he answered his own question by posing another, "Did Sinclair put you up to it?"

"No, no, nothing like that. He merely said to do whatever it took to get you to remember and that he would make me a partner to share some of the gold from your cavern if I did. Hiding away your little Scottish sweetie was something I decided to do to help you remember, ami—" Oritz stopped, then corrected himself, saying, "Mister Caleb," deferring to Caleb's earlier request. "We would not have truly hurt her and would merely have kept her captive until you found the cavern."

Caleb doubted that most sincerely. In his brief conversations with Kitty, he'd discovered that the scar-faced bandit she'd despatched at Farley's had been ready to do much, much more than just 'keep her captive'. And now, to learn that Sinclair had promised this bandit a share of the cavern's gold for his treachery, Caleb realised his earlier instincts about the Scotsman had been entirely accurate.

Of course, once he did locate the golden cavern, Caleb had almost no doubt that the small man in the bowler hat would attempt to increase his share of the partnership through Caleb's 'accidental' death.

Leaning forward at the table, Caleb took another sip of his beer. He enjoyed this one quite a lot. The bottle's label said it was 'imported' from Eastern Canada. Moosehead was its name, and it was quite tasty but not quite as good as the true nectar of Ireland that he preferred when he could get it, Guinness Stout. He placed his glass back on the table and sighed, saying, "I'll make you a deal."

Jesús's smile disappeared, and he tilted his head, saying, "I am all ears."

"I will give you my entire share of the gold in the cavern." He'd been doing a lot of hard thinking and had concluded he wanted to be done with the cursed cavern. He could get some honest work, find a peaceful and quiet spot in this beautiful valley, and settle down with Kitty.

Smiling broadly once more, Oritz leaned closer and said, "That is a very generous proposition. And I will tell you what, I will accept it, with one exception."

"And what's that?"

"You must take me inside the cavern so I can see the gold before I will release you from our agreement. But if you cross me, I will have two dozen men here in a week, all looking for you."

"Deal then," Caleb said and stuck out his hand. Oritz did the same, and they reached across the table to shake.

Rufus jolted from his nap near the door and raised his head, suddenly tense and alert.

Just as they clinched hands and began to shake, Caleb thought some trickery was occurring on the part of the small Spaniard on the table's far side. The man seemed to start vibrating, and then everything around him did the same.

An alarmed look replaced Oritz's grin, and he released his grip at the same time as Caleb and shouted, "Earthquake!"

Across the room, Brown had grabbed his bottle of whisky, and he and Cookie were clambering under the safety of the sturdy table they'd been sitting at only moments before. Bottles were shaking with a musical tinkle behind the bar, and several tumbled to the floor with a crash as Muddy tried to save dozens more but found his number of hands far too few for the job. At his back, Jesús had risen from his seat and staggered on unsteady feet toward the batwing doors as the world all around him shimmied and shook.

The group of volunteers sharing a drink scattered as the room trembled around them, some heading toward the batwing doors as Jesús had, and others clambering under their tables like Doc Brown and Cookie. From the kitchen came a horrific shriek of someone in pain, a woman, possibly Kitty.

Caleb struggled from his chair to see what was happening, but the shaking room around him seemed bent on keeping him from his destination. However, he was determined and kept going, finally making it to the side of the room. He hugged the wall as he moved along and now neared the kitchen.

From above, a huge, five-point set of antlers came crashing down. They slammed into the floor, missing him by mere inches, the long, pointed tines penetrating deeply into the hardwood flooring.

Though the shaking seemed to be worsening, Caleb was committed to his course of action. When he'd swept Kitty into his arms only hours before, he had vowed to himself that he would do whatever it took to keep her safe, and it was a vow he meant to keep or die trying.

CHAPTER TWENTY-SIX

The pot from which Maggie had pulled the ant was rattling and bouncing and getting dangerously close to the edge of the wooden island. Kitty danced back from where she stood as the shaking became worse and worse. She couldn't even steady the pot since she was having a hard time enough just standing upright at the moment.

With a shriek of dismay, Kitty's reservations about the pot's stability proved accurate all too soon. It bounced off the island's edge and sloshed its near-boiling contents across the floor, some of it splashing onto Maggie's cotton skirt at the same time. Now, it was the cook's turn to utter a cry, this one of pain.

The other girls staggered out of the way as the hot liquid rushed across the floor toward them, and none wearing footwear that would in any way protect them.

Now near the door to the saloon, Kitty looked out just in time to see a huge rack of elk antlers slam into the floor with deadly force in front of Caleb. She shrieked again, this time in fear for her Irish beau instead of herself. Here they were, finally back together and now the pair of them about to be killed in an earthquake.

Caleb saw her just as he looked up from his near-death experience with the antlers and called out, "I'll come to you!"

Nodding, Kitty waited where she was for Caleb to do just that. He approached on unsteady legs, but fortunately, nothing else fell on or near him, for the moment.

Over at the bar, the large pendulum clock next to the alcohol availability sign dropped from its hanging place, its inner workings making a resounding and musical 'clang' as they struck the bartop. Muddy stopped trying to save the bottles of alcohol from falling and dived out of the way as the 'saloon rules' sign detached and joined the clock on the floor behind the bar.

Despite everything shaking like it was about to come down around their ears, it didn't. After several more seconds of terror, the vibrations began to lessen more and more, and soon, the ground stilled once again.

Doc Brown crawled out from underneath his table just as Kitty emerged from the kitchen and joined Caleb in the saloon, their eyes as wide and staring as the doctor's. Taking in the disarray around the room, Brown said, "That's my first experience with an earthquake, and I hope it's my last." He moved to his group of patients in the corner. One man had fallen off his table during the tremor and was now in need of assistance getting back up.

His arm around Kitty's shoulder, Caleb nodded at Brown's comment and said, "I felt one down in Chile just after I first made land there. Let me tell ya, it made me rethink my decision pretty quick, but by then, the ship I worked my way over on had sailed, so it was too late."

The girls entered the room from the kitchen, Monique and Lucy helping Maggie, one on each side. The cook's skirt was now held up with a hairpin, her leg exposed beneath, a nasty red welt forming where the hot stew had struck her. Lucy followed behind moments later, her hair hanging down, a towel in hand with something wrapped inside. She handed it to Maggie, saying, "Here, get some of this ice on it. There's not much left in the icebox, but I think it should help cool you down."

Carla pulled out a chair, and Maggie sat with a pained wheeze. The cook placed the dripping towel on her leg with a grateful sigh and said to Lucy, "Thank you, dear."

Kitty looked to Maggie and said in a quiet voice, "It's like the legend you told me of your ancestors."

"How's that, dear?" Maggie asked.

"You said, many, many years ago, your people had experienced the land shaking, and then the black things had shown up. This is almost the reverse of that—the black things showed up, and now the earth moved!"

"Any more legends you should be tellin' us about, Maggie?" Caleb wondered.

Maggie shook her head sadly and appeared about to speak when Sandy burst through the front doors, saying, "The water is goin' away!"

As everyone inside the saloon moved to the sidewalk outside to see what Sandy was talking about, there came a flurry of gunfire. Silver moonlight was just starting to shine down through broken clouds, giving things an otherworldly luminescence.

Jesús stood next to Lucias in the street. They fired their revolvers at the black creatures that writhed and coiled in the mud, easy to spot now that they'd been left marooned by the floodwater's rapid departure.

"What happened to the water?" Kitty wondered.

Brown stood to one side of her and Caleb, looking down the street. Though the moon was waning, it was still large enough and bright enough to illuminate the scene. "There must be a fault somewhere at the other end that it drained into."

The lack of water so suddenly had not been good for the black beasts, and the street was rife with them. Dozens and dozens flipped, flopped, writhed, and coiled, casting about as they looked for refuge in nearby water but could find none. Their short, stubby limbs were not strong enough to move them far on the streets and side alleys now thick with heavy mud.

Sandy had moved off down the sidewalk toward the police station, saying, "I want to check this out."

In the side alley near the haberdashers where Kitty and Caleb had been stranded, the boy came upon something they couldn't see. He paused briefly and stomped his size fourteen boot onto whatever he'd found, grinding it into the gravelly mud, then moved on.

After a few more tense moments, the tall man-boy arrived in front of the police station, and he hollered back to the group, "There's a big crack in the road down here!"

Brown smiled grimly, saying, "Just as I suspected."

Kitty asked, "D'ya think it swallowed up some of those things?"

"It appears to have drained away like a very large bathtub," Brown observed. The lower end of town had been underwater by several feet, and all of it had suddenly emptied into some other, heretofore unknown cavern through the fault in the ground. Brown added, "It must have created a good bit of suction as it drained."

The beasts that hadn't been sucked away were left stranded and were now fair game. Lucias and Jesús were joined by some of the slightly inebriated volunteers who were shooting at the stranded water beasts. They seemed to be having a great time while doing so, judging by the number of 'yeehaws' and 'woohoos' that could be heard between the shots.

"Well, this is a bit of a bad news, good news situation it would seem," Brown concluded. "Though we have some damage to the town, it would appear mother nature is working in our favour at the moment."

Some damage had indeed been incurred, with the Bank of Montreal next to the still smouldering husk of Vicker's Five and Ten suffering the most harm of any building they could see. Perhaps caused by the ants undermining its foundation, the brick structure now leaned at a drunken angle with one side several feet lower than the other.

"I'm sure there will be more bad news to come," Kitty said, wondering what else this valley had in store for them.

As if in answer to her question, Thomas Sinclair pushed through the batwing doors at Caleb's back, Angeline at his side. With a shake of his head, he said, "Well, that was altogether unexpected." The small Scotsman stood with his thumbs hooked into the sides of his vest, his round belly on prominent display beneath the shiny satin fabric.

"It looks like that shakin' has dried things up a bit for your trip tomorrow."

"Can't you stop and take a breath? D'ya have to go right away?" Kitty wondered.

Nodding, Caleb said, "Yes, I do. I want to get this over and done with." He looked deeply into Kitty's eyes as he spoke, and she knew his mind was made up. He finished, adding, "And when this is all over, I want to get on with my life—my life with you."

Kitty hugged him tight and said nothing, her eyes blurring with tears.

Sinclair cleared his throat and continued, "I've had Lucias and Muddy put together those things you requested. They're in the storage room when you want to take a look."

Caleb nodded, and Sinclair moved to the bottom of the Nugget's steps but didn't step down into the mud, his shiny leather boots not made for such conditions. He beckoned Lucias and Jesús, who joined him for a private conversation.

While Caleb's 'partners' confabulated, Kitty looked into her beau's eyes, searching for something to reassure her that this wouldn't be the last evening she'd ever spend with the man. But she could see nothing and said, "Tell me you're comin' back."

Silent for a long moment, Caleb eventually said, "Don't worry, I'm comin' back, and I don't even care about that gold at all anymore."

"Really? Why?"

"I found the one true treasure I've been looking for my entire life, and I don't intend on losin' it now."

With that, he kissed her, and Kitty hoped he would never, ever stop.

CHAPTER TWENTY-SEVEN

The early morning breeze was cool, almost chilly, in fact. Kitty pulled her shawl closer about her shoulders. Caleb put his arm around her, partly out of protectiveness and partly trying to warm her. They watched the sun rise over the ragged mountain peaks in the east, its rays just now warming the ridge at the back of the valley. Tufts of cotton cloud skidded across the cerulean sky, but they were in no way threatening. The storm and the destruction it had caused now seemed long gone.

On the main street, mud was already beginning to solidify, embedding the carcasses of numerous black water beasts, though a few smaller ones had survived in puddles. However, the puddles were now mostly gone, and the small fry lay gasping in the thickening mud, soon to join the rest of their monstrous family in the next world.

But Caleb's mind was currently occupied with a different kind of family, the human kind. He thought of Kitty and love and having someone to go through time with, perhaps even starting his own family. These thoughts and more had gone through his mind, over and over, for the last few hours, and he couldn't stop thinking them.

Last night, he and Kitty had spent several of their last few precious hours making love with an urgency that belied their true passion. Caleb had been exhausted afterwards and slept solidly for a few hours but had woken from that fit slumber and experienced broken sleep since.

And so, he had risen sometime after four, the edges of the mountains outside tinged mauve with dawn. It was still several hours before the sun would creep over the mountaintops. And so, he'd left Kitty sleeping while he'd gone downstairs to once again inspect the gear that Sinclair had left for the expedition.

Piled in the corner of the sizeable main-floor storage room were several bundles of rope and other supplies, including some of the new calcium carbide headlamps he was so enamoured with. And even Maggie had gotten in on the act, providing several dozen hearty oatmeal flapjack biscuits wrapped in tin foil. They sat next to the supply of jerky and other lightweight food supplies salvaged from O'Malley's Outdoor Supply Store, which Sinclair also owned.

While Caleb dreaded returning to the cavern, he at least looked forward to having the higher intensity lights this time. It would be interesting to see what else the series of caves contained since much of it had remained hidden in darkness from his single, dented kerosene lantern. And though there were provisions, with the number of fish in the lake, he didn't think finding something to eat would be a problem for them in the long run up there. After all, these supplies were just to help them find the place again, and it wasn't like he wanted to go on another tour of it. The rest of the men would be welcome to explore it while he returned to town and to Kitty's soft, slender arms.

Last night, there had been some discussion around the girls wanting to return to the rustic cabin they shared with Kitty. However, it was decided they should wait for the morning. The way to the cabin could be challenging to traverse, and the light of a new day was judged to be best before they ventured out. The girls had agreed and spent the night in their rooms, although they had done so alone to the best of Caleb's knowledge. Of course, he didn't know for sure due to the noise he and Kitty had been making.

With the sun now well above the mountaintops, Kitty and Caleb moved back into the saloon. Around them, the volunteers using the floor as their bed had begun to stir.

"Ah! There you are, Kitty!" Doctor Brown exclaimed as he rushed toward them. "I want to run back to my office and gather up the little addition I've been working on for Caleb's expedition!" Without waiting for confirmation, the doctor departed, leaving Kitty ministering to his remaining tabled patients.

With Kitty busy, Caleb returned to the storage room. He'd begun to assemble a pack for himself from the supplied items when a voice spoke at his back.

"I hope everything is to your likin'," Thomas Sinclair inquired.

Startled, Caleb spun in surprise and said, "It seems like you've got just about everythin' a fella could want for spelunkin' about in the bowels of the earth."

"I've had my fair share of doin' just that," Sinclair said. Standing in the doorway to the storage room, the Scotsman added, "Come into my office for a moment if you could, lad. There's something I want to show you before you get goin'."

A few moments later, they were in Sinclair's office, the door closed. Lucias and Angeline were nowhere in sight.

Caleb sat in the leather chair opposite Sinclair at his desk.

His host didn't seat himself right away and instead moved to the display case off to one side of the room. "There's more than just gold to this valley. You know that, don't ya?"

"You've got that right. It's like trouble is drawn here."

"More than that," Sinclair said as he opened the curio case and withdrew something from the top shelf. Returning with a silver tray in hand, he placed it on the desk between them with what seemed great reverence. Black fabric nestled around three black stones in the centre of the tray. He eyed them with a gaze that bordered on obsession as he said, "These are very precious to me."

"I can see that."

Three obsidian stones gleamed darkly in their nest of black velveteen fabric, seeming to absorb the light of the single oil lamp on the desk. With a puff, Sinclair sat opposite Caleb and said, "D'ya know what they are?"

"Pieces of obsidian?"

"More than that. These are stones of power."

Caleb leaned forward, something in the pit of his stomach going sour as he looked more closely at the black gemstones. "There's something about them, to be sure."

"Yes! And it was one of those that drew us here, not the gold. That was just an added bonus."

"Us?" Caleb wondered.

"Well, it was actually Angeline who was drawn here. Amongst her other gifts, she has these feelings she can't explain that guide her sometimes."

Kitty had told him of Angeline, saying something was not quite right about the woman. Well, now he knew the reason why. "So, you're sayin' she's like a psychic or a clairvoyant, and she could sense these stones?"

"Much more than that." Sinclair continued, "Those stones are very powerful, and we've only ever found them along the grid."

"The grid?"

"Ley lines. Perhaps you've heard of them."

Caleb shook his head.

"They're quite a new and controversial topic, but some believe they contain power that flows through the earth beneath. In fact, two of these ley lines intersect right here under our feet." Sinclair pointed to the topmost stone in the velvet triad and said, "This one is from beneath this very building." Next, he directed Caleb's gaze to the stone on the bottom left, "That one was from Scotland, near my ancestral castle." And to the third stone, he said, "This is from North Africa. "In fact..." he trailed off as he swivelled in his chair to look to the second shelf of the cabinet where an ebony box sat. "That was where we found the ebony box as well."

"You found that buried in the ground?" Caleb looked toward the dark box in the cabinet, noting its white pearl trim.

"Not quite buried in the ground. But with it, we found several stones already inside. And now, with the others I've gathered since, there seems to be a power emanatin' from them, as well as that box. And it continues to get stronger the more of them we bring together. In fact, I had more stones in the past, but they were stolen from me before I could discover their true power."

"And you've only ever found them along these ley lines?

"Aye. And I don't rightly know how many ley line junctions there are across this globe, but I intend to find all that I can and collect as many of these stones when I do. I've long been fascinated by electricity and power of all kinds, both physical and metaphysical. And I believe that something big will happen once I've amassed enough of these gems."

"Something big? An explosion, you mean?"

"Hardly. I think it will be much more than a mere explosion, you can be sure of that. And I don't care how much money it takes; I intend to find every last one that I can. And that is why I am pointing them out to you. I was going to show you the situation where I found the one beneath this saloon. I should have shared it with you the first time I took you down there. However, that's beside the point. The elevator is out because of the damned earthquake now, so it's not possible at the moment. But I'm showin' them to ya now so you can keep your eyes open when you find your cavern again."

"And you think there's more of them up there?"

"We don't know. Angeline says she's unsure because the power concentration of the stones together here masks any signs of others nearby. But I thought if you saw them here and perhaps felt something as you looked at them, you would be familiar with the sensation when you were up there in the dark."

"Well, if I feel any tinglin', I'll double-check around me. But I have to tell ya, as of right now, the only thing I feel is a chill."

"Aye, they all share that property. Most people can feel that much." Thomas stood and removed the tray from the desk, placing the stones back in the curio case. "But others, like my Angeline, can feel so much more than that."

Caleb recalled something from their earlier conversation down below, and he asked, "Did ya hear the voices before you found that stone?"

"Why do you ask?" Sinclair said as he sat back down, his chair giving a squeak of protest.

"Because you asked me that same question about my cavern," Caleb replied. He'd suddenly recalled his initial encounter with the spider up in the hills, along with his additional thoughts that he might not have been alone there.

Upon hearing the clatter of rocks, Caleb had thought of the People of the Ground or the Ancient Ones he'd heard rumour of in his travels up through South America. After encountering the spider, he'd thought nothing more of the noise and figured it had been the arachnid moving around in the dark. But now that he'd learned of these stones and how people were drawn to them, he wondered, were other things drawn to them as well?

Sinclair clarified, "Well, actually, it was only after we found the stone below that we started to hear them."

Caleb thought this quite interesting. Only after removing the stone did they hear the voices. Was whoever, or whatever the stones belonged to, searching for it? Was it the Ground People Lucias had heard when he'd been alone near those bottomless tubes below? And why only a single stone? Curious, he asked, "Were there ever any instances of more than one found at a time?"

Sinclair shook his head. "Nay, only one at a time that we've ever seen, except for what was inside that box when we found it."

Was the stone found below this saloon somehow linked to the existence of the beasts that filled his golden cavern in the hills above? And how many more stones were out there? These were all questions for which there seemed no answers at the moment, and indeed, Caleb felt unsure if he wanted to know them, even if there were.

But if he did or didn't was a moot point because it seemed his current destiny was to find out, whether he liked it or not.

CHAPTER TWENTY-EIGHT

Doctor Brown had returned to his practice, his mind awhirl with what he intended to do with the spiders. They were one of the most dire threats still remaining, but he thought he had matters in hand now, thanks to his new creation, the Brown Pest-Away Fumigator. It was almost complete, but before he could put the finishing touches on it, he needed to finish up with something else first: his little addition to Caleb's upcoming search for his golden cavern.

He looked at Mama and scowled. The arachnid hung upside down from the top of its cage, its numerous eyes seeming to study Brown as intently as he studied it. Cornelius shook his head and said, "You are a troublesome one. You and your numerous little ones. And as much as you want to propagate your species, we can't have you doing that. If Mr. Darwin is to be believed, you've already had your chance tens of thousands or even hundreds of thousands of years ago. Right now, we don't need another apex predator lurking in the shadows around this valley or any other."

Thankfully, the creatures with the biggest appetites, the vicious red ants, were now less of a concern due to the hail and flooding that had occurred. And though that flood was initially a boon for the black beasts, the subsequent earthquake had sent them on their way again; he just wasn't sure where.

Any of the black monsters that hadn't been sucked into the fissure at the lower end of the main street had been stranded on land when the water drained away. But the question was, where did the water and the beasts go? Did they drain through an underground channel to the river and, ultimately, the lake? Or were the obsidian creatures now cut off from the world in another water-filled subterranean cavern similar to where they'd first been found? And there was one alternative still; perhaps everything had drained away into the fracture, and there was no cavern. Instead, the creatures were now wedged in the spaces between the rock, where they would die of hunger and dehydration.

Brown kicked the mop bucket where the small black beast was contained, and it sloshed and roiled about in the shallow water at the bottom. The little monster looked like it had grown even more despite his not feeding it. And though the earthquake had helped with the things in town, how many of its kind still swam in the trio of pools at the park, let alone the river? He hoped the animals were communal creatures like some fish and that they travelled in schools. If that were the case, then maybe they had all escaped the pools yesterday, only to be betrayed by the earthquake, making Mother Nature responsible for both their liberation and their ultimate demise.

And what of the scaly animal before him? He knew this small, ugly creature would turn into a large, monstrous creature, and he couldn't keep it in the bucket forever. Even the washtub would eventually be too small for it. Whatever he did, he wouldn't have long before he had to make a choice. After all, it wasn't as if he could just release it back into the wild.

Brown shook his head to clear it of his speculations. Time was short, and he needed to get back to the Golden Nugget to see Caleb and the others off on their grand adventure. He was eager for the Irishman to try his other new invention, which he'd just wrapped in burlap to protect it until needed. Though not specifically designed for the upcoming expedition, the device was something he was close to testing as it was, and now it looked as if it would get a thorough workout courtesy of Caleb instead.

Though the doctor desperately wanted to go up the mountain with them, he knew it wasn't in the cards. The thought of rappelling down a rope hundreds of feet was one thing, but climbing back up was another. Cornelius had never been one of the most athletic boys growing up. On top of that, he was rail-thin because of his drinking, and his lack of exercise over the years had not been kind to his muscles. As Caleb had also pointed out, apart from climbing, there would be a fair bit of crawling and possibly swimming, amongst other things. Cornelius didn't feel particularly old most days. Still, since he had recently celebrated his sixtieth birthday, he realised Caleb was right, and he should leave the early spelunking and discovery of the cavern's layout to the younger men. Perhaps once things were more established up there, he would get his chance to have a little look-see.

The bell jangled over the door, and to Brown's surprise, the subject of his thoughts entered the office.

"Hey, Doc! D'ya have a minute?"

"Caleb! I was just heading back to the Nugget to see you off."

"Well, we're almost ready, but I wanted to talk to you in private before I go.

"Really? About what, my boy?"

"About my condition."

"What's wrong?" Brown asked with concern.

"It's about what we discussed yesterday."

"You mean your magical powers?"

"Is that what you're callin' them now?"

"Well, I don't know how else to categorise them. What with those knife wounds you say you had—"

"I didn't just say I had them. I felt the knife go in!"

Brown held his hands up placatingly, "I wasn't questioning you, my boy. I phrased that incorrectly. I meant the wounds you described. There was no evidence of anything recent, and when I examined them, there was only some slight scarring."

Caleb shook his head, "I don't know what to tell ya. You saw the blood. And I know I got cut by Oritz because I felt it. And what about all the blood around those holes in my clothes? It didn't belong to Oritz; it belonged to me."

"It's not the healing that's unprecedented; it's the speed. The fact that your broken ankle has also seemingly mended in a little over a week instead of six, well, it almost seems magical." He pointed to Caleb's leg and interjected, "Speaking of which, any more pain?"

Caleb shook his head. "Nope, I feel fit as a fiddle."

"It's quite fascinating, really. And it makes me wonder."

"About?"

"About your recent miraculous convalescence and how your recuperation seems proportional to your accelerated constitution.

Caleb shook his head and looked at the doctor with a slight

squint. "What d'ya mean, Doc? Pretend like you're talkin' to an idiot."

Brown gave a small smile and said, "If the wounds were as deep as you say," he held up a hand in a 'before you say something' manner and continued, "and if they healed in less than an hour. And keeping in mind such an invasive wound, depending on the complications, could potentially take almost as long to heal as a broken ankle, which you no longer have…"

"Yes?"

"Well, if all of this is related to that bite you received in the cavern from our slithering black friends. And now, the way things are accelerating for you…"

"Wait a minute! Are ya tryin' to say that if I broke my ankle again or my arm, it might heal in a matter of hours?"

The doctor shrugged slightly. "I wouldn't want you trying such a thing just to find out if my supposition is accurate, but yes, that seems like it's a definite possibility. However, there are a couple of caveats I would add."

"And they are?"

In a lower voice to emphasise his words, Brown said, "Firstly, keep this to yourself."

Caleb shook his head. "I wasn't about to start shoutin' it from the street corner like the town crier, that's for sure."

"Good. Well, in a nutshell, I've been giving your condition quite some thought, as I do with most things, and there's a good chance you shouldn't go at all."

"What?"

Brown shook his head and said, "You really should be

under observation. Your accelerated healing might not stop at just that. But then again, even if I were there with you, or if you were down here, there is probably little I could do if it got more aggressive.

"Meaning?"

"I mean, it might metastasise and spread like cancer throughout your body, over-accelerating your cells until your body eventually consumes itself."

"Say what now?"

Brown held both palms out and said reassuringly, "Or it might be nothing at all. It's only supposition."

Caleb gave a small sigh and a slight shake of his head. "Well, thanks for putting my mind at ease, Doc. I think."

Brown nodded, hoping his ramblings made some sense to his friend. "Always a pleasure, my boy."

A slosh came at their backs, and they turned to see the black creature in the mop bucket had managed to get its head up high enough, so it was now resting its toothy little maw on the top edge. It regarded them both with its cold, soulless eyes for several moments, then splashed back into the bucket. It made Cornelius wonder about Caleb in the water with the black beasts yesterday. Those creatures hadn't touched him in the least, and now this small one seemed more than interested in him for some reason.

"Looks like our friend there is getting a bit big for its britches, Doc."

"Yes. I noticed that just before you came in and was trying to decide what to do with it."

"Maybe you can have a fish fry," Caleb said, his eyes

trained on the bucket.

"I was thinking of pickling it, actually."

"Doc! You don't want to go and try eating that thing!"

The doctor looked to Caleb with confusion for a moment and then laughed, saying, "Oh no, not that kind of pickling, my boy! The kind done with formaldehyde in a large jar, in the name of science! In fact, I could get some from Ezra's once it's cleared of arachnids."

"Oh, right!" Caleb nodded and added, "Of course, that's what you mean. It's just with everything trying to eat everything else around here, I thought you might be trying to get in on the act!"

As if in response to Caleb's words, the earth began to tremble around them as if hungry once again and ready to swallow up more than just the black water beasts this time.

Caleb braced himself against the counter and said, "Not another one!"

"Relax, my boy, this is only an aftershock."

"After what?"

The building vibrated around them as if rattled by a giant's hands. Jars and bottles tinkled together in a small cabinet behind the counter, and the scoop net clattered to the floor from the wall where it had been propped.

"An aftershock; they sometimes occur after earthquakes. I suppose you could say it's the ground settling into its new position and getting comfortable. It's a fascinating emerging field, seismology. I can tell you more of the subject sometime if you wish."

Still clinging to the counter as the ground wobbled around them, Caleb said, "Can you tell me how long this will last?"

"Shouldn't be for much longer than the original quake."

Within a few moments, the tremor began to lessen and then stopped all of a sudden; the show was apparently over.

Now that he could walk without swaying more than usual, Brown moved to a shelf near his barbering chair and removed a large book almost a foot and a half long by one wide. Its cover read, 'The Illustrated Book of Human Anatomy - Revised Edition'. With a knowing nod, he said, "I figured this would come in handy someday." Brown placed the book across the top of the bucket and then positioned a large piece of copper ore on top. "There we are. No more playing jack-in-the-box for you, my foul little friend."

Inside the bucket, the black beast reared up and tried bumping its head into the book to dislodge it, but the ore on top held it firmly in place.

"You go and try eatin' some of that anatomy, ya dirty little bugger," Caleb said with a dismissive tone.

"At least his brethren are no longer roaming the streets. So that is one less worry, along with the ants seeming to be vanquished, for the moment at least."

"It's just your spider friends now, Doc."

"They're hardly friends," Brown said, moving to the spider. "But they need to be studied."

"And killed."

The spider still hung upside down in the cage. It poked a couple of its legs out and tapped them against the bars of its avian prison as if beckoning Caleb to come a little closer and say those words.

"If they could be kept in captivity, it would be such a scientific breakthrough."

"Keep them? For what?"

"Their venom. It needs to be studied. I think it could be a valuable aid in medicine, especially in the field of pain relief and patient sedation. You saw how potent its poison is. Just one nip and it can paralyse a man."

Caleb nodded, "Sandy's lucky he's so big; otherwise, he woulda been put down and..." he trailed off, shuddering slightly. "Just the thought of going back up to that cavern where that beastie came from gives me the willies."

"But the fortune you might acquire must make the risk more acceptable, doesn't it?"

Nodding slightly, Caleb said, "I might have thought that a couple of weeks ago. But if it were just me, knowin' what I do now, I might just leave it there. I swear that cavern is cursed the way everythin's been goin'."

Seeming as if in response to Caleb's words, Sandy burst through the door, saying, "Mr. Caleb! You better come quick; we got a problem!"

Brown looked to his friend and said, "I'll catch up with you. I need to get one more thing ready for you while you deal with your little problem."

Shaking his head, Caleb moved toward the door, saying, "That's the trouble. Even the little problems around here can be deadly."

CHAPTER TWENTY-NINE

The pair of big brown eyes regarded Caleb with two things: one was recognition, and the other was hunger. Getting tongue-lashed a second time, Caleb cried out, "Okay, okay! Fine! I'll get you some more sugar, don't you worry your pretty little head, Emily."

"If I didn't know better, I'd say she was hooked on the stuff!" Sandy observed.

Whether Emily was or wasn't addicted to sugar didn't matter much to the mule because she wanted it nonetheless. She nudged Caleb's hand again and licked it front and back, then nudged her nose at his pockets as she quested for sugar somewhere on his person. Not finding any, she seemingly decided to continue what she had started, her sit-down strike, and so she remained where she was, seated comfortably on the straw-covered stable floor.

"She plunked herself down just before the earth started shakin' again, and now she won't get up. I don't know if she's afraid it might start movin' again or what." Sandy tried to pull the mule up with his one arm but stopped after a moment, grimacing slightly, and leaning to one side. Emily remained where she was, seeming quite happy to do so. "I can't even pull a mule up at the moment with my pulled muscles on top of my spider arm," Sandy said with a sad shake of his head.

Emily was essential to Caleb's plan, for whatever it was worth. Without her help, he wasn't sure if he could find the cavern. But he wondered at her reluctance. In the past, he'd heard of mules being sensitive to impending disaster. Was her unwillingness to move a result of the earth tremor, or was it because she could sense something calamitous in the offing?

Despite some recent helpful flashbacks, none had brought Caleb any closer to recalling the actual location of the cavern's entrance—where he'd released the mule from her duties.

So, that brought him to his current plan. It had been formed by another partially recovered memory: his act of giving the mule a dose of sugar before he sent her fleeing down the mountain. He hoped it would be a location that had left a memory somewhere between Emily's two long ears, a place she would remember because of her mixture of delight at the sugar and fear from his shouting at the same time. And his logic went, if he gave her more sugar, it might spur her to remember the spot somewhere up on that golden ridge.

But now, before he could accomplish that, he would have to get her up and walking, and that didn't seem to be on the cards at the moment, at least until he got his hands on some more—

"Sugar?" a melodic voice inquired at Caleb's back.

Caleb turned to see Kitty Welch, a lovely smile on her face. The sunlight made her hair fire, bright eyes sparkling beneath like sapphires. It was a moment so unexpected it took his breath away. His thoughts of reluctance regarding the climb back up to the cavern were now gone. He wanted to find it more than anything and then be done with it. Sinclair and Oritz could duke it out for ownership of the gold without him needing to worry about constantly looking over his shoulder as he had for the past few months. Then, he and Kitty could begin their new life together.

Kitty held out two sugar cubes to the mule.

Emily stood almost immediately and began to nibble the cubes from Kitty's palm as daintily as could be, leaving a generous helping of saliva in return as thanks.

Caleb nodded his own thanks and said with a smile, "Leave it to you to be so sweet."

Kitty blushed slightly and replied, "You mentioned that you were thinkin' of bringin' Emily with you today. And I also recalled what you said motivated her, so I put a couple of cubes in my pocket just in case."

His heart swelling with love for this thoughtful woman, Caleb said, "It seems that Emily thinks you have some more."

The mule nudged Kitty's hand, searching for more sugar from her person, but found none and gave a snort of disappointment. Kitty responded, "You can have more at the saloon. There's a whole bag of it waitin' for ya there."

Caleb grasped Emily's bridle and led her out of the stable before she could decide to sit down again. With Kitty at his side, they moved down the street toward the Golden Nugget to load up the supplies. Kitty held his hand, seeming not to care who looked as they made their way.

"I've been thinkin'," Caleb said slowly.

"That always gets ya in trouble."

Laughing, Caleb replied, "Aye, you're not wrong, lass. The last time I got a bright idea, I ended up being on the run for my life."

"And ended up splashin' down in the river before me."

Caleb clenched Kitty's hand a little tighter and added, "It hasn't been all bad. I've made some great friends, and I met you." Had he not had a mule attached to his other hand, he would have stopped and kissed Kitty right then and there, impropriety or not. But seeing as they had just gotten Emily moving again, he didn't want to stop until they reached the saloon. He continued, saying, "I was thinkin', though I know it's soon, and we really don't know each other all that well, but before I went up the mountain, I wanted to ask you a question."

"And what might that be?" Kitty tilted her head, sparkling eyes interested, red lips creased with concern.

They were halfway to the saloon, and Caleb glanced up ahead for a moment and then back to Kitty before speaking as if to make sure they were still alone. When he turned around, he had a serious look in his eyes. "For most of my time on this planet, I've led a solitary life with few friends. I knew some lads in the army, but once I was discharged, we fell out of touch after playing postal tag for a half-dozen years. Since then, I've never stayed anywhere long enough to make too many more friends. And I've never been with a woman, for longer than an evenin' that is."

As that admission escaped Caleb's lips, he suddenly looked mortified and quickly added, "And it wasn't that often at all, mind you! I mean to say, I wasn't ever serious with a woman before. I don't want you thinkin' I'm a man of loose morals, more so than you already do."

Kitty smiled, saying, "I don't think you have to worry about that, Mr. Caleb Cantrill. Now, what was your question? Time is growing short." It was Kitty's turn to glance up the street. They were almost to the Nugget.

"Right, the question. Would you, Miss Kitty Welch, be able to find it within yourself to make a man like me very happy."

Caleb reached into his pants as he spoke.

Kitty's eyes widened in surprise at this development, and she said, "As much as we're not mindin' what other people think about our buddin' romance, are you sure you want to pull that out in the street, luv?"

Caleb stopped the mule, no longer caring if she sat down again. Clearing his throat, he opened his hand and held out the remaining golden nugget from the cavern. His voice low and serious, he said, "Miss Kitty, would you find it within yourself to do me the privilege... That is to say, would you allow me the pleasure of asking you... I mean, if you can find it in your heart, I would like you and I to, well—"

With a small laugh, Kitty interrupted and said, "Are ya askin' me to marry ya?"

Caleb swallowed hard and nodded solemnly. He looked deeply into Kitty's eyes and said, "Well, will ya?"

It was Kitty's turn to look into Caleb's eyes, searching for something deep within them. Whatever she sought, he hoped to heaven she could find it.

Pursing her soft, round lips, she said, "When?"

Caleb wrapped Kitty's hand around the nugget and said, "Once I come back down the mountain."

Kitty looked at the gold, then up at Caleb and said, "That would make a fine ring, I'm sure." She paused a moment, then added, "Since my father is no longer in this world for you to worry about askin', that does make things a little easier for ya. Because I'm sure he'd have somethin' to say about your heritage. But fortunately, that doesn't bother me."

His eyes wide and unblinking, Caleb said, "And?

"Yes, I'll marry you, Caleb Cantrill. When you get back, we'll set a date."

Caleb's eyes lit up, and he said, "You have made my day, month and year, Miss Kitty Welch!" He gave her a passionate kiss, which she returned, and both seemed reluctant to part until a voice spoke at their side.

"Sorry to interrupt, Mr. Caleb and Miss Kitty, but we're almost ready." Sandy had run ahead of them and had been working on bringing out the supplies for the trip to the front steps of the Golden Nugget." He held up a small box, saying, "And I have this for you from Mr. Lucias."

In Sandy's large hand was one of the more dangerous aspects of the expedition.

"Sweet Heaven to Sunday! Careful with that, lad!" Caleb handed the mule's rein to Kitty, saying, "Would you mind?" then gingerly took the small box that Sandy proffered.

"I was careful not to shake it," Sandy added.

"I'm glad of that. Since you wouldn't be standin' here now if you had." The box was not large, perhaps half a foot wide by four inches square, labelled 'Danger! Extreme Care! Explosive!' Caleb slowly opened the lid. Inside were five vials of nitroglycerine packed in diatomaceous earth, as Lucias had promised.

His face a study in concentration, Caleb took each vile gently from the fine earth and carefully placed them into the small pockets of the vest he now wore. It was something else he'd picked up at Vicker's Five and Ten when he'd gotten his new hat and Kitty's basket. The black leather vest looked similar to what Lucias would wear. Close-fitting, it had several pockets, and he could separate each vial so they wouldn't swing or sway against his body or each other as he walked. It was a much-needed improvement from carrying them in a knapsack as he had.

As they pulled up to the Nugget, Rufus tried to come bounding down from the front steps where he'd been sitting but was stopped short by a rope tied to his collar. And so, sitting on the bottom step, the wolfhound greeted them instead with several 'woofs'. Sandy ruffled the dog's fur, saying, "I made sure this fella was kept from jumpin' up while I was givin' you your nitro."

"A great thought, my lad," Caleb said.

Sandy smiled broadly at such a compliment and bounded up the steps to gather the supplies.

Kitty tied Emily to the hitching post and gave her a cube of sugar, saying, "I found one more in my pocket for ya, my dear."'

Emily happily gobbled the cube down as Sandy began outfitting provisions to her back and sides. Jesús gave him a hand, along with his grizzled sidekick, Cookie.

The expedition was travelling lightly and doing so on foot, wanting to bring along as little as possible. They'd discussed going on horseback, but Caleb had pointed out that if they all went down into the cavern, they didn't want to leave a bunch of mules or horses loitering around outside the entrance. Doing so would announce their presence and make the place stand out far too much. Discretion was the word of the day, after all.

Lucias stood nearby, today sporting blue jeans and a brown cotton shirt. He still wore his black hat and boots. Overtop was his usual duster to complete the look and also hide some of the other armaments he'd brought along for the journey.

Sandy lumbered out with the final bit of gear. It seemed

his pulled back muscles must be feeling better in the few minutes since he was at the smithy and had managed two loads already. But then, Sandy wasn't the type to complain, even if he were in pain, much like Caleb. The boy's lame arm now seemed able to move and lift light items. According to the Doc, he should be right as rain in another day or two.

Caleb's buoyant mood was quickly scuttled when Thomas Sinclair plowed through the batwing doors, Angeline trailing behind. To Caleb, he called, "Great things are afoot, laddie. I can sense it!"

Nodding toward the Scotsman, Caleb replied, "That's what I like about you, your optimism."

Sinclair laughed. "It's more than that, lad, much more." The Scotsman moved to one side of the walkway to confer with Lucias and Angeline. Jesús joined him as Cookie moved down the Nugget's sidewalk as far from the dog as he could.

Finished loading Emily, Sandy said to the mule, "That's all of it, girl." He nodded to the bundle he had just attached and then addressed Caleb, "If'n you wouldn't mind tightenin' that down, Mr. Caleb. I tried to get it as tight as I could, but my tyin' arm ain't quite back to full strength yet, though it is feelin' better by the hour."

"Not a problem, lad." Caleb let go of Kitty's delicate hand, though he felt reluctant to do so, knowing his time with her was limited. After a moment, he'd secured things to his liking on Emily and grasped Kitty's hand once again.

The second-floor girls flounced out of the saloon's entrance, followed by the cook, Maggie and Muddy the bartender. It seemed that almost everyone was out here to see them off today.

Now on the steps in front of the Nugget, Lucias called out, "Hey everyone, listen up!"

Sinclair stepped forward and said, "This is an auspicious moment. My two new business partners are preparin' to leave on a quest that will benefit all involved."

From behind Jesús, Cookie quietly observed, "But mostly him."

Not turning his attention from Sinclair, Jesús raised his arm and held his index finger up in warning, and the cook's jaw snapped shut.

The Scotsman continued, "As a way to commemorate this event, I would like to take a photograph of the moment." He turned and faced the man behind him, police constable Albert VanDusen and said, "The new acting chief of police, Albert VanDusen, will do the honours."

Tall and fit, VanDusen stepped out from behind Sinclair and moved down the stairs with a small wooden box and matching tripod. Caleb had seen them before. A Kodak, he believed it was called.

An American he'd met in Chile had shown Caleb one of the cameras. Working on a photo shoot for National Geographic Magazine, the man had boasted of the Kodak's abilities. For the rather exorbitant price of twenty-five US dollars, you got the camera with a roll of film inside capable of taking one hundred pictures. When it was full, you mailed it to Kodak to have the film processed and printed. And, he'd added proudly, for only ten dollars more, you could have the photos and negatives mailed anywhere in the world. From what Caleb understood, it had completely revolutionised the news and magazine industry.

Albert VanDusen placed the Kodak on its tripod in the middle of the street and told people to line up in front of the Golden Nugget. After some muddling around trying to get everyone situated, Caleb found himself on the group's periphery, standing next to Kitty, who was with the other second-floor girls. In front of them stood Thomas Sinclair. Next to him, tall and mysterious, was Angeline. She was flanked by Lucias and the doctor. Sandy stood off to one side of the girls near the back, towering above all. To one side of him, almost out of frame, stood Jesús Oritz, grinning for all he was worth, Cookie beside him with a glum expression. In the very front of the group, now untied from the steps, sat Rufus, panting heavily from excitement, his tongue lolling out one side of his mouth.

With everybody situated, Albert called for them not to move and snapped several pictures, one after the other, to ensure he got a usable shot. Most of the girls smiled, trying to look like Lillie Langtry, but the men were mostly serious like they were next in line at the dentist's office.

Caleb marvelled at how quickly these newer cameras took a picture compared to when he was a little boy in the 1860s. He recalled one photo session with his family and the length of time they'd had to hold still to have their picture taken. Back then, no one smiled in photos since it was so hard to keep a grin for the number of seconds it took to capture the photograph. And for the longest time when he'd seen photos growing up, he thought people from the past never smiled because it must have been a grim time. But in these modern times, photographers could now snap away when they were outside, shooting pictures almost as quickly as some men could fire a gun.

When the photo shoot was over, Thomas Sinclair pulled Caleb aside to have a few words in private. Gesturing to the small crowd, Thomas said, "Ya know what all this is, don't ya?"

"A going away party?"

Sinclair shook his head. "Nay, this is your last chance, laddie. If you don't recall where the gold is up there, you're goin' to have serious problems when you get back down here."

"What d'ya mean, problems?"

"You'll be beholdin' to me for the gold I repaid Mr. Oritz on your behalf. As well as the cost of this little expedition. Nothing comes cheap around these parts, as ya know."

"Don't worry, Thomas, you'll get more gold than you can ever imagine."

"I can imagine an awful lot."

"I'm sure ya can. But trust me when I say you won't be disappointed."

"I'd better not be because trust me when I say you will be disappointed if you come back empty-handed. I might just have to send a telegram to Scotland Yard regardin' your Scottish sweetie. And I'm sure the Northwest Mounted Police would be more than interested to know where one of the men that robbed the Bank of Montreal in Red Deer on the Victoria Day holiday has gotten to."

The Scotsman meant every bit of what he said, Caleb could see that. Well, perhaps this new stress would help him remember where the entrance to his cavern lay, or so he hoped.

As of right now, the only other individual who might know the cavern's location wanted another sugar cube. With a shake of his head, Caleb realised he'd better stock up if he ever wanted to locate his golden cavern again.

CHAPTER THIRTY

It was now several hours since the gold-finding expedition had departed. Doctor Brown still wished he'd had the opportunity to go with them but knew it wasn't in the cards. Hopefully, things would go well for his Irish friend up the mountain, and he would still get that chance in the future.

Cornelius had put aside his work on the fumigator over the last couple of days since he'd been hurrying to finish the other project he'd been toiling away on, which he'd given to Caleb just as he'd departed.

While Kitty tended to the wounded this morning, the doctor had taken a quick nap. Afterwards, he'd worked further on his spider problem, and just a short while ago, he had finally finished his prototype of the fumigator. He felt quite excited since he would be trying it out momentarily.

Approaching Ezra Randall's funeral parlour, the doctor and Sandy found the ground soft and squelchy. Most of the water had drained into a two-foot-wide crevasse just down the street from the undertaker's. Unfortunately, the ground around it was having a harder time drying out than up near the Nugget. Down here, it was much boggier, and despite the drainage, it was still quite soggy. He was glad he'd worn his Wellingtons. Sandy had only his work boots, currently caked with mud from top to bottom.

In his better hand, Sandy held the prototype of the Brown
Pest-Away Fumigator. The device was relatively simple to
operate, and if all went well with this first test, now that he
knew what he was doing, Cornelius could quickly slap
together another one for Farley's house.

"Gosh, Doc, I don't know about this. Here I am, just gettin'
the feelin' back in my arm, and I'm goin' right back to the
same place where I lost the use of it!"

Brown shook his head and said, "Fear not, my boy. We'll
only peek inside first to see if we can even attempt to fumigate
the establishment." Before arriving at the door to the chapel
where they now stood, they'd circumnavigated the house to
verify all the windows were closed, and it seemed to be sealed
shut from all appearances. Of course, whether or not the
spiders could get out of the chimney was another concern,
and it would depend on whether or not the flue was open.
Being summer, he was hopeful that Ezra hadn't been using his
fireplace and that it was currently closed.

"Well, you go first then, Doc." Sandy nodded toward the
door handle. "After all, you're the one with two good hands
and the fancy hat."

Cornelius said, "Very well then." On the doctor's head was
a beekeeper helmet he'd charged to Sinclair's account at
O'Malley's Outdoor Supply. In addition to that, he wore thick
leather gloves and the same heavy winter jackets he'd worn to
the ice house with Caleb. The heat of the late afternoon was
stifling, enough to make him feel like he was roasting alive,
but he wanted the extra layer of protection just in case. Of
course, once they were inside the funeral parlour, the heat
would be far worse.

Sandy wore a trapper hat with the ear flaps down and tied
under his chin, a scarf wrapped around his throat several

times for good measure. In addition to overalls made of heavy duck cloth to protect his legs, he also wore a winter coat like the doctor.

Brown readied the fire extinguishers slung over each shoulder. Though the first was primed and ready to go, it wasn't quite full. He wanted to be prepared and adjusted where the second nozzle hung so it was within easy reach. Both contained a combination of cider vinegar, red wine vinegar and the remainder of his acetic acid. After giving his backup supply to Angus for the pumper wagon, he'd only had a small amount of home-brewed acid left and no time to make any more, so he'd had to improvise.

The backup extinguisher clanged against his side, knocking into a silver flask filled with whisky in his vest pocket. It was something kept on his person strictly for medicinal emergencies or situations of high stress, just like the one presently occurring. However, he didn't want to remove his beekeeper's helmet just to steady his nerves, so he would forgo it for the moment.

And so, Brown took a deep breath, turned the handle, and said, "Into the fray together we go," then entered the funeral chapel with Sandy close at his back.

Everything seemed quiet. At least no spiders were in sight, so that was a good sign. Of course, it had been the display room in front where the boy had found them, so that was understandable, and also where they were headed next. The soles of their boots clattered on the chapel's mud-covered hardwood floors, the air around them hot and filled with the scent of dank earth.

Still in the lead, Brown moved slowly down the aisle, scanning the pews on both sides as he went with the tip of the extinguisher's nozzle, more than ready to let loose a blast of acid at the slightest hint of motion.

A row of coffins lined one wall in the showroom, or at least they had. Several had succumbed to the flood waters and subsequent earthquake and now lay on their sides, with one completely upside down.

"That's the one that I found Ezra in." Sandy pointed to an oak coffin in the middle of the group. No longer propped, it lay flat on the floor, split lids still closed. Its fine wood was now smeared with the muddy water that invaded the funeral parlour, and it appeared some may have seeped into the coffin.

"Hang on a moment, Sandy. You keep an eye out while I do something that will help." He began to spray the floor around the coffin, the acid easily soaking into the mud-caked wood.

"What're ya doin', Doc?" Sandy placed the fumigator on a table near the room's entrance and moved next to the doctor to watch while casting his eyes about the room at the same time.

"I want to give our little eight-legged funeral crashers an unfriendly welcome." That said, the doctor continued to spray the area around the coffin for another short time, making sure everything was well soaked, making it into an acid mud bath for anything happening to crawl over it.

Brown reached into his satchel and pulled out a couple of short lengths of coiled rope, each perhaps a dozen feet long. He tied one end of each to the gleaming handles on the top and bottom half of the infested coffin's lid, then passed the ends around a brass rail that ran the length of the wall about four feet up. The edge of the display coffins had rested along this rail when propped open so as not to damage the wall. Now, using the rail as a pully, Sandy could tug the ropes to open the coffin lids while standing out of harm's way, and Cornelius could spray the inside of the coffin as they swung open.

Handing the end of the rope to Sandy, Brown said, "Don't pull these quite yet."

The doctor positioned himself directly in front of the coffin and said, "Well, we can have some small hope that a few of them might have drowned in the flooding."

Taking a deep breath, Brown readied his fire extinguisher and said, "Okay, my boy, pull the bottom rope as smoothly and as slowly as you can so I can juice them as it opens!"

"Sure enough," Sandy said, his voice slightly higher than usual. He pulled the rope forcefully but smoothly, and the coffin eased open.

Dozens and dozens of hand-sized spiders surged out of the gap and dropped to the floor. They were quickly coated by the doctor's spray and curled their legs as they jiggled and jerked in their death throes. Those missed by the spray danced and spasmed as they tried to move across the acidic mud coating the floor.

Any spiders that were fortunate enough to make it through the mud still had to deal with Sandy. He stomped on them angrily, obliterating them in an explosive gush beneath his size fourteens. "Consarned spiders! Makin' me all weak and scared! Take a bootful of Sandy for your troubles!"

Abruptly, Brown's extinguisher sputtered the last of its spider juice, and he dropped the now useless nozzle to his side and grabbed the second, continuing his deadly spray with hardly a pause.

He called out to Sandy as he pumped a steady stream of juice on the curling and spasming arachnids, "I'm glad I brought that second tank now!"

After another moment or two, the flood of spiders had

finally lessened to a crawl, pun intended, Brown thought. He breathed a slight sigh of relief and said, "Hopefully, that's the last of them!" He swiped at the sweat dripping down his forehead but couldn't get to it. The mesh of the beekeeper's helmet served only to smear it around, and it ran down into his eyes, stinging them and blurring his vision. Tasting the salt of his sweat in the corners of his mouth, Brown said with more enthusiasm than he felt, "Okay, now for the top!"

As Sandy creaked the top half of the casket back, Brown was relieved to see it appeared devoid of spiders, which seemed promising. But one thing it did contain was the desiccated remains of Ezra Randall. He hid beneath a gown of spider silk, the centre of his chest below the sternum a gaping cavity where the gestating baby spiders had eaten their way out. This time, they hadn't had their maturation cycle interrupted like the ones back at the office with Farley Jones.

"Careful, Doc, don't get too close!" Sandy squeaked.

"Don't you worry, my boy. I'll give this a good spray as well!"

Brown leaned in slightly and aimed the nozzle at the corpse's chest, but before he could pump, one of the larger female spiders launched itself from the billowing web behind Ezra's head. It easily jumped the gap to Cornelius, who was far too close.

The beast wrapped its spiky legs around the doctor's hand holding the nozzle, then sunk its poison-filled fangs into his forearm.

CHAPTER THIRTY-ONE

Emily halted suddenly, and Caleb held his hand up to stop the procession behind him. The mule looked into the forest on both sides of the narrow trail, sniffing the air like a dog. Then, with a considerable snort, she carried slowly on in the direction she was going. Presumably, whatever had caught her attention wasn't worth her time, judging by her dismissive snort, and that seemed a good thing.

Caleb spurred her to walk a little faster with another sugar cube of encouragement. Kitty had given him a sack containing two pounds of the sweet little cubes, personally pilfered from the kitchen's pantry by none other than Maggie, so he had plenty to get the mule up the hill and keep her motivated.

At his back was Jesús, followed by Lucias, with Cookie trailing along at the rear. When they'd departed, the old man had been situated just behind Caleb. He had happily babbled to anyone who'd listen about his new pots and pans, recently charged to Sinclair's account at O'Malley's. They'd clattered against Emily's side, the cook chattering away about the biscuits and stew he was planning for the evening meal once they reached the bottom of the ridge. But the other men could only bear to hear so much of his cooking advice, so he was relegated to the back of the line.

Thinking of food, Caleb's stomach grumbled again. With back bacon, sausage, Maggie's fancy 'hash brown' potatoes and pancakes and syrup, breakfast had been a feast that had filled him completely. At least, that was until about an hour ago. He was quite surprised his stomach was already growling like a Nile crocodile and wondered if it was linked to his bite and rapid healing. Was his body now working so hard that it burned through its daily calories much quicker than it ever had before in his life? In the past, if he'd had a comparable breakfast to this morning's, he wouldn't be thinking about dinner until five or six p.m.

Now, here he was, ravenous again. But it was more than that. He was as ravenous as a... At first, Caleb refused to think of the possibility, but his always helpful mind offered the suggestion nonetheless: as ravenous as a black beast from the cavern. Reluctantly, he realised he was right. Those obsidian monsters seemed to be quick growing and always wanting to eat whatever wandered by, much like the ants. Was his appetite, like his accelerated metabolism, another by-product of his bite? It seemed entirely possible. He shook his head, sad that the beast hadn't also given him super strength, not that he'd tried any strongman's feats to verify, but he didn't feel any stronger. Oh well, accelerated healing was something he would take as a consolation prize for the moment.

Emily's tether was looped around Caleb's wrist, allowing her plenty of room to manoeuvre the trail. Every once in a while, the group would stop as she sniffed something or other near the path's edge, sometimes stopping to eat a particularly colourful wildflower discovered there.

Once outside of town, they'd followed the trail along the river for several miles. Just recently, they had branched away to a different trail, this one heading slightly uphill as the ground began to gain elevation toward the ridge and glacier beyond. The air was fresh and clear here, but as he looked back the way they'd come, the remnants of the fire from the day before were sorely apparent.

Many trees were blackened by the inferno's ferocity, and much of the terrain along the river seemed to have burned, along with half the town. Had it not been for yesterday's natural calamities, their little expedition would have probably already been attacked by ants or spiders by now. Thankfully, it seemed what the fire hadn't scorched or killed, the hail and rain had washed away, and they had seen no monstrous threats yet.

That thought gave Caleb some hope for things up at the cavern. If the tsunami he'd created in the underground lake had washed most of the ants out, along with a majority of the black beasts, then it might be a little less deadly up there than he remembered from last time. Of course, there might still be some more spiders and centipedes, but surely they were the worst that the cavern still had to offer. At least, he hoped that were the case.

They had made good progress in the last few hours and were now well over five miles outside town. The ridge was not that far, sitting about fifteen miles or so from the townsite. Wider than it was long, this bowl-shaped valley ran about twenty miles deep and maybe forty wide. Their goal was to make it to the base of the ridge before nightfall and then climb to its top tomorrow.

The narrow trail widened for a short distance, and Caleb paused, pulling out the field glasses Sinclair had supplied. He squinted through them, scanning the valley, the heat hammering down on his head. With a sigh, he put away the glasses and took off his hat, wiping the sweat from his brow with the bandana around his neck. As he placed his hat back on his head, a slight nudge came at his back, and out of habit, he reached into the pocket of his dungarees for a cube of sugar from the handful he'd transferred from the sack.

As Emily crunched her cube, a feeling of déjà vu crept over

Caleb. It all seemed so very familiar, and he was sure he was on the correct track. Thanks to his earlier recollection about the waterfall, he at least had a marker to search for as he moved along and scanned with the field glasses. The new glasses weren't as nice as the pair from his army days, which he'd left in the cavern, and he hoped to retrieve them once back inside.

Jesús appeared at Caleb's side. He struck a match and lit a cigarillo, hand cupped around the flame to stop the breeze from blowing it out. He took a deep drag, blew the smoke out, and said, "How is your memory, Mister Caleb."

Caleb noted the sarcasm in the man's voice. Since his blowout about Jesús calling him amigo and friend, the man had taken to calling him Mister Caleb like Sandy did. With a shrug, he said, "I've had some more feelings of 'been there, done that'."

"So, that is a good thing then."

"Aye, I think it is."

Oritz looked to the sky and the lengthening shadows on the mountains and said, "How much further do you figure?"

"Today or to the cavern?"

"Both"

"I think we should be able to make it to the base of the ridge in the next few hours and then make our camp there for the night. If all goes well, we should be in the cavern sometime tomorrow." Caleb hoped this to be true and was feeling optimistic about the experience so far. Keeping Emily supplied with sugar cubes and having her retread the steps they would have taken toward the ridge seemed to be working.

However, it was tomorrow and afterwards that he was more worried about. At the moment, Caleb knew himself to be a valuable asset. He was sure neither Jesús nor Lucias would want to see any harm befall him too soon, so he didn't have to fear for his life at this point. But once they were inside the cavern, he was sure all bets would be off.

If anything, Lucias had been more of a help than a threat so far. But Caleb didn't know what the man's ultimate assignment was regarding his life expectancy. He was quite sure that Jesús must also be wondering the same thing. Sinclair would be more than likely to extinguish any agreement between himself and the bandit, that was, as soon as the gold's location and existence were verified.

"You are sure the ridge holds the destination of our quest?"

"Like I was tellin' ya, we can wind our way up there in the mornin' and find out. I won't really be sure of anything until I'm back inside that cursed cavern."

Filled with sugar for the moment, Emily began to wander forward, tugging gently on the reins. They again fell into a single file as the trail meandered back into deep forest. Seeing a chance to check something as they walked, Caleb reached for his satchel, slung over one shoulder. He retrieved the burlap-wrapped item the doctor had given him as they'd prepared to depart civilisation.

Brown had only said he hoped Caleb would find the device helpful in his explorations, and hopefully more than once, he'd added. About the size of a small loaf of bread, the device seemed quite weighty. After marvelling at it for a moment, Caleb began to read the note that had been tied around it with string.

'Caleb, my boy. I was hoping to be able to test this out myself beforehand but figured you might be able to use it right now. I was designing it for the gold mining industry in step with my gold extraction process. Bear in mind you will be using it for the first time live in the field. I have tested it in my office but not with any great lengths of wire. However, I have supplied you a spool of copper wire for your use, located elsewhere in your supplies.'

Hand-painted lettering on one side of the device proclaimed it to be the Brown Static Detonator. To attach the aforementioned spool of wire, there were two knobs on one end, and a small hand crank was recessed in the other. Under a square metal cover in the centre was a silver toggle switch where the doctor had added a humorous touch. One side was labelled 'Off' and the other, 'Kaboom'.

The note went on to explain the details of how to work the detonator and that he would no longer have to worry about using slow and outdated gunpowder fuse. Brown added that the spool of wire would hopefully survive several uses, barring it getting caught in a cave-in and Caleb not being able to retract it. The whole procedure seemed relatively simple. After winding the crank for several seconds to build the electrical charge up, he only needed to flip the switch from 'Off' to 'Kaboom' to detonate his nitro.

"Well, I'll be jiggered! This is a handy bit of kit, to be sure!" He had seen large static generators when he'd been in the army, but never one as small as this, especially one capable of detonating explosives. Hopefully, the device would work as the doctor indicated, and tomorrow might just be the day he got to give it a trial run.

CHAPTER THIRTY-TWO

"Omilord! Doc!" Sandy called as he witnessed the oversized spider from hell sink its fangs into the arm of the doctor's jacket.

Brown slapped it off and sprayed it with a drenching rain of acid solution. The monstrous spider curled into a ball the size of a cantaloupe, looking surprisingly compact in death compared to the size it appeared with its appendages extended.

"Are you okay, Doc?" Sandy asked, eyes wide in wonderment. Now that the spiders seemed under control, he edged a little closer to Cornelius.

The doctor finished spraying his nozzle inside and around the desiccated corpse of Ezra. He stopped and pulled up his jacket sleeve slightly to show Sandy his arm, saying, "When I was at O'Malley's, I also grabbed a couple of these archery bracers. I knew I'd be poking my arms around enclosed spaces that might not be the safest, and it now seems like a good thing I did."

Thanks to the saturating spray Brown had given the coffin, a couple of smaller, hand-sized spiders suddenly dropped from behind the cadaver's head. They fell to the silk covering the corpse's upper chest, their legs curled tightly as they joined Ezra in death.

Giving a satisfied nod, the doctor added, "That looks about it for these crawlers. But we'd best check the rest of this establishment just in case."

"Do you think there's more?"

"I suppose we're going to find out." Moving up the staircase to the second-floor loft, Brown called, "I'll check up here. I don't think there's room for both of us. Maybe you can check the parlour and kitchen!"

"Sure enough, Doc."

Sandy looked to the front parlour, still feeling uneasy. After his recent bite, he was deathly afraid of getting another one. He hoped to get a couple of guards as the doctor had, and maybe something for his legs, too. However, he doubted they made such a thing large enough for his muscular body, not to mention how uncomfortable it would be to wear leather like that in this heat for any length of time.

There were only a couple of chairs and a small loveseat in the front parlour, and Sandy only gave it a cursory scan as he peeked under each. Moving into the kitchen and embalming room beyond, he discovered the smell of death lay heavy in the air. The coating of mud from the flood had helped to partially mask it, but now that he was in the same room with it, the stench of rotting flesh was almost overpowering.

The partial remains of Sam Shepherd still sat on the embalming table where Sandy had left them the day he'd got bit. The smell from the cadaver was horrendous. Left in this warm, sealed building for the last couple of days, it had made it rot faster than usual. And though Ezra Randall had been dead inside his coffin almost as long as Sam had been in pieces, the smell in the front display room hadn't been that bad, surprisingly. Maybe the spiders eating him alive as they developed had played a part in that. With a shiver, Sandy looked closely about the room.

The oiled tarp around Sam's body was seeping dark fluid around its folds as the ravaged remains inside became more and more corrupted with each passing minute. Sandy looked about to see if there was anything he could do and saw the row of three doors across the room.

They weren't full-sized doors but square, and just a little larger than a body. Ezra had shown them to Sandy when he'd brought over Farley Jones. It was Ezra's 'filing cabinet'. When he needed to store a body for a day or two, he just added some ice to a metal pan inside each drawer, allowing him to store them far longer than normal. But there was no ice inside the filing cabinet since the ice house no longer existed. Still, Sandy reasoned, placing the rotting cadaver inside one of the drawers would certainly help things smell-wise. He realised they'd have to be back soon to take care of burial since, along with Sam, they still needed to inter Ezra, as well as little Teddy Malone, currently behind one of the filing cabinet's doors. And Sandy had a pretty good idea which door it was.

A puddle of water seeped out from beneath the leftmost door of the filing cabinet. The ice that had been keeping Teddy from corrupting before burial had melted. Sandy wondered if Teddy's ghost still walked this house, lost and alone, as he looked to finally move on to his final reward.

In addition to mysterious worlds beneath the earth and submarines from twenty-thousand leagues under the sea, another of Sandy's favourite kinds of story was a ghost story. And the more he thought of ghosts, the more he wondered what the ghost of Teddy's wasted, spider-riddled corpse might look like.

Adding fire to Sandy's smouldering embers of fear, there came a sudden tapping for a moment, then nothing more.

What was that, Sandy wondered, his eyes like an owl's. The noise had been so faint, he could hardly hear it but felt sure he knew where it was coming from—the lefthand drawer, Teddy's drawer.

A small rectangular card on the outside of the leftmost door of the filing cabinet bore the name, 'W. Malone'. That was strange, and Sandy wondered about it for a moment. W. Malone? Then he recalled Teddy sometimes went by his middle name of Wally, depending on where he worked. At the ice house, when he was doing his delivery boy chores, he went by the name of Wally, and when at one of his other part-time jobs, he went by Teddy.

One day, Sandy had asked the boy about it, and he'd said it was due to new child labour laws. It was something that Sandy himself had dealt with when he'd applied at the Nugget. When the working age was raised to twelve over the last few years, many children trying to make money to help their families lied about their age and names. Or in the case of Wally, used a middle name for one part of his life and his first name for the other. He'd said by doing that, it kept his hours as a delivery boy separate, and he could work twice as long if he wanted without getting in trouble with the law.

The noise came again. Tap-tap, tap-tap.

Was the boy somehow still alive after being consumed from within by spiders? No, it couldn't be; Sandy knew that much. The body they'd seen at the ice house was already wasted away. So, if it wasn't Teddy's ghost, what was inside there wanting to get out? He could think of only one answer.

At his back, a clatter of footsteps descended from the loft. Brown entered the preparation room, saying, "No sign of anything upstairs. Have you had any luck?"

Sandy nodded toward the filing cabinet and said, "I don't think the upstairs is where we need to be lookin'." He tilted his head and added, "Listen."

From the drawer came another slight tap-tap-tap, as if the cadaver inside was getting a little claustrophobic and wanted to be let out for a quick breath of fresh air or perhaps needed to get to another job somewhere.

"That is curious, indeed. I suppose we should investigate." Brown adjusted his nozzle slightly as he spoke.

"You got enough juice in your squirter, Doc?"

Shaking the extinguisher, Brown replied, "I think I have half a tank."

Sandy stood with one gloved hand on the cold steel handle of the filing cabinet door. He nodded to the doctor.

"I'm ready, my boy. Give it a yank."

Leaning in from as far away as he could and still reach the handle, Sandy pulled it hard and scampered rapidly back out of the way.

As the door swung open, Doctor Cornelius Brown stepped back in horror, uttering a cry of surprise and disgust as he did.

CHAPTER THIRTY-THREE

Though the tabletops were hard, as wooden objects were prone to be, Kitty's patients had been made comfortable with extra blankets and pillows from the boudoirs upstairs, which the rest of the girls had assisted in bringing down. And even they, too, were acting as angels of mercy as she, flitting about from patient to patient and helping where they could while Kitty's attention was elsewhere.

Kitty swabbed the brow of the man on the table before her. He was one of several injured in the battle with the ants and later the black river beasts.

Ned Belmer had been sweating up a storm but now seemed a bit more chipper than he had a few hours before. Kitty discovered just how chipper, moments after she'd tended to his needs. When turned to check on a tablemate of his across the way, Ned had tried to grab her keister.

"That'll be enough of that, Mr. Belmer!" Kitty said as she spun around, a bit more anger in her voice than she'd intended. More kindly, she added, "I'm glad you're feeling a little better, but you need to keep your hands to yourself. I'll have you know I'm acting as a nurse now, not a second-floor girl!"

With a lecherous smile, Belmer said, "That's even better! Now turn around again!"

Kitty shook her head and smiled but didn't give the man the opportunity he requested and moved on to check the other half-dozen patients. Two men had their hands badly mangled as they'd tried to fend off the ants which had dropped onto them from the rooftops. Several others had lost hands, feet or entire limbs from the bite of a black beast.

But no matter what had caused their wounds, all received a taste of the doctor's surgical steel. Cornelius had been forced to amputate above some of the more egregious wounds, removing the jagged gristle that remained, the men screaming in agony as he'd done so. Well, some of them had, at least. Those patients that drank, the sensible ones (on this occasion, Kitty thought), had screamed much less since they'd taken the option of as much whisky as they could down over ten minutes before the operation. As a result, most were already three sheets to the wind by the time the doctor had started to saw.

Her employer, Thomas Sinclair, had been generous enough to cover the cost of the alcohol option to the patients wishing to imbibe, and many had taken him up on his offer. But those who didn't drink had been given the option of morphine instead of whisky, but most had eschewed its use. Instead, those men had received a leather strap to chew on while the doctor evened out the trim the ants and water beasts had given their digits and limbs. And through it all yesterday evening, Kitty had been standing by, assisting the process, and feeling like she was about to lose her lunch through most of it.

Now, with the amputations and requisite sutures behind him, Brown had borrowed Sandy and gone in search of some spiders at the morticians. The doctor had told her he had a new process he wanted to try that involved gassing the spiders. Kitty just hoped he didn't accidentally gas himself and Sandy in the process.

And so, finished tending her patients, at least for a few moments, Kitty moved to the bar. She'd just started a grateful sip of a glass of water she'd received from Muddy when a familiar voice spoke at her back.

"Mr. Sinclair wants to see you."

Kitty's heart sank as she turned toward Angeline. "Oh my. I hope it's nothing serious."

"He wouldn't say. But I'll stay here and keep an eye on your patients with the other girls while you go and see him." With that, Angeline turned and swept off to the saloon to check on the wounded.

With a heavy heart, Kitty returned her glass to the bar and moved down the long corridor to Thomas's office. With Caleb on his way to hopefully find his cavern of riches, she presumed her job as spy must be over, and yet here she was being called into Sinclair's office once again. What could the man want of her now?

The door was open a crack, and she knocked tentatively.

"Come in, woman! I'm expectin' ya!"

Kitty pushed through the door and stood indecisively for a moment.

Sinclair said, "Close it behind ya! There's no need for anyone else hearin' our business."

Kitty cringed inwardly and closed the door quietly at her back, then stood beside it for a moment longer.

"Come all the way in, girl! I'm not gonna bite!"

Not quite one hundred percent convinced, Kitty moved slowly toward the chair in front of Sinclair's desk. As she sat, it gave out a small squeak as if she'd just sat on a mouse.

Thomas squinted at Kitty as if lost in thought and didn't speak for several moments. Making a small "Hmmph", he pulled a cigar from his desktop humidor, a richly carved cedar box with a large S in the centre of its gleaming lid. Once his guillotine had decapitated his cigar, he struck a match with a flourish on his golden match safe. Eyes focused on the cigar's tip as he lit it, he said, "Your new beau certainly seems to think highly of ya."

Kitty nodded slightly. "Yes, he does, as I do him." She didn't think there was any point in denying their relationship since most everyone had seen them kissing outside and holding hands after the ant attack and again this morning.

Sinclair laughed.

"D'ya think that's funny?" Kitty asked indignantly.

"Nay, not funny. It's charmin' that the two of you got together, a bank robber and a cat-burglarin' floozy."

With a flash of fire in her eyes, Kitty said, "That's not all we are."

Sinclair nodded and said, "This is true. Your man is also a thief who would steal from his own kind and you, a soiled dove who thinks her feathers are still unsullied."

Kitty's mouth was a flat line, and she held her tongue, knowing the man was just goading her on and trying to get a rise out of her. And what could she say to that after all? He was correct on all counts. Of course, he couldn't know of all the other things they were: their hopes and shared fantasies, her ambition to have an eating place of her own or Caleb's thoughts of getting some land and trying his hand at ranching. Ignoring the man's remarks, she asked, "What d'ya want of me now?"

"Want I want of ya? Nothin'! It's about what I've been asked for ya."

"Asked somethin' for me? By who?" There could be only one answer. And she was about to speak it when Sinclair answered the question for her.

"Caleb Cantrill, of course." Thomas puffed on his cigar for a moment, peering at her through the cloud of smoke as he watched her reaction.

Her eyes widened slightly, but she didn't speak for a moment, then said incredulously, "What would Caleb have asked from you on my behalf?"

Sinclair smirked and puffed, then said, "Your welfare."

"My welfare? Why would he ask that?"

"In case he didn't come back, a course."

"What do you mean?"

"He told me he hoped to heaven it all worked out, but he wanted peace of mind just in case it didn't. Since he agreed to go up that mountain in good faith as part of our agreement, he asked for one more thing in return. And that was if he never came back—"

"Don't say that!"

Sinclair continued, "In the event of unforeseen circumstances, he wanted me to swear that I would make sure you were looked after."

Kitty felt about to cry as she heard this. If Caleb had such misgivings about going back up into that cavern that he would ask that of this man, of all men, then maybe he shouldn't have gone at all. Instead, they should have stolen away in the night before this nightmare could have finished playing out. Her heart ached, and she wished they had met under different circumstances. In fact, any other circumstances would have been better.

Thomas continued when he saw she had nothing more to say or was in too much emotional turmoil to be capable. "And though I am many things, one of the main things I am is a man of my word. And if your beau never comes back, and we never find that gold, you can rest assured I will make sure that you'll not want for anythin' from here on out."

Still speechless, Kitty placed her face in her hands and wept. She wept with a certainty she now found frightening. Her heart felt broken, and though she was never a woman to have premonitions, deep in the pit of her stomach, she knew that Caleb would never come back now, especially not after making a request like that.

"And there's somethin' else you should know."

Things just keep getting better and better, Kitty thought dolefully. "What's that," she asked in a small voice.

"Those stones you helped steal from Tullibody."

"What of them? I told you I never saw any of the money."

"That may be the case, but there is so much more happening to which you are unaware. However, your compliance in their theft is something not in dispute, yet your involvement in all this is much greater than you think."

How was that possible, Kitty wondered. She'd helped William McLeod steal some jewellery from a store owned by Joseph Tully. Jewellery, it turned out, Thomas Sinclair had more than a passing interest in. But that was over a half-dozen years ago, and she'd had no involvement with that scoundrel since.

Thomas wheeled his chair to one of the curio cabinets across the room, smoke billowing behind him as he did. He retrieved something from the cabinet, then puffed back. As he rolled to a stop, he placed a silver tray in the centre of his desk. Resting in soft velvet on the shining silver, three coal-black gemstones gleamed darkly.

Sinclair flicked some ash from the tip of his smouldering cigar into a heavy crystal ashtray to his side. He took another puff, then said, "The stolen stones were being appraised for me by Joseph. They were stones just like these." He gestured to them with the tip of his cigar, adding, "They are very rare and very powerful."

Not sure of Sinclair's claim about power, Kitty looked to the obsidian stones and felt something stir deep down inside her nonetheless. Though she hadn't received any money or jewellery in the heist, there was something she'd received after all: a memory. Either forgotten due to the passage of time or because she had chosen to forget, whatever the reason, she'd never shared it with anyone because she'd never dared.

CHAPTER THIRTY-FOUR

A scuttling wave of spiders washed out of the storage drawer where Teddy Malone's body had been sequestered. Obviously, the cadaver was not quite as devoid of arachnids as Cornelius had thought back at the ice house.

When Ezra had returned to the funeral parlour with the boy's corpse, some had obviously still been inside and escaped, leading to the tragedy in the display room where they'd found the undertaker's body.

Now, there seemed to be no end to the hand-sized spiders. Cornelius pumped and sprayed and cursed and prayed as he tried to get every last one of them. Unless he could contain the little beasts, another tragedy would be in the offing, his death and Sandy's.

Several scampered off to one side, but Sandy's size fourteen feet were standing by, and he squashed the escaping spiders, stomping them to a greasy paste on the hardwood floor.

Another contingent of spiders escaped the doctor's spray and fled in the opposite direction. Sandy was near the shelf with the embalming liquids, several labelled 'Arsenical Fluid' and others 'Formaldehyde'. He recalled Ezra saying he kept those chemicals for his 'special occasions' when he had to store a body for any length of time or have it transported to another destination.

"This seems pretty special to me!" Sandy cried as he swept the bottles from the shelf with his able arm. They shattered in a spray of glass and toxic fluid, which flooded across the floor.

The escaping spiders were washed with the solution, almost immediately curling into little balls of death as it touched them. But now, from the floor, a white vapour formed, swirling and twirling around as it grew higher and higher.

"We need to get out of here immediately!" Brown called. "Those fumes are deadly! Try not to breathe!" Giving a shake of his head, Brown realised he was getting a chance at fumigating the spiders after all, just not in the manner he'd imagined, with him and Sandy still in the building.

No sooner had he spoken when not one, but two, of the giant female spiders scurried from the depths of the cabinet. It seemed the males had been the protectors and the first line of defence, ensuring the females were unharmed and able to breed and spread their scourge far and wide.

The monstrous arachnids moved with surprising speed, hissing as they scuttled out of the cabinet. Fortunately, Sandy's chemical experiment seemed effective on them as well. As the creatures dropped from the drawer into the growing mist below, they began to spasm and stagger as if drunk. Without warning, they both collapsed into the toxic puddle and ceased moving, their legs curling tightly around them in death.

Following the doctor's move and backing quickly from the room toward the chapel, Sandy said with a tremor in his voice, "That was a whole lot of spiders, Doc."

"Yes, my boy. It seems there were a few left inside of Teddy after all."

The mist followed them, their motion creating enough of a draft in the sealed building to carry the poisonous vapour along. It grew higher as they moved and was now at their knees, increasing in volume by the second.

Once they were at the chapel entrance, Brown was about to close the doors when he spied the fumigator Sandy had set down when they'd battled the coffin spiders. "Might just need this." He grabbed it and handed it back to Sandy, then quickly closed the double doors, the breeze of his doing so temporarily blowing back some of the toxic gas.

They walked rapidly down the aisle to the pulpit where the exit lay, more vapour pouring under the gap in the chapel doors at their backs.

Nodding to the fumigator in Sandy's hand, Brown said, "It seems we'll still have a chance to use that since we need to make one more stop."

Sandy looked to the doctor and said with apprehension, "Yeah, Farley's house."

Nodding, the doctor patted the extinguisher hanging from his shoulder and said, "After what Kitty described to me of her adventures at Farley's, it doesn't sound like whatever solution I have remaining will do us much good."

"Why's that, Doc?"

"Because she said there was a whole bedroom and attic full of them."

Sandy looked at the small box in his hand and said with wonder, "And this little thing is how we're gonna kill them?"

Brown nodded and said, "That's why we brought it. And speaking of killing things, let me remind you once again of using extreme caution as you carry that. Try not to shake it or tilt it in any way."

"Yessir. This sounds as dangerous as Mr. Caleb's juice."

"His juice?"

"Boom juice," Sandy clarified.

"Yes, use as much caution as you did with the nitroglycerine because the fumigator could kill you almost as quickly, though you'd at least die in one piece. Just picture the mist you made at the funeral parlour when those chemicals mixed. The fumigator does the same, only quicker."

"I'll do my best to be careful," Sandy said with a very gentle nod.

The walk to Farley's wasn't a long one, but the day was heating up, and their protective winter garments made them sweat profusely. Sandy had removed his hat and wiped his forehead with the back of his jacket sleeve. "I hope we don't have to wear this stuff for too much longer, Doc."

"Yes, it does feel a little humid at the moment. But fear not, my boy, we'll be back in our summer apparel when we're done at Farley's."

Sandy placed his hat back on his head and nodded, saying, "Glad to hear it. I think my brain is gettin' cooked in this hat."

The part of town where Farley's house was located had been underwater for longer than the rest. It was closer to the river and also lower in elevation. The ground was soft and muddy, and sucked at their boots as they squelched up the walkway to the front door.

Finding the front door locked, Sandy said, "There's no key, Doc."

"Very well, my boy. Why don't you give it a little encouragement!"

Sandy's eyes grew wide. "Ya mean break in?"

"I don't think Farley much cares anymore."

Sandy nodded at that and said, "That's a good point. Okay, here goes nothin." He leaned his three hundred pounds of muscular bulk against the heavy oak door and said, "Open says me."

A cringe-inducing crack was followed by a groaning creak as the door complained of Sandy's sudden violent termination of its house-securing duties. But even with that done, the door would only open a few inches.

Furniture and other items had floated around when the house's ground floor had been underwater, and it seemed that much of it had settled toward the front entrance as the water receded. A couple of kitchen chairs were the main culprits barring the way, along with several small wooden fruit crates and a sodden seat cushion from a love seat, also close by.

Swamp water was the only thing Cornelius could think of as he stepped inside, wrinkling his nose at the pungent scent. All around them, the walls and floor were stained with drying mud almost five feet up.

Sandy crystallised Cornelius's thoughts when he said, "It smells like my uncle's barnyard in Rock Creek when it gets a good rainin'."

"Yes, there is something to be said for keeping one's house dry, to be sure."

Brown handed the fumigator back to Sandy, having held it so the boy could break in without killing them both. As he peered into the front parlour, looking everywhere at once, he announced, "According to Kitty, the arachnids are contained to one of the bedrooms upstairs and the attic."

Breathing a sigh of relief, Sandy said, "That's good news."

"But that doesn't mean they didn't somehow escape," Brown added, looking carefully around as he spoke.

They moved from the living room to the small kitchen. The remaining two kitchen chairs and the dining table were upside down and pushed against one wall. Across the room, the trap door was open near the clothes drying rack.

During some of the surgeries at the saloon, Kitty had described her harrowing experience and how she'd escaped through the trap. Perhaps the door had been left open by the bandit, Oritz, as he'd chased after her, or maybe the floodwaters had pushed it open. It was hard to say since there was nothing visible in the crawlspace right at the moment except some standing water that hadn't yet drained away. In fact, several properties just beyond Farley's were still flooded.

The two men stood listening for a long moment, but the house was deathly silent. The only sound, apart from Sandy's rapid breathing, was the dripping of water through the open trap door.

Brown took the lead down the narrow hall to the second-floor stairs. There seemed no sign of spiders on the lower level, and it appeared they had remained contained to the room where Kitty said she'd clocked her captor with the candle holder.

The situation with the bandit in the room upstairs was an interesting one. Cornelius presumed he would be a cadaver by now, or close to it. But if the scar-faced man still clung to life, the fumigator would be a mercy to him. However, right now, the question was, how to get the fumigator into the bedroom without getting swarmed by spiders.

The stairs were rather steep, and Brown clung to the hardwood banister as he crept upward, the nozzle of his remaining extinguisher at the ready.

With a sigh of relief, Cornelius arrived at the top of the stairs and stood on the small landing outside the two bedroom doors, one to each side. But his feeling of relief didn't last. It smelled stale here, like old, mothballed sweaters, and the heat was stifling.

There was a single window in the wall of the small landing between the bedrooms. It was currently closed, as were both doors. The remains of several spiders were smeared across the floor, having been stepped on and ground into the hardwood. This must have occurred when the bandit, Oritz, opened the door and discovered his crony's predicament.

Brown jiggled the extinguisher under his arm, the fluid sloshing hollowly inside. "I think I have a quarter tank left." That would be barely enough for any significant number of spiders. And they had another problem: he didn't know which door it was, and Kitty hadn't specified.

"What do you think, Sandy?"

"About what, Doc?"

Nodding to the bedroom on his left, Brown asked, "Should we try door number one..." He trailed off and looked to the bedroom on the right and finished, "Or door number two?"

"Gosh, I don't know." Sandy looked from his good arm to his recovering arm and said, "I guess door number two since I'm lookin' forward to havin' two good arms once again when this freezin' poison runs its course."

Cornelius repeated, "Freezin' poison? Oh yes, the venom. Quite so, my boy. Door number two it is."

Sandy watched as Brown began to spray the floor in front of the rightmost door, as well as around the door jamb and lintel overtop, soaking things thoroughly.

"What're you doin' now?"

"Making sure our eight-legged friends stay in there when we open the door. The only problem is getting the fumigator into the centre of the room without having to walk in there, especially if it's full of spiders. If I set it on the floor and push it in, it will only go so far, and then the spiders will swarm us. I need a way to shove the fumigator in quickly, all at once."

Sandy looked to the door for a moment, then back to Brown, then down the staircase and finally back to the doctor. "Hang on a sec, Doc."

After handing the fumigator to Brown, Sandy moved down the stairs a third of the way, holding the banister railing as he went. He paused there, took a breath, and with one mighty heave, pulled the railing from the wall in a shower of plaster and squeal of nails.

Stomping back up the stairs, Sandy proudly displayed his handiwork to Brown, saying, "Once you open the door, I can just slide the fumigator in with this, and nobody has to enter the room!" In preparation, he placed the banister on the floor, one end facing the door.

Brown nodded and said, "Well done, my boy! All right, we're going to have to make this quick. As soon as I pull that insert out from between the sodium cyanide and sulfuric acid, we'll have to get out of here like nobody's business."

"And if we don't?"

"We're dead."

"Sure enough," Sandy said, readying his grasp on the banister.

CHAPTER THIRTY-FIVE

Kitty had been the one who'd had the misfortune to find the obsidian gemstones. Hidden away in a corner of the jewellery store, they'd been separate from other gems nearby and she'd known right away they were special.

Three of the biggest gemstones Kitty had ever seen, she'd known there was something special about them right away. They'd sparkled like dark stars in the light of the flickering gas lamps outside the shop window, somehow seeming even deeper than the night itself. They begged her to touch them and make them her own, and she'd been overwhelmed with desire to do so, but when she made contact, it had been a different story. Though she'd been wearing fine kid gloves, the obsidian stones had felt cold beneath her fingers, bitterly so. And there had also been the things she'd seen.

They burst through her mind in a billion blinding flashes. Things she would never have imagined in a million years. Things that were amazing, mysterious, frightening and beautiful, yet nothing she could recall with any great detail now. The only thing she strongly, truly and completely remembered was that after she had dropped them in the jewellery sack, she'd never wanted to have anything to do with them again in her life. William had gathered them up along with the rest of the jewels when they'd fled the scene of the crime moments later, and that was the last she'd ever seen of them.

William McLeod had always been the man in charge of fencing the loot. As soon as a job was done, the group would go their separate ways, none with any evidence of a crime on their person. Only once pounds sterling had been exchanged for the stolen jewels did William divvy the proceeds with the rest of the gang. From Kitty's brief time with the group, it had worked quite well until William was arrested.

From her brief time working with the gang, Kitty had managed to save a bit of money. And so she'd fled Europe, booking passage on an Allan Line Royal Mail Steamer from London to Halifax. Once she'd departed the East Coast of Canada and begun moving inland, she kept going west until she'd ended up in this nameless little town in British Columbia. She had no desire to get back into the life of crime and who she used to be, and she had thought she'd been done with the whole affair. But now, here she sat, half the world away from Scotland, staring at what appeared to be the exact same stones.

Pointing the tip of his cigar at the obsidian gems in the centre of the desk, Sinclair said, "Your young protege seems to have an affinity for them as well."

"My protege?"

"Sandy," Sinclair said, then blew several smoke rings.

Had Sandy touched those stones as well now, Kitty wondered. From her limited exposure all those years ago, her one contact with them had seemed enough for her to never forget them, though she'd tried. And now, had the boy had an experience similar to hers?

Sinclair continued, "I think you were drawn to their power back in Tullibody, just like the young lad was here. Both drawn to them for different reasons." Thomas puffed on his cigar as he let his words sink in.

Kitty pondered that. Had she been drawn here? Over four thousand miles away from home, and she'd somehow ended up in a place that had more of the exact same stones as the ones she'd stolen. In a small voice, she asked, "But how is that possible? Across all this distance?"

"I told ya. They're very powerful. They first came to my attention at my ancestral castle back in Glenrosa. They were what started my fascination with the occult and artefacts thereof."

Haltingly, she asked, "Artefacts?"

"Aye, things with dark power. The kind that draws certain people. So, I think it's more likely they found us rather than the other way around. Or, in your case, they found you, and you stole them. But that brief contact was enough to leave their mark on ya. And that is why you've ended up here with us after all those miles and all these years."

"Us?"

"That's right, us," Angeline said from the office doorway. She swept past Kitty and then stood at Thomas's side. With a cold smile on her lips, she ran her long, bony fingers through Thomas's tufts of wild red hair as she regarded Kitty.

Sinclair said, "Angeline was the one that had first contact with them. And afterwards, she seemed changed, and like a divinin' rod, she's now drawn to their power."

"I know you felt them as well," Angeline said in a soft voice. "You touched them, and now you are drawn to them."

"But these aren't the same stones."

"Nay, they're not, but they're the same nonetheless."

"What do you mean?"

"They all function as one," Angeline said.

"Aye. The more you have together, the stronger they get. After Glenrosa, Angeline led us to Austria, then India, and we found a single stone in each. Eventually, we landed in North Africa, where we found these three, along with that ebony box."

"Box?" Kitty's mind was awhirl, and she was having difficulty keeping up with all the travelling and touching. And now there were boxes?

Sinclair looked to the curio cabinet where an ebony box with pearl trim sat. "Aye, that one."

Kitty gazed at the dark box, lost in thought. Had she been drawn from Aberdeen, across the ocean, and all the way here to this backwoods little town in British Columbia, all due to her initial contact with those obsidian stones? And was it because Thomas had collected several of them together that she'd been more easily drawn?

"These stones all have something else in common, apart from their power," Thomas added.

"What's that?"

Angeline answered, "Wherever we've found them, there's usually one of two things, but sometimes both at once."

"And that is?" Kitty wondered, not sure if she really wanted to know the answer.

"Immense wealth like gold or diamonds," Thomas said.

"And what's the other."

"Great misfortune, suffering, and death," Angeline said softly.

"Why are you telling me all this," Kitty asked.

"Because I want you to track down those stones from Tullibody that you stole," Thomas replied.

"Me?"

Angeline nodded. "Since you made contact with them, you will be able to find them. They will call to you."

"How will I know? I didn't even realise I was drawn to those stones here in this town. I just ended up here. And how am I goin' to find those stones after all this time? It's been over six years since I've seen William McLeod."

"Then it's about time for the two of ya to get reacquainted," Thomas said with finality.

"But I wouldn't know where to start."

"Well, I do," Sinclair said. "And don't worry, you'll have plenty of help."

CHAPTER THIRTY-SIX

Doctor Brown crouched near the door. With one hand prepared to initiate the fumigator's chemical reaction, his other turned the handle.

The door swung inward, and the doctor temporarily froze in place, staring in wonder at the room beyond the threshold.

Sandy had indeed chosen wisely.

Spider webs were draped everywhere about the room, from ceiling to floor and wall to wall, yet there were no arachnids anywhere in sight. In the centre of the bed lay a figure. Kitty's would-be assailant, upon which she'd unleashed the wave of spiders.

Swathed from head to toe in a thick, silken cocoon, there were only the slightest movements under the shimmering silk as the man inside struggled for air. He seemed to have a bad case of consumption, with each breath a phlegmy rattle. The incubating spiderlings in the egg sacs around his lungs were no doubt growing larger and larger, crowding out his room to breathe with their wriggling, multi-legged mass.

Releasing the breath he didn't realise he was holding, Brown said, "That's odd. I would have thought they'd be thick as thieves here, but it seems to be only webs."

"I dunno, Doc. Looks bad enough to be worth pullin' your tab right now!"

Seeming in response to their voices, a sudden jiggling of the thick webbing that ran into the ceiling hatch signalled they would soon be welcomed to the spider's kingdom, and their hosts were now on their way.

"Hold your breath!" Brown exclaimed.

Vapour began to pour out of the top of the fumigator as soon as the doctor pulled the tab separating the acid from the cyanide. In a shrill voice, he cried, "Okay, my boy! Get it into the middle of that room, now!"

Brown scampered aside and let Sandy do his thing.

Like a curler at a bonspiel, Sandy pushed the square wooden box into the centre of the room. It spun slightly as it slid across the polished hardwood and finally bumped up against the leg of the bedframe. Thick clouds of toxic vapour now poured from the top of the fumigator as the chemical reaction got well and truly underway.

Instead of retracting the banister as Cornelius expected, Sandy jigged it over slightly and then pushed it further into the room, saying, "Don't want to pull it out and find any eight-legged surprises on the end!"

As if the attic were overflowing, spiders began to pour from the open hatch in the ceiling, seeming excited to welcome their new guests. Some scurried down the web, while others spilled into the air, tumbling acrobatically to the bed below in a deadly shower. At the rear of the welcome wagon, several larger, head-sized females began scuttling down the thick web hanging from the hatchway.

Brown pulled the door rapidly shut, the breeze from the motion blowing the growing cloud of toxic fumes back into the room and buying them a slight reprieve. He backed away, looking everywhere around him for escaped arachnids, examining his arms and the rest of his clothing at the same time, afraid a spider might have dropped onto him when he'd been pulling the door shut. Upon reflection, Cornelius realised he could have used another short length of rope to pull the door shut but had left the only two strands he'd brought at the funeral parlour tied to the casket's handles. Well, hindsight was always sharper than foresight, it seemed.

Turning to face Sandy, Brown saw the boy had already turned toward the stairs. As he moved to join him, he glanced back and saw the first tendrils of poisonous gas begin to waft from under the closed door. The fumigator seemed a resounding success, and he was sure the spiders were already feeling the effects of the gas. Unfortunately, so would they, and all too soon, unless they got out of there. "We need to depart with some alacrity, my boy!"

Sandy had moved down the stairs about halfway and then stopped, his hand resting on the remaining banister railing. "I thought I heard something down there, Doc."

"Heard what?"

"I dunno. It was a kind of a thump, like something dropping onto the floor in the kitchen."

The kitchen, Brown wondered, where they'd been forced to leave the trap open, its door now in several pieces, presumably torn off in the flood by furniture that had floated up against it.

At their backs, the growing cloud of poison gas from under the door moved inexorably toward them. "We need to move, Sandy!"

Sandy took a couple more steps and then stopped again—and just in time, it appeared.

In a flash of black death, a water beast slapped into view at the bottom of the mud-covered stairs, using its little prehensile limbs to pull its glistening, muddy body along. It hissed like a snake gargling whisky, then coiled the rest of its sinewy body into sight, preparing to wriggle itself up the stairs toward them.

"No ya don't, ya ugly bastard!" Sandy said, adding, "Pardon my French." He ripped the remaining banister rail from the wall with his 'weak arm', proclaiming, "Now that's feelin' more like it!" He changed his grip from underhand to overhand and jabbed the banister railing down at the obsidian creature.

The rounded end of the railing had all of Sandy's three-hundred-odd pounds behind it, and it rammed down the black beast's throat as it hissed and sputtered up the steep stairs toward them. Sandy bore down, and the beast thrashed and coiled as it was force-fed the wooden rail, but the stress was too much for the slender hardwood, and it began to bow slightly, then suddenly snapped in half.

Sandy stomped on the broken rail, and it bounced up in the air. He snatched the jagged shaft and drew it back like a spear, then threw with all his might at the beast in one fluid motion.

Still dealing with the remaining lumber that Sandy had stuffed down its gullet, the animal never saw the shaft of wood coming. It shot into the side of the monster's thrashing head, pinning it to the lath and plaster wall across from the foot of the stairs.

The creature squiggled and hissed, but it wasn't going anywhere. Sandy finished the job with a fruit crate that had settled in the narrow hall after floating from somewhere else in the house. He scooped it up and slammed it repeatedly into the beast's head, fracturing its skull into numerous fragments and stilling its agitated movement. With a cry of disgust, he said, "That's for Sam Shepherd and Chief Hildey!"

"Well done, my boy!" Brown cried, adding, "Now we need to get the hell out of here!" The doctor clambered down the remaining steps, the cloud of toxic fumes at his back ready to envelop him and allow him to sample its mystifying scent.

Sandy held his breath and flew toward the front door, kicking aside detritus that had ended its flood-filled journey on the floor of the short hallway. Once free of the house, he trundled down the front steps. He gasped for air, now willing to breathe once again.

The doctor was close at his back but paused at the door, his hand on the knob as he looked back. Noxious gas poured from the stairwell like liquid cloud and puffed into the hallway they had vacated only moments earlier. The upper rooms and attic of the tiny house were no doubt already filled with it.

A smile crept across the doctor's face as he softly closed the door. It seemed the Brown Pest-Away Fumigator was doing its job quietly and efficiently. He sauntered down the steps, taking a moment to breathe in the fresh, hot air of the blazing summer afternoon.

His hands on his knees as he took in great heaving lungfuls of air, Sandy said, "Tell me that's the last of those blessed things, will ya, Doc?"

Exhaling slowly and feeling some tension leave his body, Brown nodded and said, "I believe things around here might just be ready to take a turn from the worse for a change."

Deep down in his chest, something began stirring that Cornelius hadn't felt in quite a while: a small glimmer of hope—hope that the worst of the creature problems plaguing this peaceful little mountain valley was now far behind them.

CHAPTER THIRTY-SEVEN

The ridge towered high above, and beyond, sheer rock face swept up to a massive entity resting on its mountaintop throne, the glacier Natánik. The waning moon cast everything in monotone, save for the ancient ice, which shone silver-blue in the early summer twilight.

Fresh wood was thrown on the crackling fire courtesy of Lucias, and escaping sap hissed and popped as it began to burn. The gunslinger had found a pine downed by the storm nearby and had been busy chopping chunks off it for their evening fire with a machete. Just using his good hand, he had hewn a substantial amount of arm-thick fuel in a short time.

Thanks to the roaring fire, Cookie finally had a chance to try out his new pots and pans and had produced a very tasty stew with plump dumplings floating on top.

Scraping his tin plate and burping contentedly, Caleb now saw why Jesús kept the cook around despite his grating personality.

Stars stretched from mountain peak to mountain peak, glittering like billions of diamonds whose worth would be immeasurable. Caleb recalled the last time he'd seen what he'd believed to be diamonds. His greed-filled thoughts of boundless wealth soon changed to fear-filled thoughts of self-preservation once he'd seen the red menace that dwelled in that small tunnel.

Just before they'd stopped for the night, they'd come upon some rock freshly fallen in the recent ground shaking. Some chunks were as big as a stagecoach, and others as large as a house. They must have thundered down the mountainside as they'd dropped.

As they'd set up camp among the large boulders, Cookie had complained that they were taking a chance since some loose rock might still want to come down the mountainside and join its brethren on the ground. Jesús dismissed his concerns saying that anything that could have fallen, would have fallen by now, and they'd left it at that.

Sitting across the fire from Caleb, Jesús asked, "Do you think you will need to do much blasting?"

"I don't know," Caleb admitted. "It all depends on what that earthquake might have done up the mountain here. If it shook as much inside that cavern as it did down in the valley, some of the chambers I entered earlier might now be blocked or even collapsed." He picked up the Brown Static Detonator and examined it as he spoke.

Jesús narrowed his eyes slightly and said, "Do not worry. I have plenty of dynamite if you need some extra assistance."

Caleb nodded, saying, "I'll bear that in mind." He looked back down at the detonator in his hands. He'd pulled it out once again as he'd wracked his brain to remember the location of the cavern's entrance. It had to be a hole in the ground wherever it was because he remembered waking up from his fall and staring up at the dangling rope. Another part of him knew he had seen a waterfall outside somewhere just before that; if he saw the rushing water again, he was sure more would come unlocked from his reluctant brain at that time.

A whinny caught Caleb's attention, and he looked up from his ruminations. Over near a small copse of trees, Emily was supposed to be bedded down for the night, but that didn't seem to be the case at the moment. She stood at the end of her rope, apparently on her way to visit Caleb for another sugary fix but had been betrayed by the short length of her tether.

Caleb smiled and stood, saying, "What's the matter, old girl. Are ya needin' another dose of your medicine?"

His wood chopping done for the moment, Lucias sat and leaned against a tree nearby, saying, "That stuff is going to rot her brain."

Reaching into his dungarees, Caleb fished out another couple of cubes as he walked over to the mule. She gobbled the sugar from his hand as he replied, "Well, I hope it's not all that bad."

"Don't make no sense," Cookie observed. "That stuff is gonna make the darned thing go squirrelly!"

"But why are you giving her constant treats and gratification?" Jesús wondered.

"I want to keep her happy."

"Happy?" Cookie asked.

"Yeah, because she's our map."

"Your map?!" Lucias snorted.

Caleb nodded. "I'm convinced she knows the route to the hole in the ground I fell into. And I'm hopin' tomorrow she'll take us up the rest of the way to where that is."

"D'ya really think she knows the spot?" Cookie wondered.

"I'm bettin' on it," Caleb replied with a slight nod, his lips a grim line.

***

The night skies were just beginning to lose their velveteen coat of stars, and the first hint of the day yet to come was gradually brightening the edges of the eastern peaks when Cookie began to scream.

Jesús bolted upright, torn from a dream of sweet Spanish sherry and an equally sweet senorita that had looked suspiciously like one of his ex-wives. Blinking his eyes blearily, he looked about.

The cook wasn't at his post, though he was supposed to have been on guard duty. Lucias had taken the first two-hour shift, then it had been the Irishman, then him. The cook had had the last shift but also the most sleep. Jesús didn't think the man would've dozed off after all that sleep, but it seemed he had done so, and now something had happened.

Cookie shrieked, "Bear! Omigod! It's a goddamned grizzly!" He should have been shooting, but he didn't seem to have a gun at the moment, though he'd been given one as part of his guard duties. Whatever the reason, the mule was now under attack by a massive brown grizzly, and it wasn't listening to Cookie.

Emily whinnied in fear and kicked out with her hind legs. She'd pushed into the copse of trees as far as her tether would allow and now squealed and brayed as the furious bear roared and lashed its claws at her.

Oritz was in the process of drawing his revolver when three quick cracks of gunfire erupted, and the bear dropped to the ground. A trio of neatly placed holes were now centred between its beady brown eyes, and its lifeblood quickly soaked into the earth and pine needles around it.

"Nice shootin', Lucias," Caleb said from one side.

Holstering his sidearm, Lucias nodded at the compliment, then turned and said to Cookie, "Weren't you on guard duty?"

"I was!"

"Then where's your rifle? I gave one to you!" Jesús said, his eyes wide with anger.

"I was taking a leak behind a couple of trees over there, and when I heard the mule start to squeal, I couldn't find where I'd put the rifle in the dark! But if that bear hadn't found the mule first, it could have easily been me!"

Jesús snarled, "Too bad it was not!" Standing near the cook, he made as if to backhand the man but then held his hand at the last minute and instead said, "Pendejo," his voice low and menacing.

The old man cringed and held up his hands defensively as if expecting the blow still to fall, but it didn't. He squinted his eyes open and blinked in disbelief.

With a shake of his head, Oritz said, "I will deal with you later."

"Well, that puts a slight crimp in our plans," Caleb said. He was now kneeling next to Emily and stroked her mane as he spoke quiet words of reassurance to her. The mule sat on the ground, dark blood oozing from the gouge she'd suffered in her side when the bear had sprung out of the darkness and pounced upon her.

Noting that the animal's eyes were even wider than usual,

and her breathing ragged from fright, Caleb wanted to distract her and decided what better to use than his old standby, and he fed her another cube of sugar.

Emily quickly gobbled it down and began to lick his hand, searching for more.

Taking a closer look at the mule's wound, Caleb added, "If this girl doesn't bleed to death first, without proper treatment, she'll likely be dead from sepsis within a day or two." He spoke from experience and had seen it happen to some of his army mates in Africa. Shaking his head, he looked to the group of men and concluded, "If we don't find the entrance to that cavern very soon, my sugar-eatin' map on four legs is goin' to go to uncharted places that we can never follow."

CHAPTER THIRTY-EIGHT

While Cookie ministered to the animal's wounds, Caleb stroked Emily's mane and patted her as he whispered calming words. After washing out the wound on the mule's flank as best he could, Cookie bandaged it using a spare shirt of Caleb's with a piece of one of the bedroll blankets tied around it. He shook his grizzled head as he finished up and said, "Can't say as I ever patched up a mule before."

"I've found this valley is a real 'first time for everything' kind of place," Caleb replied. Around them, the day grew brighter. The sky was now deep purple in the west, fading to pale pink closer to the eastern horizon, the still-hidden sun painting the mountain's craggy tips a glowing yellow-orange.

Jesús examined the dead grizzly in the growing light while the other men worked on the mule. He poked and prodded at the corpse for several moments, then said, "I think I found what caused this bear to attack."

The other men crowded around, and he pointed to two separate spots on the bear's mud-covered legs. Caked blood was soaked into the fur all around, and one of the wounds, a bite mark, looked very familiar to Caleb.

"It's been battling something, and whatever it was

wounded it gravely," Lucias said.

"What woulda caused that?" Cookie asked, looking around at the brightening day, perhaps thinking something might be lurking in the bushes nearby.

His mouth a grim line, Caleb said with a knowing nod, "One of those black beasts." The bear's wound was quite similar to the one he'd received during his own encounter with one of the monsters in the underground lake, though fortunately, he hadn't had a chunk taken out of him as the bear had.

Jesús looked up from where he squatted and said, "It must have been out of its mind with pain and attacked the first thing it could find to vent its rage."

"This doesn't look fresh." Lucias prodded the wound with the tip of a branch he'd broken off a nearby tree. "Might have happened a day ago, back when those things were freed from the river in that flood."

Caleb wondered at that. Though he had suffered a bite from a black beast, as of yet, he had only experienced things which seemed beneficial, such as his rapid healing. But was there more to it than that? Were the effects of the bites dependent on what the creatures bit? Perhaps it brought out the innate tendencies in bears and other aggressive species? And maybe it worked more quickly on the lower animals, especially those with more sizeable wounds like the bear had. Whatever the cause, he was left with a queasy stomach at the thought.

Once they'd packed up camp, they'd had a quick breakfast of griddle cakes and bacon. Though he hadn't thought he would have had an appetite after working on Emily, Caleb managed to wolf down a half dozen of the large fluffy cakes along with several rashers of bacon. The lot of it had been liberally smothered with butter and maple syrup and washed down by some surprisingly good coffee.

Emily had picked at some long grass but seemed to have no appetite, which wasn't surprising. However, several sugar cubes perked her up, and after a short while, she began to lead them up to the ridge.

There were several points where a natural switchback in the mountain led off in a couple of different directions. Yet each time, the mule had seemed to know where to go. And so, Caleb had continued to feed Emily sugar, hoping she would be able to keep going through sweets alone.

By mid-afternoon, the sun was baking down on them again. The climb had been quite laborious and slow in places, but now, they'd finally reached the top of the ridge. The men took a moment for a water break and to gaze upon the valley below and marvel at the distance they'd come. But not Caleb; he scanned along the base of the rock face where it met the ridge for the object of his quest: the waterfall. Peering through the field glasses, it all seemed so familiar, but so far, he hadn't had much luck with his memory apart from more déjà vu.

Caleb felt a nudge against his shoulder and turned. He rubbed behind Emily's ear as he fed her a couple more sugar cubes. "Emily, my dear, how're you holding up?" He'd been keeping an eye on the poor mule as they'd made their winding way up toward the ridge. The usually perky and spry animal was slower than usual, and he could see she was favouring her wounded side as she walked.

Emily nuzzled her nose into Caleb's hand, her long pink tongue exploring his palm for any remaining traces of sugar. "You can have some more soon, girl." He shook his head, unsure how much more of the remaining sugar would be eaten by the mule before she passed. The climb, though not completely vertical by any means, was still a challenge, even for a healthy person. And though Emily wasn't a person, she was far from healthy. And, of course, it had also been extra challenging for the men because of that fact. In her weakened condition, Emily could not carry as many items, and they'd had to divvy up some of the stores she'd had on board.

As if reading his mind, Lucias approached and said, "Your friend there has lost a lot of blood. He nodded toward the animal's side and the makeshift dressing over the wound.

Caleb said, "Aye, I've noticed that. She's a lot slower. I think the sugar is the only thing keeping her going now."

"You're probably not too far wrong." Lucias looked to the mule again and added, "When the time comes, I'll put her out of her misery for you."

"Aye, thanks. The way things are goin', I don't know how much longer that'll be."

Interrupting the conversation, Jesús and Cookie approached. "What have you remembered, Mister Caleb?"

"I'm goin' to have another scout about, alone. You can mind the store." He handed Emily's reins to Jesús and proceeded along the ridge for several dozen yards through the small rocks and assorted scree that had tumbled down the mountainside.

Caleb felt déjà vu threaten to overwhelm him once again. The earthquake looked to have dropped more fresh scree and rubble from above. Taking a breath and slowly exhaling to steady his hand, he peered through the field glasses again, sweeping them slowly along the rocky wall in the distance. Despite the feeling of familiarity, there seemed to be nothing but rock, rock, more rock, and—

"Well, I'll be a daft, addled leprechaun!" Rising up from behind several large boulders was a waft of steam. He moved along for another short distance to get a different angle and then looked again. Sure enough, behind the steam on the other side of a boulder was a small waterfall, possibly the one he recalled seeing just before the cavern, the one where he'd had his brilliant idea, or so it had seemed at the time.

A clatter of rock came at Caleb's back, and he turned, reflexively putting his hand on the Remington at his hip. Though not a man to usually carry a revolver, he had made an exception in light of the company he was now keeping and the hazards of the wild in this valley. And so, he had accepted one Lucias had loaned him from what turned out to be an extensive collection.

Back at the Golden Nugget, the man in black had taken Caleb to another room, its door located in the corner of Sinclair's office. He had first presumed it an indoor toilet for Sinclair's private use or maybe a powder room for Angeline. But it wasn't either and had, in fact, been another room almost as large as the storage room where all of the expedition's supplies had been located.

There were no windows in this room, and as Lucias had lit the lamp when they entered, Caleb had stared in slack-jawed awe. He hadn't seen such an armoury since his time in Her Majesty's Fifth—everything from Deringers to daggers and Colts to clubs. Hanging from pegs and hooks, one wall seemed to contain almost every brand of firearm Caleb had ever seen. Another wall had stabbing and slicing weapons, from swords and battle axes to pearl-handled straight razors and ebony-clad stilettos. On the far wall had been bows and arrows, along with crossbows and what looked like bolas that he'd seen Argentinian cowboys use to bring down errant cattle. All in all, it had looked to be a playground paradise for a man like Lucias, in the business of using assorted weapons as he was.

Caleb dropped his hand from the revolver when he saw it was Lucias knocking about some of the smaller rocks as he approached. The man now stood next to him but didn't speak, in keeping with his generally silent demeanour. Caleb looked back through the glasses for a moment, saying nothing himself.

The gunslinger squinted at the base of the rock face across the field of scree, then asked, "Is that waterfall something you've been looking for?"

His jaw dropping slightly, Caleb let the glasses hang from his neck and cupped his hands around his eyes to try and see the waterfall unaided but had little luck. As he turned back to face Lucias, the shining brass casing on the glasses glinted warmly in the golden, late afternoon light, dazzling his eyes. "You can see that from here? I can barely see it with these glasses!"

Lucias looked from the rock face to Caleb, his squint not changing significantly despite also being dazzled by the reflected light off the polished brass. He said flatly and without braggadocio, "I can shoot the wings off a fly at a hundred yards."

With a nod, Caleb replied, "I can believe that." He glanced over his shoulder toward the distant waterfall and said, "And in answer to your question, I think that's the first part of the puzzle."

The sun once more began to slip behind the rugged mountaintops, and Lucias nodded toward it, saying, "I think we should be able to make it across these rocks by nightfall, and we can camp there."

"That's exactly what I was thinkin'. And if that's the waterfall I'm lookin' for, it might trigger some more memories once we get there." In fact, Caleb really hoped that would be the case. Despite seeing something that looked like it might be part of the flash he'd had; he still wasn't sure it was the correct waterfall. He began to move back toward the bandits and Emily when Lucias caught his elbow and said, "There's something I need to tell you."

Caleb halted and turned, placing his hands on his hips as he said, "And what would that be? Are you goin' to threaten me again?"

Lucias shook his head and said, "Nah, this isn't business; this is off the record."

With a tilt of his head, Caleb said, "Okay, speak your mind."

"As you know, Mr. Sinclair has me here protecting his investment."

"Aye."

"And since you're a smart guy, you know those bandits are probably going to try and kill you and me, if and when we find that gold, right?"

Caleb nodded again and said, "I pretty much figured that out on my own."

"Well, I thought I should tell you; I've got orders to do the same to them if and when we find that gold."

"Well, I almost figured that would be the case, too."

"I'm not done yet."

"Go on then. Light's a wastin'."

"And I'm supposed to kill you, too."

Giving a sad shake of his head, Caleb replied, "I wish I could say even that much came as a surprise, but sadly, no, it doesn't either." He began to move back toward the bandits.

"Listen," Lucias said, grabbing Caleb's arm again. "Despite what Mr. Sinclair wants, I just wanted to tell you that I want to give you a chance when we find it."

"You don't say." This was a surprise coming from the man in black, and he inquired, "What kinda chance?"

"I'll let you live if you promise never to come back to this valley."

"I was almost thinkin' of just givin' your boss all the gold in that cavern anyway, though I'd like to take just enough to get myself set up elsewhere, me and Miss Kitty, that is."

"That's the other reason I don't want to kill you. I've always been kinda partial to Kitty. She reminds me of my kid sister. Anyway, I wouldn't want to see her hurt. And my killing you would do that, so I am going to allow you to live for that reason."

"That's very generous of you."

Lucias frowned and said, "Let me finish. Whatever you can load on a mule, you can take with you and have no further claim to the gold in that cavern or any in this area. As far as Sinclair will know, you died up here 'accidentally' just like he wanted."

Caleb nodded and stuck his hand out. "We have a deal."

They shook briefly and did so with their backs to the bandits to not tip them off that some sort of deal was in the making. Their agreement complete, they began to pick their way back through the rough rock to Emily and the bandits.

This new deal with the gunman was rather unexpected, Caleb realised, but at least it offered him a faint glimmer of hope. Now, he only needed one more fortuitous revelation at the waterfall. Thinking that, he crossed his fingers since whatever Irish luck he had remaining was most likely wearing very, very thin.

CHAPTER THIRTY-NINE

The light was almost gone by the time they'd picked their way through the field of scree. Caleb was in the lead with Emily. Lucias, Jesús, and Cookie trailed behind, all laden with supplies since the mule could no longer carry anything.

Almost to the waterfall, Caleb felt a tug on the reins and turned. Emily had stumbled, now kneeling on her front legs and seeming unable to go on. He knew that if she went all the way down, they would never get her up again. Caleb reached into his pocket, took a handful of sugar cubes, and fed them to the mule. At first, Emily seemed reluctant to partake, and he almost thought she might be done there and then.

Earlier, Caleb had wondered if he would use his entire sugar supply before Emily succumbed to her injuries, and he now saw that might yet come to pass. Over the last couple of hundred yards, the mule had just stopped walking three times, and each time, he'd given her several cubes to get her going again. The gashes from the bear had been too broad, and Cookie had been unable to stitch them together. Now, blood was seeping through the makeshift bandage, and Caleb was sure that her blood loss was getting critical since she felt cool to the touch in places despite the heat of the day.

In South Africa, Caleb had seen numerous lads slowly

bleed to death. Part of the process involved the body pulling the remaining blood to the vital organs and shutting down its pumping to the limbs and musculature. Compounding things with the blood loss was the dirt and mess that the bear's claw had left in the wound. Though the cook had rinsed it as best he could before applying the dressing, he hadn't gotten everything. Her skin now seemed inflamed, and flies were rife around the wound. Emily was close to death, and there didn't seem to be anything they could do to stop its arrival.

Even after munching down the cubes, the mule still kneeled, and it wasn't until Caleb offered her more sugar that she finally stood again but did so with great difficulty.

With a few more minutes of sugar powering Emily along, they wound the remaining way through the rocks to the waterfall. The closer they got, the surer Caleb felt they were on the right path. As they drew closer to the rock face, he looked upward and marvelled at the size of the glacier resting at the top of the mountain.

As his gaze settled upon the ancient ice, a memory made another flash in Caleb's mind. This one was of the sun and the moon, and he suddenly thought of the aboriginal name of the glacier once again, Natánik. However, his forgetful mind wouldn't help him discern any more. But now that he'd recalled thoughts of this gigantic piece of ice before finding the cavern, it seemed another positive sign.

Steam and mist swirled into the early evening air as the small waterfall dropped into a pool at the base of the rock face. From there, a narrow stream emptied into the surrounding scree. Well, it wasn't Saturday, Caleb realised, and with the temperature that the water looked, he certainly wouldn't try to bathe in that even if he was as dirty as the devil himself.

As that thought occurred, another flash struck, and Caleb recalled what he'd done upon first seeing the little waterfall—

and this time, he also saw a flash of the gold sovereigns from Red Deer. He remembered squatting down and sticking a finger in the small stream, then yanking it back out immediately, having burned himself slightly.

Caleb dropped Emily's reins and moved closer to the rock face as if in a daze.

The waterfall splashed onto a massive slab of rock and poured into a pool below, then streamed away and disappeared into the surrounding scree. He'd definitely done more than just stick his fingers into this water; he was sure of it now. Caleb tore his gaze from the waterfall to the slab of rock, then the mountainside sweeping up into cloud, then down to the pool, and finally back to the waterfall again.

With a wailing howl, Caleb dropped slowly to his knees and almost pounded his fists in frustration on the ground before recalling the nitroglycerine on his person.

Lucias had been watching this display of emotion and asked, "What is it? What's wrong?"

"The gold! It's gone!"

"What gold is gone?" Jesús asked as he and Cookie arrived on the scene.

"All of it. The gold from the bank job."

"What? Where?" Lucias asked.

"There!" Caleb pointed at the steaming pool as he stood. He now remembered everything about the waterfall and, in particular, the pool below. Because that was where he had tossed the bags of stolen gold. Once under the churning surface of the steaming waterfall, they had been very hard to see. But now, viewing them was much more difficult, and in fact, it appeared they would never be seen again.

At the time, Caleb hadn't stopped to think how he would ever have gotten them out of that boiling pool. But considering the amount of gold he'd hidden there, he was sure he'd have had more than enough motivation. Except now, there was no way to get to them, even if he could figure something out.

Hundreds of tons of rock now lay on top of the glittering gold, rendering the point moot. During one of the recent earth tremors, a thick slab of rock had fractured off and slammed down like a coffin lid on top of the hidden gold, burying it forever.

Shaking his head in abject sadness, Caleb lamented, "I finally remember the gold sovereign's hidin' spot, and there's no way to ever get to them now!"

"That is very unfortunate," Jesús said.

"Good thing you have your other caverns filled with gold," Lucias said as he moved past Caleb to check the mule's wounds.

"Aye, caverns I still can't remember the location of!"

"Then let us hope your mule survives a bit longer," Jesús responded.

"Aye, that's somethin' I've been worryin' over, too."

Shaking his head, Jesús added, "I think that sugar has been the only thing keeping her going."

Caleb nodded, saying, "Part of me knows that she's not going to make it and should be put down, and it truly pains me to see her as she is. But another part of me needs her alive to help find that cavern tomorrow. So I'm going to keep giving her sugar while I have it and hope she lasts." He moved to

Emily and stroked her ear. She whinnied lightly, but not how she used to, and it seemed she was in rough shape.

"Here ya go, old girl." Caleb fed the mule another trio of sugar cubes, and she greedily gobbled them down.

As Caleb and Jesús talked, Cookie had lit a small, alcohol-fuelled camping stove from their supplies. With that done, he now crouched at the pool's edge, about to scoop a potful of the water when Lucias said, "Hang on there!"

The cook jerked his head up and said, "What's the matter?"

The gunslinger rubbed his fingers together, saying, "This stuff's no good for cooking or washing."

"Why not? It's already boilin'!"

Pointing to the stream, Lucias answered, "I was going to use some of that water to clean the mule's wounds, but as soon as my fingertips touched it, I could feel my skin react. Whatever is in that water, I had to rinse off with some drinking water to stop it from burning." He held his fingers up, and they appeared slightly reddened at the tips.

"Yeah, I was going to mention that too, but the gold's predicament distracted me," Caleb added.

"Well, that don't help me make dinner none," Cookie groused.

Lucias said, "There's another stream about a half mile back you can fill your pots from. That was cold and clear, probably from that glacier up top, not from the bowels of hell or wherever this water comes from."

Cookie groused some more and said, "I'm gonna need some help getting water then."

Jesús said, "I will help."

With Cookie carrying a lantern, the two men departed for the stream in the growing darkness, each carrying a pot, and Jesús had a water skin over one shoulder to top up their drinking supply.

While the gang members were otherwise occupied, Lucias and Caleb moved aside some of the roughest rocks and made spots for their bedrolls on the rocky ground.

About twenty minutes later, the bandits returned with the pots and water skin filled. Within the hour, Cookie had once again whipped up a somewhat palatable dinner of rehydrated beef and potatoes he'd brought along, making a rather tasty hash.

The evening was late by the time they were done. After giving Emily some solid food and more sugar, the group bedded down for the night. Being away from the horrors in the valley below, it was decided they didn't need to have anyone stand watch. And soon, all were asleep beneath the midnight stars.

***

The meadow was filled with golden light; butterflies dipped and danced over the flowers that swayed in the gentle breeze.

Emily was here, eating something hidden just out of sight in the grass. Caleb moved closer to see what had so engaged her senses that she didn't see him. He arrived at her side and was surprised to see her eating from a big blue ceramic bowlful of sugar cubes.

"Ya can't have all those, girl! Ya need to have some real food to help with your wounds!" He looked to her side and saw the bandages were now gone, and the gouges raked into her flesh by the bear now healed and whole. It was surprising to see her heal so quickly, and he wondered if she'd been bitten by a black beast like he had. "Well, whatever it is you're doin', keep on doin' it!"

Emily looked up from her bowl of sugar and regarded him, her long, thick lashes fluttering in the breeze. The mule's big brown eyes seemed to possess an intelligence and heart he'd never noticed. He felt glad she was well now and realised how much he come to think of Emily as a friend after all their miles and adventures together.

Caleb began to stroke Emily's mane, just behind her ears, where she liked it, when she suddenly said in a rough male voice, "Wake up! It's Emily!"

"I know it's you, girl! I'm talkin' to ya," Caleb muttered as he came up from the depths of his dream. He'd only had a couple hours of sleep, having been uncomfortable not only with the rocky bed on which he lay but also uncomfortable that he didn't recall any more of where the cavern lay.

And now, just as he'd been dozing off fitfully, he was being awakened again. Rubbing at his eyes, Caleb said, "What in the name of heaven is happenin'?"

"Caleb," Lucias said. "It's Emily. She'd dead."

CHAPTER FORTY

Emily was buried where she dropped since there was no way to move her. At close to one thousand pounds, when the word 'buried' was used, it was used loosely. Despite some grumbling from the two bandits, the men had assisted in moving some of the smaller rocks and piling them onto the mule's corpse. She had been a reliable travelling companion and deserved that, at least. It was for their benefit as much as Emily's, of course. Leaving a dead mule out in the open would cause vultures to circle overhead and draw attention to their position. After all, they wanted as few people to know of the cavern's location as possible until they could find the entrance and secure things to their liking.

And that thought brought Caleb to his current dilemma. How to find the cavern. He stood lost in thought, arms folded, one hand raised, his index finger tapping his lips as he pondered the situation. With his four-legged mule friend now eating sugar cubes in the meadows of his mind, Caleb was at a loss as to what to do next.

The sun's piercing rays were just cresting the eastern mountains, their brilliance bathing the ridge as a new day began. Above, the glacier's time-worn ice glowed golden in the rich, early-morning light.

Jesús approached, crunching through the scree. "Where are we going now, Mister Caleb."

Shaking his head, Caleb said, "That is the question of the hour."

Caleb looked back toward the boiling acidic stream with longing. If only he'd been able to get to that gold from beneath the waterfall. He'd felt so cunning when he'd hidden it, thinking that no one would ever have thought to look there. And now, no one would ever have the chance.

The sun just then hit the stream, its honey-coloured rays dappling over the surface of the burbling water. Caleb was just turning away when a flash of yellow caught his eye. Yellow was a colour that he paid attention to around these parts, and he glanced back.

His eyes widening, he said, "Ello-ello! What have we here?"

Glinting from the bottom of the stream bed was something that looked very familiar—something round and about the size of a golf ball.

"I need a piece of kindling!" Caleb called urgently.

Several pine trees had dropped from the cliffside in the recent quake, and Lucias hacked at a limb of one with his machete. He returned with a branch the thickness of his wrist and handed it to Caleb saying, "Hope this will do the trick."

"Thanks. I'm hopin' that thing in the stream is what I think it is." Leaning over the boiling water, he saw there were two nuggets, not one. With the tip of the branch forming a convenient Y, Caleb easily fished the two golden stones from the water and placed them on a flat rock nearby to let them cool down. But his impatience won out, and he decided to pick the nuggets up after only a few seconds, saying, "Shite on a shamrock! These are bleedin' hot!"

Caleb tossed one of them over to Oritz, who eyed it greedily and tossed it from palm to palm as it cooled. Cookie crowded next to him, his own eyes lighting with avarice.

"This is what you say was all over the floor of that first cavern?" Jesús wondered.

"Aye, and a couple of others as well." Caleb tossed the remaining nugget to Lucias and said, "Here, you can keep it."

"Gee, thanks," the gunslinger responded. Though he was sarcastic in tone, the way he eyed the golden nugget showed he was impressed nonetheless.

As the men compared the two nuggets' similarities, Caleb had other thoughts going through his mind. If these lumps of gold were the same as the cavern, had they somehow been dislodged during the quake at the same time the giant slab had fallen overtop the gold sovereigns? That would explain why this stream looked an awful lot like the ones he remembered on the floor of the cavern he'd had the displeasure to fall into.

More interestingly, he had seen similar stones of gold not only on the floor but also in the boiling pools and streams that dotted the cavern. He wracked his brain as he tried to recall more of the layout of the cave system. One of the streams had run off in the opposite direction from the others, and he now wondered, where had that stream flowed to?

He craned his neck toward a smaller ridge several hundred feet above where the stream of water exited the rock face. Caleb felt growing certainty he'd found a route up to explore that smaller ridge. And the more he thought about it, though still hazy in his mind, the surer he became he had done so with Emily in tow. And it was there that he had tied her to a tree and...

Caleb's eyes widened as he looked up to the narrow ridge, then back to the waterfall, then to the ridge and then back to the waterfall once more. A startling revelation came to him as he realised the smaller ridge above was, in fact, the roof of the cavern he'd fallen into! And the 'hole' he'd shimmied down was a natural chimney leading into that rocky horror show below.

Lucias's keen eyes had been watching Caleb, and he asked, "Having another moment, are you?"

Still looking to the waterfall, Caleb replied. "I'm havin' more than that, my son."

"This is all well and good," Jesús said, approaching with the single nugget in his hand. "But are there any more?"

"Yes. Many, many more."

"What're ya gonna do now?" Cookie wondered.

A plan was forming in Caleb's head. "I think we might not have to look for a hole in the ground after all." As he spoke, Caleb retrieved the Brown Static Detonator from his satchel. He placed it on a rock and then reached slowly into one of the pockets of his leather vest and extracted the reason the other men had been doing the physical labour around him on this quest so far.

It was not that he couldn't help out. But if he did and then slipped and fell or jolted himself in some way, perhaps laden with a heavy pack, the consequences for him and everyone around would be dire. It was one of the few saving graces of being loaded with enough nitroglycerin to destroy a city block. It was also the reason why he didn't fear any bodily harm from either of the bandits at the moment, unless they were suicidal.

"Not looking for a hole? What do you mean?" Oritz asked, his eyes narrowing as he watched Caleb work.

"I mean, what we came up here for might be just on the other side of that rock." Caleb temporarily replaced the nitro vial in its pocket, wanting two free hands as he moved to examine the small waterfall pouring from the rock face.

When he'd been here before, he was sure that the amount of water coming out of it had been less substantial than now, but he needed to get closer to check the outflow.

Fortunately, the edge of the slab of rock that had entombed Caleb's gold sovereigns also served as a ledge of sorts, which now ran just above the steaming stream. Taking a breath, he edged cautiously along the slab's edge, its surface slick from the waterfall's spray but made it to the rupture in the rock without incident. The water's flow seemed strong enough that any round nugget like the ones from the stream below was liable to be flushed through this gash in the rock, especially since it had now been slightly enlarged by the earthquake.

Working quickly but smoothly, Caleb placed some of his blasting cotton into a small crevice next to the waterfall's exit. He made sure the wire tips were a small distance apart, as the doctor had mentioned in his instructions, and inserted them gently into the cotton. Removing the vial from his vest pocket, Caleb poured out a moderate amount of boom juice, not wanting to get carried away but, at the same time, not wanting to have too little, either. Satisfied he had the right balance, he gently capped the vial and returned it to his vest. Cautiously moving back along the ledge, he joined the other men, now standing off to one side.

To remind Caleb of what he'd said in the note, the doctor had written some brief instructions in ink on the side of the detonator. After loosening the thumb screw terminals on the top, he wrapped one nitro wire around the first and tightened it down but left the second unattached until ready to blast. Making sure the toggle switch was set to 'Off', Caleb withdrew the recessed handle at the end and gave it a dozen good cranks.

"I'd recommend you gentlemen find yourselves a seat for the show." With his cranking complete, Caleb spooled out a bit more wire and moved behind a sizable boulder which rested nearby.

Once everyone was hunkered down, Caleb wrapped the loose wire around the other terminal, flipped the safety cover off the toggle switch, and paused with his thumb ready to hit 'Kaboom'.

CHAPTER FORTY-ONE

"Fire in the hole!"

A thunderous blast rang out, and fragments of rock rained down around the men, with one the size of a human head slamming into the ground next to the boulder where Caleb and Lucias squatted.

Hunkered behind a different boulder, Cookie was not quite concealed from the blast since Jesús took up most of the spot. Due to the cook's exposure, a rock the size of a fist glanced off his partially exposed shoulder, resulting in him reciting a choice selection of blue words.

The noise from the blast echoed up and down the valley like thunder, as if, despite the clear blue day, the recent storms were now back for a second round.

A moment of silence reigned over the group, and Jesús spoke first. He poked his head over the boulder he'd hidden behind, saying, "That was very impressive. Now, I wonder if all that noise did any good or if we'll need some of my good, old-fashioned dynamite?"

Dust hung in the still morning air. Caleb stifled a sneeze, not wanting to violently shake his body, not with a vest full of nitroglycerine. He held his nose, still feeling like he wanted to sneeze out more dust and moved around the boulder to see the results of his handiwork.

At his back, Lucias muttered, "Gesundheit."

Caleb nodded in thanks and wiped the dust from his face with the bandana he'd hung around his nose in anticipation of the blast. Lucias also sported a bandana, as did Jesús. Unfortunately, the cook was without, and he coughed from the now-settling dust.

The haze of dust gave way to grey rock and then to blackness as Caleb moved closer. There was more than just a fissure in the rock face now. There was a gaping hole. It wasn't huge by any means, but it was a way in, nonetheless. From one side of it poured the boiling stream, its volume now greater but not substantially so since the explosion hadn't changed the course of its flow.

Looking toward the man-sized hole Lucias said with admiration, "Well, I'll be a son of a bitch. You did it!"

The gunslinger's pedigree notwithstanding, it seemed Caleb had indeed done it. He stood with his hands on his hips, peering up at the black entrance into the unknown. It was his cavern, as far as he knew, at least if the gold they'd found outside was anything to go by. However, this entrance looked temporary, and the next time the land settled, it might just collapse. In addition, they would have to crawl through since it wasn't more than three feet high on the outside and quickly narrowed as it progressed.

The Spaniard spoke at Caleb's back, saying, "Are you ready to find out if this is your cavern?" Jesús inquired.

"I'm supposin' so," Caleb said with a slow nod, but we need to get ready first."

Indeed, if this was his cavern, they needed to be well prepared before they went inside. First, they needed their calcium-carbide lamps lit, and second, they would need their gloves to protect their hands as they crawled over the jagged stone of the cavern's new entrance.

"It's a little small, ain't it?" Cookie whined as he rubbed his shoulder where the rock had struck him during the new cave opening's explosive entrance to the world.

"You're an observant man," Caleb replied. "I think we're goin' to have to go one at a time and push our packs ahead of us and wriggle through like worms."

"Worms?" The cook groused. I don't wanna wriggle like no consarned worm."

"Yes, you do," Jesús said, "And you are going to push your pack with your eyes open and your mouth shut."

"I'll go first since it's my hole," Caleb said. "But I need to do things a bit differently from what I told ya because of the boom juice I'm wearin'."

Before beginning his crawl, Caleb checked that his vest wasn't loose, and everything was tied and buttoned up where it should be. Having it flap open and strike the rock wall as he crawled along on hands and knees would be a tragedy.

While Caleb prepared, Lucias began igniting the calcium carbide headlamps. He handed one to Caleb, saying, "Just don't go swimming with this."

"Why? What would happen?"

"Too much water too fast could cause the carbide tank to rupture."

"Well, that doesn't sound good. I'll keep it in mind." Caleb carefully attached it to the front of his brown felt hat. Once outfitted, he tied a short piece of rope onto his satchel and gently lowered himself to his knees, then began to crawl through into the darkness, dragging the bag behind.

The distance was not far, and soon, Caleb popped his head into the cavern beyond. Unfortunately, due to his closeness to the ground, there was not much more than water vapour visible at the moment. But that was to be expected since the cavern he recalled had a shifting, vaporous fog that wafted about, making it difficult to see the yawning pits to hell that dotted the cavern floor.

Standing slowly through the ground-level fog, Caleb stared into the cavern beyond with wide-eyed wonder and apprehension. The waterfall's stream next to him flowed from out of boiling pools further inside the cavern, pools which looked very familiar. Through the foggy mist, the cavern floor seemed covered with the familiar rounded stones, just like the ones beneath the Golden Nugget Saloon. But unlike Sinclair's cavern, which had been picked clean of the golden nuggets, this cavern was not, and there was an abundance of rocks with a familiar yellow gleam. He picked up several fine examples and stood, saying, "Well, well, aren't you a lovely lot."

He returned to the small hole out to the world and heard the men calling to him and asking if he was all right.

"More than all right," Caleb called back with a laugh, then chucked the handful of golden nuggets through the hole. Cries of surprise and delight came from the other side as the men discovered the treasure he'd tossed.

Despite his amazement to see this familiar and deadly cavern again, there was something he needed to relay to his compatriots on the other side of the hole. When he'd crawled through, he'd noted how unstable the rock opening had looked. Calling through to the other men, he pointed that out, saying, "Watch yourselves as you come through!"

"Why, what's the matter?" Lucias called.

"These rocks look pretty unstable, so I'd suggest you don't dally on your way through and try not to bump them if you can help it!"

There was a murmur of voices from the other side as the men no doubt discussed the order of entry. After a moment, a bundle of supplies popped through. Caleb grabbed it and pulled it out, and then Jesús scuttled from the hole like a crab.

"Madre de Dios!" the small Spaniard exclaimed as he stood upright. For once, his golden grin paled in comparison to the gold that surrounded him. With numerous nuggets on the floor and veins of precious yellow metal coiling off into the darkness along the closest wall, it was a king's ransom ready for the taking.

More supplies popped out of the entrance hole. Jesús grabbed them, and Lucias came next.

One more to go, Caleb thought, then we'll all be together in this underworld of horrors.

Instead of a bundle of supplies coming through the hole next, it was the cook. He groused and moaned as he clambered from the hole, "Ain't no way I'm bein' a wiggly worm! And how come I don't rate gettin' a light of my own? It just ain't right!"

"Where are your supplies?" Jesús demanded.

"Got them behind me on some rope. Couldn't a pushed it through first, what with the pots and pans, they woulda got stuck on something for sure."

"And you didn't think the same might happen if you went

before them?" Jesús queried.

The cook shook his head slowly and said, "Nope, didn't think a that."

Jesús muttered something in Spanish and pushed the cook aside. He began to reef on the rope in anger and pull the bundle through. The pots and pans clanged and clattered on the rocks for a moment, and then they got stuck.

"Tonto! Why did you do this?"

"Here, let me try," Cookie said. Jesús handed the rope to the cook.

Cookie got close to the hole and squinted into the daylight that shone through the short passage. "I think I see the problem!"

Behind him, Jesús scowled at the back of his cook's head and said, "So can I, so can I."

Cookie called over his shoulder, "One of my consarned fry pans looks to have gotten wedged!" He turned back and muttered, "But I think if I pull the rope this way instead of that way, it should—"

With a grunt of surprise, the cook fell backwards as the rope either snapped or came loose from a poor job of tying. From within the passage came a clang as the wedged pan came free at the same time.

This sudden movement seemed enough to shift some rock already loosened by the passage of the three men since Caleb. Whatever it was, the short rock tunnel crumbled in on itself with a rumbling crash, crushing both their food and cookware and sealing them inside in absolute blackness.

CHAPTER FORTY-TWO

One of the men bitten by a black water beast had passed away during the night. He'd lost most of one leg up to the knee, and his blood loss seemed to have been too great. That had been a particularly hard amputation, and the man had taken several shots of whisky before the procedure. It had helped with the pain but hadn't helped with his blood coagulation since alcohol never did, from Brown's experience. And though he'd sewn the blood vessels shut and cauterised the wound, it had continued to seep, and the man passed overnight.

Fortunately, there was some good news: a couple more victims had become well enough to get back on their feet this morning or at least not need a 'bed' on top of a table in the back corner of the bar anymore.

Sandy's arm was almost as good as new now, and he'd helped the doctor bundle up the man's body. He'd placed it temporarily in the cold storage room in the Nugget's basement until they could bury it. There was no ice to cool the cadavers since the ice house had been ravaged by the fire, and it would be a deep winter before the area saw any more.

Despite the good news with Sandy's arm, the boy seemed somewhat sombre but wouldn't say why. Brown suspected it was due to his new job offer from Sinclair, which was creating some inner turmoil. Whatever the cause, it didn't seem to affect his appetite. After downing enough breakfast for three men, the boy departed with the rest of the volunteers who were going about town cleaning up the mess.

Thinking of Sandy's new, gloomy attitude, the doctor had seen Kitty Welch acting strangely as well. Part of it, he realised, was Caleb's departure weighing on her. The Scotswoman was currently across the room, bathing the forehead of a man who'd suffered several nasty bites to his legs by the razor-sharp mandibles of the ants. For whatever reason, the bites didn't seem to be healing.

In keeping with things not being whole or healed, business was not quite back to normal at the Golden Nugget either, which was understandable. Despite everything that had happened, there had still been a few sourdoughs who'd come down from the hills for their monthly bath and fancy meal, wondering what had happened while they'd been busy digging in the dirt. But otherwise, it was slow since most of the town's population was still busy trying to recover their lives and livelihoods after the catastrophic events of the past little while. Those misplaced because their homes had burned down now had no place to sleep, but thankfully, the United Church had opened its doors and floors to them.

Maggie, along with assistant cook Mike and waiter Ed, had been kept busy feeding the volunteers and had provided a hearty breakfast of bacon and eggs to get them on their way. Cornelius had been tending to patients at the time and, with a shudder, had watched the crowd gobbling down their food, unable to fathom partaking in solid food so early in the morning. But now, with midday approaching, he finally felt his stomach begin to rumble for his noon-hour breakfast.

Cornelius made his way to another man who'd been bitten by a black beast. Like Caleb, he was fortunate and hadn't lost any digits or limbs. Though he'd had some complaints of fever yesterday, it had broken overnight, and he appeared fine this morning. This man was also very familiar with the saloon, but not in the same way as Cornelius, his view usually from the other side.

"How are you today, Muddy?" Brown inquired as he approached the bar.

Despite his bite, over the last couple of days, Muddy Wilson had insisted that he felt well enough to work. He now stood polishing a beer glass behind the bar. At the doctor's inquiry, he set the glass down and massaged his thigh, saying, "Not bad, Doc. It's strange, but yesterday I felt like my insides were burnin' up, and this mornin', I feel hungry like I could eat a horse."

Brown nodded and said, "Well, that is good news. I'm not sure if Maggie has anything with hooves back there, but she must have something tasty to fill you up.

"That'd be great. I suppose I don't need a whole horse. Maybe a whole chicken or two would hit the spot, though."

Brown wondered at the man's hunger. His Irish friend had been having the same increased appetite as well. He would have to keep an eye on this man for the next little while. Not that that would be a problem, thanks to Cornelius's constant patronage at the saloon and current part-time residency. But it made him think that a blood test of some sort would be in order, though he'd be unsure what he'd be looking for once he got it under the microscope at his office. He knew what blood looked like under magnification and could tell if a person was anaemic or had parasitic issues, but that was about it. Still, it would be worthwhile taking a look and was something he wished he'd done with Caleb's blood.

The doctor was yanked from his reverie by a cold feminine voice at his back that could only belong to one person, a voice which said, "Thomas wants to see you."

Cornelius placed his best grimace on his face, one he hoped would pass for a smile, and turned to Angeline. "See me, dear lady? Well, as much as I'd like to, I'm quite busy making my rounds, and I'm up to my elbows in patients at the moment. Can't it wait?"

"You won't find any patients here at the bar, Doctor Brown. And Mr. Sinclair waits for no one." Angeline's hazel eyes seemed to probe inside Cornelius's brain for a moment before she turned briefly away and called out, "Kitty, come here!"

Kitty Welch made her way to where they stood, her face troubled, most likely because she had to deal with Angeline again. "Yes, ma'am?"

"I'll need you to keep an eye on all the patients for a few minutes while the doctor has a conference with Mr. Sinclair."

Kitty nodded, and Angeline moved off toward Sinclair's office, presumably expecting Cornelius to be in subservient pursuit.

Brown looked to Kitty and asked, "Are you going to be okay, young lady?"

Kitty nodded and said, "As right as I can be, I suppose. I'm just worried about Caleb on top of everything else happenin'."

Cornelius was about to ask Kitty what else was happening since this was the most vocal the girl had been all morning. But he didn't get the chance since Angeline called quite harshly from the office corridor, "Doctor Brown! If you please!"

Brown gave Kitty a gentle pat on the shoulder and a small smile, one hopefully better than the grimace he'd supplied Angeline. He called out, "Be right with you!" From the side of his mouth, he said quietly to Kitty, "Reluctantly."

Kitty smiled slightly. Just seeing a little bit of that positive emotion break the girl's dour expression made Cornelius feel somewhat better as he marched off to whatever fate Thomas Sinclair now had in store for him.

CHAPTER FORTY-THREE

"Now what are we supposed to do for food? And how are we gonna get out of here?" Cookie wailed.

"There's plenty of fish, amongst other things, in the lake further back," Caleb replied. This was true; it was just a matter of catching them without getting eaten by the other things that swam in the midnight lake.

"We can always blast our way out. I still have my dynamite," Jesús said dismissively.

"And I, my nitro," Caleb added, lightly placing a finger on the vest where he carried his boom juice. He was feeling the warmth of the cavern now, the leather garment not breathing too well. However, he didn't want to loosen it and have the vials start jiggling against his body as he made his way across the cavern's treacherous terrain.

Lucias adjusted the drip of water onto the sodium carbide in his lamp, and its beam grew brighter. He looked about the cavern and said, "Lots of mist around here, too."

"Aye, and you'd best watch your step in this cavern and others nearby since some mighty deep holes are hidin' in that mist."

Jesús ignored the conversation, busy picking up gold nugget after gold nugget and stuffing them in his pockets. "I cannot believe the riches in here! This is going to fund the gang for many decades to come!" The Spaniard grinned broadly as he stood and placed another few nuggets in his bulging pockets.

"You'd best take care," Lucias said. Looking to Jesús's trouser pockets, he cautioned, "You wouldn't want that added weight to affect you adversely in an emergency."

"And there's plenty of things in these caverns that are great at creatin' those," Caleb said, brightening his carbide lamp as he spoke. He scanned the environment, looking for any spiders, centipedes or ants in the immediate vicinity. Fortunately, from what he could see through the swirling mists, the ground was clear of anything slithering or scuttling for the moment.

"So, what do we do now?" Cookie asked.

Without saying anything, Caleb began moving further into the cavern, a specific goal suddenly springing to mind.

"Where are you going, Mister Caleb?" Jesús inquired as he trailed along behind.

"I figured we might well make use of what's already down here."

Caleb had arrived at a familiar spot and looked with a pain-filled wince at the short length of rope still coiled on the ground next to where he'd regained consciousness. Close by was his bundle of goodies that he'd lowered into the cavern before beginning his descent. It all felt like it had happened decades ago in light of everything that had occurred so far.

The bundle contained some food, mostly jerky and

possibly a few random sugar cubes that may have gotten out of the paper sack he'd been carrying for Emily. He generally travelled light and relied on his hunting and fishing ability when he was on the move, something he hadn't needed so much since he'd come to Canada. But on the way up, he'd hunted and cooked his fair share of creatures from the tip of South America well into the Southern US. And the most surprising thing he'd found was how many of them tasted like chicken, even some of the more disgusting-looking things he'd found under a rock when he was really desperate for food.

"This is what's left of my base camp," Caleb said as he went through the bundle of things, looking for anything he might need. Several rocks looked to have fallen down from the chimney in the earthquake, and he wondered if that route was also blocked.

"Not much of a camp," Cookie observed. "Where'd ya do your cookin'?"

Caleb shook his head. "I didn't get a chance to do much of anything. I'd been plannin' on comin' back here that first day, but then some of those giant buggerin' ants changed my plans right quick."

After some short discussion, it was decided to leave some supplies here and make it the official camp for the expedition's first few days.

With great caution, they began navigating the section of the cavern containing the bottomless tubes scattered invisibly on the foggy floor. "Watch your step here, my lads. Spots in this floor have an awful long drop." He paused and picked up a handful of gold nuggets, then flung them into the black abyss of the closest hole.

"What're ya doin'!" Cookie called. He reflexively grabbed for the nuggets and began to lose his balance at the edge of the hole. Suddenly, he was pinwheeling his arms, and gravity seemed about to do its job.

Lucias reached out one long arm, his unbandaged hand snagging the man's belt at the last moment, and he reeled him back to safety.

In a shaky voice, Cookie said, "Much obliged, mister."

Jesús removed his bowler hat and swatted Cookie with it. "What are you doing? You imbecile! There is more than enough here that we need not worry about a few small nuggets!"

Cookie held an arm up to stop the bowler battery being inflicted upon his person and said, "It was just a reflex seeing good money bein' thrown away!"

"Well, you're goin' ta need better reflexes than that in here," Caleb said, then added, "And you may or may not have noticed somethin' else in all the excitement."

"And that is?" Lucias asked.

Caleb looked down into the hole, his lamp illuminating the first couple of dozen yards, and then darkness swallowed the light. "None of those pretty little stones have made any sound of hittin' bottom as of yet."

Nodding, Jesús said, "I did notice that." He grinned and added, "This would make a wonderful place to dispose of uncooperative people."

"Aye, that it would," Caleb said. He made a mental note to keep a good distance between himself and the small Spaniard, especially near any precipices. He was sure Lucias must be thinking the same thing as he without needing it pointed out, or at least Caleb hoped so.

Despite what the man in black did for a living, Caleb had

come to respect his no-nonsense attitude and his helpful intervention with the ants and water beasts over the past few days. Though not a friend, he found Lucias was at least a man of his word. And thanks to their recent conversation, he hoped the man would stick by his promise to let him disappear with Kitty and a mule-load of gold, after he got another mule that was.

A pang of loss and guilt came over Caleb as he thought of his four-legged rambling companion. Emily had been better company than many men he'd had the displeasure of travelling with over the years and had gone most places he'd led her without complaint.

Now at the back of the cavern, Caleb paused, the group of men behind him doing the same. They were at a spot he'd been dreading a return to, where he'd first discovered what horrors this cavern contained, at least regarding its wildlife.

"What is it?" Lucias queried.

"I'd suggest you all keep your wits about you, gentlemen. Keep checkin' not only the floors and walls but the roof up there somewhere as well. As Caleb spoke, he'd turned his head this way and that, his sodium vapour light cutting through the darkness before them, its brilliant light casting capering shadows all around.

"Can I ask why?" Cookie wondered.

With a pinched expression, Caleb replied, "We're about to enter the land of the spiders."

CHAPTER FORTY-FOUR

"Have another drink, doctor," Thomas Sinclair offered. He pushed the crystal decanter toward Cornelius with a slight smirk playing at the corners of his lips.

Whether it was contempt or pity, Brown didn't know and didn't care. He only cared about the offer of free booze. The day looked to be less eventful than the last several, and he felt he could have an extra shot or two this morning before lunch in celebration of all of his hard work over the last few days. He'd been forced to remain mostly sober since he'd been so busy, he hadn't had a chance to drink to excess as he usually did. But now, with a quieter day, he figured he could let loose a little.

Nodding appreciatively, Brown said, "Well, it's been a long morning, and things are looking a little better out there in the temporary ward next to the bar. And it must be four o'clock somewhere..."

"That's the spirit, Doctor! Enjoy yourself, you've earned it."

Angeline perched on the edge of the settee across from Thomas, saying nothing for the moment but watching everything with keen interest.

"Don't mind if I do", Brown said.

That smile played across Thomas's lips again as he watched Cornelius pour several fingers of the scotch into his crystal tumbler. Brown took a sizeable sip, enjoying the burn as the alcohol ran down his throat after so many days without. With a slight "Ah" of satisfaction, he asked, "And what can I do for you today, Mr. Sinclair."

"Thomas is fine. After all, I should be on a first-name basis with my new personal physician."

Brown had been sipping some more of his drink and almost spit some of it across the desk, but fortunately, his mouth's grasp on good whisky was a strong one, and it all remained inside. He swallowed, feeling the alcohol sear its way down like never before, as if it were burning through his belly and all the way down to hell. He placed his tumbler on the cork coaster Sinclair had slid across the desk and cleared his throat. "I'm sorry? Your personal doctor, you say?"

"Aye, that's correct."

"But I thought I was only being blackmailed to help find the gold mine! And with that now underway, I figured our deal was done."

"Done, doctor?" Sinclair shook his head and said, "Nay, we've hardly gotten started."

"What do you mean?"

"Some may speak negatively of your enjoyment of alcohol, but I also tip back my elbow on occasion. And I've seen your ingenuity during the crises that have arisen around our wee town over the last little while. Despite your drinkin', it seems ya can handle your booze almost as well as I."

"Just trying to steady my hand as I do my part to keep the

public health as any good doctor would."

"Aye, but we both know you're not a doctor, of humans at least. But don't take that as a slight against ya, Doctor Brown. I think your experience with animals has been of benefit with regard to our cleanin' up some of that mess that Mr. Cantrill brought down the mountain with him."

"Thank you for noticing, and I believe you're correct." It was a backhanded compliment from Sinclair, to be sure, since the man still felt the need to state that he was not a 'real' doctor aloud once again. Perhaps it was his way of establishing he was still in control, which seemed most likely. Brown took another swallow of scotch, and Sinclair continued.

"And thanks to your ingenuity, I'm goin' to send ya on a little holiday as a reward."

"A holiday?" Cornelius wondered, almost choking on his whisky again. Going on holiday wasn't something he particularly wanted to do. That was what a person took to get away from things. He was already 'getting away from things' at the moment, on this, his permanent vacation here in the West Kootenays of British Columbia, Canada. In fact, in order to have a holiday, he didn't need to go anywhere except to the bar in the saloon outside the office door at his back.

"Aye, but it's a workin' holiday, however."

That was more like it, Cornelius thought. There's always a catch.

Before he could respond, Angeline broke her silence and, as if reading his mind, added, "And don't worry, it's nowhere near Vancouver."

"But why would you need me to go with you on vacation?"

"What I need is your brains, at least what's left of them, to go along with the brawn and the beauty that I already have," Sinclair said cryptically.

"I beg your pardon?" The small, round Scotsman was many things, but brawny and beautiful were not two of them.

"I wouldn't be goin' with ya." Sinclair stood and moved to a glass cabinet in the corner. He returned with a black box moments later and placed it on the desk. It looked to be ebony, with pearl inlays around the edges. Cornelius's eyes widened as he looked more closely. The box didn't have pearl trim after all; he could see that now. Squinting slightly as he looked closer, he said, "Are those..."

"Aye, doctor. Those are human teeth, as far as we know."

"Where in heaven's name did you get that?"

"Oh, I doubt heaven has much to do with any of this." Sinclair opened the box and showed Brown what lay within its velveteen folds. "These are what you're goin' ta look for."

"What are they?" Cornelius peered in awe at the contents of the box. A half dozen black gemstones rested inside, but it looked to have room for over a hundred or more.

"The obsidian stones are power. But I don't know how to harness it yet. And what needs to go inside this box is more of these stones."

And what would happen when they filled those empty spots, Cornelius wondered. He knew Sinclair's interest in electricity and had heard talk of a proposed electrical dam on the local river. But he'd never heard of power coming from stones. He had to admit, this piqued his curiosity, and as a practitioner of medicine and a would-be scientist, he was quite interested to know more. "Power, you say? From those jewels?"

"Aye. These six, plus three in that display case across the room, which I have collected over the past decade. I had initially had three others and was having them examined by an associate of mine back in Scotland when they were stolen."

"Stolen, you say?"

"Aye. And the young lady responsible for that is one of the people you will be goin' on your little vacation with, Miss Kitty Welch. Together, you will help track them down."

"But how long will this be for? I have a practice to keep, you know."

"As long as it takes, Doctor Brown. Miss Welch is the only lead I have on those stones, so I am sending her to try and track them down. I believe she is drawn to these due to her contact with the original three. And it drew her halfway around the world to here." Sinclair had noticed Brown's stare at the black box and added, "Go ahead, doctor, touch the box if you wish."

Cornelius reached out to tentatively touch the ebony box but hesitated when his fingers were close. Cold seemed to emanate from its surface, so intense he felt as if he'd get frostbite if he made contact. Whatever the power these stones possessed, he realised, it was not a power of light, warmth and good; that was for certain. "It's like it's been stored in ice. How could you handle touching it just now?"

"After you've been around it a while, the effect doesn't seem as strong."

"You become inured against it somewhat?"

"Somewhat. The cold is tolerable since the aura the stones and this box exude is irresistible."

"But how were you initially drawn to them?"

"He wasn't," said Angeline's at Cornelius's back. He almost sloshed his drink, forgetting the woman was in the room, so taken as he was by the ebony box. She'd moved from her perch on the settee and now crossed the room to Thomas, putting her hand on the back of his chair when she arrived.

"You, dear lady?"

"Yes, me," Angeline replied but would say nothing more on the subject.

Brown looked to Sinclair and asked, "And what do you want me to do exactly on this little gem hunt?"

"You're goin' to oversee things for me. With your medical background and obvious brains, you're goin' to be a valuable asset to the Sinclair Corporation. You'll have Kitty Welch guidin' ya like I said. She knows where the stones last were and who to contact to discover their whereabouts, if she can find the man. And that's where you'll come in handy as well; you can help her deduce his location to try and find out what he did with them. You'll also have someone along to help you persuade anyone unwilling to assist your little enterprise. Because those stones are mine, and I want them back."

"And what Thomas wants, Thomas gets," Angeline finished.

"Your takin' up practice in this town wasn't a coincidence, doctor, not after everything that's happened here over the last little while. You, Kitty, and Caleb were all drawn to this area for a reason. In fact, we all were."

Nodding, Angeline replied, "Wherever we've found these stones, we have found wealth, power, and people as well. Some were called by the stones themselves, but others felt it seemed like a place they needed to be for whatever reason."

"Aye," Thomas agreed. "Now that you have an idea of what we're talkin' about let me tell you the rest of your duties."

For the next several minutes, Sinclair explained more of Brown's obligations as the new Sinclair Corporation physician, along with further details of his upcoming trip. He finished by telling the doctor to begin the process of closing down his practice since he would be gone for many months.

Brown stood, feeling slightly wobbly, and it wasn't just from the two tumblers of alcohol he'd recently consumed. As he wandered back out into the saloon, he wondered what was going to become of him and Kitty and who the persuader was that would accompany them. He presumed it might be Lucias. Well, whoever it was, together, they would be seeing some of the world, whether they wanted to or not.

CHAPTER FORTY-FIVE

Fragments of lamp glass lay scattered on the cavern floor near three diverging tube-like tunnels. The glass was in front of the smaller of the three, located in the middle, the one Caleb had thought of as more of a nook, which, in reality, had turned out to be a lair.

"Have your handguns ready, lads," Caleb advised. He nodded his chin toward the waist-high hole and said, "That's where that eight-legged freak first attacked me. And I don't know if it was the same one that came down the waterfall with me or if that was its cousin. Either way, be on your guard."

"You heard the man," Lucias said, drawing his Colt and cocking it in one smooth motion. Though shooting left-handed now from his injury, he had two guns; the one holstered on his right side faced backwards so he could draw it easily once his left-hand weapon was spent.

Jesús extracted his sidearm and readied it, saying, "Those things are as ugly as they are fast."

Cookie edged back into the darkness slightly at the mention of spiders. He was the only one of the group to have a kerosene lantern since the calcium carbide lights were limited to three, and the cook was at the bottom of the illumination totem pole. As well, he was the only one weaponless.

Keeping well back from the nook-sized hole, Caleb crouched and shone his headlamp into its depths. There was no movement he could see, and the newer, high-intensity lamp seemed to be paying its way since he saw all the webs in the back of the tube quite clearly. More of the ubiquitous gold swirled through the walls of this smaller tunnel, just like the rest of the cavern, but of the spider, whether singular or plural, there was none. But where was the beast then, Caleb wondered.

"Seems empty at the moment," Lucias observed as he crouched next to Caleb. "More gold, though. Seems to be a whole lot of it up here, like you said."

"More than enough for everybody," Caleb replied.

"Did you hear that, Oritz?" Lucias asked.

In a grin so broad it threatened to outshine the cavern walls, Jesús said, "Yes, more than enough." He seemed to have a faraway look in his eyes as if a part of his mind were elsewhere, perhaps planning something treacherous for the group or perhaps simply how many whores he could afford with his share of the gold.

"We have a couple of choices now," Caleb said as he stood.

"And they are?" Lucias asked, standing as well, and dusting off his black boots with one hand.

"Well, if we go to the left, we'll end up at that cavern I told you about, with the lake, the black beasties, and the ants. It might be clear now, what with that huge wash of water when that rock wall collapsed."

"What caused that anyway?" Lucias asked.

"I tried doin' some exterminatin' with my boom juice. And as I was fightin' for my life, the wall of rock collapsed into the lake and flushed me and everything else out of the cavern."

"That'd do it," Cookie said.

"And if we go to the right?" Jesús inquired.

"I don't know, I've never been that way. Might be more gold, hard to say."

"And you say the caverns on the way to the lake all have gold?" Lucias asked.

With a nod, Caleb said, "Pretty much."

"And critters as well, I'll wager," Cookie said.

"Them, too," Caleb agreed.

Tilting his head to the rightmost tunnel, Jesús said, "Then perhaps we should find out?"

"Lead the way," Caleb said, gesturing toward the unexplored tunnel.

Giving Cookie a slight shove from behind, Jesús said to his henchman, "You heard the man."

"Me? But what if there're more critters down that way?" Cookie asked, his voice rising shrilly. "I ain't got no weapons!"

"We will defend you from behind," Jesús said in a cold, flat voice, a grin no longer on his face. "Do you have a problem with that?"

Shaking his head and moving into the tunnel on the right, Cookie held his lantern high and said, "Nope, I suppose I don't, and it wouldn't matter if I did."

***

The corridor sloped downward for several hundred yards, its walls dotted with the odd whorl of gold, but Caleb noted it was nothing as significant as he'd found in the tunnels on the way to the lake-filled cavern. After another short distance, the tube levelled out as it opened into another cavern. This, too, had ground mist like the first cavern and no doubt more vertical tubes of doom. "Keep an eye out!" Caleb called. "There's bound to be more black holes in the floor of this cavern, too."

Squinting into the expansive darkness, his lamp doing little good, Lucias observed, "The whole place is like Swiss cheese."

"I wish it were. Then we'd only have to worry about mice," Caleb replied as he moved along next to Lucias. As the cavern widened, the men had spaced themselves accordingly as they'd moved. Cookie was on the right, with Jesús separated from him by several yards, then it was Lucias and Caleb on the far left.

"This is one large hole in the ground," Lucias said, shaking his head at the cavern's size as they moved into its vastness. The ground fog seemed thicker here than near the main entrance. The ceiling was also higher, so high, in fact, the stalactites, which had been visible using their headlamps in the previous caverns, were now nowhere in sight.

They moved cautiously across the mist-covered floor toward a wall barely visible on the left. Caleb meant to move clockwise around the cavern until they found another exit. Patches of what seemed to be moss covered the ground in numerous places, like little islands amongst a sea of bare rock.

"What's that?" Cookie wondered. He toed at something in the moss and knocked it out into the open, and it rolled a couple of feet before stopping. It was about the size of a moderate-sized rat, but a rodent it most certainly was not. Pale and squirming slightly, it almost seemed an oversized aphid, albeit a bloated one and legless to boot. Cookie held his lamp closer and saw numerous other pale, squirming creatures in the patch of moss and all the moss in which he cared to look.

"I wonder if I could fry it up?" Using a spatula that hung off his belt at all times, the cook poked at the creature with its tip, and the pale beast wriggled pathetically, but that was all.

Looking at the moss, Caleb thought suddenly of the underwater lichen he'd seen in the lake and wondered if this were related to it somehow. He stopped the water's feed to the calcium carbide lamp on his hat, then turned off the gas. His lamp's flame gradually diminished and went out, and he said, "Douse your lights, boys!"

"What?" Cookie said.

"For what purpose?" Jesús wondered.

Lucias looked to the darkness around them and then to Caleb and asked, "You sure?"

With a nod, Caleb said, "Aye, I need to check on somethin'."

Grumbling, Cookie complied, as did Jesús and Lucias.

As Lucias's light sputtered to darkness, for a moment, Caleb thought he was wrong, but after a few seconds, his vision adjusted, and he was relieved to see that he'd been quite right after all.

"I don't understand what this is about, Mister..." Jesús trailed off and amended his statement, saying, "Oh! I see now what you were wondering about!"

Cookie said, "What're ya talkin' about? I don't s—" He stopped in midsentence, looked toward the grubs in the moss and finished saying, "Well, I'll be! These little buggers glow in the dark, and so does this moss!"

Whatever was in the moss seemed to make the creatures that ate it glow as well. The aphid-grubs squirmed and squiggled in and around the moss, seeming to give the luminescent plant matter a life of its own.

Thinking of life below ground in these caverns of horrors, Caleb pondered what also lived around here that might eat these pale, disgusting creatures. Ants sprang to mind once more, but not the ones from these caverns. On his travels in South America, he'd seen colonies of ants that kept aphids as a food source and milked the little things like cows for their nectar. Was there something here that did the same?

The men relit their lamps and scanned about the cavern, their lights flashing back and forth and cutting through the darkness as they continued toward the cavern wall. They were now close enough to see the texture of the rock face. Caleb was looking toward this wall when something flew past his head, giving him a start and making him duck slightly. "What in blue blazes was that?"

"What're talking about? Where?" Lucias asked, turning his head this way and that.

"There!" Jesús exclaimed as something zoomed past his lamp's beam. As they grew closer to the far wall of the cavern, there seemed to be more and more of whatever the flying creatures were.

"Bats!" Cookie cried.

"No, not bats," Caleb said, swiping at another winged creature that shot past his light's limited view of the world.

What in the hell were they, he wondered.

Suddenly, one of the winged creatures lighted upon an aphid-grub and the men were able to see it in its full glory. Not a bat or bird, but rather, "A moth!" Cookie exclaimed. Well over two handspans wide, it was a sight to behold.

"What?" Jesús moved closer to the creature for a better look. As he did, another landed nearby and settled on one of the grubs. At this point, the men saw things for what they were—the moss fed the grubs, and the grubs fed the moths.

A small tube with a wicked-looking hook on the end extended from the moth's mouth. It pierced the grub's semi-translucent skin, and the moth began greedily sucking the vital fluids from the creature. These giant moths gorged themselves on the plenitude of juicy grubs that squiggled and squirmed in the glowing moss, acting as vampire bats like Caleb had seen in South America. And in fact, if they were to douse their lights, he was almost certain they would see these winged horrors glow as well.

"Well, at least they don't seem to find us as appealing as these grubs," Lucias observed.

As those words left the gunslinger's mouth, one of the giant moths fluttered over to Cookie and landed on the small of his back between his shoulders. He gave a startled, "What the heck!" and tried to sweep the creature from his shoulders but couldn't quite reach.

"It seems to like you," Caleb said.

"Yeah," Cookie chuckled slightly, saying, "I guess I'm like a candle. I attract 'em!"

Caleb thought about that. Cookie's lantern had a yellow cast, while their calcium carbide headlamps gave off more of a white light. Another moth soon landed on Cookie's arm that held the lamp. And he giggled slightly at the feel of both creatures padding around on his back and forearm. He marvelled at the size of the one on his forearm and said, "Lookit the backs of these things!"

That was what Caleb was already doing. The moths had a circular pattern on their backs with two smaller black circles inside the larger one, making it look for all the world like the eyes in a skull—a death's skull. He was about to warn Cookie that, from his experience, everything in these caverns seemed to have only one thing in mind, and that was to eat you.

But before he could do so, Cookie suddenly shrieked and reached over his shoulder with his free hand to swat at the moth on his back again, and this time, it fluttered away. "Darn thing nipped me!" he said, alarm growing in his voice.

As he spoke, the creature on his forearm wrapped its wings around his limb. There was a faint clicking sound as its chitinous proboscis unfurled, and then the hooked tip pierced deeply into Cookie's flesh. He shrieked again, this time much more loudly.

As the creature dug in, Cookie released his grasp from the lantern's handle, and it shattered on the cavern floor, coating the moss and grubs in flammable oil. With a 'whup', the fuel ignited. Hissing and popping, the aphid-grubs wriggled and spasmed, giving off a sickly-sweet odour as they cooked in the heat of the kerosene's fire.

Cookie wrenched the moth from his arm, and it fluttered, wounded, to the ground. "Consarned thing bit me!" He raised his foot to stamp on the creature.

Caleb saw this at the last moment, his introductory experience with the ants coming back to haunt him, and he called, "Wait! Don't kill it!"

But it was too late. Cookie stomped on the fluttering,

injured moth, and it let out a squealing hiss of pain as he ground its guts into the floor. "Bite me, will ya?" He stomped on it again and again.

The flickering light of the burning oil spread across the mossy floor and continued to brighten the cavern around them, further exposing the horrors it contained. The wall they had been approaching suddenly rippled, like wind catching a ship's sail or a wave washing across a beach.

Except there was no wind or water. The movement was from the colony of monstrous moths that clung to the cavern wall. Hundreds, upon hundreds, of the grub-sucking, now blood-sucking creatures fluttered their wings in agitation, their grey and brown mottling helping them blend with the rock face as they rested there.

But now, the creatures were no longer resting, and it seemed an alarm or threat response had been triggered throughout the colony. As one, they peeled away from the wall in a massive wave, fluttering here, there, and everywhere as they sought to discover what had happened to one of their own.

"We need to move now!" Caleb cried as he turned and began to hustle as smoothly as he could back the way they'd come.

Perhaps it was the blood that dripped from Cookie's arm, or maybe it was the adrenaline that coursed through his body from the response to the injury. Whatever the attraction, the fluttering creatures seemed drawn to Cookie as moths to a flame.

As the other men rushed back toward the subcavern's entrance, several more moths lighted on the cook as he ran, and he began to scream even louder. However, it was somewhat muffled by the dozen or so winged creatures already on him and fluttering around preparing to land.

Caleb felt a moth settle on his shoulder but was able to knock it gently away before it could bite him. Lucias and Jesús were also swatting the moths as they ran. It seemed the creatures were suddenly unparticular about which of them they landed upon.

The gunslinger had tried shooting at several moths and hit them without issue. However, there were so many that it was overwhelming, and he just gave up and ran, breezing by Caleb and Jesús as he did.

Shrieking like a banshee, Cookie caught up to the group of men with surprising speed. He was covered in moths from head to toe, all seeking to sample whatever made his blood so special. Something about him attracted the winged monsters, possibly his sweat or the stench of his fear. Cookie was something new and exciting they'd never encountered before and something of which they wanted more.

The cook was unable to see where he was going and, in his panic, ran blindly. In this cavern, it was a deadly mistake.

As they neared the entrance, Cookie veered off to one side, and unfortunately, this side contained a lava tube—one that was vertical rather than horizontal. Another shriek escaped the cook, but this one was not pain. This was a scream of surprise as he found himself suddenly hurtling into the black depths of the tube. His scream faded quickly as he fell, but it didn't end in a thump or a thud as he hit bottom since there seemed no bottom to hit. Instead, his scream continued growing fainter and fainter as he plummeted into the abysmal void.

CHAPTER FORTY-SIX

Moving to the exit as swiftly as he could, Caleb swatted at the moths as he went but did so carefully due to his explosive-filled vest. He had to run smoothly and evenly and couldn't jiggle as he ran.

Lucias and Jesús had no such restrictions, and they made it to the exit well ahead of Caleb, moving as if their britches were on fire.

From his vest, Caleb pulled the half-empty vial of nitroglycerine he'd used to put the front door into the cavern. This was another door and one they needed to close quickly. Uttering a silent prayer to Mother Mary, he lobbed the vial underhand toward the edge of the tube, just where it widened into the cavern.

When the nitro hit, he was already moving in the other direction. If he were caught in the blast, it would knock him over, and it would be game over. There was a bend in the tube close at hand, and as the explosion shook the cavern, a gust of hot air pushed at Caleb's back as he moved around the corner. Thankfully, he was able to keep his footing and continued to move swiftly forward, hoping the whole time he didn't trip.

Back at the junction, the other two men stood before the

small nook, panting slightly after their narrow escape, and waiting to see if Caleb had also made it.

As Caleb hurried around the corner, Lucias said with a nod, "Glad you're still in one piece."

"Me, too. Thanks," Caleb replied. He brushed the remnants of the explosion from his shirtsleeves, then gently swiped his hands down his pant legs to remove the last of the dust. Resisting an urge to sneeze, he looked to Jesús and shook his head instead. "I'm sorry about your friend."

Jesús shrugged. "It was no great loss, but it is unfortunate he took our cooking supplies with him when he went."

When he went? Caleb wondered at that expression, taken aback at the Spaniard's lack of compassion regarding the death of the last of his gang. Oritz made it sound like his cook had decided to take a quick vacation rather than plummeting to his death down a bottomless hole. From his own admission, Jesús had arrived with a dozen men in his charge, and now, all had died in the pursuit of Caleb and the gold sovereigns. Though many of those men had not been upstanding paragons of virtue, and many were robbers like himself, they didn't need to die as they had.

The weight of the deaths of so many men, innocent or not, was a burden on Caleb's shoulders and upon his very soul. And that wasn't even taking into account the deaths of Hildey Dugrodt, Ezra Randall, Farley Jones, Melinda Vicker and at least a score more who had died during the battle for the town. And who knew how many more yet to be found? All had died because of his finding this cavern. Now more than ever, he well and truly believed this was a cursed cavern and that nothing good would ever come to anyone who found it or its gold.

Lucias said nothing at Oritz's callous comment, but the look in his eyes spoke volumes. He pulled out his gleaming

Colt, and at first, Caleb thought the gunslinger was going to use it on Jesús, but instead, he popped the chamber open and removed four spent cartridges, then replaced them with ammo from his gun belt. He looked up to the other men as he snapped the chamber closed and said, "Well, I guess that's our official welcome to this underground hell."

"It can only get better from here," Jesús suggested, one hand caressing the gold that swirled off into the largest of the tunnels on the left.

"I wouldn't hold your breath, but you keep thinkin' those happy thoughts," Caleb replied with a shake of his head.

Jesús grinned and said, "I am already thinking happy thoughts about the amount of gold we will take out of this cave system."

"If it'll let you," Caleb added.

"What do you mean?" Lucias asked.

"These caverns are cursed. At least I think so, judgin' from the monstrous blight that's come out of the place."

"Be that as it may," Lucias said, checking his Winchester as he spoke, "We have a job to do here."

"Aye, you're right. Well, I guess the rest of the grand tour is in order then," Caleb said as he moved past Jesús and into the large tube.

They negotiated their way carefully through the next cavern containing the plethora of boulders that blocked direct access from one side to the other. Once through, they arrived at the low lip of rock left behind when Caleb had blown the beautiful blockage and discovered his centipede welcoming committee.

Fortunately, no more multi-legged monsters were waiting for them in the darkness on the other side. The remains of the bug roast crackled and crunched underfoot as they stepped over, and Caleb couldn't help but shudder at the sound. It didn't appear to have been disturbed by anything else moving about in the cavern, at least from what he could see at this point. Of course, that didn't mean there wasn't something else even more deadly around the next corner.

Soon, and surprisingly without incident, they stepped through the misty entrance into the lake-filled cavern. On their way through the final tunnel, they'd still seen no further sign of any spiders, and Caleb hoped it had indeed been washed away in the tsunami.

For the next few moments, they stood marvelling at the cavern and size of the lake. The water gently rolled against the soft sand covering the shore, and it was quite serene.

Since they were a safe distance from the water, Caleb reached for his headlamp once again and said, "Douse your lights."

"What? More moss?" Lucias wondered.

Caleb shook his head and said, "No. Trust me, this is worth it."

The men did as instructed, and the cavern plunged to near blackness. However, after a moment, their eyes adjusted, and the group stood gazing in wonder upon the glowing lake. Caleb felt the same awe and astonishment he had experienced upon his first introduction to the body of water. The lichen continued to glow softly along the sides of the steep shore, then faded away as the lake descended into limitless depths.

"We just need a rod and some line," Lucias said as he watched the plethora of colourful aquatic life that glowed and pulsed in the crystalline water.

"No, this is always quicker for fishing." Jesús pulled out a stick of dynamite from his jacket pocket and moved toward the shore. Caleb thought the man was going to try a little explosive angling right then and there. But when he arrived at the water, the Spaniard said, "Judging by our last adventure, we might want to keep this handy," then stuffed the stick back into his jacket.

For a moment, Caleb was tempted to forget to tell Jesús what else swam in the lake alongside the glowing, colourful fish. But since he wasn't a complete bastard, he said, "You might want to not get too close to that water."

"Why not?" Jesús had planted his hands on his knees and now gazed into the depths of the pellucid lake.

Caleb was about to mention the obsidian beasts when his introduction suddenly became unnecessary.

Up from the depths came one of the creatures in question as if summoned merely by the power of his thoughts. It splashed to the surface a couple of feet from Oritz, and he stepped back rapidly, stumbling and landing on his bottom.

"That's why not," Caleb said quietly.

The black beast swam back and forth near the shore, perhaps sensing Caleb since he seemed to have some strange bond with the monsters now. Thankfully, the slight slope from the lake was enough to keep the black thing in the water, and it didn't attempt to crawl out as the beasts had done down in town.

"Your black friend seems eager to greet us," Oritz observed.

Lucias said, "I think you mean eager to eat us."

"That's a bit more accurate," Caleb said. He struck a match and relit his headlamp, then peered about, his light cutting into the darkness. The beach ran a short distance to the right and dwindled away, replaced by more rock face, the body of water disappearing beyond into shadow. To the left, the beach met the cavern wall barely visible in their headlamp's beams. If they went that way, they would wind up on the small ledge that had allowed access to the ants' kingdom.

Caleb could hear the faint hiss of the waterfall in the distance and wondered again if the tsunami had actually washed all the ants from the cavern. If it had, then they could explore further in that direction. With their exit possibly blocked for good near the front entrance, he thought again of the airflow he'd felt from the small tunnel tube where he'd first encountered the glittering diamond-like eyes of the ants. If those red devils were no longer squatting in the tunnel, perhaps they could find another exit leading them out of this cavernous hell hole.

With that in mind, Caleb said, "There's more to the cavern, but we need to go for a bit of a stroll along the water." He was keen to see the result of his last explosive exit from this cavern. Perhaps the collapsing rock wall had revealed a way out through the ice?

A short while later, Caleb ventured once more onto the narrow ledge. Lucias was behind him, and Jesús was at the back of the line. Moving slowly, Caleb saw they had a companion. The single black beast followed them silently, slithering along in the water and keeping pace since introducing itself to Jesús back at the beach.

"Go away, ya buggerin' thing!"

The obsidian creature didn't seem to hear Caleb's request and continued to track them.

The ledge narrowed precariously as it came to a small

outcropping in the stone wall. Caleb paused momentarily, saying, "Sweet mother of Sundays, that was a lot of rock." The spot where he'd tossed his knapsack with the last of the nitroglycerine at the pursuing ants had done a very impressive job.

Blue-white ice shone in Caleb's headlamp like fine Italian marble. The rock face the glacier had been scraping along was now gone, and the massive body of ice lay exposed to the world, perhaps for the first time in millennia.

Moving carefully, Caleb noted several dark shapes further back in the ice, which were hard to discern, his lamp's light distorting their shape. Whatever they were, they seemed more than just rocks and looked much larger than the other detritus from the glacier.

The ledge was much narrower along this section due to the explosion, and Caleb had to watch his footing. He called back over his shoulder, "Watch your step here, lads! She gets a bit narrow."

"Yeah, you ain't just whistling Dixie," Lucias said, coming around the corner behind Caleb.

Now past the narrowest part of the ledge, Caleb arrived at a wider section and breathed a sigh of relief. About to turn and check on the progress of the other men, at his back came a brief shout of surprise and a splash as someone fell into the deadly water.

CHAPTER FORTY-SEVEN

The dark water churned in the light from Caleb's headlamp as he rushed back along the ledge. Jesús stood there looking suspiciously unconcerned that Lucias was now in the water.

"What happened?" Caleb cried as he grew closer.

"He was just ahead of me, and his foot slipped," Oritz explained as he looked at the water.

Lucias was swimming back toward the ledge as quickly as he could. Surprisingly and fortunately, the black beast was nowhere to be seen. Perhaps it had gone in search of easier prey in the sizeable lake.

"Well, help him outta there!" Caleb said. He wondered at the claim Oritz had made. Lucias's foot had slipped, had it? It was hard to imagine the man in black being careless, and he wondered exactly how much assistance Jesús had given the gunslinger into the water.

Oritz leaned forward slightly but looked unable or unwilling to help. The ledge was so narrow where he stood that if he bent any further, he would have risked falling in himself.

Caleb remembered his fall into this lake when the explosion had blown him from this very ledge. How had Lucias gotten so far away from it, Caleb wondered, unless he'd been pushed. He knew Oritz had been close behind the gunslinger, and he wouldn't put it past the Spaniard to have done precisely what he assumed he had done.

All at once, Caleb recalled he still had the short section of rope he'd salvaged from where he'd fallen into the cavern. He'd gathered it up when he'd collected items from his bundle and was now glad he had. Pulling the rope from the belt loop of his dungarees, he lashed it out toward the gunman, saying, "Grab hold of this, Lucias!"

"Son of a bitch!" Lucias sputtered. As the gunman grabbed for the lifeline, he looked toward Oritz.

Caleb wondered if he missed part of what the gunslinger had said. And had it, in fact, been preceded by the pronoun, 'You'?

Lucias had almost grasped the floating rope when he was suddenly tugged from sight.

"Bugger me!" Caleb called and tried lashing the rope out once again. It slapped over the spot where Lucias had been, and he figured the worst had come to pass when the gunslinger suddenly resurfaced with a huge gasp of air.

"Grab the rope!" Caleb called again.

This time, Lucias grabbed hold and wrapped the rope around one wrist. He looked to Caleb as he was reeled in and said, "Something had me by the foot and pulled off my boot! At least, I think that's all it pulled off!"

No sooner had the words left Lucias's mouth when things changed dramatically, and not for the better. The lantern he'd been wearing had been submerged along with the rest of him but hadn't fallen off, though its flame was now extinguished.

Unfortunately, excess water had seeped into the chamber that held the calcium carbide, and it had a devastating effect. The gas pressure suddenly spiked inside the calcium carbide tank, and it ruptured with a resounding pop.

The acetylene gas inside was lighter than air, and it dissipated quickly. Unfortunately, the calcium carbide pellets were not, and they cascaded down onto Lucias's face. Some bounced off and hissed and foamed as they reacted with the water. He coughed and gagged, having difficulty getting air because of the gas being created around him.

Lucias suddenly cried out in agony and let go of the rope as he tried to wash the rest of the carbide from his face. But it was too late since it was already melting through his skin, the additional water only accelerating the process.

Caleb had begun to cast the rope again when the gunslinger was suddenly tugged beneath the surface, and he watched in horror as Lucias was dragged down into blackness.

Jesús approached where Caleb stood, still staring in shock at the spot where Lucias had been only moments before.

With a shake of his head, the Spaniard said, "That is both tragic and unfortunate, to be sure."

"You son of a bitch!" Caleb said. "You pushed him in, didn't you? Hopin' he'd be eaten by one of those black beasts!"

With a look of surprise, Oritz said, "I do not know what you are talking about."

"Yeah, and I'm Scottish," Caleb said with no trace of humour. Had it not been for the vials of nitro on his person, he would have grabbed the man, shaken him by his lapels and finished what he started back in the alley in town. And if his intention were to kill them both, then that would be a great way to do it. But despite everything, Caleb wanted to live, and he could do nothing more than scowl at the man.

They were close to the section where the ledge dropped down, the spot that had slowed Caleb as he'd been chased by the ants. It wouldn't be far now until they were on the other shore of the lake.

After Caleb stepped down to the lower ledge, he turned back to Oritz, who was preparing to follow him. In a low, cold voice, he said, "You can keep your distance for the rest of the way. I don't need you too close to my back." Whether Oritz had pushed Lucias or not was something he would never know, but in the meantime, he wasn't going to trust the rotund reprobate any further than he could throw him.

Jesús held out both hands, palms up, to show he intended no harm, and Caleb scowled even harder at the man. He began to make his way, and the Spaniard hung back for a moment to give them some distance.

It seemed the earthquake had also affected this section of the cavern. The rock face, which had been spiderwebbed with cracks, had crumbled away in places, and huge chunks of stone lay scattered in various spots all along the narrow shore of the midnight lake. And one of those places looked to be just over the entrance to the ants' domain.

This was their last chance at a way out. If they couldn't carry on from here, they'd have to retrace their steps and try to blast their way out the front entrance or maybe climb the chimney to get to the frayed rope. There seemed no other choice. Before arriving at this lake-filled cavern, they'd checked one of the other tunnels, but rather than lead to an exit, it ended at a precipice with a black void beyond. A waterfall jetted out of a gash in the rock across the way. Presumably, it was the same one Caleb had ridden over when he'd been flushed from the cavern. Looking into the void, he'd wondered how in heaven he'd ever survived the fall, but survive it, he had, and he thanked his ever-dwindling Irish luck for it once again.

"Mind yourself. This is where I first encountered those six-legged red bastards. I don't know if the flood that happened up here cleared them all out or not. If it didn't, we have one less gun to deal with them."

Jesús shrugged with a look that said, 'What am I going to do about it?'.

Caleb shook his head in exasperation. "But it might not matter since the tunnel out of this cavern could be blocked."

Oritz held up the stick of dynamite from earlier that afternoon and said, "Then we will unblock it."

"Nope, if it's blocked, we'll have to hope there's another way through. If we blast here, the whole damned ceiling might come down."

Taking a deep breath, Caleb moved toward the entrance to the ant's world, Oritz a safe distance at his back. Numerous rocks had already fallen, and from the looks of things, it wouldn't take much more than a low rumble to bring down the rest of it. In fact, the way his luck had been going, he wouldn't have been surprised to have the whole thing crumble on top of him as he stood there looking at it.

Though several large boulders blocked the route directly, Caleb was eventually able to wind his way through the obstacle course. At the small tunnel's entrance were some smaller chunks of fallen rock but nothing too much to scramble over; still, it looked like a tight squeeze.

Strangely, there were carcasses of fish scattered amongst the fallen rock. The stench was horrendous. But despite the smell, it made Caleb's hope rekindle. That meant the lake had sloshed into this section during the tsunami and washed away the ants. After all, he reasoned, the fish would have already been eaten if the red devils were still around.

Caleb turned to Oritz and said, "I'll go first since it looks like we'll need to go single file. Once I make sure it's clear, I'll call you in." Caleb removed the small satchel he'd been carrying with the static detonator and blasting wire and pushed it into the tunnel ahead of him. Once through the obstructed entrance, things looked a bit more solid. He was glad to have the head lantern since it freed his hands as he crawled. But judging by what he could see so far, the way ahead looked empty, and as he replaced the satchel over his shoulder, he released a breath he hadn't realised he'd been holding.

Now, several yards in, it appeared the tunnel branched into a Y. One direction seemed blocked at the moment, but the other wound off into darkness and appeared the only way to go. Caleb shivered slightly. The temperature inside this tube was quite cold for some reason, much more so than any other part of this cave system so far, where hot and steamy seemed to be the order of the day. Yet, in this tunnel, he could almost see wisps of his breath.

Just about to call Oritz to follow him in, Caleb paused when he realised there were still things glinting around him in the light of his lamp. Dark and multifaceted, they had looked much like the eyes of the ants when he'd first encountered them, and he may have confused the two. But since there were no ants here right now, what was shining in the lamplight? He leaned closer to one of the walls, and his eyes grew wide.

As he'd suspected when he first found this tunnel, there were indeed gemstones embedded in the rock on both sides. But these gemstones weren't diamonds, and he laughed heartily at the thought of everything this cavern seemed to contain. Everything from gold to monstrous beasts out of time, and now, shining darkly from the walls around him, dozens and dozens of the mysterious obsidian gemstones Sinclair coveted.

From the tunnel entrance, Jesús called, "What is funny? Are you all right?"

Caleb called back, "More than fine. I just discovered more that this cavern contains."

"More wealth?"

"I suppose it is, to the right person."

Hearing this news, Oritz began to push his bag through the small gap and eagerly scrambled into the tunnel. With a greedy grin, the small Spaniard only stooped slightly as he approached, while Caleb had to stand with his back hunched over like that fella from Notre Dame.

"What is it? What did you find?" Oritz's breath steamed from his mouth as if his internal furnace were stoked by his insurmountable greed.

"These stones." Caleb gestured toward the walls of the tunnel.

"Ah, the black stones! Thomas had shown them to me and told me of their power. This is phenomenal!"

The Spaniard began to worry away at one of the stones with the blade of a Bowie knife he'd had tied to his thigh. "At the very least, we must take some of these while we are here."

"You go right ahead. I'm goin' to check out where this tunnel goes."

"Fine, you do that. I will catch up with you once I have extracted a couple of these."

With that, Jesús continued to pry one of the obsidian gemstones from the wall as Caleb moved into darkness.

CHAPTER FORTY-EIGHT

Jesús wormed the razor-sharp blade into a small gap between the volcanic rock and the shining black gemstone. His breath came in snorting gasps like a bull charging a red cape, all his attention focused on the stone before him. So much so that he failed to notice the slight noise that came from the section of tunnel that had been blocked at the Y branch.

"You need to come out of there right now, my pretty," he said to the glistening stone. But it paid him no heed and remained where it was. Despite the cold, Jesús was dripping wet and hot with excitement, feeling the need to free the stone and hold it in his hand. He pressed harder with the blade, feeling sure it would snap, but it didn't.

Finally, with a hollow pop, the gemstone came loose and tumbled into the palm of his hand.

And then Jesús began to scream.

The stone felt as if it were melting into the flesh of his palm. He tried to pull it free with his fingers but couldn't gain purchase because of the blood that seeped from the wound. As if acid, the stone ate its way down to the bones along the back of his hand, and no matter how he tried, he couldn't pull it free. Though he was sure he had inflicted such pain upon others, never in his life had he felt such agony.

Oritz grabbed the knife from the tunnel floor where he'd dropped it, then jammed it into the raw flesh next to the stone and screamed again, long and hard. He pried at it, slicing into his palm as he did and continued to shriek in agony, white-hot pain consuming his world.

However, there was one thing that managed to take his mind off of his current predicament.

Like brittle bone, the ceiling let loose a crack, and the ground began to shake and shimmy around him.

Jesús snapped his head in the direction Caleb had gone and watched as that section of the roof crumbled and fell into the tunnel, blocking it completely. He spun and began to move toward the small opening he'd crawled through, but it, too, was blocked as the massive rock wall on the other side crashed down, dumping hundreds of tons of rock in front of the only other way out. He was now trapped inside the tunnel and effectively buried alive.

For several more seconds, the aftershock rumbled, and Jesús feared the passage might collapse completely, but fortunately, the roof held. Abruptly, the shaking stopped, and the small tunnel was silent once more, apart from Oritz's ragged breathing. He was relieved he could still see the dust hanging in the air, his calcium carbide lamp thankfully undamaged.

The section of the tunnel that had been blocked at the Y junction had partial access again. Part of a supporting wall had crumbled away when the ceiling collapsed, and a small opening into the passage on the other side was now visible. There didn't seem much room, but he thought he might be able to wiggle through if he moved some rocks. That was, once he dealt with the searing pain in his hand.

Once more, Jesús began to worry his blade at the stone fused to his palm. And once more, he heard the noise, the one he'd only partly paid attention to as he'd first attempted to free the gemstone from the wall. The sound was louder now and coming from the newly opened passage. With heart-stopping certainty, he suddenly realised it was a sound he recognised.

Dozens upon dozens of diablos rojo swarmed through the small opening to the other passage, keening shrilly and clacking their mandibles. They were returning with enthusiasm to the treasure their colony had been guarding for generations until a recent separation—the glistening obsidian stones. And then they discovered the threat to their treasure, one that would be neutralised at all costs.

The red beasts were too quick and too numerous to allow Jesús to shoot his gun or even light the dynamite in his pocket. Very shortly, he no longer worried about removing the gemstone from his hand, for he no longer had a hand, or an arm, or legs, or much of anything else, in fact.

In his last, brief moments of life, there was nothing Jesús Oritz could do but shriek in impotent rage and excruciating pain as he was eaten alive by the swarming mass of red death. He could go nowhere, while the ants, on the other hand, could go everywhere.

***

Caleb had moved slowly through the tunnel at first, leaving Oritz to retrieve his gemstones. The passage grew narrower and narrower as he went, and he was about to turn back and tell the man to hurry up when the ground began to shake and shimmy. The roof of the tunnel collapsed at his back, separating him from the Spaniard.

He'd turned and hustled as fast as he could in the direction he'd been exploring, stooped over with both shoulders brushing against the rock walls of the rapidly narrowing tunnel. As the world trembled around him, he hoped it wouldn't be enough to agitate the boom juice in his vest.

Fortunately, the saints seemed to have been watching from above, and Caleb praised them most highly when he suddenly stumbled out the other end of the tunnel. He only stopped himself from falling and self-terminating by placing his hands out in front of him before he hit the ground. He ended up positioned like he was doing a push-up back in the army, something he was now glad he'd kept doing since Africa.

As he stood, he stared about like a slack-jawed yokel at the county fair.

The other caverns in this system had been large, and some, he thought, enormous, like the moth cavern and the midnight lake. But where he currently stood made the other caverns pale in comparison. Though his lamp still burned brightly, it illuminated barely any of the immense space now surrounding him.

To the darkness, Caleb said, "I don't think I'll be gettin' back to Kitty any time soon." It was quite true; there was no way he could ever go back the way he'd come. He didn't know what had happened to the Spanish bandit, though just after the shaking stopped, he thought he'd heard a muted scream, several, in fact, but they hadn't lasted long. No, it seemed he would have to keep going forward into this unknown world until he found a way out. And that might be easier said than done.

Nearby was an abundance of moss that looked similar to the stuff in the cavern where the blood-sucking moths drained Cookie. However, the area around him seemed devoid of winged threats at the moment, and he was thankful for that. But it made him wonder about the ground cover around him. He turned off the gas, and his flame guttered to blackness.

As his anxious eyes gradually adjusted, he soon discerned a slight glow from the nearby moss, but it was not as strong as in the other cavern. However, there was something else that was a bit brighter—mushrooms, and quite a few, from what he could see.

Thoughts of seeing Kitty any time soon grew smaller and smaller as his night vision became clearer and clearer. Lichen, similar to that found in the lake, lined the embankments of a stream which looked to contain fresh water. It burbled down a slight slope and pooled in the cavern floor, with more flora and moss growing around it. Without exception, the vegetation all shared the same characteristic and glowed with their own internal light.

His eyes now coming to terms with the darkness, Caleb looked about, taking in more and more of his surroundings. This was not just a cave or a cavern but seemed like an entire world. Though not as bright as daylight by any means, the illumination allowed him to see other patches that grew in what seemed a valley below, stretching for miles. The cavern ceiling arched hundreds of feet above, with distant stalactites barely visible in the dim distance.

Somewhere above, reigning over all, was the glacier, Natanik. As large as the sun and the moon was what he now recalled of the glacier's Aboriginal meaning. It seemed an appropriate name for the massive piece of ice, which might just serve as his grave marker if he couldn't find a way out.

With a sigh and a quiet prayer, Caleb Cantrill moved down the slope to see what his new world contained, hoping he might yet make it back to the one he'd left behind and the woman he would never forget.

EPILOGUE

Kitty Welch sat across from Doctor Brown in the stifling coach, the earthy must of the lanolin-coated seats quite strong in the August afternoon's heat. Sandy was out at the horses, whispering gently in their ears, calming them greatly. Whatever power the boy seemed to have over animals seemed to be something that might come in handy on their journey. Especially his power over the two-legged variety, thanks to his experience as bouncer at the Golden Nugget Saloon. Considering some of the people Kitty suspected they would be dealing with, Sandy's ability to persuade them to 'listen to reason' could come in very handy.

The horses had been stamping their feet, impatient for the stagecoach driver to climb aboard and begin guiding the trio on their journey over the mountain to Sproat's Landing. From there, they would take the Canadian Pacific Railway to Calgary and beyond to Halifax. White Star Lines would then steam them to England, and it was there that their quest would truly begin.

Doctor Brown was adjusting something inside a small wooden box on his lap. He'd told Kitty what it was, but the description had been over her head. And so, she'd just nodded and smiled politely as she'd listened to the doctor's animated description of the device's attributes. His ability to find solutions to problems and be on the cutting edge of science as he was, would make the doctor another valuable addition in their search for the stones.

And thanks to Cornelius's insights and creativity, he seemed to have rid the town of the spiders thanks to his fumigation techniques. From what Brown had told her, Thomas Sinclair had been quite impressed and requested he make several more of the fumigators for 'just in case' while they were away. Of the ants, they'd seen no signs either. Brown said there was a very good possibility they'd either been crushed in the hail, drowned in the flood, or swallowed up in the earthquake that followed. He'd added if there were any that survived all that, they were no doubt so far downriver now they were someone else's problem.

Thinking of problems, when they arrived in London, Kitty was unsure what they would do apart from taking another train, this time to Edinburgh. That was the last place she'd known William McLeod to be after he'd been released by the bobbies. He'd sent her a letter, which her mother had forwarded to her after she'd landed in Halifax. In it, he'd said how sorry he was that her name had come up during the interrogation, adding it hadn't been his intention to drag her into it, but the questioning the police had given him had been painfully persuasive, and he'd told them many things he wouldn't have otherwise. He'd ended the letter begging her forgiveness, and that had been the last she'd ever heard from him.

That had also been the case with Caleb and the rest of the men on the gold quest. Her heart ached, not knowing what had happened to them. It had been almost a month now with no word at all. She feared they'd been crushed in a cave-in when that third earth movement had struck a couple of days after they'd left. She supposed there was a chance they were still alive and somehow trapped within the mountain.

There was another, worse possibility, and Kitty thought of

the bandits that had gone with Caleb. Had they done something most foul and betrayed them all? Whatever had happened, no one that went up the mountain that day had ever returned. And despite the ache in her heart, she still felt that Caleb was somehow alive, though she didn't know why. If he were dead, she would feel it somehow, she was sure of it, and she'd not felt anything like that, at least, not yet. So, for now, she would focus on the journey ahead, try to forget about Caleb Cantrill and hope for the best. Who knew, when she returned from Europe, he might be finally back and ready to regale her with tales of his adventures.

And besides, Kitty had other things to worry about. She and Caleb had shared a couple of amazing nights together that she would never forget. Though their intimate interludes had been brief, their passion had been intense enough for a lifetime, or that's how it had felt. Another part of her, just a little lower than her heart, ached with longing for the electrifying moments they'd spent together those two evenings. However, that brought her to her other concern.

Usually, when she went about her job on the second floor of the Nugget, Kitty would insist that the men she saw wear some sort of protection as they went about their business. There were all sorts of different prophylactics available in these modern times, and if her client didn't have one, she would send them just around the corner to get one at the chemist's.

But with Caleb, she'd relaxed those standards, wanting to feel every sensation of their lovemaking those two nights. And so, having relaxed said standards, Kitty was late for her time of the month. She hadn't shared this with anyone, not even the other second-floor girls, since she still wasn't sure if it was truly the case. She'd been late other times in her life due to an illness or stress, amongst other things. But it was now a little over two weeks, stretching the boundaries of possibility quite far.

Well, at least she was travelling with a medical doctor and a man-boy so devoted to her safety that he would likely kill for her. Not that she would ever entertain the thought of asking Sandy, or anyone else, to do such a thing on her behalf. Fortunately, as far as she knew, it was something the boy had never done for Thomas Sinclair, unlike Lucias, the Scotsman's now-missing enforcer.

The telegraph line had been fixed a couple of days after Caleb's departure, and Thomas had been on it quite heavily, ordering everything he could think of that the town would need for rebuilding. And it was not that the man was particularly altruistic and wanted to help anyone in particular, except perhaps himself. The supplies he brought in would be for sale in his stores, where he would sell them at a tidy profit; of that, she was quite sure.

Sandy clambered inside, quite literally jostling Kitty from her reverie, his muscular bulk rocking the coach like a North Sea squall.

"Gosh! This is gonna be great, ain't it?" he asked the doctor and Kitty, his face bright with excitement.

"Isn't it, my boy," Brown corrected.

"Ain't it what, Doc?"

"Going to be great." Brown said, "It's isn't, not ain't."

"It ain't?" Sandy wondered.

Brown sighed, and Kitty smiled, saying, "Don't worry, Doctor Brown, you'll have plenty of time to work on it during our trip."

"That is quite true, dear lady. I will have to write these things down for Sandy, and he can use them for bookmarks when reading that fantastic fiction he so likes."

"Aye, that's a great idea," Kitty said with a nod and a smile.

"I like learnin' new words. Thanks, Doc."

"My pleasure, my boy."

Sandy had shown up at the stagecoach with one small bag, which had been mostly filled with books. He'd said he'd decided he wanted to read them all several more times since he loved the high adventure in them. Kitty had pointed out to him that they were also going on an adventure, and he might be able to write about their journey as they travelled. She figured a travelogue penned by Sandy would be a great exercise for him to get better at reading and writing. They were also fortunate he was travelling so lightly because they were not.

Kitty and the doctor each had a steamer trunk up top and a small day bag on their person below. Unsure what to bring, Kitty had said as much to Sinclair. He had informed her she would be travelling under the expense umbrella of the Sinclair Corporation, and they would not have to worry about feeding or clothing themselves while on their quest. The entire trip must have cost Thomas a small fortune, easily over five thousand dollars, according to the doctor's calculations. But it seemed the stones in question were worth whatever expenses they incurred in the group's pursuit of them.

Though several years had passed since Kitty had last touched the Scottish gemstones, she hoped they still stood a good chance of finding them. Now that she'd been reintroduced to the obsidian stones by Sinclair, she felt she might be able to guide them somewhat, along with the help of the other device they were bringing for that purpose.

That had been the box the doctor was talking about. He'd somehow figured out that since the stones were drawn to each other, they could also be located through a device that

contained one of the stones. When he'd finished his earlier
long-winded speech about the directional box he'd made,
upon seeing her befuddled expression, Brown had simplified
things, saying it functioned almost like a compass. And this
particular compass would theoretically point them to the
stones and other high-energy points on the planet where
stones like them were concentrated.

The little town they were now leaving appeared to be one
of those spots and not the only one in this province. Angeline
had given Kitty a crash course on the stones, including how
and where she and Thomas had found them over the years.
From what she understood, one location was up the coast
from Vancouver, a picturesque place very much like this one.
But unlike the glacier here in this valley, that little town,
Entwistle, lived in the shadow of the ominous-sounding
Overseer Mountain.

Whatever their future may bring, Kitty felt sure it would
not be dull. If she were to give birth to a son of Caleb Cantrill,
she would do so in high fashion, at least for the time being.
And if anything happened to her during childbirth, she knew
the infant would be cared for in the capable, if slightly
besotted hands of Doctor Cornelius Brown and protected by
the massive fists of Sandy.

With a jolt, the carriage began bouncing down the dusty
main street, still in the midst of repair after the earthquake.
Kitty watched the facades of the shops pass by: lawyers and
assayers, banks and saloons, shops and bakeries, and many
more. She wondered how much this nameless town would
have changed when they returned from their adventure. With
Thomas Sinclair at the helm, big things would no doubt be
afoot, of that she was absolutely certain.

***

A gentle summer breeze, as soft as a caress, brushed
Kitty's cheek as she watched out the coach's rear window.

They were nearing the top of the Golden Mile Pass, the late afternoon sun glinting off the glacier. Somewhere back there was the man who had captured her soul like none other.

Whatever they encountered in their search for the obsidian stones, Kitty knew she would be coming back to this valley. From its verdant trees and resplendent mountains to its rushing rivers and clear blue skies, the West Kootenays held many things for her, but the most important it would ever hold, was her heart.

The stagecoach jolted over a bump, and the valley disappeared from sight.

Kitty sighed, feeling both hopeful and terrified, all at the same time.

Across the aisle, Sandy gave a resounding "Yahoo!"

From beside Kitty, Cornelius Brown uttered an encouraging, "Well said, my boy!"

The trio were well and truly on their way, and Kitty felt sure it would prove to be the adventure of a lifetime.

FIN

FINAL WORDS

Well, it's been quite a ride, but we finally made it to the end of this journey, the final installment in this rather tall tale of gold, greed, guilt and grit.

What was only an idea in the back of my mind for a long time is now living in your mind. If I have done my job correctly, you've grown as attached to some of the characters as I have.

If you've been entertained and would like to share your thoughts with others, please leave a review; they are critical to a book's success. To make things easier, here is a direct link to the Amazon review page for CLAW Emergence Book 3: Return to Darkness, so you can leave a few thoughts while everything is fresh in your memory:

Amazon.com/review/create-review?&asin=B0CQWRM7N1

Please make sure to sign up for my newsletter, The Katie Berry Books Insider, for further novel updates, free short stories, chapter previews and monthly giveaways. To join, click here:

https://katieberry.ca/become-a-katie-berry-books-insider-and-win/

Good health and great reads to you all,

-Katie Berry

CURRENT AND UPCOMING RELEASES

CLAW: A Canadian Thriller (November 28th, 2019)

CLAW Emergence Novelette – Caleb Cantrill (September 13th, 2020)

CLAW Emergence Novelette – Kitty Welch - (November 26th, 2020)

CLAW Resurgence (September 30th, 2021)

CLAW Emergence Book 1 (December 24th. 2022)

CLAW Emergence Book 2 (July 1st, 2023)

CLAW Emergence Book 3 (December 24th, 2023)

CLAW Resurrection (Spring 2024)

ABANDONED: A Lively Deadmarsh Novel Book 1 (February 26th, 2021)

ABANDONED: A Lively Deadmarsh Novel Book 2 (May 31st, 2021)

ABANDONED: A Lively Deadmarsh Novel Book 3 (December 23rd, 2021)

ABANDONED: A Lively Deadmarsh Novel Book 4 (July 15th, 2022)

BESIEGED: A Lively Deadmarsh Novel (Fall 2024)

CONNECTIONS

Email: katie@katieberry.ca
Website: https://katieberry.ca

SHOPPING LINKS

CLAW: A Canadian Thriller:
Amazon eBook: https://amzn.to/31QCw7x
Paperback Version: https://amzn.to/31RYPK7
Amazon Audible Audiobook: https://amzn.to/2Gj3j45
(Also available on all other major audiobook platforms)

CLAW Resurgence:
Amazon eBook: https://amzn.to/2YeDdZt
Paperback Version: https://amzn.to/31RYPK7
Amazon Audible Audiobook: https://amzn.to/36nLSgk
(Also available on all other major audiobook platforms)

CLAW Emergence: Tales from Lawless – Kitty Welch:
Amazon eBook: https://amzn.to/37aSnAn
Large Print Paperback Version: https://amzn.to/3tTsoa9
Audiobook on Audible: https://amzn.to/3szAmXM

CLAW Emergence: Tales from Lawless – Caleb Cantrill:
Amazon eBook: https://amzn.to/3ldYoC3
Large Print Paperback Version: https://amzn.to/3meDVg9
Audiobook on Audible: https://amzn.to/3qkKvUe

CLAW Emergence Book 1: From the Shadows:
Amazon eBook: https://amzn.to/3VnB6di
Paperback Version: https://amzn.to/3Xjv5Q1
Audiobook: August 29th, 2023
(Also available on all other major audiobook platforms)

CLAW EMERGENCE Book 2: Into Daylight:
Amazon eBook: https://amzn.to/3JEC9Tf
Paperback Version: https://amzn.to/3NwKfhG
Audiobook Version: https://amzn.to/41y2lGR
(Also available on all other major audiobook platforms)

CLAW EMERGENCE Book 3: Return to Darkness:
Amazon eBook: https://amzn.to/3GUVe1B
Paperback Version: Coming Soon
Audiobook Version: Coming Soon
(Also available on all other major audiobook platforms)

ABANDONED: A Lively Deadmarsh Novel Book 1 – Arrivals
and Awakenings
Amazon eBook: https://amzn.to/3jM3GDX
Paperback: https://amzn.to/3yruNLL
Audiobook: https://amzn.to/3yNot0o
(Also available on all other major audiobook platforms)

ABANDONED: A Lively Deadmarsh Novel Book 2 –
Beginnings and Betrayals
Amazon eBook: https://amzn.to/3BTn4a9
Paperback: https://amzn.to/3BTneyh
Audiobook: https://amzn.to/3FrwcVF
(Also available on all other major audiobook platforms)

ABANDONED: A Lively Deadmarsh Novel Book 3 – Chaos
and Corruption
Amazon eBook: https://amzn.to/3HpBNMM
Paperback: https://amzn.to/3IOGTE7
Audiobook: https://amzn.to/3PtVyqr
(Also available on all other major audiobook platforms)

ABANDONED: A Lively Deadmarsh Novel Book 4 –
Deception and Deliverance
Amazon eBook: https://amzn.to/3wo6XqF
Paperback: https://amzn.to/3Qh5t3m
Audiobook: https://amzn.to/3NVOdC9

(Also available on all other major audiobook platforms)

Manufactured by Amazon.ca
Bolton, ON

37255299R00206